It Started
with a Secret

IT STARTED WITH A SECRET

JILL MANSELL

THORNDIKE PRESS
A part of Gale, a Cengage Company

Simultaneously published in 2020 in the United Kingdom by Headline Review, an imprint of Headline Publishing Group, a Hachette UK Company.
Thorndike Press, a part of Gale, a Cengage Company.

Thorndike Press® Large Print Softcover Romance and Women's Fiction.
The text of this Large Print edition is unabridged.
Other aspects of the book may vary from the original edition.
Set in 16 pt. Plantin.

LIBRARY OF CONGRESS CIP DATA ON FILE.
CATALOGUING IN PUBLICATION FOR THIS BOOK
IS AVAILABLE FROM THE LIBRARY OF CONGRESS

ISBN-13: 978-1-4328-8091-0 (softcover alk. paper)

Published in 2021 by arrangement with Sourcebooks, LLC.

Printed in the United States of America
1 2 3 4 5   25 24 23 22 21

IT STARTED
WITH A SECRET

CHAPTER 1

Lainey could hear the helicopter before it came into view over the tops of the trees. The powerful *thud thud thud* of the rotor blades was quite thrilling out here in the depths of the French countryside. She wondered what it would be like to actually take a trip in a helicopter.

Blinking, she shielded her eyes from the bright afternoon sun. "Here they are then, right on time."

Bill, standing next to her on the ancient stone steps of the chateau, said, "Remember, anything they want, they get. Before they even know they want it."

The faint tremor in her boss's voice signaled just how vital it was that this stay was a success. Lainey passed him a tissue so he could mop his brow.

"Everything's going to be fine." They'd worked so hard; every eventuality had been covered. What could possibly go wrong?

Well, apart from water pipes bursting, ceilings falling in, or the electronics blowing up, but now wasn't the time to think about things like that.

Together they followed the gray-and-silver helicopter's trajectory as it drew nearer, descending from a cloudless cobalt-blue sky and aiming for the landing pad in the center of the front lawn.

Bill puffed out a lungful of air and wiped his palms with an already damp and mangled tissue. "Everything has to be better than fine. It needs to be perfect."

Lainey felt his pain. Behind them, Bill's wife was shrilly calling out to everyone to gather on the steps in order to greet their all-important guests, *Downton* style. Bill and Biddy, in their late fifties, were lifelong Francophiles who had made the decision two years ago to take the plunge and exchange their immaculate semidetached home in Hounslow for a dilapidated twelve-bedroom chateau in the Loire valley, with the aim of living the good life, enjoying the warmer weather and spectacular scenery, and socializing with like-minded expats and friendly locals alike. In order to finance the dream, the plan had been to host guests at the chateau and hold weddings and special events there too.

In theory, it had sounded like everyone's idea of an idyllic existence, but it hadn't turned out to be nearly as easy or as much fun as they'd envisaged. A centuries-old chateau was an always-ravenous money pit, and the small bequest left to them by Biddy's parents had soon been swallowed up. The moment the fences were repaired, the drains collapsed. Once the leaking roof was fixed, fifty huge window frames needed replacing. No sooner were the chimneys unblocked than the ancient plumbing system disintegrated and the floorboards developed dry rot.

But Bill and Biddy had valiantly plowed on, addressing the locals in loud, mangled Franglais and getting frustrated when they were unable to make themselves understood. A year ago, they'd taken on several members of staff, Lainey among them, and finally opened their expensively refurbished doors to paying guests.

Today's were the most VIP visitors by far. Wyatt Hilstanton, a member of a hugely wealthy Boston banking dynasty, had relocated to London several years ago and was arriving here with his British girlfriend, Penny, with the intention of proposing to her. It was to be the ultimate romantic surprise, and every last detail had been planned for weeks. The chateau was full of Hilstantons, who had arrived earlier and were currently hiding upstairs until it was time to celebrate.

Best of all, Wyatt's father had booked the chateau for an entire week in August for the wedding itself.

As Lainey straightened her shoulders, footsteps sounded behind her, and a hand came to rest lightly on her bottom. Turning, she glimpsed the flash of a grin before Anton raised his eyebrows in a *Who, me?* protestation of innocence. But his hand stayed where it was, and now it was her turn to smile. Maybe when they were off duty later tonight, they could celebrate Wyatt and Penny's engagement in their own way.

The helicopter settled at the very center of the landing pad. When the rotor blades had stopped turning, the guests alighted and made their way across the grass. "Just remember, everyone," Biddy murmured, "be *nice.*"

"Welcome, *welcome* to Chateau de Rafale!" Bill pumped Wyatt's hand in greeting and bowed, then shook Penny's hand even more energetically and did a kind of manly curtsy. Biddy followed his lead, while the rest of them stood there and beamed until their cheeks ached.

Lainey studied Penny Carter, Wyatt's girlfriend, and was relieved to see she wasn't an obvious gold-digger type. Unless this was the nifty double bluff employed by all the most successful gold diggers. But no, she was pretty certain that wasn't the case here. While Wyatt was encased head to toe in Ralph Lauren, possibly a size too small for him, Penny was dressed in a white sleeveless cotton top, a plain knee-length pink skirt, and sensible low-heeled espadrilles. Her hair and nails were short and unadorned. She had a pretty heart-shaped face and a sweet smile.

"I can't believe how beautiful this place is," she marveled. "I've never stayed in a chateau before!"

"Everything's ready for you," said Bill. "Let me show you upstairs to your rooms."

"My favorite stepson," Majella exclaimed with delight when she heard Seth's voice on the phone. "Hello, darling! How are you?"

"Good, thanks. I've just taken a look at the ad on the website." As always, Seth came straight to the point. "Did you write it?"

"No." Majella was frantically searching the kitchen for her car keys. "I called the agency and explained what we needed, and

11

they told me to leave it with them. Oh dear, is there a problem?" She hadn't spotted any errors, but that didn't mean there weren't any.

"Right, let me read it out to you: 'Live-in domestic couple, fulltime permanent position, cleaning and organization. Competitive salary. Cornwall.' " Seth paused. "And that's it."

"Oh. Is it wrong?"

"It's so . . . *bland.*"

Majella sighed. "I know. But that's what those kinds of adverts are like."

"Remind me what you said about the couple you interviewed on Monday."

"They were boring." She pulled a face at the thought of them; they'd actually been the king and queen of boring. The prospect of having to spend her days in their company was just too awful to contemplate.

"And have there been any more applicants since then?"

"None." For goodness' sake, where *were* her car keys?

"Well, that's probably because they fell asleep reading the advert. What's that noise?" said Seth.

"Sorry, just dropped the cookie tin. I'm looking for my keys. Oh, Glenda, no, that's *naughty* . . ." But she was too late: the little dog had already snaffled up two cookies and was racing out of the kitchen, her tail helicoptering with joy at the unexpected gift.

"You need to rewrite the ad," Seth advised. "In your own words. Say what you're really looking for and let the applicants know what they'd be getting themselves into."

"Ha, they'd run a mile."

"Just be chatty and informal and honest, like the way you used to write to me when I was at school, remember?"

"Of course I remember." Warmed by the memory, Majella nodded. "Yes, you're right. Thank you, darling. I'll do it tonight. Now, d'you have any idea where I might have left my car keys?"

"No, but the last time you couldn't find them, you'd put them in your bra for safe keeping."

It was ten to six. The plan was that at six o'clock, Wyatt would suggest to Penny that they go for a stroll around the grounds of the chateau before dinner. Along the way, they would "accidentally" discover a tiny stone crypt tucked in among the trees with its old wooden door standing slightly open. Wyatt would wonder aloud what might be inside, and they would venture toward the building to find out. Then, as they entered and closed the door behind them, Penny would be greeted by the sight of dozens of candles burning like tiny stars inside glass holders, silver heart-shaped helium balloons bobbing from the ceiling, and hundreds of crimson rose petals strewn on the ground.

Lainey hadn't been so sure about the heart-shaped helium balloons, but Wyatt had insisted. Nor had she been entirely convinced by the music he'd chosen to start playing as soon as the door was closed, because in all honesty he didn't have the best singing voice and "My Heart Will Go On" was a demanding song at the best of times. But apparently it was "their" song and he'd made the recording specially. And as Bill had stressed several hundred times, Wyatt's every wish was their command.

At six on the dot, showered and changed into smart evening clothes, the couple arrived downstairs and headed outside for their predinner stroll in the grounds. As soon as they'd made their way out through the front entrance, Lainey and her friend and fellow employee Kit collected together the silver ice bucket, the chilled vintage Bollinger, a silver tray, and two crystal champagne flutes. Having filled the bucket with ice, they slid out through the side door of the kitchen and raced over to the crypt.

"This bottle cost eight hundred euros," Kit murmured as he positioned it at an angle in the ice bucket. "I didn't believe Bill when he told me. But then I Googled it."

Lainey had spent the last hour pulling petals off roses, which had made her feel like a murderer. Now she took them out of their bag and scattered them across the flagstone floor. Above them, the helium balloons swayed in the faint breeze coming through the open door. She made sure the phone was set up on the docking station and slipped the remote control into her pocket. Right, all done. Time to escape and silently lurk behind the handily positioned stone wall to the left of the crypt.

They were joined there by Bill and Biddy. A few minutes later, they heard Penny and Wyatt making their approach. Biddy beamed excitedly at Lainey.

"Oh, hey, look at this place," Wyatt exclaimed. "Wonder what's inside?"

"We shouldn't go in there." Penny sounded concerned. "It might be someone's home or something."

"Honey, it's fine. We're not going to get into trouble. Come on, let's take a look. Give me your hand . . ."

The group hiding behind the wall heard

the door close with a heavy clunk, and Lainey pressed play on the remote control. The walls of the crypt were thick, so they couldn't hear the music nor whatever else might be happening inside.

"It's so romantic," Biddy whispered gleefully. "She's such a lucky girl! When Bill and I got engaged, we'd missed the last bus back to Swindon and were walking home in the rain. Bill said, 'Oh, by the way, my mum wants to know if we're getting hitched. What d'you reckon I should tell her?' And that was it! That was my proposal!"

Bill was laughing quietly. "Did the trick, though, didn't it? You said yes. And we haven't done too badly, have we?"

Seven minutes later, Kit said, "They're taking their time. I thought they'd be out by now." His task was to take lots of photos when the couple emerged into the sunshine in a daze of just-engaged happiness, while Bill, Biddy, and Lainey provided the enthusiastic applause and congratulations.

Another few minutes went by, then they heard the unmistakable sound of a champagne cork being popped.

"At last!" Lainey exhaled with relief because the relatives were all assembled in the main hall back at the chateau for the next stage of the surprise.

The heavy wooden door creaked open, and they launched into a frenzy of clapping and cheering until the look of absolute horror on Penny's face and the fact that Wyatt wasn't with her made them realize there might not be much call for congratulations after all.

"Oh God," Kit muttered. "Don't say she's shot him." They'd all heard the pop.

Penny's pallor was startling. "Have you been waiting here the whole time?"

"Um, yes. But we weren't listening. We couldn't hear anything," Lainey added hastily.

"Now I know why he didn't want me to come outside." She shook her head. "Wyatt asked me to marry him. I said no."

"But why?" Biddy's voice rose as she spread her hands. "He loves you!"

"And I like him." Penny squeezed her eyes shut for a moment. "He's a really nice guy. But I don't love him, and I can't marry someone just because I don't want to hurt their feelings." She shook her head. "If I'd known he was going to do this, I'd never have agreed to come here. I should leave."

"His family's here too," Bill blurted out. "All waiting to celebrate."

"Oh God, please no! Are you serious?" Aghast, Penny began to back away. "They're

17

going to hate me. I need to get out of here right now."

Lainey's heart went out to her and to Wyatt too. All that careful planning and no expense spared. It just went to show, sometimes a perfect proposal turned out not to be so perfect after all.

CHAPTER 2

At midnight, Lainey climbed out of bed and went over to the window. From her tiny room high up in the south-facing turret, she had a view over the wooded border of the grounds on that side of the chateau, and she could definitely hear noises. Something was happening out there.

Penny had left; she would be back in the UK by now. Biddy had instructed Kit to drive her to Charles de Gaulle airport outside Paris. The young woman had been shaken and upset by the unexpected turn the day had taken. Escaping the wrath of Wyatt's furious relatives had been her number one priority.

When Bill and Lainey had finally ventured into the crypt, they'd found Wyatt swigging from the bottle of vintage Bollinger. The soundtrack he'd recorded, of himself singing that his heart would go on, had still been playing. The dozens of tea lights were still flickering, the helium balloons still bobbing in the cool air.

"Well, that went well." He had wiped his mouth with the back of his hand. "Lucky I didn't make a complete idiot of myself, eh?"

That had been six hours ago. They'd taken him back to his family and tried to reassure him that it really wasn't the end of the world. Lainey had assumed that, from that point on, he would be consoled and taken care of by his parents and brothers, but it was definitely Wyatt she could see down there, weaving his way across the lawn.

And he was on his own, heading for the trees.

It was a moonlit night; otherwise, she might not have been able to identify him.

She watched as he paused, swaying visibly, and gazed up at one of the largest trees. What was he doing? Searching for squirrels? Or seeking out a branch sturdy enough to take his weight should he decide to —

No, don't even think it; of course he wouldn't do something so drastic.

But once the possibility had occurred to her, how could she ignore it? Pulling on a pair of shorts and her pink denim jacket to cover her thin nighttime T-shirt, Lainey hurried down the many flights of stone steps and let herself out through the side door.

Wyatt was sitting on the grass by the time she reached him. He wasn't looking his best.

"Hi." Lainey's heart went out to him. "How are you doing?"

"Never better. Really, best day of my life." He shook his head, pulled a balled-up handkerchief from his trouser pocket, and roughly wiped the pouches beneath his eyes. "I'm not crying, OK? It's hay fever. Oh man, what a nightmare."

It wasn't hay fever. Lainey lowered herself to the ground next to him. "I'm so sorry. It's a rotten thing to happen."

"You know what, though? I'm a nice guy. A really nice guy. And loaded too. I mean, I'd have given that girl everything she wanted. She'd have had a great life with me. Why would she turn down an offer like that?"

"I don't know, but isn't it a good thing she did?"

"And you expect me to say yes to that?" Wyatt stared at her. "Are you out of your mind?"

"I mean, in the long term. Because you're right," Lainey told him. "You are a catch. Lots of girls would be only too delighted to go ahead and marry you, because they'd know they could bail out six months later and walk away with more money than they

21

could ever earn. And Penny could have done that too, but she didn't. She did the decent thing. So at least you know she wasn't a gold digger."

Belatedly, it occurred to her that this just made it worse.

"I already knew she wasn't like that," Wyatt retorted. "It was why I wanted to marry her in the first place." He threw down the handkerchief and raked both hands through his hair, rocking back and forth with frustration. "And now I've been publicly dumped. I'm going to be a complete laughingstock. Just wait till everyone at work gets to hear about this."

"But they don't have to know! You can ask your family not to say anything. They're on your side," Lainey reminded him. "They love you. If they don't breathe a word, how's anyone else going to find out? You can just tell your friends at work that things didn't work out between you and Penny and the two of you broke up."

"How's anyone else going to find out?" Wyatt gave a snort of disbelief. "Are you kidding me? I have three brothers who can't wait to tell the world what a total loser I am." He rose clumsily to his feet. "And they'd be right."

"You aren't a loser."

"I am. I'm a joke." He was squeezing his eyes shut now, shaking his head. "I've never had any luck with girls. All I've ever wanted to do is fit in, find someone my mom would like, then get engaged and settle down."

"But loads of us are like that. I never have any luck with boys," Lainey exclaimed. "Honestly, I'm a walking disaster, always have been. Every single time, I fall for someone I think is amazing, and then he turns out to be just as rubbish as the rest of them." She didn't tell him about gorgeous Anton, who was on course to reverse the pattern and bring her some much-needed happiness at long last. Poor Wyatt, there was no need to rub his nose in it.

"You're a good person. You're trying to make me feel better." He eyed her blearily. "And guess what? It isn't working. But it's nice of you to try."

"You should get to bed," Lainey said gently.

To her relief, he nodded. "I guess I should."

Whoops! He wasn't too steady on his feet. Lainey grabbed the crumpled handkerchief he'd left on the grass and stuffed it into her jacket pocket, then held out her hand to grab him and keep him vaguely vertical.

"I just wanted to get married." He mum-bled the words brokenly. "Is that too much to ask?"

Poor Wyatt, what a terrible day he'd had. Still supporting his swaying body, Lainey said, "It'll happen one day. You'll get over this, I promise."

A thousand kilometers away, in St. Carys, Majella put down her pen and finished her glass of rioja. There it was then. For better or worse, she'd done the rewrite.

This evening's first attempt, on her laptop, had been a disaster. Then, remembering Seth's advice, she'd found herself a felt-tip pen and writing pad and curled up on the violet sofa in the living room. Casting aside the stiff, official advertising language used by the agency, she had written as if she were chatting away to the kind of people she would love to employ.

The ad now said:

HELLO! AMAZING COUPLE REQUIRED
— COULD IT BE YOU?

We live in a gorgeous beachfront home in north Cornwall. We're a happy but untidy family who need taking in hand. Are you orga-nized, energetic, and delight-

24

ful to have around? Would you like to restore order from chaos and look after us?

Must love cats, dogs, teenagers, and the occasional tricky geriatric. You'll have your own flat, use of a half-decent car, and flexible hours.

So what do you think? Would you be our Mary Poppins . . . and Bert? Come on, give us a go. It'll be hard work, but lots of fun too, we promise!

Having read through it again, Majella took a photo of what she'd written and emailed it to Seth.

He replied a minute later: *So much better. Well done. X*

Succinct and to the point, as always.

Majella sent a second message: *Should I mention Richard, do you think?*

This time the reply was almost instantaneous: *God, definitely not.*

The next morning, a drastically hungover Wyatt and the rest of his family departed for the airport in a small fleet of limousines.

"I feel so sorry for him," Lainey told Kit as they washed up after breakfast. Seven hours later, she was feeling even sorrier, but this time it was for herself.

Bill and Biddy had gathered everyone in the office. The only other guests, a strapping German couple, were currently out on a day trip to La Rochelle.

Biddy closed the door behind them, and Lainey saw that her eyes were red-rimmed. In that moment, she knew what was about to happen.

"We've run out of money." Bill didn't beat around the bush. "I mean, we've spent everything we had, and everything we borrowed on top of that. I'm afraid we've reached the end of the line, folks. We're going to have to let you go."

The bookings had thinned right out, he went on to explain, although they'd already guessed as much. At midday, a bachelorette party of twenty had canceled their imminent stay, and, of course, Wyatt's extremely lucrative summer wedding was now off the cards too. As an absolute final straw, another section of floor had collapsed in the north tower, and an ominous crack had appeared in the ceiling in the cavernous drawing room.

There was nothing more they could do, Bill continued with resignation. Their long-held dream had failed, and the chateau was going on the market; hopefully, someone with deeper pockets would take it off their hands and enable them to pay off the considerable amount of money they owed the bank.

"We can pay you up until today, but that's it. I'm so sorry." His shoulders were slumped, and he looked exhausted; after months of desperately trying to keep all the plates spinning, the time had come to let go and give up.

But it wasn't as if each of them hadn't been expecting it to happen sooner or later. Lainey's heart went out to the couple. She stepped forward and hugged first Biddy, then Bill. It wasn't their fault, after all. They'd spent the last two years working their socks off.

"Thanks, love." Biddy wiped her eyes. "Oh dear, I feel like we've let you all down. I just hope you manage to find yourselves new jobs."

"Don't worry about us. We'll be fine."

Biddy glanced across at Anton on the other side of the room. "Will you two find something together, d'you think?"

Lainey had already asked herself this same question and decided that they would. It made sense. They were pretty much the perfect match, and they were crazy about each other. Why wouldn't they continue what they'd started so promisingly two months ago?

She gave Biddy a reassuring squeeze. "Of course we will."

Heading upstairs ten minutes later, Lainey found Anton packing his belongings into the two suitcases he'd arrived with. As she let herself into the room, he was wrapping up his beloved Victorinox kitchen knives; they had been his parents' gift to him on his twenty-first birthday and were his absolute pride and joy.

"Hey." She slipped her arms around his waist. "Are you OK?"

"Not so bad." He gave her a brief kiss.

"What happens now? Any ideas, or is it too soon?"

"No definite plan." He shrugged and carefully wrapped the final knife in soft white cotton. "I'm going to head south — Cannes, Antibes, maybe Saint-Tropez. See what turns up."

"Sounds good to me." Lainey nodded and inhaled the scent of his body. The soft white cotton, she realized, was one of the chateau's pillowcases.

"How about you?" said Anton, and she smiled knowingly.

"Well, I thought I might head south too. I know, what an incredible coincidence! We could go together. How about that?"

"Actually . . ." Anton hesitated. "I was going to call a friend, see if I could stay with her for a while."

"Oh." *Her?*

"She's based in Saint-Tropez and knows pretty much everyone, so she'll be able to put the word out, find me work on one of the yachts, that kind of thing."

"Oh." Lainey felt the familiar sensation of her hopes for a happy ending slithering away, like an adder disappearing into undergrowth. "Right, of course. That sounds . . . brilliant."

"Hey, you and me, we've had fun." Anton surveyed her with a lopsided grin. "Haven't we? But it was never going to turn into anything serious, we both knew that. It's been great, but now it's time to move on to the next adventure."

Not to mention the next girlfriend. Ah well, this was the kind of thing you got used to when you had a fatal attraction to pretty boys and were gullible enough to get your hopes up.

Again.

His eyes were roaming over her face and body, probably so he'd be able to remind himself who she was should their paths happen to cross in years to come. The next moment, he hooked his index fingers through her belt and drew her toward the unmade bed, breaking into the kind of playful grin that had gotten her into trouble in the first place. "I'm not leaving for a couple of hours. No reason why we can't take our time and say goodbye properly."

CHAPTER 3

"So did you?" Kit raised an inquiring eyebrow. "Say goodbye *properly*?"

"No I didn't. I turned down his most generous offer." It was the truth, although Lainey was beginning to regret it now.

"Let me guess. You said no so you could feel good about yourself, but you kind of wish you hadn't."

Lainey tipped her head back until it was resting against the wall behind her. "I hate how you always know these things."

He gave her a companionable nudge. "If it were me, I'd be exactly the same. Actually, I wouldn't. I'd have wanted to say no, but I couldn't have walked away. So I would've given in and gone for it, then felt even more rejected and miserable afterward."

"I've been there too."

"So you were right to turn him down,

even if you are feeling like rubbish right now."

"Thanks," said Lainey.

"And you'll find someone else sooner or later. You know you will," Kit said kindly.

That sounded familiar. Oh yes, it was pretty much what she'd told poor rejected Wyatt last night.

On the bright side, at least she wasn't as miserable as Wyatt.

"It isn't going to happen." The decision came out of nowhere, like a comet, but as soon as it entered her head, Lainey knew this was what she needed to do. "Not for the rest of the year at any rate. I'm not going to let it."

He frowned. "What does that mean?"

"Men, boyfriends . . ." She flapped her hand dismissively. "All that . . . *sex* stuff — it's just so much more hassle than it's worth. You see someone, you fancy them, you get to really like them so you think about them *all* the time, and then sooner or later, it all goes tits up and you end up feeling completely rotten until the next one comes along, and the whole stupid circle starts all over again. And if you aren't upset, it means it was a waste of time anyway, but if you *are* upset, it's just the most horrible, empty feeling in the world. So that's it."

She rose from the bench and gathered together her mismatched cases, because the train was approaching the station. "I'm taking the rest of the year off. From now until Christmas, at the very least, I shall be a man-free zone. Me and the opposite sex are on a break."

Ooh, that feels quite empowering. Go me!

Kit said mournfully, "Some of us have been on a break since the beginning of the year, even though we didn't want to be."

"Ah well, by this time tomorrow, you'll be back home in London." Lainey gave his arm a reassuring squeeze. "More beautiful boys than you can shake a stick at."

"Actually, I wasn't planning on shaking a stick at them," said Kit.

Biddy had driven them this morning to the Gare d'Orléans. She'd pressed a packed lunch on them to keep them going during the long and tedious journey home. Thirty minutes after boarding the train to Paris, Lainey had finished hers.

"You're an animal." Kit shook his head in disbelief.

"I can't help it. Traveling makes me hungry." She licked her fingers, brushed baguette crumbs off the front of her sleeveless black top, and neatly folded the paper bags that had contained her food. "I don't understand how you can not eat yours."

"Easy. Because six hours from now, I'll still have mine to look forward to. And you'll be hungry again."

"I'm pretty sure in six hours' time, I'll have bought some more food." Lainey's phone beeped with a message. She read it and groaned.

"Problem?"

"It's from my dad. He didn't want to say anything yesterday, and of course I can still stay at his place for a while if I really want to, but his girlfriend's kids are in the bedrooms, so I'd have to sleep on the sofa, and the boys like to come downstairs at six in the morning to play games on the Xbox before school. So if I'd rather find somewhere else, they'd completely understand."

Kit grimaced. "Bummer."

"Pretty much." She'd only met the two boys once, last Christmas; they were friendly enough but incredibly loud.

"My mum wouldn't mind you staying with us for a bit if you're desperate."

Lainey smiled at him. "I bet your mum's as lovely as you are."

"Well, nearly. I mean it, though. You'd be welcome. She'll try to feed you up too."

"That sounds wonderful."

"Not really," said Kit. "She's a shocking cook."

Lainey intermittently dozed and daydreamed for a while, her head resting against the cool glass of the window. She loved her dad and knew he loved her too, but their lives had diverged following the death of her mum from gastric cancer eight years ago. "I don't want you wasting your life here, thinking you have to look after me," he'd said, knowing she wanted to travel and work abroad. "Get yourself out there and see something of the world, love." So she'd gone ahead and done exactly that. It had felt a bit strange to see her dad moving on, rebuilding his life with a series of girlfriends who were the opposite of her mum. He seemed happy, and of course she was glad about that, but her bedroom had long gone, and with her jobs providing live-in accommodation, it had meant fewer visits to see him and no longer any actual place of her own to call home.

Oh well, never mind. It would happen one day. The dream she'd harbored for years was to save as much money as she could, find a tumbledown property — close to the sea perhaps — and do it up herself, then open it as a bijou but perfect B&B.

Which might be a tad unrealistic, but

everyone was allowed to have a dream, weren't they? Her own business — something that could gradually be built up and expanded — would make use of the knowledge she'd gained while working for other people in the hotel and leisure industries. Caring for her mum during those difficult teenage years might have decimated her school exams and put paid to any plans for university, but she knew she had a good brain, her cooking skills were excellent, and she certainly wasn't afraid of hard work. She just needed to get enough money together first. And who was to say that twenty years from now, she wouldn't be running her own boutique hotel?

Anyway, it was nice to be offered a temporary place to stay by Kit's mum, and there was always her own Granny Ivy, who would be glad to put her up if she was really stuck. But her grandmother was hosting friends from Canada for the next month, which meant her cottage was full. Lainey knew that what she really needed was to find something more permanent for herself and a job to go with it.

Reaching Paris at last, they carted their cases on the Métro to Bercy in the 12th arrondissement, then boarded the bus that would, nine hours from now, deposit them at Victoria Coach Station in central London.

Right, time to take another look at the jobs website she'd bookmarked earlier.

Hooray for the magic of Wi-Fi.

For the next hour, Lainey pored over the many and varied vacancies advertised online. Next to her, Kit finally unwrapped his packed lunch and began to eat.

"Look, there's a parrot up there in that tree!" She pointed out of the window.

Kit said equably, "There could be a pterodactyl out there, and I still wouldn't look if it meant taking my eyes off my food. Not while I'm sitting next to you anyway."

Lainey blew him a kiss — he knew her so well — and turned her attention back to the situations vacant, preferably with living accommodation included. There was a crisply worded ad for a housekeeping assistant required to join an existing team on a private Highland estate in Sutherland. A hardworking gardener was needed for a large country house in North Wales . . . hmm, gardening definitely wasn't her forte. A companion was required for an elderly lady in Kensington; that might be promising . . . Oh, fluency in German essential. The only German she knew was *Sprechen Sie Englisch?* Which probably wouldn't get her the job.

"You're sighing," Kit remarked ten minutes later. "You sound like a walrus."

Well, thanks!

"They should add video clips to these adverts, so you can see what kind of a situation you'd be getting yourself into. There's one here for a mother's helper. It says you have to be calm and efficient, and look after four small boys who are rambunctious but adorable." Lainey pulled a face. "Does that mean they're actually obnoxious monsters, completely out of control? A bit of secret camera work would come in handy."

But when she emailed the agency, they replied within minutes to say the job was no longer available.

The next ad required someone to work as a cleaner and companion for an elderly ex-academic gentleman who lived in Durham. The successful candidate, it stated, must have plenty of patience and a thick skin, and be capable of engaging in prolonged periods of vigorous political debate.

Maybe not.

Then again, who was to say that any of these people would even want to employ her? To be on the safe side, she should probably be applying for every job on the list to see if anyone was remotely interested.

As soon as she started reading the next

ad, however, she knew that this was the job she wanted.

Just typical.

"Oh God, why did I even read this one?" Puffing out her cheeks in exasperation, she passed the phone over to Kit. "It's *perfect.*"

When he'd finished reading, Kit said, "Sounds great. Go for it."

Lainey knew it was nothing but a fantasy, but she really felt as if she could picture the house by the sea and the woman who had placed the ad. She took back her phone and said, "I can't. They're advertising for a couple."

He grinned. "If you get down on one knee and ask really nicely, I'd probably agree to marry you."

Two days later, they left Kit's mother's flat in Wimbledon and traveled by train down to Cornwall. By midafternoon, they'd almost reached St. Carys.

"Put it away," Kit ordered.

Lainey couldn't help herself. Sometimes she could take or leave Facebook, but now wasn't one of those occasions. Anton had arrived in Saint-Tropez and was evidently wasting no time in moving on. He'd just posted a slew of photos of himself settling nicely into his new life on the Côte d'Azur.

39

Fifty-seven photos, in fact, and she'd felt compelled to scroll through the lot of them. There was Anton on the deck of a super-yacht, sitting outside a bar on the seafront, taking selfies on the beach, looking happy and handsome, for all the world as if he wasn't missing her at all. But that was because he *wasn't* missing her, was he? And think of all the stunning bikini-clad girls down there who'd be only too delighted to rub sunscreen into those beautiful brown shoulders . . .

"Stop it." This time Kit took the phone away from her, switched it off, and dropped it into his shirt pocket.

"I love it when you're being masterful."

He studied her face. "Are you really missing him?"

Was she? Lainey considered the question and exhaled. "I just wish he weren't having quite such a brilliant time, that's all."

Basically, her pride was bruised. Then again, at least she was used to it. "Look, I haven't said this before, but the rest of us thought Anton was a bit of a smug git."

Deep down, Lainey knew Kit was right. But it was always hurtful hearing someone else say that kind of thing; it felt as if they were criticizing you for being stupid enough to have gotten involved with someone like that in the first place.

"I mean, he had a pretty high opinion of himself," Kit continued. "Thought he was God's gift."

"Yes, yes, all right."

"All I'm trying to say is, he's not worth moping over. You could do so much better."

"Except I'm not *going* to be doing any better because I'm not planning on doing anything at all. Man-free zone, remember?" With raised arms and pointy index fingers, Lainey drew a bubble around herself. "And I'm not moping anyway. Just because I've been flicking through a few photos doesn't mean —"

"Why don't you stop arguing," Kit interjected, "and start paying attention instead? You haven't even looked out of the window yet."

She followed the direction of his nod and did a double take. What felt like just a few minutes ago, the train had been rattling through the countryside, surrounded on all sides by rolling fields and verdant countryside. But while she'd been hunched over her phone, busy scrutinizing every last detail in Anton's photos, they'd reached the coast. There before them was the sea, glittering in the sunlight and bordered by a sweeping crescent of yellow sand. As the little train chugged around a bend in the track, the seaside town of St. Carys came into view.

"Wow," Lainey breathed. Of course they'd looked the place up online, but the real thing was already better. "I want to live here. Do you have a good feeling about it? Because I do, I definitely do."

"Don't go getting your hopes up." Kit was the practical one. "We haven't passed the interview yet."

They were early; their appointment at Menhenick House wasn't until four, which left them with thirty minutes to kill. Since dragging their overnight cases across the sand wasn't ideal, they stopped at the end of the esplanade overlooking the harbor and grabbed a table at a café topped with a blue-and-white-striped awning.

"OK, we're a ten-minute walk away." Double-checking the map on his phone, Kit pointed to the left. "Up that hill and over on the other side of town. It's straightforward enough."

"Do you think they'll like us?"

"I don't see why not. I'm fantastically lovable, and you're just about bearable when you make an effort."

"Do we look like a couple, though? Do we *behave* like a couple?"

42

"We could quickly go and buy a couple of matching 'kiss me quick' hats, if you think it'll help."

"Maybe we should practice holding hands." Lainey didn't regard herself as a devious person or an untruthful one, but on this occasion, it was a necessary fib. The family had advertised for a couple to work for them, and the accommodation they were supplying was a small one-bedroom apartment. If other genuine couples were in the frame, being two unattached people might be all that was needed to tip the scales against them and lose them the job.

"If we were a couple, we wouldn't hold hands during the interview," Kit pointed out.

She pushed aside her coffee and reached across the table. "Come on, humor me. Let's give it a go anyway."

Kit did as she asked, lacing his fingers between hers. "Like this?"

"How does it feel?"

"Bit weird. The last time I held hands with a female, it was my mum and I was six."

"Give us a kiss." Lainey leaned closer and playfully pursed her lips. Kit did the same and blew a kiss across the table.

The woman in charge of the café, coming over to clear the empty table next to them, said cheerfully, "Now that's what we like to see, a nice bit of romance to cheer us all up! Down here on your honeymoon, are you?" She tilted her head, checking their clasped hands for brand-new wedding rings.

"Maybe one day." Kit showed her his ring-free finger. "She hasn't asked me yet."

A couple of minutes later, Kit disappeared to the bathroom. Since her phone was still confiscated, Lainey sipped her coffee and watched the flow of people making their way in and out of the shops along the curving esplanade. Her gaze was on a young mum attempting to console a screaming toddler when she was distracted by the sight of a tall man in his thirties making his way past. He was wearing jeans and a black polo shirt, with sunglasses hooked over the V at his throat, and it was the way he walked that caught Lainey's attention because it was such a beautiful, *easy* walk.

Narrow hips, long legs, flat stomach — if she'd had a checklist, it'd be full of ticks by now. And he was good-looking too. Even from this distance, she could see the excellent bone structure, the dark eyes and defined eyebrows.

OK, men might be off the agenda for the foreseeable future, but it was still possible to admire a physically attractive specimen.

The next moment, an older woman swerved into his path and held her arms out as if to waylay him. Without slowing or missing a step, the man diverted past while completely ignoring her. Mystified, Lainey watched as she clasped her hands together and called out, "Oh, *please,*" but the man continued as if she simply didn't exist, heading on toward the café, then abruptly turning left and disappearing into one of the narrow side streets.

The woman, visibly dejected, trudged away in the other direction. And Lainey realized that it didn't matter how physically attractive you might be; nothing could make up for a cruel and uncaring attitude. How could he just ignore someone like that? Was the woman his mother or some other relative? Was she an ex-employee, summarily dismissed? Because she hadn't appeared to be begging for money nor had she approached any of the other passersby.

Now that they'd both vanished from view, though, it was highly unlikely Lainey'd ever find out. She checked her watch, eyed the delicious-smelling cheese-and-bacon toasted sandwich being delivered to one of the other customers, and wondered if she had time to order one before they needed to set off for their interview.

CHAPTER 4

Menhenick House might not be chateau-standard spectacular, but it was still pretty impressive. It gleamed white in the sunshine, a rambling country property surrounded by lawns and gardens that would have been stunning if only they weren't so desperately overgrown.

The gates had been open, and a dusty, red Audi stood on the weed-strewn driveway. The house looked to be a mishmash of styles, probably Victorian but with Edwardian additions. Cobalt-blue wooden shutters flanked the sash windows, and the front door was painted blue to match. Now that they'd made their way around the curving path, they could appreciate the stunning sea view and hear the waves breaking on the beach below. The lawn sloping down from the terrace was in need of watering. One rectangle of grass had been neatly mown, but the rest of it was over a foot high.

"Oh God, I hope they like us," Lainey whispered, because how amazing would it be to live in a place like this?

Kit *rat-tat-tat*ted the heavy lion's head door knocker. "I hope *we* like them. Because if we don't, the deal's off."

Nobody answered the knock. Kit tried again. Then Lainey knocked a third time. "There's someone in there, I'm sure of it."

The next moment, they heard a shrill voice call out, "Hang on, hang on," followed by the rapid thud of footsteps galloping downstairs. The door was wrenched open to reveal a teenage girl in an oversized T-shirt, with a purple towel wrapped turban style around her head. "Sorry about that. I was in the bathroom. Are you here for the interview?"

"We are." Kit gave her a friendly nod.

"Oh, but you're early! It's only four o'clock."

Lainey said, "We were told to be here at four."

"Well, Mum said five, and she's not here. She's taken the dogs out. Look, you'd better come in. Sorry about the mix-up . . . Honestly, this is why we need people here to sort us out! Sorry about the mess too." She led them across the hall, along a wide corridor, and into a vast kitchen. "Now you can see what you'd be up against! Have a seat, both of you. Is it OK if I leave you here? Only my hair's at a bit of a crucial stage, and if it falls out, it'll be your fault, so I need to get back upstairs. Help yourselves to tea or coffee or anything else you fancy. I'll message Mum and let her know you're here, but who knows if she'll see it? She's completely hopeless with texts."

She disappeared out the door. Kit and Lainey looked at each other.

"Pretty girl," said Lainey.

"Messy kitchen," said Kit.

He wasn't kidding; to call it cluttered would be an understatement. Every surface was covered with packets of food, discarded mugs and glasses, bits of makeup, books, DVDs, sunglasses, plates, and magazines. The sink was piled high with dirty dishes, and there were dog baskets lined up against the far wall, various pet toys piled between them, and an emerald-green surfboard propped against another wall.

"I suppose we just wait," Kit went on.

"I wonder where the bathroom is," said Lainey. "I could do with a wee."

"Should have gone before we got here, like I did."

"Well, I suppose I can't go nosing around looking for it." She pulled out a chair, removed an empty potato chip packet and a baseball cap from the seat, and sat down.

"We don't even know how many people live here. Could be four, could be twenty-four." Kit paused. "All we know is that they can't be bothered to clear up after themselves. Look at this!" He pointed to half a piece of toast on the table.

"Ooh, maybe it's a test! Maybe we should do the dishes, then when the mother gets back, she'll be dead impressed."

He shook his head. "And what if we're doing that and one of us manages to break a priceless crystal glass? What would we do then?"

"Wrap the pieces in newspaper and bury them in the bin. I can't seriously imagine they'd ever notice."

"Well, we can't do it anyway." Kit indicated the empty plastic bottle next to the taps. "They've run out of dish soap." He opened the right-hand door of the huge American-style refrigerator and shook his head as he surveyed the contents. "Hmm."

"What's wrong?"

"A bag of spinach six weeks past its sell-by date."

Lainey shrugged; who could blame them for not eating it? Spinach was gross.

"You should never keep eggs in a fridge."

Kit reached for a plastic packet and waved it accusingly at her. "And look at this! Who lives in a house worth millions and buys cheap ham?"

Twenty minutes later, they heard the front door open. The next moment, there was a noisy skitter of claws on the parquet flooring out in the hall, followed by two dogs bursting into the kitchen.

"Ernie, Glenda, be gentle! Hello!" A woman hurried in behind the dogs — a lumbering golden Labrador and a small bouncy terrier — and shook hands with Lainey and Kit. "I'm Majella. So lovely to meet you both. Sorry about the mix-up. India told me you were here, so I came rushing back, but we were right over on the other side of St. Carys. I could have sworn Seth said you'd be here at five, but my brain's a bit of a sieve."

Majella was in her midforties, with green eyes and an engaging smile. Her blond hair had been ruffled by the sea breeze, she was wearing fuchsia-pink lipstick, and her billowy white shirt had come untucked from her pink-and-white-striped trousers, possibly because the trouser button was missing. They sat opposite her at the cluttered scrubbed-oak kitchen table with mugs of tea and answered her questions about their references and previous jobs. Apart from the small fib about them being a couple, everything else was aboveboard.

Afterward, Majella took them across the graveled driveway to the little flat above the garage.

"The bedroom's not huge, but it's a nice, comfy bed," she promised. "And look, you can just about see the sea from the window!"

"It's perfect." Lainey nodded; the gray sofa wasn't massive, but they could take it in turns to sleep on it.

Majella beamed. "And how long have you two been together?"

"A year. We aren't married," Kit explained. "I hope that's OK. I mean, we can arrange it if you really want us to."

Lainey looked suitably enthusiastic; well, it was good of him to offer.

"Of course it's OK," Majella assured them. "No problem at all! Now, let's get back to the house, so you can meet everyone. Violet and Harry should be home from school soon, and Seth's around somewhere . . ."

In the kitchen once more, she filled them in on the rest of the family.

"Like I said in the advert, I'm afraid we aren't the most organized. Well, I'm sure you've already noticed. Up until a month ago, we had Maisie living with us, but she's had to move to Coventry to look after her grandchildren. And to be honest, it was an awful lot of work for one person, so that's why we've decided to go for a couple." With her elbows on the kitchen table, she began counting on her fingers. "Now let me tell you who's here. There's me, for a start. My husband, Tony, died five years ago, so I'm battling on without him, but clearly I need a couple pairs of helping hands. Then we have the girls, Violet and India, who are seventeen —"

"Twins?" asked Lainey.

"Yes, but not identical. In fact, they couldn't be less identical if they tried. And then there's Harry, who's eleven and a complete boy — sports mad and eats more than his own body weight in food every day. Next there's my father-in-law . . . Well, it's actually his house . . . and when he's away, traveling around the country, he'll need someone to drive him and generally keep him in check." She paused, glancing at them both. "Just so you know, he's quite a character. Then there's Ernie and Glenda, obviously, and we also have two cats — Radley and Peanut, which are the kind of names you end up with when you're daft enough to let a pair of seven-year-olds decide what to call their new kittens. And finally there's Seth, who's my husband's son from a previous relationship. He splits his time between here and Bristol. But he's around more often than not, and I work for him too in his travel business. And that's us!" She sat back and gestured around the room. "We're a happy household . . . well, most of the time, when the girls aren't having one of their epic fallouts! But those never last long . . . Ah, here's Violet and Harry now."

The two of them had just arrived home from school. Sports uniform and gear was thrown into a corner of the kitchen, and Harry set about making himself a mountain of lopsided sandwiches stuffed with cheese, chips, and ketchup. Introduced to Lainey and Kit, he greeted them cheerfully and asked if they played football, then glugged down a pint of chocolate milk. He was skinny and blond, with an impish grin and cheeks so freckled they looked painted on.

Violet dumped her schoolbag on one end of the table and pulled out an assortment of textbooks followed by an extremely flattened packed lunch.

"Don't you want that?" Harry spoke through a mouthful of sandwich. "I'll have it."

"I was too busy writing an essay at my lunch break." Violet whisked the squashed items out of reach. "I'm eating them now, you glutton."

"If you're eating them now, that makes you the glutton." Playfully he grabbed a hair band that had fallen out of his sister's bag and pinged it at her head.

"And if you're a pain in the neck," Violet retorted, "no one's going to want to come and work here." She shook her head at Lainey and Kit. "Boys, they're just a total nightmare."

"Apart from me," said Kit. "I'm not a nightmare at all."

"I like boys." India arrived downstairs with her head no longer swathed in a towel. "Apart from my little brother." She struck a *ta-da* pose and waited for everyone to admire the transformation. "Well, what do we think? Fabulous or what?"

Lainey grinned. "Your mum did say the two of you were the opposite of identical."

"Trust me, if I were identical to Violet, I'd chuck myself off the nearest cliff. Mum, d'you like it?" India swished her hair from side to side like a shampoo ad.

"If I were identical to India, I'd move to Australia," said Violet. "And get a face transplant."

Harry swallowed a mouthful of chips. "You look like a parrot," he told India.

Lainey said, "Honestly, I think it looks fantastic."

Only half under her breath, Violet squawked, "Who's got purple hair? India's got purple hair, *kwaaaaarrckk!*"

"At least I'm not sad enough never to have dyed it. She's the thin, dreary one," India explained to Kit and Lainey. "Whereas I'm curvy and spectacular."

Lainey studied the two of them. Violet's hair was straight, collar length, and natural blond. She was wearing her navy school uniform and no makeup, and her only jewelry was a tattered gray friendship bracelet around her left wrist. She was small and serious looking, her fair eyebrows unplucked, her fingernails bare.

And then there was India, whose generous curves were poured into an emerald-green Lycra dress that hugged every inch of her body and contrasted spectacularly with the Cadbury's purple hair. Her darkened eyebrows were immaculately shaped, her makeup a riot of peacock-blue eyeshadow, iridescent highlighter, and crimson lipstick.

"Next year, I'll pass my exams," said Violet. "And you won't."

"That's because I don't need to pass

them. Some of us have our dazzling personalities to get us through life."

"Fine, just don't come whining to me ten years from now, when you can't afford another stick of mascara."

With a splutter of laughter, India came up behind her sister and gave her an extravagant hug. "And that's why I love you so much. Who else could call a tube of mascara a stick?"

"Get off me," Violet grumbled, but she was smiling too. "You're such a weirdo."

"They do love each other really," Majella assured Lainey and Kit. "If anyone else dares to criticize either of them, the other one piles in like a tank."

"Have you had many other applicants?" Kit asked.

"Four other couples so far. Well, three," Majella amended.

"The first couple were *sooo* boring." India mimed a yawn. "The second ones were plain weird. The third thought *we* were a bit weird. And Seth messaged the fourth couple and told them not to turn up." She smiled brightly, shrugged. "And that's all of them to date."

"Good one." Violet rolled her eyes. "Now these two are going to be wondering how we'll be describing them as soon as they've left."

"I can juggle," Kit offered. "And ride a unicycle, if that's any help." He paused to think. "Does that make me boring or weird?"

"I don't suppose I'm allowed to ask," said Lainey, "but I'm dying to know why the fourth couple got canceled."

A figure appeared in the kitchen doorway and a clipped male voice said, "When I checked them out online, they hadn't done a good enough job of covering their tracks."

CHAPTER 5

Lainey's heart did a panicky double thud of alarm because this had to be Seth, and what was he actually saying here? Did this mean he'd checked her and Kit out online and discovered they weren't a couple? She'd made her own social media accounts private and told Kit to do the same, but maybe he'd forgotten. Had Seth discovered the lovingly curated photos of Kit's Hollywood dream list, currently featuring a top three of Chris Hemsworth, Ryan Reynolds, and Zac Efron?

Well, a boy could dream.

And if this was the case, he was probably here now to order them out of the house.

Then he stepped out of the shadows and into the kitchen, and Lainey's breath caught in her throat because this was Majella's stepson, and now she recognized him — he was the one she'd watched earlier determinedly ignoring the woman who'd been pleading with him down by the harbor.

Early thirties, dark-brown eyes, black hair slicked back, and frankly intimidating carved cheekbones teamed with a straight, strong nose and chiseled jaw; it was definitely him.

"Well, this is Seth," said Majella. "As you've probably guessed! Seth, this is Lainey and Kit."

He shook their hands in turn, his gaze cool and appraising. Lainey swallowed, because it was as if he was committing every last detail of her face to memory, and a mixture of this and liar's guilt was making her palms slick.

But he either knew the truth or didn't, and since they no longer had anything to lose, she said cheerfully, "What did you find out about them? Were they drug dealers? Bank robbers on the run?"

"Let's just say they weren't altogether truthful about themselves." He moved aside as Harry and the dogs raced past them out of the kitchen. "And if we're going to have people living and working here, honesty is important. You have to be able to trust them completely. Why are you looking at me like that?"

Goodness, he was direct; it was like being interrogated in court. Lainey said, "We arrived in St. Carys early and stopped for a coffee down by the harbor. I saw you walking along the esplanade." Maybe the woman who'd tried to waylay him had been someone he'd rejected for the job.

"And you recognized me from somewhere?" He tilted his head in inquiry.

"Well, no, because I didn't know who you were then, did I?" She lightened the reply with a little laugh because his manner was so abrupt. "I recognized you when you walked into this kitchen one minute ago."

"And you're still interested in the position?" There was a glimmer of something combative in his eyes. "Despite having met us?"

"Everyone else seems great," said Lainey. "Although I haven't made my mind up yet about you."

Next to her, Kit muttered under his breath, "What are you *doing*?"

But India and Violet were already high-fiving each other, demonstrating their approval. While India clapped, Violet said, "She's good, Seth. We like her."

"So do I," said Majella before hastily reaching over and touching Kit's arm. "And we like you too."

Kit nodded gravely. "Thank you. Everyone always likes Lainey best, but I don't mind. I'm kind of used to it by now."

Lainey grinned at him and said, "Thanks, darling," then wished she hadn't, because it felt so strange. Worse than that, it sounded completely unconvincing; this was something they really should have practiced beforehand. She tried giving Kit a loving look instead and saw the suppressed laughter in his eyes.

Then his gaze slid to the open window behind her and amusement turned to shock. Hearing footsteps on gravel, Lainey turned to see who he was looking at, but the moment and the footsteps had passed. She raised her eyebrows at him and mouthed, *What's wrong?*

He looked as if he'd seen a ghost.

"I just . . ." Kit was shaking his head. "Was that . . . Is that . . . Did I just see who I thought I saw?"

"Well, if you thought you saw Beyoncé," said Seth, "then no, you didn't."

At that moment, Lainey became aware that everyone in the kitchen was watching her and Kit, waiting to gauge their reaction. Finally, the door opened and a tall, thin figure entered the kitchen, grumbling, "There I was, all settled down ready to watch *Pointless,* and it's a bloody repeat. Oh, are these the latest contestants? Hello, hello, don't mind me, just looking for the gin. You're a couple of pretty young things, aren't you? Quite a step up from the last ones; what a pair of Quasimodos they were. Darling, have we run out of gin? Because if we have, I shall need to declare a state of emergency."

If it was possible, the voice was even more recognizable than the face. Kit was still gazing at him, slack jawed, but Lainey didn't react outwardly. Until this moment, it hadn't occurred to her that the family surname could be significant, but it now became apparent that it was. The tricky old gentleman mentioned in the advert was Sir Richard Myles, and all of a sudden finding yourself in the same room as him was kind of overwhelming. No wonder Kit was looking dumbstruck.

He must be close to eighty now, but those bright-blue eyes were undimmed with age. In the 1960s, the young Richard Myles had burst into the public consciousness upon landing the lead role in a movie called *Wherever You Are*. Epic, sweeping, and madly romantic, it had broken box office records worldwide, and Richard Myles's boyish good looks and charismatic personality had confirmed his place in the Hollywood firmament. Together with a wild group of fellow actors, he had dominated the party scene, burned all the candles at both ends, and almost single-handedly kept the gossip columnists in business. Quick-witted, self-effacing, and with buckets of charm, he'd worked nonstop for decades and downed enough alcohol to fill countless swimming pools. One by one, his hard-drinking actor friends had died, but against all the odds, and to everyone's amazement, Sir Richard and his ironclad liver had survived.

He was an actual national treasure, currently wearing a Hawaiian shirt and cream linen trousers while he rummaged in the fridge before finally locating a can of Fever-Tree tonic.

"If you finished the last bottle," Majella said patiently, "there isn't any more gin."

"Well, this is a disaster." Richard clutched his heart in dismay. "It's *worse* than a disaster. Darling girls, which of you two would like to pop down to the store and pick me up a liter of Tanqueray?"

"Grandad, they won't let us buy it." By the sound of Violet's voice, this wasn't the first time they'd been asked. "We're only just seventeen."

"But surely you can use your fake IDs?"

India said, "They know we aren't eighteen, though." She grinned at Kit. "It's the price of fame."

"I'd go myself," said Sir Richard, "but my hip's playing up." His forehead creased with the kind of despair conveyed by a castaway on a desert island when the rescue plane flies off without spotting him. His shoulders drooped and the fingers of his free hand rested against his sternum in defeat.

"I know where the liquor store is," said Kit. "We passed it on our way here. If you'd like me to, I could go."

The shoulders lifted and the agony in Sir Richard's face was replaced by sheer joy. The pilot of the rescue plane had spotted the castaway after all and was coming back to save him.

"Well, I didn't like the other couples anyway." He slid a couple of twenty-pound notes out of his wallet and handed them to Kit. "But now you're indisputably my favorites."

"I'll shoot down there as soon as we've finished being interviewed," Kit assured him.

"Oh, but I was rather hoping you could run down there now, dear boy. My liver's starting to think my throat's been cut. Besides, how would I know for sure that you'd be back? You might bugger off with my money and we'd never clap eyes on you again."

"I wouldn't do that. I'm very honest. We both are," Kit assured him. "You can trust us completely."

"Good to know, dear boy. Right then, off you pop. We'll see you back here in no time."

Sir Richard ushered Kit out of the house, then put his head back around the kitchen door. "If anybody needs me, I'll be in the garden."

"You're supposed to be sitting in on the interview." Seth sounded exasperated.

"I've already told you, I like this couple best."

"What about the questions you wanted to ask?"

"Fine." With a sigh, Sir Richard leaned against the doorjamb and fixed his gaze on Lainey. "Have you ever been arrested?"

"No."

"Not even once? How disappointing. Do you drive too fast or too slowly?"

"Neither," said Lainey. "I drive just right."

"Ever been stopped by the police for speeding?"

"Yes."

"And did you get a ticket, or manage to talk your way out of it?"

"Talked my way out of it."

He beamed his approval. "Good girl, that's what I like to hear. And do you like mustard?"

"Can't stand it." Lainey pulled a face at the very idea.

"No more questions." Sir Richard turned his attention to Seth and Majella. "Passed with flying colors. This is the one for me."

Once he'd left, it was the twins' turn. They asked Lainey about her favorite TV shows, the kind of music she liked, and her top three websites when shopping online for clothes before giving Seth and Majella a cheery thumbs-up and disappearing upstairs. Majella's phone rang and she excused herself, mouthing apologetically, *Work.*

"And then there were two," Seth commented once they were alone. "Still, they seem to like you."

"But you haven't made your mind up yet. And I've worked out why."

He raised an eyebrow. "Go on."

"Sir Richard." Lainey clasped her hands loosely together on the table in front of her. "The advert didn't mention him, but you're wondering if we knew who we'd be working for and whether that's why we applied for the job."

"Correct."

"It's not rocket science. And for the record, we had no idea. But then I suppose we would say that, wouldn't we?"

A flicker of a smile. "I suppose you would."

"That's why you were watching us so closely. I wondered what that was about."

"For what it's worth, I'm veering toward believing you. Your boyfriend certainly looked surprised when Richard walked past the window."

Lainey nodded. "What's made you so wary then? Something's obviously happened in the past."

"The couple whose interview we canceled? When I did a bit of online investigation, I found out they're members of the fan club."

"Ah." God, imagine having your own fan club. Did it feel as strange as it sounded?

"We had an undercover journalist apply to work here three years ago." Seth's eyes narrowed with disdain. "And there was a gardener once who tried to sell stories to the press. Not to mention the cleaner we caught auctioning things off on eBay."

OK, maybe he had a reason to be suspicious. Lainey said, "What kind of things?"

"Empty cologne bottles. Items of clothing." He paused. "A toothbrush."

"Seriously? People are weird."

"You don't have to tell me." His tone was wry.

"We aren't weird. And we have our police

background checks." He and Majella must surely have checked those out already. "Four days ago, Kit and I were perfectly happy, living and working in a French chateau. Then the owners ran out of money and had to let us go, which is why we came back to England and set about finding somewhere else to go. We were on the bus when I saw the ad Majella wrote, and it just felt like it was meant for us. I wish I could take a lie detector test to prove to you that it's all true."

"Actually, we could do it on my phone. There's an app you can download." He was giving her another of his appraising looks; was this a bluff, or was he serious?

Lainey stood her ground. "Great, let's do it."

A pause, then the corners of his mouth lifted. "Maybe not. I can't imagine they're accurate. But good answer."

"Thanks."

"So the two of you met when you went out to the chateau. And that was a year ago."

"Correct. We got together pretty much straightaway."

"What happens if you break up?"

"I don't know. We'd just have to cross that bridge when we came to it. But hopefully that won't happen. We're happy and we're really good together. I love him and he loves me." Which was all true, in the platonic sense. Who could fail to love someone as good-natured and easygoing as Kit?

"What happens if you don't get this job?"

"We catch the train back to London and apply for other positions, keep going until we find something." But she knew the other members of the family were on her and Kit's side; surely by now the odds were tipping in their favor?

"Woof."

It was one of the dogs, but neither of them had come back into the kitchen.

Lainey glanced around and spotted a baby alarm propped up on the dresser, largely hidden behind a fruit bowl and a set of weighing scales.

No wonder the bark had sounded a bit tinny.

She turned back to Seth. "Do you have a baby in the house?"

He shook his head. "It's for the dogs. If either of us is working upstairs in the office and they're down here, we like to keep an ear out for them, make sure they're not up to mischief."

Which made perfect sense, but there was something more; the smoothness of the explanation was the giveaway. After a moment, Lainey figured it out.

"You arranged for us to arrive early, so we could be left alone here in the kitchen. You were up in your office listening to see if we said anything about your grandfather."

And there it was, the tiniest flicker of amusement lifting the corners of his beautifully shaped mouth, confirming that she was right. Lainey smiled too, because they'd passed the test. Better still, they hadn't inadvertently given away their own secret. Thank goodness.

Aloud, she said, "That's quite an underhand trick to play. Might even be illegal."

"It isn't. But it can be informative."

Mentally backtracking, Lainey tried to remember everything she and Kit had discussed. Oh God . . . Hastily she said, "I was joking about the broken glass."

"I should hope you were. And when your boyfriend gets back," Seth continued smoothly, "you can tell him the cheap ham in the fridge is what we give the dogs."

Before long, Majella finished her phone call and rejoined them. Ten minutes after that, a pink-cheeked and slightly out-of-breath Kit arrived back from the liquor store with the Tanqueray.

"Let's see how you mix one, then." Sir Richard, summoned in from the garden, set the challenge and oversaw the pouring of the gin, the addition of six ice cubes, the perfect amount of tonic, and a large wedge of lime.

He took a sip and gave a nod of approval. "Good, good. Bit of oomph, that's what I like." He turned to Seth. "Have we taken them on yet?"

Seth narrowed his eyes. "Not yet, but well done for trying to force the issue."

His grandfather affected outrage. "Oh, come on! Aren't I allowed to throw in my two pennies' worth? Pretty young couple, madly in love, capable of pouring a damn fine G and T . . . what more could we possibly ask for?"

"It isn't just your decision, though. I think we need to discuss it." His tone pointed, Seth added, "In private."

"And how long before you make up your mind? These kids could get bored waiting and go somewhere else, then you'll be sorry. Look, they've got their cases with them. They're here, all ready to start. If you let them leave, they might get a better offer and we'll never see them again."

Silence. As situations went, could this one be anymore uncomfortable?

Majella and Sir Richard were both looking at Seth, who for reasons of his own still

71

evidently had doubts about taking them on.

"Well, this is awkward." Lainey checked her watch. "I tell you what, if you don't have any more questions, we'll go now. The next train leaves in forty minutes. If you think you'd like to take us on, give the agency a call. And if you decide to go with someone else, that's fine too. Either way, it's been lovely meeting you all."

Well, most of you.

They waited on a bench on the station platform. The train was now due in seven minutes and neither of their phones had rung.

"I'm glad we didn't do their dishes for them now," said Kit.

Unless it was the fact that they hadn't done the dishes that had annoyed Seth. Lainey heaved a sigh. "They don't have any other candidates. They'll just carry on advertising until they find what they want." The sun, lower in the sky now, was shining directly into her eyes. She closed them and said, "It's so frustrating, though. We didn't do anything wrong. Why didn't he want us? I mean, who wouldn't? We're lovely, and we'd have been great there."

"Maybe he'll change his mind." Kit was ever the optimist.

72

"He won't. It's not going to happen." She scuffed the soles of her sandals against the sand-dusted tarmac. "Not in a million years. He isn't the type."

"Oh God," Kit murmured, and she guessed information had just flashed up on the display board that their train was delayed, because of course it would have to be delayed before the long, hot, and tedious trip home. Except it wasn't even home, was it? It was the spare room at Kit's mum's place, with the discarded knitting machine next to the —

"Sometimes he's the type," said a voice that didn't belong to Kit.

Lainey's heart did a leap, her eyes snapped open, and there was Seth, standing before them with his hands in his trouser pockets, calmly surveying her.

"You really need to stop eavesdropping on other people's private conversations," Lainey told him.

"Not my fault your eyes were closed. So why am I not the type to change my mind?"

"Because you're a businessman who enjoys making split-second decisions and sticking to your guns. Backing down would be seen as a sign of weakness."

"Well done." Seth pointed an index finger at her and nodded in agreement. "Absolutely right, ninety-nine percent of the time." He seemed to specialize in significant pauses, Lainey was already discovering. "But I'm also man enough to know when I need to back down."

Lainey held her breath. So did this mean . . . ?

"That house needs two people to keep it in order. Richard and Majella and the kids and the animals need two people to keep *them* in order. I'll be there some of the time, but I move around. They like you, they want you, so I'm deferring to their wishes. If you're interested in the position, it's yours." He glanced across at the departures board; their train was now due in two minutes. "If you'd rather head back to London, then come down and start work next week, not a problem. But if you want to move in right away, that'd be great." He gestured to the left of the tiny station. "And I can give you a lift. My car's over there in the parking lot."

"Well, this is interesting, but we'll need some time to discuss it. In private." Lainey eyed him coolly as the approaching train hooted in the distance. "If you could give us a few minutes, we'll —"

"Stop playing games," Kit blurted. He

rose to his feet and stuck out his hand to Seth. "Thanks very much. We accept."

CHAPTER 6

"You know, I'm enjoying being your girl-friend."

"My first and only." Kit held out the mug of tea he'd made for her. "You should be honored."

Lainey wriggled into a half-sitting position inside her sleeping bag on the sofa and took the mug from him. It was seven in the morning of their fourth day in St. Carys, and they'd already settled into an easy living-together routine. Kit's mum had arranged for the rest of their stuff to be sent down to them, and it had been delivered yesterday. Since Kit was almost six feet tall, it had made sense for him to take the double bed. Lainey, at five foot four, was sleeping on the sofa, which wasn't brilliant, but it was bearable. The first night, they'd both occupied the bed, but Kit was a restless sleeper and no slouch in the snoring department, so they'd picked up a sleeping bag in the big supermarket outside St. Carys. Each morning, it was rolled up and hidden away in the cupboard behind the front door, where the vacuum cleaner was kept.

"We're quite compatible, aren't we?" Lainey sipped her tea, made just the way she liked it, and watched as he deftly spread her slice of toast with butter, then Nutella.

"If I could only persuade you to enjoy watching football on TV, you'd be perfect."

She took the plate from him; he'd even cut the toast into geometrically perfect triangles. "I love you, but that's never going to happen."

"You don't know what you're missing." Kit put two more slices of bread into the toaster for himself. "I feel sorry for people who don't love football —"

There was a brisk triple knock on the door. Kit had left it on the latch earlier, and it started to swing open. A glance at the outline of the figure through the frosted glass told Lainey the early-morning caller was Seth. With a triangle of toast sticking out of her mouth, she launched herself to her feet and began hopping toward the bedroom. It was ridiculous, like a one-woman sack race, but quicker than trying to wriggle out of the sleeping bag or struggle with its temperamental zip.

Once in the bedroom, she overbalanced and landed with a thud on the bed. But Seth hadn't seen her, that was the main thing. Peeling herself out of the bag, she hastily threw on shorts and a navy sweater, fluffed up her hair, and headed back out to the living room.

"Are you OK?" Seth raised an eyebrow. "I heard the crash. Sounded like you'd fallen out of bed."

"I did. I panicked. Thought we didn't have to be over at the house until seven thirty."

"Sorry, you don't. I dropped by because I'm heading up to Bristol. Harry's just remembered he has a school trip today, so he needs to be there twenty minutes earlier than usual or he'll miss the bus. Plus he needs a packed lunch and swimsuit."

"Right, that's fine. Thanks." Harry's school was thirty minutes away by car; they could still make it.

"We've searched everywhere for his swimsuit. No luck so far."

"Ah, OK." What was he staring at behind her, and why was he looking so horrified?

"Is that yours?" He pointed at the plate of toast.

"Yes." Had there been something in the small print about it when they'd signed the employment contract? Was balancing a plate on a piece of furniture strictly forbidden in case it tipped over and dropped food onto the carpet?

"Nutella *and* butter?" From the way he said it, you'd have thought it was fried wasps.

"So?"

"That's . . . disgusting."

Lainey was instantly on the defensive. "No it isn't."

"It is," Kit chimed in. "How many times have I told you it's wrong? You're supposed to have Nutella on dry toast."

Honestly, talk about disloyal. Although, on the upside, it did make him sound like a boyfriend, if an unsupportive one.

"I can have Nutella however I like." She reached for the plate and offered it to them. "Hey, don't knock it till you've tried it."

"Some things you don't need to try," said Seth.

Their loss. She put the plate down again. "You don't know what you're missing. Anyway, don't worry. We'll get everything sorted. I'll be over in five minutes."

Just as soon as she had a chance to put on a pair of panties and a bra.

Majella had spent the morning hard at work in the office dealing with queries from clients of Seth's company, Faulkner Travel. At midday, driven by hunger pangs, she made her way down to the kitchen. The windows were sparkling clean, the flagstone floor was crumb free, and the piles of clutter had been reduced by 90 percent.

"You're a miracle worker," she told Lainey, who was busy in the adjacent utility room, shoveling clothes out of the washing machine and into the tumble dryer. "You both are. I'm already so glad you chose to come here."

"We are too." Lainey's streaky blond hair was escaping from its scrunchie, her cheeks were pink, and the sleeves of her navy sweatshirt were damp. "Oh, I managed to find Harry's swimming trunks. They were hiding under a pile of towels in the airing cupboard."

Through the clean window, Majella could see Kit out in the garden, hacking away at the mass of honeysuckle threatening to smother the roses beneath the pergola. And now Lainey was piling vegetables onto the chopping board at one end of the kitchen table and fetching a big glass ovenproof dish from the cupboard and a sharp knife from the drawer. It would be disloyal to say so, but this cheerful girl put Maisie, their last housekeeper, to shame.

She could think it, though. And tell Seth when he returned, so he'd know he'd been wrong to doubt the new couple's capabilities.

Aloud, she said, "You both work so hard."

"We're used to it. As soon as I've made the casserole, I'm going to scrub down the skirting boards. Honestly, it makes a difference," Lainey assured her, because Majella was clearly looking as bemused as she felt. "Just you wait. By the time we've finished our blitz, this house is going to look amazing, like something out of a magazine."

They were angels in human form. Getting back to having a home they could be properly proud of was the answer to Majella's prayers. She went to the fridge and found a wedge of Brie to have with crackers to quell her rumbling stomach. Then, settling herself at the table, she watched as Lainey expertly diced her way through a small mountain of carrots, onions, and potatoes for the casserole.

"I remember the first time we set eyes on this place. It was fifteen years ago, just after Richard bought it. We all came and spent a summer down here, and I couldn't believe how perfect it was. That was back when Richard was still spending months at a time over in LA, and his financial adviser told him he should rent it out. So for the next few years, that was what happened, until Richard had his heart attack and realized the time had come to slow down."

"That must have been terrifying for you."

Majella nodded. "It was touch and go for a few days. But he had his bypass op and came through it. Then he decided he wanted to up sticks and live here full-time, and he asked us to move down with him. But Tony was working in Kensington, and it just wasn't practical. So Richard gave up on that idea, married Ava Delucci, and moved into her villa on the edge of Lake Como instead."

"I remember that." Lainey pulled an oh-dear face, because pretty much everyone on the planet knew that his marriage to Ava had been a catastrophic error of judgment. It had ended with the excitable Italian actress stopping traffic in the center of Rome in order to bellow through a megaphone that she couldn't stay married for another minute to a man who would rather play poker in a casino than visit the opera with her. In response, Richard had gravely informed a TV journalist that attending the opera was almost as much of an ear-splitting experience as being married to Ava.

"So then he moved back to London and took a suite at the Goring, as you do,"

Majella added drily. "That was seven years ago, just before Tony was diagnosed with cancer . . . Oh, it was an awful time." The familiar wave of grief swept over her, and she put down the cracker in her hand. "I know it's a massive cliché, but life really is a roller coaster, isn't it? We were so happy up until then. Except you never properly appreciate the good times until they stop being good and you find yourself up to your neck in misery instead."

"We don't have to talk about it." Lainey had stopped chopping carrots; her tone was gentle.

Majella shook her head. "It's OK. I've had plenty of time to get used to it. It's been almost five years now since he died. For the first couple of years I couldn't say his name without crying, but it's easier now. This is my new life, and it's up to me to make the most of it."

"Look, am I allowed to ask a personal question?"

"Fire away." She knew what was coming.

"Violet told me last night that you don't go out on dates. She said there hasn't been anyone since Tony."

"That's true. There hasn't." Majella shook her head.

"And is that because you aren't interested?

Again, just say if you don't want to talk about it," Lainey added hastily. "Or have you thought it might be nice to meet someone else but it just hasn't happened?"

"I honestly don't mind talking about it." Majella smiled briefly. "I joined an online group for widows after I lost Tony, and quite a few of them have met someone else. I think I wanted to concentrate on the children, make sure they were getting through it OK. But I've done that now. And I suppose it would be nice to meet . . . well, someone nice . . ." An unexpected surge of emotion caught in her throat, and all of a sudden, it was necessary to swallow hard. After years of resolutely reminding herself how lucky she was to have the children here to keep her going, she seldom allowed herself to admit she felt lonely.

"You're ready to meet someone," said Lainey. "That's good."

"There's no hurry. Maybe the right man will come along someday. But you can't make it happen."

"You took me on because you wanted a Mary Poppins to make your life better and easier." Lainey gestured cheerfully with a knife in one hand and a potato in the other. "Well, that's my mission. I may not be able to make it happen, but we can definitely figure out how to tip the odds in your favor."

CHAPTER 7

It was five in the afternoon when Seth Faulkner arrived back in St. Carys a week later. The drive down from Bristol had taken just over two and a half hours, thanks to a fast car and, miraculously, no holdups on the motorway. He parked in the driveway of Menhenick House and let himself in only to find it deserted.

The air was warm, the sea was delphinium blue, and seagulls wheeled overhead as the sun hung low in the sky; it didn't take MI5 to work out where everyone would be. He made his way down through the garden, then farther down still, until he emerged at the top of the smallest of the three beaches in St. Carys Bay. Beachcomber was the farthest west, then there was Mariscombe; all three were stunning, but this one, Menhenick Bay, was the most hidden, the most sheltered, and his personal favorite.

And there too, down on the sand, were

his favorite people. India and Violet were sprawled next to a picnic blanket, helping themselves to food being offered to them by Majella. Richard, wearing sunglasses and his beloved panama hat, occupied a folding chair and was watching an energetic game of Frisbee being played by Harry and the new couple while feeding bits of sandwich to Ernie and Glenda, stretched out in the patch of shade beside him.

Seth zoned in on Kit and Lainey. Even if he hadn't seen the already noticeable difference in the house and garden, he was aware of how thrilled Majella was to have them here, basically because she kept sending him texts and emails telling him so in order to prove that he'd been wrong not to want them and she'd been right.

No one had yet spotted him up here, and Seth continued to watch unobserved.

The girls had always been happy to play beach games with sports-mad Harry when they were younger, but at seventeen, their enthusiasm had waned. Luckily Lainey and Kit were really throwing themselves into the game. All three were wearing shorts and T-shirts, and when Harry sent the Frisbee sailing into the sea, the other two raced in after it. Kit tried to reach it first, and Lainey, refusing to be beaten, pushed him to the left so he overbalanced and landed on his knees. With a shriek of delight, she danced past and launched herself at the Frisbee. Up to her thighs now in the turquoise water, she waved it above her head and did a gleeful victory dance, then pretended to throw it to Kit before sending it flying high over his head instead to Harry on the beach.

Realizing he was missing out, Ernie abandoned the secret supply of sausage rolls — which was a miracle in itself — and tore over to join them in the water. And really, who could blame him? As Richard had observed last week, Kit and Lainey were an attractive couple. With his rugby player's physique, tousled fair hair, and winning smile, Kit had a clean-cut, all-American look about him. But it was Lainey — surprise, surprise — who drew Seth's attention to such a degree that he was finding it almost impossible to look away. Her dark-blond hair, wavy and windswept, flew behind her as she high-stepped through the waves, chasing Ernie. Her white shorts were wet, her tanned thighs gleamed with droplets of seawater, and the wide neckline of her red T-shirt was slipping off one shoulder. Ernie abruptly went into reverse and launched himself at her, and Lainey tumbled into the water, screaming with laughter as the dog, tail wagging madly, attempted to lick her face.

It was the strangest sensation; there was just something about this girl. Seth had no idea what it was, but he knew he couldn't allow himself to think it. Nor was he enjoying feeling this way; it wasn't ideal, to say the least. The more he looked at her, the more strongly he felt as if there were some indescribable connection between them; a sense of recognition, almost, as if they'd known each other before.

Although he was equally certain they hadn't; thanks to his excellent memory, he'd always been able to place familiar faces from the past.

The riotous game was in full flow again now. Wonder of wonders, even India had been persuaded to put down her phone and join in. Seth smiled to himself as Glenda promptly leaped up and entered the fray, then found his attention turning once more to Lainey, who was grabbing the hem of her boyfriend's T-shirt in order to hold him back so Harry could dive past and seize control of the Frisbee.

As Seth settled himself on the rock behind him, he wondered just how tricky the coming months were likely to be. He hadn't been entirely truthful with Majella and Richard. When Majella had said in bewilderment, "But *why* don't you think we should hire them?" he'd replied, "I just think an older couple would be better. These two have only known each other for a year, so who's to say they're even going to stay together? They could have a massive fight next week and break up, and then we'll be back to square one."

As a rule, in both business situations and life in general, Majella accepted his advice and decisions. This time, however, she'd made up her mind and wasn't allowing him to change it. With a shake of her head she'd said firmly, "And maybe they won't break up. Don't be such a pessimist, Seth. Just because you get bored with your relationships doesn't mean everyone else does. They seem like a brilliant couple, the rest of us like them, we've decided we want them here, and that's that."

It was surprisingly frustrating, he'd discovered, not getting his own way. "But —"

"Seth, stop trying to argue with me." Majella had stood her ground. "Even if they do break up, I'd rather have Kit and Lainey for a few months than be stuck with some boring middle-aged couple who'll stay together for the rest of their lives."

That was the moment Seth had known he was beaten. He'd been forced to give in with good grace, drive down to the train station, and relay the news to Lainey and Kit that they were hired.

And now they'd settled in just as effortlessly as Majella had predicted they would. The rest of the family was absolutely delighted to have them here.

Whereas he . . . wasn't.

He expelled a stream of air from his lungs and reminded himself that he could do this. He had to. Yes, he was drawn to Lainey; he'd experienced that jolt of attraction the moment he'd first set eyes on her in the kitchen last week, so powerful it had almost taken his breath away.

And he was accustomed — always had been — to getting whatever or whomever he wanted.

But this time it wasn't going to happen; it couldn't happen. He might have something of a reputation where women were concerned, but the one thing he'd never done — never would do — was deliberately try to break up a relationship.

Especially not if the couple concerned were working for his own family.

Which meant he was just going to have to keep his feelings for Lainey to himself. It wouldn't be easy, but it was doable. Just because you found yourself drawn to someone didn't mean you had to act on it. When they weren't available, you simply put the idea out of your head and carried on as if it hadn't happened.

Not by so much as a flicker would he give himself away. And with a bit of luck, his notoriously short attention span where the opposite sex was concerned wouldn't let him down. Give the situation a few weeks, and the attraction would fade away of its own accord.

"Seth!"

They'd spotted him. Faces had turned in his direction, Majella was waving and India was beckoning him to join them. "Come on down. You can be on our team!"

He hesitated and wondered whether to feign an urgent business call, one that would require him to head back to the house. At that moment, the phone in his pocket began to ring. Great, talk about karma; now it *would* be an urgent business call, requiring hours of work to sort out.

But when he glanced at his phone, he saw Dawn's name on the screen, which was far easier to deal with.

She'd left two messages already while he'd been driving down the M5. Oh well, one more couldn't hurt.

And it would be ridiculous to try to avoid Lainey and Kit; they lived and worked here, for goodness' sake.

He let the call go to voicemail and put the phone back in his jeans pocket, then rose to his feet and made his way along the sandy path that led down to the beach.

No problem. He could do this.

An hour later, when Dawn's name flashed up on his phone for the fourth time, he answered it.

"So you are still alive," she exclaimed. "I was beginning to wonder."

"Sorry, I was on my way home, couldn't answer while I was driving. Then I ran out of battery. All sorted now."

"Well as long as you're not trying to avoid me." She laughed. "Because I'm not used to that happening."

"I can imagine," said Seth, and he meant it. They'd met for the first time a couple of weeks ago, had been introduced by mutual friends on the terrace of the Mariscombe House Hotel. She'd moved down from Durham last month to join a small firm of solicitors in St. Carys, and interest among the thirtysomething crowd at the hotel that evening had been intense.

Even now, Seth realized he was mentally comparing Lainey and Dawn; he couldn't help himself. If you were to stand them next to each other and ask people who was the most beautiful, most would say Dawn. She was physically impressive, tall and perfectly proportioned, with immaculate makeup and glossy dark hair snaking down her back. She had a swaying, slinky walk, an air of absolute confidence, and a low-pitched Joanna Lumley voice. She looked like one of those go-getting, high-powered legal types in the US TV show *Suits.*

Lainey, in comparison, was more . . . How could he phrase it? Down to earth. She was attractive, but in a completely different way. In his imaginary lineup, Seth couldn't help picturing her as she'd looked on the beach earlier, with her cheeks glowing, her eyes bright, and her streaky brown and blond hair whipped by the sea breeze into a mad tangle. Sand had dried on her arms and legs, a strand of seaweed was caught up in one hoop earring, and a trickle of blood had slid down her shin where she'd sliced open her knee on a broken mussel shell during a particularly energetic dive tackle.

The red T-shirt had stretched out of shape and the white denim shorts had been drenched and clinging to her thighs, but she'd been having too much fun to care how she looked; basically, she'd radiated joy.

If he had the choice, Seth knew, he would go for Lainey every time.

OK, time to stop comparing them. Because he didn't have a choice, did he?

Lainey wasn't available, and the one currently on the other end of the phone was Dawn.

Who clearly wasn't accustomed to having to call a man four times before getting to speak to him.

"Sorry about that," he continued. "It's good to hear from you. How are things?"

"*Things* are fine, thanks so much for asking." She sounded amused. "Although I did think you might have been in touch before now. You told me you would be."

"I know. The last couple of weeks have been crazy at work. I've been up in Bristol most of the time." Which was true enough.

"But I can hear the sea, which hopefully means you're back now," said Dawn. "I was wondering if you'd like to come over to my place for dinner this evening."

She wasn't shy, you could say that for her.

"Dinner sounds good," said Seth. "Or we could go out to eat, if that's easier. I've heard great things about the new French place on Silver Street."

"Tried it last weekend. My food's better than theirs." Modest too.

"In that case, you'd better tell me where you live and what time you'd like me there."

"Eight sharp. I'll text the address. You won't regret it," said Dawn. And confident.

Well, he was in need of some distraction, and she seemed keen to supply it.

Seth told himself it was the sensible thing to do.

At 7:45, ready to leave, he headed downstairs and made his way through to the kitchen, drawn by the smell of fried onions and sizzling bacon.

Lainey, also showered and changed, was wearing a pink dress splashed with yellow stars, her hair tied up in a messy topknot. Busy putting the finishing touches to a tray of burgers, each one piled high with onions, sliced tomatoes, and melted cheese, she looked up and noticed him eyeing them.

"Hi, I know you said you didn't want anything, but there's plenty here if you change your mind."

"It's killing me, but I mustn't." Oh God, though was there anything better?

Seth watched as she deftly crisscrossed strips of streaky bacon on top of each burger before pressing the upper halves of the buns onto the stacks. His mouth watered.

"Suit yourself." She placed the last two strips of bacon on a small plate and pushed it across the table in his direction. "Although these'll just go to waste if you don't eat them."

As Seth finished the second one, he realized they'd just whetted his appetite and made a bad situation worse; now he *really* wanted one of the giant burgers.

"Thanks." He checked his watch. "I have to go."

"Darling, are you off?" Majella came into the kitchen with Richard. "What time will you be home? Oh God, ignore me. Force of habit. You're not one of the girls!"

"I'm not," Seth agreed. Were there really no more leftover strips of bacon?

"And am I allowed to ask who you're seeing?"

"Her name's Dawn. She's the new lawyer at Berry and Dexter."

"Ooh, I've heard about her! I gather she's causing quite a stir in St. Carys. Stunning *and* supersmart."

Seth noticed that Lainey paused for a split second and glanced across the table at him. He shrugged. "She seems pretty smart."

"And of course she's a stunner," Richard chimed in. "He wouldn't be wasting his time on someone who wasn't. Let's face it, he's not going to go out with a warthog."

CHAPTER 8

At ten o'clock, while she and Kit were stretched out in front of the TV, Lainey's phone rang.

"It's Biddy." Leaning over the edge of the sofa, she reached for it. "Why would she be calling?"

"All going well?" asked Biddy, and Lainey assured her that everything was fine.

"Well, that's good news." Biddy had clearly felt dreadful about letting them go at such short notice. "Now, I know you're not going to be able to help with this, but I promised I'd get in touch with all of you and ask, just on the off chance. We had a call from Wyatt this afternoon. He's only gone and lost the engagement ring, hasn't he?"

Lainey sat up. "What? Lost it where?"

"Well, if he knew that, it wouldn't be lost," said Biddy. "Silly boy. He went to return it to the shop this morning, and when he opened the box, the ring wasn't there."

"Oh my God, you mean it's been stolen? But who would do that? And when did it happen? It wasn't me!" The little hairs on the back of Lainey's neck prickled with alarm; was it weird to feel instantly guilty even though you knew you were innocent? At the age of eight, a boy at school had shoplifted a packet of fruit gummies and promptly told the shopkeeper she'd forced him to do it. The horror of being unjustly accused had haunted her ever since.

But Biddy was laughing, keen to reassure her as Lainey switched to speakerphone so Kit could hear what was going on too. "Oh no, love! Of course it wasn't you, nobody's saying it was. Wyatt's blaming himself, what with being so distraught and getting so plastered. He thinks he has a vague memory of going up to his room that evening and taking the ring out of its box, but apparently it's all a bit of a blur from then on, so it could be anywhere . . . he could have dropped it or thrown it into the lake. We've searched the chateau as best we can, and Bill's been outside all afternoon with his metal detector, but it's hopeless. I'm just calling on the complete off chance that you or Kit might have spotted him with it at some stage."

"I wish I had, Biddy. But I can't help you. And neither can Kit," Lainey added, because he was right next to her, shaking his head. "I mean, I went out to talk to Wyatt at around midnight — you already know that — but he didn't mention the ring then and I didn't see him with it. But I can tell you where he was — under the trees directly across the lawn from my room. He was looking up at the biggest tree with the low, spready-out branches . . ." OK, tree names weren't her forte. "The one that looks like a belly dancer waving her arms and wearing a fringy costume."

Kit shook his head in disbelief. "Biddy? She means the weeping blue cedar."

"Well, that's where he was when I found him. And it's where we sat down on the grass to have a chat." Lainey paused, because watching Wyatt trying to conceal his tears had been absolutely heartbreaking. "I was just doing my best to cheer him up, make sure he didn't do anything drastic. So Bill could try there with the metal detector."

"We'll give it a go in the morning." Biddy sighed.

Kit said, "It was insured, wasn't it?"

"Apparently not. Wyatt thought he'd wait until they were engaged, poor lad."

"And do you know how much it was worth?" said Lainey.

"I do. He told me. That's why Bill's been spending so long trying to find the damn thing." Biddy lowered her voice, as she always did when discussing money. "Apparently it cost him forty thousand pounds."

Lainey gasped; that much for one ring? "Oh no, poor Wyatt! What a nightmare."

"And he can't even remember where he left it. What a dingbat," said Kit.

It just went to show, you never could tell how a first date was going to pan out. Well, that was life, Seth reminded himself. You might think you knew what was likely to happen, but you could always be proven wrong.

Which didn't normally sit well with him, what with preferring to be right all the time, but in this case, he was happy to go along with it. Plus, it made his life a whole lot easier.

Because when superconfidence was a woman's particular unique selling point, the last thing you expected was to end up drying her tears in the kitchen.

"I can't believe it. I can't believe it's all gone so wrong. I thought I could do it." Mortified by the extent of the failure, Dawn had shaken her head and made a grab for his plate. "You can't eat that, don't even try."

"It's fine." But this was a blatant lie, and he'd let her take the plate, with its over-cooked whole quail, rock-hard potatoes, and that ill-advised blue cheese sauce with its mysterious undertones of dish soap. She had marched into the kitchen and tipped the contents of both plates down the waste disposal. When she'd pressed the button, the noise had been horrendous, as if the poor bird's fragile bones were being crunched up by a slavering dragon.

And then Seth had heard a strangled sob. In the kitchen, he'd found Dawn red-faced with shame.

"I thought I could follow the recipe and everything would be perfect. I wanted to impress you. And now everything's ruined because I *failed.*" She'd been trembling with despair, a sky-high achiever who for once hadn't achieved. He'd torn off a paper towel and carefully wiped her eyes so as not to deconstruct the layers of blended eye-shadow, liner, and mascara.

"Hey, don't worry about it. It's only a meal." As he'd said it, he'd prayed his stomach wouldn't rumble with hunger.

"But it's a meal I prepared, and I wanted

you to be dazzled by my brilliance."

She'd looked so miserable that Seth had given her a hug. "Would you believe me if I told you it's made me like you more?"

He'd managed to get her over the disappointment. Then, since he hadn't been able to stop thinking about the food Lainey had prepared earlier, he'd left Dawn to clear away all evidence of her failure and headed down to the new gourmet burger place behind the esplanade to pick up takeout for the two of them instead.

Now, making his way home at midnight, he reflected on the irony of the way things could turn out. He'd meant what he'd said about the disastrous dinner making him like her more. When everything about a person seemed perfect, from their brain to their outward appearance and the sleek, stylish furnishings in their modern apartment, it was endearing to discover they were human after all.

The tide was out, which meant he could take a shortcut across the uncovered sand separating Mariscombe from Menhenick Bay. The stars were bright overhead, the sea was calm, and the beach was deserted apart from a couple of late-night dog walkers and a small group of teenagers perched on the rocks, their lit cigarettes glowing in the dark.

But as he continued around the curve of still-damp sand, finally reaching Menhenick Beach, he was just able to make out another solitary figure sitting above the tide line.

Lainey heard the sound of footsteps on wet sand and turned her head. By the time it occurred to her that they could belong to a murderer, she'd recognized the walk and the white shirt and was reassured that they didn't.

Unless he went in for a spot of secret contract killing on the side. At weekends, maybe. Did Friday night count as the week-end?

As he approached, leaving the smooth, wet sand and reaching the dry, powdery kind, she said, "So, how was your evening?"

"It was . . . good, thanks." For a moment, she sensed he was on the verge of elaborating before deciding not to. "What are you doing out here at this time?"

"Listening to the sea. I just love the sound of those waves." She inhaled the magical tang of salt in the air, raised her arm like a conductor, and made a swooping gesture as the next wave tumbled over itself and slid up the sand toward them. "I'm not over the novelty of it yet."

Seth smiled. "Mind if I join you?"

"Be my guest."

He lowered himself to the dry sand and sat beside her, long legs stretched out in front of him. "Where's Kit? I'd have thought you'd be out here together."

"Oh, he's not as obsessed with the sea as I am. Plus, he's fast asleep."

Seth said, "Not very romantic."

Damn, she shouldn't have said it like that. Vigorously she shook her head. "No, he is, of course he is! He's just shattered today after clearing out the garage and rebuilding that wall. He's romantic when he's awake."

"Well, I'm glad to hear it."

Was he teasing her? Did he suspect that something was amiss with their relationship?

"And when we're on our own," she continued. "We're not going to be all lovey-dovey at work, are we? That would be unprofessional."

"Of course it would."

He sounded amused. Time to change the subject. "Can I ask you something?"

"About whether I'm romantic?"

Now he was definitely teasing. "No, about the first time I saw you. You were walking along the esplanade and a middle-aged woman was trying to talk to you. She seemed quite desperate, but you completely ignored her and walked off, and I couldn't figure out for the life of me what was going on." She turned to look at his face in profile to gauge his reaction. "Why did you do that?"

"It's been bothering you all this time, but you didn't ask me before now?"

"I wanted to, but I figured it wasn't any of my business."

"It's really not that exciting. Her name's Pauline, and she's one of Richard's super-fans. Well, she started off as a fan, then turned into a bit of a stalker. She took early retirement last year and moved down from Manchester to be closer to Richard. She's harmless, but in the last few months, her obsession's gotten worse and she's turned into a bit of a pest."

"You acted as if she weren't there," said Lainey.

"It's what we were advised to do. Any kind of engagement just sets her off and makes things worse. Oh dear." He looked at her. "You must have thought I was being incred-ibly rude."

"I did."

Seth smiled briefly. "Well, I'm really not. We used to speak to her, be nice, but it just escalated the problem. She lives in a trailer covered in photos of Richard. She writes to him almost every day. When you saw us, she was begging me to take him over to her place for afternoon tea, so she could show him her scrapbooks."

Chastened, Lainey said, "Oh," and felt bad for having harbored bad thoughts about him.

As if reading her thoughts, Seth said, "I'm really not a monster."

"OK."

"Once she realizes you're working for us, she'll probably try to get you on her side too. Just have as little to do with her as possible. And don't worry." His tone was reassuring. "As I said, she's persistent, but she's essentially harmless."

"Right." Lainey nodded and kind of wished she hadn't asked now. It meant Seth Faulkner was good-looking, charming, and *not* the cruel, ruthless person she'd originally thought he was. Just sitting this close to him was making her more physically aware of his body, his voice, and his aftershave, which was so delicious it was making her want to lick his neck . . .

OK, mustn't do that. To distract herself, she said quickly, "So you had a good time tonight. Will you be seeing her again?"

"Dawn?" For a split second, his gaze flickered over her face, and Lainey felt her breath catch in her throat. "Oh, I should think so. That is, if she wants to see me."

And now a quiver ran through her, as if an invisible feather were being traced down the line of her spine. Because given the option, who wouldn't want to see someone like Seth again? What must it be like to be him: utterly confident, pretty much perfect in every way, a stranger to self-doubt or the concept of rejection? His tone had been playful, because the idea that Dawn might turn him down was simply too far-fetched for words.

The tide was still coming in; a bigger-than-usual wave broke on the shore and moved up the sand to within a few feet of them, providing Lainey with the excuse she needed. Scrambling upright, she said, "Right, that's close enough. Time to go in."

"Into the water, you mean?" His teeth gleamed white in the darkness as he rose to his feet too. "If you're up for a midnight swim, I'll join you."

Lainey's heart was galloping inside her rib cage. He was only teasing her, but what if she said yes?

"No thanks, the sea's all yours. I'm off to bed."

"Maybe I'll leave it for tonight." Seth brushed dry sand from his hands, and together they left the beach, heading up the narrow path and through the garden of Menhenick House. When they reached the driveway, they both saw the light on in the sitting room of the apartment above the garage.

At the sound of their footsteps crunching on the gravel, Kit appeared at the window.

"Whoops," said Lainey. "He'll be wondering where I've been."

"Gets jealous, does he?"

She shook her head, thinking fast; how would someone in a normal relationship respond in this situation?

"We're a couple. We trust each other." She said it with confidence, waving up at Kit in the window and romantically blowing him a kiss. "He knows I wouldn't do anything for him to be jealous about."

Seth nodded. "Good. Well, it's nice that you're so happy together."

"We are. See you tomorrow." She moved toward the flight of steps leading up to the flat.

Seth turned to make his way back to the house. "Night."

An owl was hooting in the trees outside. Seth opened his eyes; it was 3:30 a.m., and each time he'd woken up so far, he'd heard himself being an idiot all over again.

For crying out loud, what was happening to him? When he'd seen Lainey sitting on the beach in her star-patterned dress, he should have acknowledged her presence with a friendly word, then walked on by and left her in peace. But he hadn't, had he? He hadn't been able to resist inviting himself to sit down beside her. Worse, he'd compounded the issue by coming out with the kind of cringeworthy comments he never usually uttered. Just thinking about himself saying "Into the water, you mean?" made him want to cut out his own tongue.

As for offering to join her for a midnight swim, oh *God.* He couldn't have sounded like more of a creep if he'd tried.

He closed his eyes against the fresh wave of shame. Was this how it felt to be a shy teenager in the grip of his first crush?

Oh well. On the upside, at least it was guaranteed to put Lainey off him for life.

CHAPTER 9

The plan had been for Lainey to go to the big supermarket a few miles outside St. Carys and get the weekly shopping done while Majella worked at home in the office. Then Majella had protested that she really enjoyed food shopping and why didn't they go together, which would be quicker, easier, and more fun than one person having to do it all by themselves.

Which had sounded like an excellent plan and actually might have been if only Majella hadn't turned out to be the world's most easily distracted shopper.

"Isn't it fabulous here? Don't you just love that there's so much choice? Look, thirteen different kinds of potatoes!" Exclaiming with genuine delight, she was picking up each of the bags in turn, reading the descriptions printed on them and admiring the potatoes themselves.

Even that would have been fine if Lainey

had been free to get on with the rest of the shopping, but her attempts to add other items to the cart were met with piteous cries of protest.

"Oh no, you've chosen the mushrooms! But I haven't even looked at them yet!"

Lainey checked her watch. "We've been here forty minutes already. Why don't I just go and pick up the fabric softener to save us some time?"

"What if you don't get the best one, though? I like to smell all the fabric conditioners; otherwise, how do I know which one's nicest?"

"OK, I'll go and get some of the boring stuff, then, like light bulbs and bleach and paper towels. Because it's midday," Lainey explained, "and this place closes in ten hours."

"You're making fun of me. I just don't want to buy the wrong things, that's all."

Lainey left her there and went off to collect some of the less exciting items on the list. Returning a couple of minutes later, she noticed a man watching Majella from over by the lettuce.

"Oh, I prefer the extra-soft tissues," said Majella. "The ones with balsam."

"Never mind the tissues. You've got yourself an admirer."

"The guy on the fish counter? I know, I think they pay him to flirt with the oldies. He always offers me an extra scallop."

"You aren't old. And I'm not talking about him anyway. There's someone over in the salad section who's got his eye on you. Don't look," hissed Lainey, but it was too late, Majella had already spun round like a top.

"Oh, it's OK. I know him. That's Gerry. We met at a party last Christmas. He asked me out."

Lainey's eyebrows rose. "And did you go?"

"No, of course I didn't."

"Why not?"

Majella shrugged. "Because I don't go on dates. It's not something I do."

"Maybe you should try," said Lainey. "Didn't I say it was time you started putting yourself out there again?" She smiled at Gerry in an encouraging way; he was about Majella's age and seemed normal enough. "See? He's coming over. All you have to do is chat to him, drop a few hints so he knows you've changed your mind, then keep talking until he asks you out again. And this time you have to say yes."

"Oh God, I can't do that. No *way.*"

"You can," said Lainey. "Be brave. Make things happen. Seize the moment!" Why was it always so much easier to sort out other people's love lives than your own? Having been introduced to Gerry, Lainey took control of the cart and said brightly, "You two carry on. I'm just going to make a start on the rest of the shopping." She then scooted off down the next aisle before Majella could open her mouth to protest.

Twenty minutes later, a voice hissed in her ear, "Oh my God, I did it. I seized the moment!" And there was Majella, looking flushed and as if she couldn't quite believe what had just happened.

"Brilliant! He looks great. You'll have a fantastic time."

"He asked me how I'd been, and I just couldn't help myself. I told him you'd said it was time I started dating again, then I apologized about the last time he'd asked me, and he said that was great news and would I like to go out to dinner with him, and I said yes! So it's happening!"

"Yay!" Lainey clapped her hands. "When?"

Majella's face fell. "Oh. I can't remember."

Gerry had only come in to pick up some sandwiches for his lunch. Having raced around the supermarket in search of him, Lainey finally spotted him outside, climbing into his car.

He jumped a mile when she tapped on the driver's window just as he was pulling away.

Startled, he buzzed down the window. "Yes?"

"Sorry, we didn't know where you'd gone." She gasped for breath. "Lucky I saw you in time! OK, this is going to sound daft, but Majella can't remember which day you're meeting up. She was so excited about the date that it completely slipped her mind. And thank you so much for inviting her."

"Look, can I just say something?" Gerry blurted. "I don't mean to sound rude, but this has put me in a bit of an awkward situation. I didn't actually mean to invite Majella to dinner. It was her idea . . . She just started gabbling about how nice it would be, and in the end, I felt I had to go along with it. I just didn't have the heart to say no."

Lainey was horrified. "But she's hardly Quasimodo. You wanted to go out with her before. You'll still meet her for dinner, won't you?"

Gerry looked pained. "I did want to go out with her before. She's a lovely woman. That's why I couldn't say no, because I didn't want to hurt her feelings. But I met someone else in January, and we've been seeing each other ever since. And the more I think about it, the more I think she isn't going to understand if I tell her I'm having dinner with Majella on Thursday night. So could you do me a huge favor and tell her I can't make it after all? I can't do it myself. It's too awkward."

Lainey found Majella in the freezer section, next to the ice cream. She was chattering into her phone, her face still lit up.

"Ronaldo, you're a star! Tomorrow morning at eight thirty, thanks so much for squeezing me in! It isn't until you have something special to go to that you realize how badly your hair needs sorting out. Thanks again, bye!"

Oh . . .

By the time Lainey finished explaining that the date was canceled, Majella's eyes were like saucers. "Oh no, how awful. I didn't even realize I'd forced him into it. I thought he might be a bit shy, so I was trying to help him out. I was being proactive, seizing the moment like you told me to. The poor man must have been scared out of his wits."

"I think he was. But are you OK? Not too upset?"

"I'm not upset. Just embarrassed. It's like

being sixteen all over again." Majella picked up a tub of coconut ice cream and fanned herself with it. "I've made a giant fool of myself."

"Well, the good thing is that you aren't sixteen," Lainey consoled her. "And you're not at school anymore, so you don't have to worry that he's going to go around telling everyone else what happened."

Majella dropped the tub of ice cream into the cart and heaved a sigh of relief. "You're right. Thank goodness for that."

India arrived home from school at 4:30. The kitchen door flew open and she wailed, "Mum, what did you do? I've never been so embarrassed in my *life.*"

"What?" Majella looked up from her laptop. "I haven't done anything."

"Except that isn't quite true, is it? Look at my phone! Listen to it!" India held up her mobile, where message after message was bouncing onto the screen, each one accompanied by a cheery *ting.* "And guess what? All of these, they're about *you.*"

Lainey, peeling potatoes at the sink, turned and saw the color creeping up Majella's neck.

"There's a girl in my grade called Rochelle Harris. She doesn't like me much. Also, she's an absolute cow."

"Oh dear," said Majella.

"And a few months ago, her mum started seeing this guy called Gerry."

"Oh God." Majella looked dismayed.

"So today, he told Rochelle's mum about the hilarious thing that happened to him this morning, and she told Rochelle, and Rochelle went on to tell . . . well, pretty much everyone."

Lainey winced. Majella, now crimson, covered her face and let out a sound like a strangled polecat.

"You're a complete laughingstock too. What were you *thinking*?"

"Lainey made me do it," Majella yelped.

Lainey protested when all eyes turned in her direction. "We thought he was still single."

Violet, behind India, said, "Mum, were you drunk or something? Apparently you publicly propositioned him and —"

"It wasn't a proposition." Majella was indignant.

"Well, you forced him to invite you out. According to Rochelle, you were gabbling away like a mad thing and refused to give up until he'd said yes. She said he couldn't get a word in edgewise." India held up the still-chiming phone. "Which is nice."

"I was saying it quickly to get it over and done with before I lost my nerve!"

"Well, it's a shame you didn't lose it sooner. That's all I can say." India rolled her eyes.

"Oh poor Mum, she didn't mean to be embarrassing. If anything, it's Lainey's fault for forcing her into it."

Violet had said it in a kindly way, but it was undoubtedly true.

Lainey nodded. "It is my fault. It was my idea, and I should definitely have checked first that he was still single." By way of explanation, she added, "I just think it'd be good for your mum to get back out there and, you know, find herself some . . . company."

India frowned. "Mum doesn't need any more company. She's got us."

"But it might be nice to meet someone I could spend time with," Majella ventured. "Like . . . a man of some kind. I mean, eventually."

"Well, congratulations," said India. "You've definitely done a great job of advertising that you're on the hunt for a man. Now everyone knows you're desperate."

"I'm not *desperate*." Majella sat back in

defeat. "It was just an experiment that went wrong."

Richard, who'd been standing in the kitchen doorway listening with interest, said conversationally, "And you never know how anything's going to turn out until you try. I met Elizabeth Taylor once, on a beach in Sicily. She needed a light for her cigarette, we got chatting, and I ended up asking her out."

Relieved to see the discussion moving away from Majella, Lainey said, "You and Elizabeth Taylor? Wow, amazing! And did she say yes?"

"Well, we didn't actually go *out* any-where." Richard winked, and ice cubes clinked as he took a swallow of his afternoon gin and tonic. "But we did spend a rather splendid forty-eight hours in her hotel suite."

Chapter 10

The flowers arrived the following Saturday morning, a spectacular burst of mixed late-spring blooms with an envelope attached. Lainey carried them upstairs to the office, where Seth and Majella were working.

"For me?" Seth looked surprised as she knocked and entered. "You shouldn't have."

Majella opened the envelope and skimmed the handwritten note inside. "Oh no, it's happening. I told her not to do it."

"Do what?" said Lainey, and Majella sighed.

"Jess from the flower shop said yesterday that if I'm on the lookout for a man, I should give her brother-in-law a go. I tried to tell her I wasn't interested, but she wouldn't listen, kept insisting he'd be perfect for me and said she'd get him to ask me out." She handed the note to Seth, who read it before passing it to Lainey.

Dear Majella,

Jess has decided that you and I are well suited. Are you willing to take a chance on a virtual stranger? I would be honored if you'd agree to meet me for dinner any evening that suits you. It's many years since I've been on a blind date, but I'm willing to be brave if you are. Please call or text me.

"His name's Justin Harlow, he's forty-six, and he lives in Polzeath," said Majella. "He's a bank manager. Honestly, how can she expect me to go on a blind date? It's ridiculous."

Seth turned to Lainey. "What d'you think?"

Oh no, she wasn't going to get landed with the blame again. "He looks great, but it's up to Majella. We can't make her do it if she doesn't want to."

Majella nodded, clearly relieved, and ran her fingertips over the velvety cream petals of one of the roses in the bouquet.

"Well, I think she should give him a chance," said Seth.

"What?" Majella did a double take; she clearly hadn't been expecting that.

"Look, you were brave last time," Seth

told her. "It's not your fault it went a bit wrong."

He raised an eyebrow at Lainey, who said hastily, "It was my fault, all mine!"

"But the thought of everyone *watching* us . . ."

"Which is why you don't want to eat in a restaurant," said Seth. "But how about if you invited him over here? Lainey could cook dinner. It'd just be the two of you eating together — we'd keep out of the way — but you wouldn't be alone with him in the house. How does that sound?"

Majella hesitated. "What if it all goes wrong again?"

Seth shrugged. "What if it goes right?"

"Tell us what Jess said about him," Lainey suggested.

"She just said she'd always thought we'd be a perfect match."

"So let's go with Seth's idea. I'll cook the meal. We'll be here, but we'll stay completely out of your way. Like he says, it might be brilliant."

"And if it isn't?" Majella looked fearful.

"As soon as dinner's over, you can send him home. Come on, what's the worst that can happen?" said Lainey.

At lunchtime, Lainey headed down into the

124

center of St. Carys to collect a refill for Richard's prescription heart medication. In the busy pharmacy, she spotted India over by the makeup counter, engrossed in examining a bottle of bright-pink nail polish. Amused, Lainey noted that she'd clearly inherited Majella's predilection for spending ages poring over items in shops.

Since India hadn't noticed her, she made her way over to the counter and waited for the middle-aged woman in front of her to finish choosing between two kinds of indigestion tablets. By the time she'd picked up Richard's prescription — he'd told her to stop calling him "sir" — India had left the shop. As she passed the makeup counter, Lainey paused, because none of the remaining polishes seemed as bordering on fluorescent as the one she'd seen India looking at. But she'd only glimpsed it for a moment; it was probably that fuchsia-shaded one on the right.

On the way home, leaving the esplanade and making her way up the hill, she became aware of being watched. She turned, and her heart gave a little skip when she saw who it was.

Pauline was walking up the hill on the other side of the street. When she saw Lainey looking at her, she came hurrying over. "Hello!"

It was all very well Seth instructing her not to acknowledge Pauline, but how could she not reply? It just felt so wrong. "Hello," she said cautiously.

"You work at Menhenick House." Up close, Pauline's eyes were light gray, her expression peculiarly intense.

OK, what was the correct response to this? Lainey gave a brief semi-nod. But she could hardly deny it; Pauline clearly knew.

"You look so nice. You have such a kind face. Could you give Sir Richard a card from me? It's a special day, you see." Pauline took an envelope out of her bag and thrust it into Lainey's hand. "It's the anniversary of the first time I saw *Wherever You Are* in the cinema. I wrote about it in my diary. It was forty-seven years ago today. I thought then that it was the best film ever made." She nodded vigorously. "And it still is."

"Well, that's lovely," said Lainey. "But I have to go now; they're expecting me back —"

"I love him. I love him so much. You'll make sure he gets the card, won't you? I want him to know how special he is to me."

Lainey edged away, feeling sorry for Pauline. "I will, I promise."

■ ■ ■ ■

"Oh dear," said Violet when Lainey entered the kitchen. "Let me guess, you've been Paulined."

It was probably the way she was holding the envelope, as gingerly as if it might be full of spiders. Lainey looked at Richard, who was wrestling with the coffee maker. "Sorry, she accosted me. I just couldn't ignore her."

"Darling, don't worry. A bit more practice and you'll get the hang of it. Pop it in the bin, there's a good girl."

"Not in the bin, Grandad," Violet tutted. "The recycling box."

Lainey was apologetic. "She made me promise you'd get it. Today's the anniversary of the first time she saw that film of yours."

"That film of mine?" Richard pretended to be offended. "I've made seventy-six of the damn things, thanks very much."

"The first time she saw *Wherever You Are* in the cinema."

He was pressing all the wrong buttons on the coffee maker, probably on purpose.

Lainey said, "Would you like me to do that for you? Then you can read the card."

"Fine. There's something wrong with this

machine. It never works for me." Richard plucked the envelope from her hand and opened it, pulling out a luridly colored card of a teddy bear clutching an armful of glittery crimson hearts. He skimmed the words written inside in a matter of seconds, nodded politely at Lainey, and said, "There, done. Can I have my cappuccino now, please?"

It had probably taken Pauline an hour or more to compose the closely written message. Richard passed the card to Violet, who folded it up and expertly tossed it into the recycling box over by the door. Lainey exhaled and pressed the right buttons in the right order; she clearly needed to stop being a soft touch where Richard's fans were concerned. Every day, letters and small gifts arrived in the post for him from people wanting more attention than he could give them. Yesterday a woman had written begging him to pop along to her auntie's birthday party in Norfolk because it would mean the world to her.

Working here, she was just going to have to get used to this situation and learn how to harden her heart.

Seth was in the sitting room, engrossed in the motor racing on TV, when Kit popped his head around the door at seven that evening.

"Just checking you don't need me for anything before I head off?"

"Nothing at all," said Majella. "We're fine. What are you and Lainey doing tonight? Going out somewhere nice?"

"No! Oh phew, that was close!" India, sitting on the floor painting her toenails fluorescent pink, had knocked over the bottle of nail polish and snatched it up again at lightning speed before it had a chance to spill on the rug.

Majella said, "Sweetheart, be careful."

"I *was* being careful. That's why I managed to catch it in time."

This was typical of India. Seth gave her a warning shake of his head; sometimes she was too smart for her own good.

"Sorry, Kit. We interrupted you." Majella turned her attention back to him. "Where are you two off to?"

"Well, I'm heading to the gym." Pushing the door further open, Kit revealed the sports bag in his left hand. "I've been looking forward to a proper workout. And since Lainey has never looked forward to a proper workout in her life, she's all set up for a lazy evening watching girlie stuff on TV."

"I'm all in favor of that." Majella beamed at him.

"And eating chips. She'll be eating her own body weight in chips," Kit added.

Seth was discovering that he suddenly had an irresistible urge to eat chips.

But he was seeing Dawn again in an hour. This time, since she didn't trust herself not to serve up another terrible meal, they were booked into a popular Italian restaurant overlooking the harbor.

"Off you go." Majella waggled her fingers at Kit. "Have fun."

". . . And then I stripped off all my clothes and everyone in the auditorium started to applaud."

Seth did a double take as the words belatedly permeated his brain. He looked at Dawn. "Sorry?"

She raised her perfect eyebrows. "You haven't been listening to a word I've said."

He shook his head; this was true. She'd been telling him about an international conference she'd attended last year in Edinburgh. "OK, I really am sorry. I was listening, then I got distracted."

"I noticed." Her tone was dry. "Is she pretty?"

For a split second, Seth thought she meant

130

Lainey, then realized that Dawn was tilting her head in the direction he'd been looking. It was ten o'clock at night; they'd finished their meal on the first floor of the restaurant and moved out onto the balcony for one last drink. From their table right next to the wrought iron railings, they had a clear view over the various harborside bars and restaurants below them.

Three minutes ago, glancing down, Seth had spotted Kit standing at the bar to the left of them finishing his drink and ordering a refill. He'd evidently been to the gym — his sports bag was at his feet — and had showered and changed into a green-and-white-striped shirt and black jeans. As Seth had watched from his vantage point, he'd seen Kit in conversation with the owner of the bar.

Then they'd exchanged a look and a smile, and that was when Seth had stopped listening to whatever Dawn had been telling him about the legal conference in Edinburgh. Because the owner of the bar was Tom, who was beautiful to look at, full of charm, and openly gay. He was hugely popular in St. Carys, bursting with joie de vivre, and a flamboyant dresser. Tonight his bleached-white hair was spiked up, his shirt was silver, and he was wearing tight-fitting white shorts. And while smiling at him wasn't significant in itself, the lingering look seemed . . . well, not quite the kind of look you'd expect to witness from a man who had a long-term girlfriend waiting for him at home.

Seth exhaled; meanwhile, Dawn was sitting back on her chair, visibly unimpressed by the lack of attention he'd been paying her riveting anecdote.

"I'm not looking at a girl." As he said it, he realized half an explanation wasn't going to be enough to appease her. "See the guy down there in the green-and-white-striped shirt? That's Kit."

Dawn nodded. "Kit and Elaine, yes? The couple who came to work for your family the other week?" She twisted in her seat and peered over the edge of the balcony. "Why, what's happening? Is he chatting up some other girl?"

"Not quite," said Seth.

At that moment, they both saw Tom come out from behind the bar to clear the glasses from one of the tables next to Kit. As he squeezed past, he rested a hand briefly on Kit's hip, before collecting up the empty glasses and making his way back. There was more prolonged eye contact, followed by a few more intimately exchanged words and another mischievous smile.

"Oh," said Dawn. *"Oh."*

"Yes." Seth nodded as they both took note of the way Kit was now glancing around the bar and the harborside, surreptitiously checking that the moment hadn't been noticed.

"Wow. This is pretty awkward then." Dawn's expression was serious. "What are you going to do?"

Seth had no idea. He wished he hadn't seen what they'd just seen. Or was that entirely true? Was a small part of him glad it had happened, glad that the relationship of the girl he was so strongly attracted to wasn't as rock-solid as he'd previously imagined?

Maybe.

Oh, but there were so many unanswered questions here. Did Lainey have any idea about this? Did they maybe have a completely open relationship or at least an understanding that Kit might meet other people so long as he was discreet?

Or would this news come as a bolt from the blue, a horrible shock that would break her heart and leave her devastated?

"Do you think Elaine knows?" said Dawn.

"Lainey," Seth corrected her automatically. "I don't know. And it's hardly a question you can ask. Look, maybe we've got it wrong, jumped to conclusions. Kit's a friendly guy, he's the type to get on with anyone."

"Come on. We both saw what we saw. The way they looked at each other . . . that was deliberate."

This was true.

"Maybe he's just flirting for fun, but it doesn't mean anything."

"Seth." Dawn gave him a who-are-you-kidding look.

He shook his head. "Well, I think we just have to pretend we didn't see anything. It's none of our business what Kit does in his spare time."

"Really?" One perfect eyebrow was still raised.

"Really."

"So if you were living with a girlfriend you were crazy about and one of your friends found out she was being unfaithful to you, you're telling me you wouldn't want to know? You'd rather carry on believing everything was fine, even though she'd actually been having sex with God knows how many other men behind your back?"

She was a lawyer. Arguing was one of her specialties, but Seth sensed there was more to it than that. He glanced over the balcony

134

again and saw that Tom was now serving other customers, while Kit had perched on a corner stool and was busy checking his phone. He turned back to Dawn. "It's happened to you."

"It has. Only once, but that was enough." Her tone was cool. "Discovering that my boyfriend at university had been sleeping with another girl was bad enough. But finding out that my flatmates had all known about it was fifty times worse. They didn't tell me because they didn't want to upset me. Well, guess what? They did. Because then I felt betrayed *and* stupid." Dawn shuddered at the memory and reached for her drink. "So don't you think Lainey deserves to know the truth?"

Did he? If he told her, and she and Kit broke up as a result, either one or both of them would leave Menhenick House, and everyone in the family would be furious with him.

Plus, what if Lainey were the one to go? What if she left the UK and he never saw her again? It didn't bear thinking about.

"I still don't think we should get involved," said Seth.

"Let me hazard a guess. You've been on the other side of the equation."

Oh, she was good. Yes, a decade or so ago,

he'd been caught dating two girls at the same time. But that had been back when he was young. Nor was it the reason he didn't want to get involved now.

He nodded. "Correct."

"You're a player. That's what comes of being too good-looking."

"I *was* a player. I'm older and wiser now." He smiled slightly. "I've learned the error of my ways."

Dawn raised her glass to him. "I'm very glad to hear it. But I still think Lainey deserves to know the truth about her boyfriend."

Another glance at the crowd below showed Kit finishing his second drink and slipping away from the bar without looking back or saying goodbye to Tom. Busy on his phone, he began to make his way along the esplanade. Was he heading home to Lainey? Or setting off elsewhere? They couldn't know.

Oh God, what a dilemma.

Seth said steadily, "Let's wait and see how things go."

CHAPTER 11

"Well?" said Kit the following evening. "Verdict?"

"Pretty."

"Too pretty?"

Lainey paused. It was eight o'clock in the evening, and they were heading back to Menhenick House, having been for a scouting walk around the harborside so Kit could point Tom out to her. They'd been subtle about it, observed him from a distance while he'd chatted and laughed with the customers at his bar. In his black shirt and narrow trousers, with his chiseled cheekbones and mischievous smile, Tom had the look of a young Leonardo DiCaprio about him. And yes, he was at that level of extreme prettiness that warned you not to get involved if you didn't want your heart dashed to smithereens, but everyone knew it wasn't always as simple as that.

"Maybe, but it's up to you." She squeezed

Kit's arm as they made their way along the beach. "It doesn't have to be anything too serious. You deserve a bit of fun."

He nodded. "I do." During their time in rural France, there'd been a distinct lack of opportunity to expand his social life. "On the plus side, pretty sure he'd be discreet."

"Whoops, speaking of discreet . . ." Shielding her eyes and peering into the distance, Lainey recognized the taller of the two figures heading toward them.

Kit peered too. "Who is it?"

"Well, one of them's Seth. Which makes me think the one in the red dress might be Dawn." Lainey paused, remembering. "He asked me how I was this morning. Wanted to know if everything was OK."

"Me too!" Kit looked surprised. "I thought he meant was everything OK with the apartment, so I told him the hinge had broken on the wardrobe door but that I'd fixed it. Then I got the feeling he hadn't been asking about the apartment after all. What are you doing?"

"Putting my arm around you. Now you have to put your arm around me, so we look romantic. Like a proper couply couple."

He gave her a playful dig in the ribs. "Whatever next? Sex on the beach?"

"Maybe not that. But you could give me a

kiss. You know, just a little one."

He laughed and pressed his warm lips against her temple. "They're probably not even watching."

But Lainey knew they were. As the distance between them lessened, she murmured, "Dawn's stunning. Look at her hair. And her *eyes*."

"Don't feel inferior. You have hair and eyes too." Pretending to spot them for the first time, Kit raised a hand in greeting and called out easily, "Hi, we weren't sure if it was you!"

They were now near enough for Lainey to be able to see that Dawn's swirly scarlet frock was made from peach-skin silk and clearly expensive. Up close, she was also even more stunning, with immaculate eyebrows and dark lashes that must surely have been extensions.

"How nice to meet you," Dawn said when Seth had made the introductions.

"You too!" Lainey wondered what it must feel like to be so completely perfect from head to toe, although the intensity of Dawn's gaze was making her feel a bit like a fascinating insect. Turning to Seth, she said, "How's Majella?"

"Not great. It's definitely one of her migraines." Earlier that afternoon, feeling sick and headachy, Majella had taken tablets and retired to a darkened bedroom to try to stave off the worst of the symptoms.

"Poor thing. How horrible. I'll check on her later, shall I? See if there's anything she needs."

"That'd be great, thanks. And she won't be able to work tomorrow," said Seth, "which means I'm going to need one of you to give me a hand in the office."

The way Kit was currently fantasizing about Tom was pretty much the way Lainey had been doing her best not to fantasize about Seth. As she opened her mouth to volunteer him for the task, Kit said, "Well, we've got a truck delivering a load of flagstones tomorrow and I told the guy I'd take care of the unloading, so you'd better have Lainey."

"Fine." Seth nodded; it clearly didn't make any difference to him either way.

"So where have you two been this evening? Anywhere interesting?" As Dawn asked the question, Lainey was aware of the miss-nothing gaze flickering over her from head to toe before moving on and doing the same to Kit. It was like being expertly assessed by an undercover police officer.

"We're still getting to know St. Carys, just checking it out," Kit said easily. "Exploring the bars and cafés, seeing what looks good."

"We spotted a gorgeous little bistro up on Silver Street," Lainey chimed in. "The food looked fantastic. We'll definitely have to try it out some time."

"Well, I'm pretty new around here too, so any recommendations are welcome." Dawn glanced at Kit's hand as he slid it casually around Lainey's waist. "We're on our way to the harbor for a stroll around. Anywhere in particular you think we should stop for a drink?" She was doing it again, eyeing them in that curiously intent manner that was so at odds with the ultra-casual tone of her voice.

"Come on," said Seth. "I know plenty of places we can go."

"Did you see the way she was looking at us?" said Lainey when Seth and Dawn were safely out of earshot.

"I did. And you know why, don't you?"

Baffled, Lainey shook her head. "No. Why?"

Racing ahead to avoid a clip around the ear, Kit called back, "She's wondering what on earth a gorgeous specimen like me is doing with an ugly bird like you!"

"You're an angel. And thanks so much for helping Seth out."

"Hey, no problem. How are you feeling now?" Lainey placed the steaming mug of tea on the bedside table. Poor Majella was still looking dreadful, waxily pale and utterly wrung out.

"Well, I've stopped being sick and the worst of the headache's over." Even her voice betrayed her exhaustion. "I'll spend most of today asleep. That's the thing about migraine; they always follow the same pattern, so at least you know what you're getting. By tomorrow, I'll be fine."

"OK, can I bring you anything else? How about some dry toast?"

"Nothing, thanks. I couldn't face eating." This time Majella managed a weak smile. "Just as well I've got a couple of days to recover before the big date."

"You can always cancel if you're not up to it."

"No need. I'll be back to normal by Thursday. Well, as normal as I'll ever be. Jess is excited. She's convinced meeting Justin is going to change my life. According to her, we're a match made in heaven."

"If you are, I'm taking all the credit."

Majella's smile broadened as she nodded in agreement. "It's all thanks to your little pep talk. I feel like you've given me permission to find someone and get myself out of

142

hibernation at long last. And won't it be amazing if that someone turns out to be Justin? Who'd have thought it could be so easy?"

If anyone deserved that kind of luck, it was Majella. Lainey grinned. "Fingers crossed."

The office, on the top floor of the house, was airy and bright, with views from the wide dual-aspect windows over St. Carys to the right, and directly ahead of them, Menhenick Beach. But Lainey was more distracted by the sight of Seth as he stood at his desk, leaning across it to double-check details on the screen of his Mac and continuing his phone conversation with a client.

From her position at the shaded end of the office, Lainey was ostensibly concentrating on collecting numbered pages from the printer and stapling them together. In reality, she was coming to the conclusion that if a hundred men were lined up in a row, Seth would be the most beautiful of them all.

She was also wondering if he'd come home last night or stayed over at Dawn's place and walked back early this morning. OK, time to stop thinking about it, because the next step would be imagining him naked.

And that could cause all kinds of kerfuffle. Best not.

At midday, she brought coffee upstairs to the office. Since the phones were quiet, she asked Seth how the business had come about.

"I was at university in Bristol, studying economies and management." He stirred his coffee and leaned against the edge of the desk. "In my second year, I moved out of the halls of residence into a basement flat in Clifton and took a part-time job in a travel agency in Clifton village. A man came in one day asking us to arrange a holiday for his family, who required help because they had two children with autism and a mother-in-law in a wheelchair. When he explained how much assistance they'd need, my boss said they couldn't deal with that kind of situation; it was just too complicated. Which really upset the guy, so I offered to put together a holiday plan myself."

"Brave," said Lainey.

"Either that or stupid. It could all have gone horribly wrong. I did it partly because I felt sorry for him." Seth added more sugar to his coffee and shrugged. "But mainly because I didn't like my boss."

"Good for you. And it went OK?"

"If it hadn't, it'd be a bit of a rubbish anecdote." Seth's eyes were bright with amusement. "Yes, it went really well. And the family, the Sandersons, were over the moon because it was the first time they'd ever managed a holiday abroad. Four months later, they asked me to arrange another one, for them and their extended family, and that was a success too. Then a year after that, our branch was closed down and I was let go, so I took an evening job delivering food from local restaurants to people's homes — like Deliveroo, but before Deliveroo was invented."

"It never occurred to me that students from rich families would have to take evening jobs. Sorry." Lainey shook her head. "Does that sound rude? I just assumed you'd get an allowance."

"I think you've been watching too much *Made in Chelsea.*" He smiled briefly. "Anyway, I was taking a meal to a house on Royal York Crescent one evening when who should be walking past but Ted Sanderson. He said, 'Good grief, lad, how many part-time jobs d'you have?' So then I had to explain that the travel agency had closed down and I was delivering food now instead." He paused. "Is this getting boring?"

"Are you kidding?" Lainey had been trying to carry on with addressing the envelopes piled up on her desk, but it was impossible to concentrate. She put down her pen and reached for her coffee. "I'm listening. Carry on."

"So I went into the house to unload the boxes, and when I came out, Ted was still there on the pavement, not looking happy at all. He said, 'Who's going to sort out our holidays now, then?' And I said that if he wanted, I'd carry on doing it for him. I felt sorry for him. He had tons of money, but his life was incredibly difficult, and it had made him tetchy. I gave him my contact details, told him to call me the next time he needed me to sort everything out. Two days later, he turned up on my doorstep with a proposition: if he put up the money and leased the premises where I'd been working before, would I be interested in going into business with him, setting up and running my own independent travel agency?"

It just went to show, you never knew when a small favor might be repaid with a far bigger one. Lainey said, "That's amazing."

"It was." Seth nodded. "I took my finals a few weeks later, and we opened the business to the public a month after that. Ted wanted us to be able to provide everything anyone could possibly need, and he had a lot of contacts more than happy to spread the word. We'd collect our clients from their homes and get them to wherever they wanted to go. Any special requests, we'd arrange them. Any problems, we'd sort them out. We started thirteen years ago and made a name for ourselves with our bespoke holidays and second-to-none customer service. And that's how it all took off. When the clients appreciate what you do for them, they recommend you to everyone they know. Most people don't need us, but some really do. And they're glad we exist."

Lainey nodded; she'd already realized this. On the phone earlier, he'd been arranging a nurse and childcare for a young mother with MS and her three small children, who were embarking on a cruise of a lifetime to Australia. Other clients had no health problems but required assurance that every step of their holiday had been dealt with, leaving them with an experience that would be completely stress free. She said, "I bet Ted's glad he ambushed you all those years ago."

Seth grinned. "It ended up working out pretty well. I bought him out three years ago, when he and his family moved to Guernsey. But he still makes me organize all their holidays for them."

"I should think so too. Oh dear." Lainey had glanced out of the window to where Kit, stripped to the waist, was hauling the recently unloaded flagstones across the driveway and around to the side of the garage. "Look at his shoulders."

Seth raised an eyebrow. "They're . . . fine. You can tell he works out."

It was her turn to smile. "I wasn't asking you to admire them. I meant they're getting burned." Picking up her phone, she sent Kit a brief text: Sunscreen!

They saw him look at his phone, then twist around and peer up at the window to find them watching him. He gave a good-natured shrug and nodded before gathering up the next flagstone.

"Now he'll tell me off for being a nag." Lainey returned her attention to the envelopes; clients of Faulkner Travel preferred to be sent hand-addressed glossy brochures in the post, rather than links to internet sites online.

"And how are things going with you two?"

She paused, glanced up. "You asked me that question yesterday."

"Did I?" Seth exhaled. "So I did. Sorry, just wanted to make sure you're OK, happy working here, settling in, that kind of thing."

"We're fine. No regrets so far." Lainey wished she could read his mind; it was nice that he cared, but the way he was looking at her was making —

"Woof woof woof, *woof-woof.*" The volley of barks blasting through the baby monitor signaled that a visitor had disturbed Ernie's and Glenda's sleep.

"Shall I run down and see who it is?" said Lainey, because from up here, the kitchen door wasn't visible. But then came the sound of the door being opened and Richard's voice saying, "Well, now, this is a surprise!"

Seth raised an eyebrow. "That's the thing about living with my grandfather. When a visitor turns up, it could be absolutely anyone."

CHAPTER 12

Thirty seconds later, they heard footsteps on the stairs. The next moment, the door to the office opened to reveal a fortysomething woman with wild rock-chick blond hair and a ton of sooty shadow and mascara lining her huge gray eyes. She was wearing torn jeans, an expensive-looking sea-green silk top, high-heeled crimson ankle boots, and half a dozen jangling silver bangles around her wrists.

The bangles were jangling because her tanned arms were outstretched and she was throwing them exuberantly around Seth.

"Darling!"

"Mum!"

So this was Christina Faulkner, which meant that she was actually in her fifties — older than she looked, then. Lainey registered the expression on Seth's face, a mixture of fondness and exasperation, as he gave his mother a hug.

"What are you doing here? Why didn't you tell me you were coming?"

"Because I wanted to surprise you! It's more fun that way!" Turning to Lainey, Christina said, "Hello. Haven't seen you before. Are you the latest girlfriend?"

Lainey spluttered, "No."

"OK, keep your hair on. You're going a bit pink, though, so what does that mean? Do you have a crush on my son, is that it?"

"Mum, stop." Seth was shaking his head.

"Just saying what I see, darling. It's not beyond the realm of possibility, after all. And what's wrong with having a crush on your boss anyway? It's fun!"

"Says my mother, who's never had a job in her life. This is Lainey," Seth continued evenly. "She and her boyfriend work here — they joined us after Maisie left."

"Maisie. Was that the dowdy one with the ankles? Well, I can't imagine anyone's crying themselves to sleep because they're missing her so much. What's happened to your stepmother? I thought she was working with you."

"Majella's off sick today," said Seth. "She's in bed with —"

"Ooh, a man? Bit of excitement at last?"

"Not quite. She's in bed with a migraine. Lainey's just helping me out until Majella's

151

back on her feet."

"Wonderful!" Christina beamed at Lainey. "So you can hold the fort here while my son takes me out to lunch."

"Mum, we're busy. I can't go out to lunch."

"Oh, don't be ridiculous, of course you can."

"You should have told me you were coming down. Look, I could see you this evening —"

"But that'll be too late! We're flying out of Newquay at six, heading to Marbella for a few weeks. We stopped off here specially so I could see you! Oh, come on, darling. What's more important? Spending a couple of hours in a boring old office or catching up over a bottle of wine with the woman who gave you life?"

Seth exhaled, clearly torn. Lainey now understood the reason for the earlier twist of exasperation on his face; Christina had no intention of taking no for an answer.

"Honestly, I'll be fine here," she said. "If anyone phones with a problem that really can't wait, I'll give you a call."

"There! See? You don't have to be here." Christina nodded in triumph. "You aren't indispensable after all!"

"You said 'we.' " Seth nodded in defeat

and reached for the jacket hanging over the back of his chair. "Who have you got with you?"

"Oh I can't wait to introduce you! His name's Laszlo" — Christina's kohl-lined eyes danced — "and he's your potential new stepfather."

"No problems here. Everything's under control," said Lainey when Seth returned exactly two hours later.

"Thanks. Well, there you go. You've met my mother." He took the sheet of paper with details of all the phone calls listed she was holding out to him.

"And you've met your potential new stepfather. How was that?"

"Put it this way, I won't hold my breath for a wedding invitation. He started accusing my mother of flirting with the pilot of the charter plane they flew down in. Apparently the pilot was very good-looking, with buckets of charm, which is why Mum took a few sneaky photos of him on her phone. Well, she said a few, but when she showed them to me, it was more like fifty. So I can't see her and Laszlo lasting more than another couple of weeks."

"Ah."

"Also," Seth continued drily, "I don't

know how you're picturing him in your head, but my potential new stepfather is actually younger than me."

"Oh wow."

"Quite. My mother has always marched to the beat of her own drum. For the last decade her boyfriends have been getting progressively younger. Laszlo is twenty-nine."

"And your mum is . . . ?"

"Fifty-one. She was eighteen when she had me." A flicker of a smile. "Some eighteen-year-olds take to motherhood. Mine never really did."

What could you say to that? "But she loves you."

"Oh yes, of course she does. In her own way. And I didn't have a terrible childhood, because the nannies she hired were great. But it didn't take long before I found myself spending more and more time with Dad, especially once he'd settled down with Majella. Which couldn't have been easy for Majella, God knows, but she was amazing and always made me feel so welcome, like it was the biggest treat for her to have me there staying with them." He paused, re-membering. "I always knew how lucky I was. While Mum was jetting off around the world on her adventures, it meant I still had a family I loved and somewhere to live."

The phone rang again. Seth answered it, and work resumed. An hour later, a text came through. He checked the screen. "It's from Mum. They've arrived back at the airport and she's just found out the handsome pilot is called Dan. He's also told her he's very happy with his gorgeous girlfriend Lily."

Lainey kept a straight face. "That's a shame."

Seth grinned. "On the plus side, she says Laszlo is delighted."

India's toes were still bothering Lainey.

As the girl rolled around the kitchen floor that evening, teasing the dogs with their favorite toys, Lainey said, "I do like your nail polish."

"Thanks, me too."

"Such a great color."

"I know."

Lainey rinsed a couple more plates in the sink and fitted them into their slots in the dishwasher. "Where'd you get it?"

"Can't remember, but you can borrow it if you like." India pretended to wrestle Ernie's battered teddy bear from his mouth. "Oh, Ernie, don't be so mean. Give me your teddy. Let me have him!"

"I saw one that color the other day, in the pharmacy on the esplanade." Lainey paused, then added casually, "It was weird, though, one minute it was there, and the next minute, I couldn't see it anymore."

"Maybe someone bought it." India glanced at her, then rolled over and sat up, pulling Ernie's wriggling body onto her lap. "That's usually the way shops work. I've remembered now. I bought mine ages ago from the big pharmacy in Launceston."

The too-innocent look in her eyes was what convinced Lainey she was lying.

But what could she do? She had no proof and no doubt at all that any accusations would be met with indignant denial. She murmured, "Right," and continued loading the dishwasher.

"Ernie, you great lump. You're too heavy! Come on, why don't I take you out for a walk?"

Two minutes later, having run upstairs and down again, India placed the little bottle of fluorescent pink nail polish on the counter with a glassy *plink*. "Here you are! You must definitely do yours too. Then we'll have matching toes!"

She whistled to Glenda to join her and Ernie and ran outside with them.

Lainey looked at the bottle. If she were to

paint her nails with the polish, would that count as handling stolen goods?

More to the point, India was a girl with everything she could possibly want, living the kind of idyllic life any teenager would envy. Why would she be stealing cheap nail polish in the first place?

The next morning as Lainey was driving the girls to school, they passed a gift shop on the outskirts of Launceston with posters announcing a closing-down sale plastered across the window.

"Oh no, look. What a *shame.*" She slowed and pointed. "One of my friends used to have a dear little shop like that. Poor Jen, she was distraught when it went out of business."

Admittedly, there was a certain irony in having to lie in order to make a point about the importance of honesty, but sometimes you just had to make do with whatever came to hand. She glanced in the rearview mirror, at India texting while Violet industriously made notes in a history textbook. "Can you guess why Jen had to close her shop?"

India said, "Did it sell really tacky stuff for tourists, like that one? Because I've been in there and it was pretty awful. Plus it smelled of old cabbages."

"Well, my friend's shop didn't smell of cabbages, and it didn't sell tacky stuff either. Poor Jen, she loved her shop so much, but in the end, she just couldn't afford to keep the place running. It was the shoplifters who were the last straw, you know. I mean, they probably thought it was fine to take something that only cost a few pounds, but when lots of people do it and all think the same thing, it ends up making the difference between keeping a business in profit and having to sell because you're too far into the red. And that's what happened to Jen." Another glance in the mirror, and this time her eyes met India's.

India returned her attention to the phone in her hand and carried on texting.

"It's just people don't realize what can happen. They wouldn't dream of stopping a stranger in the street and demanding money, but they think it's fine to take things that don't belong to them. And it isn't fine," Lainey emphasized. "It's stealing, it's dishonest, and it can end up wrecking other people's lives."

Violet closed her textbook. "Didn't your friend have security cameras in her shop?"

Poor nonexistent Jen. "No, she didn't."

"Well, it might have helped."

"I know." Lainey shook her head sadly. "But she couldn't afford it."

At five that afternoon, Richard ambled into the kitchen and dumped a sheaf of papers on the oak table before helping himself to a vodka and soda from the fridge. Lainey, who was at the sink peeling potatoes, watched him open the window and call out, "Girls, who'd like to give me a helping hand? Bit of forgery. Won't take long."

Lainey raised an eyebrow. From outside, Violet shouted, "Are you paying?"

"Honestly, young people today." Richard tutted. "Fine, a tenner."

India, who was sunbathing on a towel, called out, "I'm busy."

"Go on then, I'll do it." Putting her homework aside, Violet rose to her feet.

The girls came into the kitchen together, Violet to sit at the table and India to pour herself a glass of pineapple juice.

"Right." Richard pushed the papers across to Violet, scrawled his name on the uppermost sheet, and handed her his Mont Blanc fountain pen. "Two hundred of those, there's a good girl."

"What are they?" Peering over, Lainey saw that the sheets were divided into rectangular peel-off stickers, each one bearing a photo

159

in the top right-hand corner of Richard during his heyday.

"Bookplates from a big book club in Washington, DC. They invited me over to meet them, but I said I couldn't manage that, so they've sent me these instead. Once they're signed and returned, they're going to stick them into the front of the books and hold some kind of fund-raising event for charity, which was why I couldn't say no." Richard paused to swirl the clanking ice cubes in his glass before taking an appreciative swig. "Plus, my publisher told me I had to do it."

"Which means *you* have to do it," Lainey told him. "Not Violet."

He waved an unconcerned hand. "How are they ever going to know?"

She stared at him in disbelief. "No, Richard, you can't *do* that." It was slightly surreal to think that upon meeting Sir Richard Myles for the first time, she'd been overwhelmed by the experience and pretty starstruck. Yet now here she was, three weeks later, about to give him a right telling off.

"It's only a bunch of bookplates," Richard protested.

"It's dishonest. Those people will think they're getting your signature!"

"And it will look exactly like my signature," he exclaimed. "If not even better."

"You'd get into trouble if they ever found out. They'd be distraught."

"They won't find out."

"They will if I tell them," said Lainey.

"Would you?"

"I might." She paused. "Yes, I would."

"Here we go." India rolled her eyes. "Time for another lecture about honesty."

"But it matters," Lainey insisted. "It *does.* When I was seven, I loved Take That and they sent me a birthday card with little messages and their signatures, and it was my most precious possession in the world. I kissed it every day and slept with it under my pillow every night. Then a year later my uncle told me he'd sent it himself, as a joke. I was completely heartbroken."

She hadn't had to make up a story this time; it was the truth.

"The people buying my book won't be seven years old," Richard argued.

"But that's not the point. They could still love you, like Pauline and all those people who belong to your fan club. You can't cheat them out of a signature. It's just wrong."

"Another touching personal story with a moral to it," India said good-naturedly as she helped herself to a cookie. She flashed a bright smile at Lainey. "Makes you wonder if they ever really happened."

Which was extra infuriating when this one had.

Thankfully, Violet came to the rescue. She shook her head at Richard. "Lainey's right, Grandad. It would be unfair. I think you should probably do it yourself."

Hooray for the voice of reason. Relieved, Lainey added helpfully, "And then you won't need to feel guilty."

"I wasn't planning on feeling guilty anyway." But Richard's eyes sparkled as he knocked back his vodka and soda, pulled out a chair, and took the fountain pen back from Violet. "Fine then, you've bullied me into it. Now, who'd like to make me another drink?"

CHAPTER 13

Two days later, the good weather came to an end, a gray sky hung over St. Carys, and for the first time in weeks, Lainey needed to dig something warmer out from her side of the wardrobe. Finding her denim jacket, she wore it over a T-shirt and leggings to drive India and Violet to school, then stopped off afterward in St. Carys to buy the sheets of stamps Majella had asked her to pick up.

It wasn't until she was in line at the post office that she tucked her chilly hands into the pockets of the jacket and encountered something unfamiliar. Normally, there might be a few loose coins in there or half a packet of chewing gum or a scrunchie for her hair, but this was a handkerchief with something wrapped inside it. Only slightly puzzled, Lainey pulled it out of her pocket and felt the flat, circular item that was coin-sized but hollow, as well as bumpy on one side . . .

Her brain was slow to catch up with her fingers, which meant she was staring at the uncovered ring for a good couple of seconds before the pieces of the puzzle dropped into place. Her memory scrolled back to the night at the chateau when she'd thrown her jacket on over her nighttime T-shirt and raced outside to make sure Wyatt wasn't about to do anything drastic. Then, while they'd been sitting on the grass beneath the trees, he'd been overcome with emotion and had wiped his eyes with the balled-up hankie. And when at last she'd persuaded him to head back inside to sleep, he'd left the hankie lying in the grass, and she'd scooped it up and stuffed it into her pocket before helping him back to the chateau.

She'd worn the jacket on the long bus journey home to the UK but clearly hadn't investigated the pockets. Then it had been stuffed into her suitcase, with the ring still inside the handkerchief.

The ring with the stunning three-carat diamond.

The ring that had cost Wyatt forty thousand pounds . . . and the one he blamed himself entirely for having lost.

"Are you just going to stand there like a lemon?" said the irritable man behind her in line. "Because some of us don't have all day."

Lainey hurried up to the counter. "Hi, can I have some stamps, please?"

Through the safety glass, the cashier said, "How many d'you want, love?"

"Um, forty thousand." *No,* that wasn't right; Lainey hastily corrected herself. "Sorry, I meant two hundred."

Arriving back at Menhenick House, she swung the car onto the driveway. Her pulse, already racing, stepped up another gear when she saw Seth lifting boxes of glossy brochures out of the trunk of his own car.

"Hey. Everything OK?" As always, he missed nothing. "Looking a bit . . . frazzled."

"You won't believe what I've just found . . ."

"You're not OK. Oh God." The boxes landed with a thud in the trunk, and he was in front of her, visibly concerned. "What's happened? Tell me. What is it?" His gaze dropped to her hands, which were tightly clasped together. "What have you found?"

He sounded so serious, so worried. Lainey shook her head. "It's not bad news. It's something really good!"

"It is?" Seth was frowning.

She brought her breathing under control.

No one would ever know the less than saintly thoughts that had darted like quicksilver through her mind between leaving the post office and arriving back here just a few minutes later. The idea that she could sell the ring and stealthily pay the proceeds into her bank account had only ever been the briefest of fantasies. Of course she wouldn't really have done it; she was an honest person who'd never stolen anything in her life. Look at that lecture she'd given India about the nail polish.

Slowly, finger by finger, she unclasped her hands to reveal the three-carat diamond ring. At first, terrified of losing it, she'd tucked it away inside her bra, before realizing that the safest place to keep it was on an actual finger.

"What's this?" A muscle was jumping in Seth's jaw; his gaze shifted from the ring to her face. "You're . . . engaged?"

It was a look of shock mixed with disbelief, and no wonder. She burst out laughing. "Because of course Kit could afford to buy me a ring that costs more than a vintage Rolls-Royce. It's a real diamond!" She waggled her hand at him to make him understand. "This is the ring that was lost at the chateau after the proposal that went horribly wrong. I was lining up just now in the post office, and when I put my hand in my pocket, there it was!"

Seth's face cleared. "This is the forty-thousand-pound ring you told me about. I get it now." He took hold of her hand and looked more closely at the brilliant, almost-flawless diamond. "Wow."

Even on a gray, drizzly day, it was dazzling, throwing out flashes of light, but it was the sensation of his fingers closing around hers that caused Lainey's breath to catch in her throat.

"Oi, oi, what's going on here, then?" Kit rounded the side of the house pushing a loaded wheelbarrow. "Is someone else proposing to my girlfriend behind my back?"

Imagine if that were true . . .

Lainey held her hand out to him. "I found Wyatt's ring inside a hankie in my jacket pocket."

"You're kidding. That's amazing!" Abandoning the wheelbarrow, Kit came over to see it. "What are the chances?"

"I still can't believe it." Lainey shook her head.

"What are you going to do?" said Seth.

Kit raised his eyebrows. "Caribbean cruise?"

Lainey said, "I only had 2 percent battery

left. That's why I had to come home, so we can phone —"

"The travel agent, to book our Caribbean cruise?"

"If it's a Caribbean cruise you're after," said Seth, "I can recommend an excellent travel agent."

"Stop." Lainey gave Kit a nudge. "And get your phone out. If we call Biddy, she can give us Wyatt's number. He's going to be so relieved when we tell him we've found it."

Biddy was so overwhelmed, she burst into tears of relief.

"Oh thank goodness," she exclaimed between gulping sobs. "We can stop looking at last. I just felt so guilty, as if it was our fault it had gone missing. I've been having the most terrible nightmares about searching for it. Last night, I dreamed I was dredging the lake with a sieve."

Poor Biddy and Bill, there hadn't been any interest yet in the chateau, and who knew how long it might be before a potential buyer came along? Having scribbled down the number Biddy gave her, Lainey promised to keep them updated and rang off.

Now came the even better call to make.

Except . . .

168

"Oh, hi," said Wyatt when Lainey reminded him who she was.

"I just called the chateau to get your number from Biddy and Bill. Listen, you'll never guess what's happened. I've found your ring!"

"Right, OK. The engagement ring? Where was it?"

He didn't sound remotely overwhelmed. The excitement was nonexistent.

When Lainey had finished explaining the chain of events that had led to the ring being discovered in her pocket in a post office line in St. Carys, Wyatt said, "Well, that's good news, I guess. Thanks for letting me know."

"Right." Lainey was really wishing she'd kept it now; this was what it was like to be a multimillionaire who'd gotten trashed and carelessly mislaid a forty-thousand-pound diamond. It was roughly the equivalent of her losing a sock after a visit to the launderette. "So how am I going to get it back to you?"

"I'll text you my address, then you can courier it over. How does that sound?"

It sounded expensive. Lainey had no idea how much it would cost to courier something that valuable, but the thought of it was already making her nervous. Also, it was *his* ring; she was just the one who'd found it.

She cleared her throat. "Look, sorry about this, but does couriering cost a lot? Because right now I'm not sure I can afford . . ." Her voice trailed off. Oh God, now she sounded like the Little Match Girl.

"No, no, I'm the one who should apologize. Sorry, how rude of me. You're in Cornwall, did you say?"

It was endearing hearing him say it with his American accent, pronouncing it as if it were two words: *Corn Wall*. Lainey said, "Yes, St. Carys."

"OK, well, I don't want to put you out. It's good of you to call. I'm due to attend a wedding in Cornwall at the end of this month, so why don't you hang on to it till then? I'll swing by on my way to the wedding. How does that sound?"

It definitely sounded cheaper. Lainey bit her lip, longing to ask Wyatt if he was glad she'd found the ring. Because he didn't sound as if he was. Then again, the thought of it was probably stirring up sad memories. This was the ring he'd wanted to give to Penny.

But it was none of her business anyway; he would drop in to collect it, then they'd never see each other again.

"Yes, let's do that. I'll find a good place to hide it until you get here."

Whereupon Wyatt, who evidently inhabited a whole different world, said, "No worries. Just put it in the safe."

While she was showing the ring to Majella, Richard came into the kitchen. "Let's have a look then. Oh, nice. That's quite similar to the one I bought my second wife." He frowned, examining it. "Or was it the third?"

"You bought the same ring for both of them," Majella reminded him. "That's why Tatiana ended up chucking hers into the sea."

Honestly, other people treated their diamonds so casually. Lainey said, "Did you find it again?"

"Can't remember. Where are you going to keep this one, then?"

"I thought I'd wrap it up in a sock, then stuff it into the toe of my winter boots, then hide it in a box at the back of the wardrobe in the flat."

"Well, that's the first place any half-decent cat burglar would look," said Richard. "You'd be better off keeping it in my safe."

"You have a safe?" Well, that was a relief.

"Of course I do." Richard chuckled at the idea that he might not. "Where else am I going to keep all the secret stuff that would

171

land me in a world of trouble if it ever got out?"

Jet lag on top of jet lag had numbed Wyatt Hilstanton's brain. He raked his fingers through his uncombed hair and gazed out through the floor-to-ceiling windows of his hotel room overlooking Central Park, twelve stories below.

The call from the girl had woken him at five in the morning, after which he'd fallen back into an oblivious stupor. It was only now, at midday, that he was beginning to realize that his response had been less than generous. She hadn't known she was calling him in New York; it was his own fault for groggily answering the phone or for forgetting to switch it to silent.

He could scarcely remember meeting her in the first place on the fateful night of the proposal that hadn't gone to plan. Then again, was it any wonder, considering the amount of drink he'd tipped down his neck? He had only the vaguest memory of recognizing her as one of the members of staff when she'd come out to speak to him on the grounds once everyone else had retired to bed. She'd been wearing a denim jacket over her nightdress and there had been mascara smudges under her eyes; for some reason, he recalled that much. She'd also been incredibly kind to a tearful, overemotional, hopeless case, listening patiently while he'd droned on about being such a loser. But that was about as much as he could recall; he wouldn't be able to pick her out in a police lineup.

His conscience prodding him, Wyatt surveyed the aerial view of the verdant park spread out before him and realized the girl needed a better, more effusive response than the one he'd given her. Well, maybe not effusive, but she at least deserved a text. The last few weeks might not have ranked among the happiest of his life, but that wasn't her fault, was it?

He reached for his phone, headed out onto the balcony, and composed the text as it tumbled out of his brain:

Hi, it's me again. I wanted to say sorry about earlier — I'm in NYC, so was asleep when you called. My memories of that night at the chateau are vague, but thank you for looking after me then, and for letting me know about the ring too — I may not have sounded grateful, but I am, I promise.

My friend's wedding is in St. Ives on the

last Saturday of the month, so I'll see you sometime around then — will be in touch again closer to that date. Once again, THANK YOU. (And I promise I'm really not as horrible as you must think.)

Best,
Wyatt

Pressing Send, he listened as the message of apology swooshed off into the ether and across the Atlantic. There, done.

And now, having spent the last fortnight struggling to come up with a plausible reason why he wouldn't be able to attend the wedding in Cornwall, he realized he was definitely going to have to go.

Twenty minutes later, as he was heading down to the lobby in the elevator, his phone dinged to signal the arrival of a text.

Hi Wyatt,
Sorry about waking you earlier — we had no idea you were in the States. This isn't Lainey, by the way — her phone was dead so she called you from mine. (I'm Kit, Lainey's boyfriend. We were both working at the chateau when you were there and now we're here in St. Carys.) Thanks so much for your mes-

sage, which I'll pass on to Lainey. What you've been through must have been completely traumatic, and being woken by a stranger in the middle of the night would just about put the tin lid on it. I don't blame you one bit for being grumpy. Anyway, here's Lainey's number . . .

The brass-fronted elevator doors slid open and Wyatt stepped out into the marble lobby. The smartly dressed doorman opened the door for him, and there was the limo waiting, ready to take him downtown to Wall Street.

He wondered how Penny was doing. Dammit, he missed talking to her so much.

CHAPTER 14

"I feel sick." Majella entered the kitchen smoothing her gray velvet shirt over her new narrow black trousers before realizing her palms were damp with nerves.

"Well, don't." Lainey, who'd been checking on the boeuf bourguignon, closed the oven. "You haven't even tried the food yet. And you mustn't be scared either. Everything's under control here. And you look fantastic."

"Too much lipstick, though?" She'd gone for a brighter shade of pink than usual. What if she looked like a drag queen?

"No. You have a beautiful mouth," said Lainey. "So you should show it off."

"I wasn't this nervous on the morning of my wedding." Because back then, Majella realized, there'd been nothing to be nervous about. She'd loved Tony, had known it would be a day to remember forever.

Whereas this, tonight, was a blind date.

Well, practically, apart from the couple of photos they'd found on Google Images.

"You'll be fine." Lainey's tone was reassuring. "If everything goes well, brilliant. If it doesn't, who cares? You finish your meal, wave goodbye, and never have to clap eyes on him again."

"I know. I just keep imagining all the different ways it could go wrong."

"The worst thing that can happen is that the orange soufflés don't rise. And trust me, they will," said Lainey. "Because when it comes to soufflés, I'm the best."

An hour later, despite Majella's very best efforts, the possibility that anything might come of this date had long evaporated like sea mist.

"I can't believe it." Justin Harlow shook his head, exaggeratedly baffled. "You mean to tell me you're sitting at this table and it doesn't even bother you that the painting over there above the fireplace is crooked?"

Justin was better looking in the flesh than in the photos they'd scrutinized online; smartly dressed, he was charming in a bank manager-y way. He was also the most persnickety person she'd ever encountered. As in, very persnickety indeed.

They were eating dinner in the seldom-used dining room, to give them privacy and allow the rest of the family to move around freely. So far, Justin had noticed and pointed out a tiny chip on his side plate, the fact that the floor-length topaz curtains were faded at the edges by exposure to sunlight, and the way the cutlery didn't match the style of the room.

"Oh dear, sorry about that," said Majella. "It never even occurred to me that it should."

"Don't apologize. I'm sure we can manage with these." Justin gave the handle of his disappointingly non-Georgian fork a reassuring tap, then pointed to the light fittings on either side of the mantelpiece. "Well, will you look at that? You've got a forty-watt bulb in the one on the left and a sixty-watt bulb in the one on the right. Ah, thank you . . ." He smiled as Lainey eased open the door and carried in their starters of tomato-and-basil tarts. "Tell me, what kind of tomatoes are these?"

Lainey said evenly, "They're red tomatoes."

"Don't worry. It's fine if you don't know what variety they are." He nodded bravely as she set the plates down in front of them. "Just . . . are they organic?"

Fifteen minutes later, Lainey took their

plates away, and Justin excused himself in order to pay a visit to the bathroom. Majella hurried into the kitchen after her and hissed, "He's a nightmare."

"Oh God, I *know.*" Lainey was shaking her head. "When I couldn't tell him the age of the balsamic vinegar, I thought he was going to put me in detention."

"He's threatening to teach me about the different kinds of mortgages next." Majella glanced at her watch and wished she could press the fast-forward button on this evening. "So if you come in and find me with my face in my plate, it'll be because I'm comatose with boredom." She still couldn't get over the fact that Jess from the flower shop had been so certain she and Justin would be perfect for each other. Did this mean Jess thought she was mind-numbingly persnickety and boring too?

"Be brave," said Lainey. "It'll be over soon."

"The sooner the better."

"Would you like me to secretly stir a bit of weed killer into his boeuf bourguignon?"

Majella grinned. "It's a tempting offer, but I suppose we'd better not."

Ten minutes later, the possibility that Lainey had done it after all flashed through her brain as Justin's non-Georgian knife and fork clattered onto his plate and his eyes widened in alarm. But no, of course Lainey wouldn't really have poisoned him. Oh God, though were the mushrooms not mushrooms after all? Were they poisonous toadstools instead? And now his face was turning red and he was clutching in desperation at his throat, barely able to speak, seemingly unable to breathe.

"Help . . . help!"

Majella flew into a panic, her chair tipping backward as she leaped to her feet. The next moment, the door crashed open and Lainey burst in like a bullet, taking in the situation at a glance.

"You've got something stuck in your throat?" She addressed Justin, who nodded wildly and jabbed a finger at his neck. "OK, keep calm. Can you cough?"

He shook his head helplessly, by this time puce in the face.

"Right, let's try this first." Pressing her left fist against his chest, Lainey slapped him hard on the back between his shoulder blades, then repeated the maneuver twice more.

Nothing happened. Petrified, Majella said, "Shall I call 999?"

"Hang on, let me just do this." As Justin continued to flail, struggling to suck air into his blocked lungs, Lainey moved behind him and wrapped her arms around his chest. Clasping her hands together and placing them just beneath the center of his rib cage, she braced herself and said, "One, two, three," before squeezing with as much force as she could muster.

Still nothing. Paralyzed with terror, Majella sensed movement in the doorway and saw that Seth had heard her cry for help from upstairs. Thank goodness — maybe he could help. But before he could step into the room, Lainey gathered herself, counted to three again, and gave a second almighty squeeze.

A lump of beef shot out of Justin's mouth like a missile and landed on the carpet with a tiny but incredibly welcome thud.

"Oh thank God!" Majella let out a hoarse cry of relief as Justin took in huge gulps of air before collapsing on unsteady legs back onto his chair. "Thank *God* you're OK."

Hands shaking, Justin took a clean and neatly pressed handkerchief out of his pocket and wiped his perspiring forehead. When his breathing was back under control, he stared in disbelief at Majella. "How can I possibly be OK? I nearly died."

"But you didn't die. You're still alive!" Majella's voice was breaking with emotion as she said, "Lainey saved you."

"What's going on?" Harry, who'd been out in the garden playing with the dogs, now appeared in the doorway with them.

"Justin was choking, darling, but Lainey saved his life. It was —"

"She didn't save my life," Justin bellowed. "She tried to kill me!"

Shocked, Lainey said, "What? It's the Heimlich maneuver. That's how it's done!"

Red-faced and scowling, Justin shook his head. "I'm talking about the boeuf bourguignon. The chunks of beef were too big; you couldn't be bothered to cut them up properly. They were lethal."

Majella's eyes widened in disbelief. "Oh please, you had a knife and fork!"

Non-Georgian, but even so . . .

"Irrelevant. They should never have been served like that. Look, look at the size of it!" He jabbed a finger in the direction of the lump of meat that had landed on the floor, and Ernie, who'd been eyeing it intently, took this as his cue to leap forward and do his canine duty. Tail wagging, he deftly vacuumed up the evidence, then raised his head and gazed hopefully around at the rest of them for more.

"I can't believe he's just done that," Justin bellowed. "Your dog is *disgusting.*"

Harry, surveying the goings-on with eleven-year-old delight, piped up, "I saw a vet program on TV, and there was a dog on there who ate his own poo!"

Justin looked as if he was about to throw up on the spot; he glared at Harry, then at Ernie, who wagged his tail unrepentantly. "I can't stand dogs. Their habits are repulsive." Turning to Majella, he said coldly, "To be honest, if I'd known beforehand that you were a dog owner, I would never have agreed to come here for dinner in the first place."

It was like a great weight being magically lifted from her shoulders. Up until this moment, Majella had been wondering how on earth she was going to get out of seeing him again without hurting his feelings. Now she didn't have to worry about it anymore. Released from the obligation, she said cheerfully, "Well, what a shame we didn't find out earlier. If I'd known beforehand that you were tedious, finicky, ungrateful, and rude, I would never have agreed to meet you either."

In the crowded kitchen, Seth opened another bottle of wine. As he poured it into the glasses held out by Lainey, his hand brushed the inside of her wrist and he felt

183

an actual physical charge from the brief contact. Could she feel it too? Was the sensation as powerful for her as it was for him, or had she not even noticed? Oh God, this was like being back at school; what was happening to him? So much for always being in complete control of his emotions.

But no one else was paying him any attention, which was something to be grateful for. As soon as Justin had stormed out of the house, the atmosphere had lightened. Majella had announced, "Well, I'm just heartbroken that I won't be seeing him again."

Harry, giving her an enthusiastic hug, had said, "Don't worry, Mum. I told our dinner lady at school that you were looking for a new boyfriend and she said if you want her husband you're welcome to him."

And now they were here, back in the kitchen, gathered around the scrubbed-oak table. Since Lainey had made a vast pear-and-almond crumble, there was enough for everyone. When Majella had finished describing the details of Justin's pre-choking awfulness, they took it in turns finding microscopic things to criticize in a pained, Justin-style manner. Then Majella said to Lainey, "Seriously, though, he could have died. You saved his life. What you did was amazing."

Lainey's shrug was dismissive. "I took a first aid course a few years ago. You never know when it'll come in handy. Anyway," deftly changing the subject, she pointed across the table at Harry and said in a Justin voice, "I can't help noticing, young man, that your left shirt collar is sticking up at a seventy-eight-degree angle, whereas the right shirt collar is at eighty-four degrees."

Harry grinned. "I think you should sort out your eyelashes because you've got two hundred and forty on that eye and three hundred and twelve on the other one."

"No, I can't bear it!" Lainey clapped her hands over her eyes. "I demand a massive eyelash transplant this *minute.*"

The others were laughing, but Seth was still recalling the scene he'd witnessed in the dining room, where, without panicking, Lainey had reached around the chest of a man a fair bit taller than herself and successfully performed the Heimlich maneuver. Now she was making light of what she'd done, but his estimation of her had risen higher still. She was quick-witted and funny, empathetic and kind, hardworking and efficient. Everyone who met her adored her. Well, apart from Justin.

And she was living with Kit, who might or

might not be gay and might or might not have shared this information with her.

Because that was the thing, wasn't it? You never really knew what was going on in other people's private lives.

Seth said, "Where's Kit? He should be helping us celebrate getting rid of Justin. Shall I give him a call, get him over here to join us for a drink?"

But Lainey was shaking her head. "He isn't in the flat. He went off to the gym, said not to expect him back until much later."

Was this even true? Seth wondered cynically. "He seems to be enjoying going to the gym," he said.

Lainey smiled and nodded in agreement, her gaze heartbreakingly open and trusting. "Oh yes, he really does."

CHAPTER 15

The summer season was well underway now; the warmer weather had brought the tourists streaming down to Cornwall, and the beaches were getting noticeably busier.

Lainey had swum across from Menhenick Bay to Mariscombe Bay and back again. It was six in the evening, and she'd been in the water for an hour; hopefully her towel would still be there where she'd left it above the tide line on the sun-warmed powdered-sugar sand.

Approaching the shore, she spotted the purple towel waiting for her. Hooray!

It wasn't until she was emerging from the water, though, that she saw someone waving to attract her attention.

Sunglasses, pale-blue shirt, flowing amber skirt, long dark hair. Moving closer to the shoreline, Lainey realized it was Dawn. And now she was making her way across the gently sloping sand toward her, as if she'd been waiting for Lainey to appear.

Which was a tad unlikely, wasn't it? Unless Dawn's quicksilver legal brain had detected the attraction to Seth that she'd been working so hard to conceal, and she'd come here to warn her off.

Well, you never knew.

Reaching the beach at last, Lainey mentally pictured a screeching, *EastEnders*-style showdown in front of the many holidaymakers surrounding them. That wouldn't be Dawn's way, though, surely. Plus, she was smiling.

Besides, when you were that beautiful, why would you even begin to feel threatened by the idea that someone else, someone less perfect than you, was harboring a secret crush on your man?

"Lainey, look at you. You're like a Bond girl striding out of the water!"

Except a Bond girl probably wouldn't be wearing a pink polkadot swimsuit from Costco. Lainey padded across to the dry sand, reached for her towel, and wrapped it around her torso.

Dawn went on. "You don't have to rush back, do you? I wondered if we could have a chat. I called Seth, and he mentioned you'd gone for a swim, so I thought I'd come on over and find you."

"Fine." Still mystified by the friendly manner, Lainey led the way up the beach. When they were sitting on a secluded section of dry sand facing the sea, she said, "Is this about yesterday?"

"Kind of. Well, Seth told me all about the choking thing, of course. About what a heroine you were and what a prize prat the guy was."

"I wasn't a heroine. I just did something I'd learned how to do." Twisting her hair into a rope, Lainey squeezed out a thin stream of seawater. "But I'll agree with you about him being a prat."

"Well, let's just call you impressive. Which was what made me realize I needed to come here and talk to you today." Dawn's expression grew serious. "Seth doesn't know I'm doing this, by the way. He doesn't think I should. But I have to, because you deserve to know the truth."

Weirder and weirder. Lainey shook her head slightly. "The truth about what?"

"Look, I'm really not one for gossip. I don't want you to think it's that. But there are certain situations with potentially life-altering ramifications and then it's only fair to share the information, but I'm so sorry if this —"

"What is it?" Lainey cut through the

189

elongated explanation.

"OK." Dawn removed her sunglasses and visibly braced herself. "We think there's a possibility your boyfriend might be gay."

Boyfriend . . .

For a split second, Lainey thought she meant her last *actual* boyfriend, Anton, who was no doubt currently sleeping his way around every bikini-clad beach babe in Saint-Tropez. Then she came to her senses and realized she was referring to Kit.

So that was what this impassioned intervention was all about. What to do? How to react? *Quick, think . . .* To lie or not to lie?

Misinterpreting her panic as shock, Dawn said, "I'm really sorry. We saw him at that busy bar down on the harbor, with the good-looking guy who runs it. They were definitely flirting with each other."

"Right. Thanks." Lainey jumped to her feet. "Thanks for . . . um, telling me."

"Hang on." Dawn was studying her curiously. "Did you already know?"

Why did she have to be such a rubbish liar? Licking her lips and tasting salt, Lainey said, "Sorry, I have to get back. I need to talk to Kit."

"Oh my God," Dawn exclaimed, realization spreading across her face. "You *do* already know."

■ ■ ■ ■

"What?" Kit looked baffled when Lainey switched off the outside tap attached to the garden hose, dragged him away from watering the hanging baskets, and gestured for him to follow her up to their apartment. "What's going on?"

"Dawn's worked it out. She and Seth saw you at the bar with Tom, and now she knows and she's going to tell Seth." Lainey's mouth was dry, her heart thudding. "And Seth's going to be mad at us because we lied to them, and he's going to kick us out, I know he will. Because how can they trust us if we've been lying to them for weeks? We may as well pack our bags now."

Dawn didn't waste any time telling him either. Less than fifteen minutes later, Seth appeared in the kitchen. "I think we need to have a word, don't you?"

Lainey blushed and gave the floor one last vigorous scrub before resting back on her heels. "About what?"

He gave her a long look. "Don't even try it. How about the truth?"

Still on her knees, she dropped the cloth into the bucket of hot soapy water. "Fine. I'm sorry. Kit and I aren't together. We're just friends. We badly needed a job and somewhere to live, and you were advertising for a couple. A couply couple," she amended.

"So you're here under false pretenses."

"I suppose so. And we didn't like lying, because we're both honest people. But we wanted to work here even more." His all-seeing gaze was intimidating and Lainey turned her head away, wiping her wet hands on the sides of her shorts. "Like I said, I'm really sorry. If you want us to leave, that's completely understandable. We'll go." She wasn't going to cry or beg; some small amount of dignity needed to be maintained. But at that moment, Glenda came pattering into the kitchen and bounded right up to her, resting her small front paws on Lainey's lap and wagging her tail like a metronome. Oh God, she was going to miss them all so much, the family and the animals too. She stroked Glenda's ears and swallowed hard. Where was Kit? Still working in the garden? Why hadn't Seth called him in here too?

The silence lengthened. "OK, now listen to me," said Seth at last. "I don't appreciate the fact that you weren't honest with us. Is there anything else you think we might need to know?"

Lainey shook her head vigorously. "No,

nothing, nothing at all, I promise."

"Well, let's hope your promises are more reliable than the story of your personal life. What you did wasn't great," Seth went on slowly, "but I suppose I can understand why you felt compelled to do it." A longer pause. "Nothing like this ever happens again, do you hear me?"

She'd been holding her breath for so long that her head was starting to swim. She exhaled. "Yes . . . I mean, of course not. Thank you."

Seth's phone began to ring. Before turning to leave the kitchen, he pointed to the paw prints left by Glenda's enthusiastic skid across the wet floor. With the very faintest of smiles, he said, "You've missed a bit."

"So there you go." Dawn's expression was smug; she was clearly delighted with herself. "Aren't you glad I spoke to Lainey now? All sorted, everything out in the open, and everyone's fine about it. That's what I call a result."

"You were right, and I was wrong." Seth, who prided himself on never being wrong, nodded because it was expected of him. But inwardly he was torn. On the one hand, it was obviously good news for Lainey that she wasn't being cheated on by Kit. On the other hand, this meant she was now single. On the *other* other hand — and assuming she would even be interested in him — he still couldn't risk getting involved with someone who lived and worked here, because if the relationship didn't work out, they would inevitably lose Lainey and everyone would be completely furious with him as a result.

Oh, and there was the small matter of Dawn too. Drily, Seth imagined her reaction if she knew he'd just thought of her as a small matter.

"Just so you know," she said now with an air of triumph, "I'm *always* right."

Yesterday they'd discussed their previous relationships, and he'd touched on the subject of his short attention span, subtly preparing her for the strong likelihood that this one would go the same way as all the rest. Whereupon Dawn, clearly not lacking in self-confidence, had declared, "Ah, but that was before you met me."

Now they were gathered in the kitchen, and Majella was hugging Lainey again. He heard her say, "You poor thing. I can't believe you've been sleeping on that sofa all this time! We must get you one of those proper fold-out sofa beds."

"Honestly, there's no need." Lainey was

shaking her head. "I'm fine with the one we have. It's really comfortable."

"You should have told us before now. We would still have hired you."

"But we didn't know that," Lainey explained. "Not for sure. And we were so desperate to work here, we couldn't take the risk. If a real couple had come along, you might have decided to choose them instead because it would've been so much easier."

"Never. You were the only ones we wanted." Majella gave Kit's arm a squeeze as he topped up her wineglass.

Richard, helping himself to a huge slice of Dolcelatte, said, "You were, but before you get bigheaded, just remember that all the others were absolutely dreadful."

From the other side of the table, Harry said to Kit, "So if Lainey isn't your girlfriend, and now you're gay, does that mean you're looking for a boyfriend?" Since discovering his mum was ready to start dating again, he'd become fascinated by the idea of matching people — any people — up. He went on eagerly, "Because one of my friends at school, his dad's gay, so if you like, I could ask him if he wants to go out with you."

Kit regarded him gravely. "Thanks, I'll let

you know."

"Do you like beards, though?"

"Beards are OK." Kit shrugged.

"Well, Lewis's dad hasn't got a beard," Harry explained, "but he could probably grow one if you were desperate."

Seth managed not to laugh. Behind him he heard India saying conversationally, "So this has been interesting, hasn't it? After all that chat about the importance of honesty at all times, it turns out you've been lying to us from day one."

"Touché." Lainey's tone was rueful. "But it was only a white lie. And no one else suffered as a result, did they?"

"I suppose," India said good-naturedly. "Just thought it was worth pointing out."

Lainey was smiling now, he could tell from the sound of her voice. "Well, that's fair enough. I wouldn't have been able to resist mentioning it either."

Seth heard India lower her voice. "We're still glad you're here."

"Thanks. Me too."

"Lainey? Lainey!" Harry was swallowing a mouthful of chips, spraying crumbs and waving his hand to catch her attention. "If you and Kit aren't together, does that mean you need a boyfriend? Or are you gay too?"

As she turned, Seth caught the look of

genuine affection for Harry shining in her eyes and felt a surge of emotion he was almost scared to acknowledge.

"I'm not gay," she said. "But just because people are on their own doesn't mean they have to have someone else. It's completely fine to be single."

"Like me." Harry nodded. "I'm single."

She smiled. "Exactly. And look how happy you are."

"But wouldn't you like to meet someone and have a proper boyfriend if you could?"

"Well . . ."

Clearly unwilling to abandon his mission, Harry said, "Because Mr. Elliott at my school is divorced, so you could go out with him if you want."

Amused, Violet said, "You're on a roll, Harry. Go on then, tell us about Mr. Elliott. What's he like?"

"He wears green trousers every day, and he likes cycling, and he tells really bad jokes. But he's nice. Everyone likes him. And he makes up songs about geography."

"Sounds perfect." Appearing at Seth's side, Dawn reached for his hand and entwined her fingers with his. Smiling down at Harry, she said, "How old is Mr. Elliott?"

"Same as most teachers." With a careless

shrug, Harry grabbed another handful of chips. "About fifty."

CHAPTER 16

It was like sticking to a brutally strict diet for weeks on end, then finally reaching that point where you couldn't cope with the emptiness for a minute more. Wyatt took out his mobile and felt his heart rate accelerate. It was no longer a question of should he do this. He wanted, needed, *had* to.

There. And now he'd pressed the button to call the number he'd been forcing himself not to call for the last month.

She probably wouldn't pick up anyway. Right now, the chances were that she was staring in disbelief at the screen of her phone and backing away from it in —

"Hello?"

He stopped dead in his tracks. "Pen?"

"Yes. Hello, Wyatt." She sounded breathless but not horrified, thank goodness.

"Oh, Pen, I didn't expect you to answer. It's so good to hear your voice." Wyatt gazed around him at the lake, the gardens, and the bandstand in Regent's Park and felt the lump in his throat expand. How his brothers would laugh if they could see him now, overcome with emotion because he was so happy to be speaking to the girl who had humiliated him in front of his entire family.

"How are you?" There was gentle concern in her voice, as if she really wanted to know.

"Pretty good, thanks. Getting on with life."

"I really am sorry about, you know, everything."

"No, please don't, you shouldn't apologize. I was such an idiot." Wyatt shook his head as the words came stumbling out. Oh God, and now his eyes were prickling, causing him to blink hard. "What I did was wrong; it was just the hugest mistake. I put you in the most awful situation, and you were absolutely right to say no."

"I was in shock," Penny said in her soft voice. "I couldn't believe it was happening. I've never really liked surprises anyway, even if they're nice ones . . . Oh dear, I didn't mean it like that!"

"No more apologies, please. And I'm not trying to shift the blame, but it was my mom's idea, the whole thing. She saw a TV show once about a surprise proposal and decided it would be superromantic. Mom's pretty forceful once her mind is made up."

"She must have been so upset when it went wrong."

"She was. Mom wants to see me married. Right now, it's her mission in life to get me paired off. I've had my work cut out explaining it isn't going to be happening anytime soon." Wyatt watched as two swans made their way in stately coupledom across the lake. Swans mated for life, didn't they? Lucky them.

He heard a shuddery intake of breath, followed by a high-pitched gulp.

Hastily he said, "No, you can't cry! I'm not trying to make you feel bad, I promise. You did the right thing and I'm glad about that." He realized he was babbling and forced himself to slow down. "And please, don't think I've called you to see if we can get back together, because I haven't. I've just really missed you as a friend."

"I've missed you too." Penny's voice was small. "As a friend."

"Well, that's good to hear." They'd enjoyed each other's company so much, until he'd gone and ruined everything.

Two bouncy terriers nearby, waiting for their owner to throw them a ball, broke into a volley of competitive barking.

Penny said, "Where are you?"

"In Regent's Park."

"Oh, lovely! Whereabouts?"

"Down by the lake, just next to the bandstand." He knew she'd know where he meant; it had been one of their favorite walks when they'd come here together.

She sounded as if she were smiling. "Found any four-leaf clovers yet?"

"I haven't been looking."

"Oh, Wyatt, you should. Any dancing going on?" The last time they'd visited, a joyously impromptu salsa party had been in progress, and they had been persuaded to join in.

"Not right now." Wyatt searched the area for something else he could tell her about. "But there's a squirrel investigating an apple core, and a little kid taking a pee up against the steps of the bandstand. Sorry, not very glamorous."

"Hey, I'm up here in Walsall, waiting at a bus stop between a closed-down ironmonger's and a bargain booze shop. The garbage hasn't been collected, and it's piddling down with rain," Penny continued solemnly. "So don't talk to me about glamour."

He laughed. "This is why I miss you."

"And I've missed hearing your laugh. I'm feeling better already. I'm so glad we're talking again."

"Does your mom think I'm an idiot?" He'd only met Penny's mother once, but they'd gotten along well.

"Are you kidding? Mum thinks *I'm* the idiot for turning you down, what with you being so megaloaded. But you can't go ahead and marry someone just because they're rich, can you?"

"Clearly not." Amazingly, Wyatt realized, he was able to joke about it. Being friends with Penny was fifty times more important than being engaged to her.

Speaking of engaged . . . "Hey, they found the ring, by the way."

"What ring?"

Damn, he'd dreamed he'd told her, but of course, in real life she had no idea. "Sorry, I forgot you didn't know. I lost the engagement ring after you left the chateau. But it turned up a few days ago."

"Oh no, you must have been frantic! The one with the diamond? Did it cost much?"

She'd barely noticed the ring when he'd been trying to propose to her. Wyatt said, "Not too much," because she would only have a belated panic attack if he told her the truth. The next moment, he was struck by an idea that felt like the answer to everything. "It's in Cornwall at the moment. I said I'd stop by and pick it up when I go down there for Sophie and Max's wedding."

"Of course, they're getting married in Saint Ives." Penny had been invited too, as his plus one.

"I was going to cancel." He paused. "Going on my own didn't seem like such a great idea."

"Oh." She sounded sympathetic. "But it'd be a shame to miss it. I mean, Max is one of your oldest friends."

"I know. And I am going to go. It's just going to feel a bit weird being on my own when everyone else is part of a couple. But I can do it, I'll be fine." He wanted to ask her, but how could he? And why would she even want to go? It was a terrible idea.

The silence echoed between them for a couple of seconds, then Penny said cautiously, "Wyatt? Can we be friends now? Like, really good, proper friends?"

"I would be so happy if we could." As he said it, he felt his heart lift.

"Well, how about if I came with you to the wedding? We could go together, just as good friends. Would that be a nice idea, d'you think? Or it's fine if you'd rather not."

Tears of relief brimmed in Wyatt's eyes. He nodded and swallowed hard. "That would be . . . Yes, I'd like that. Very much. It'd be great."

"Let's do it, then. Have you booked anywhere to stay yet?"

"I haven't, but I will. I'll get to it today." Hastily he added,

"Separate rooms, of course."

"Of course," Penny echoed down the line.

"Separate hotels if you want."

She laughed. "No need for that."

"I'm so glad I called you." He dodged out of the way as a skateboarder whooshed past. "I've missed hearing your voice, spending time with you."

"Oh, Wyatt," Penny sighed. "Hasn't it just been miserable? I've missed our chats so much too."

CHAPTER 17

". . . and that's when all six of us ended up dancing naked in the Trevi Fountain at midnight."

Lainey was driving Richard back from his appearance at a literary festival in Dorset. His event had gone well; the audience had shrieked with laughter at his scurrilous anecdotes and the line for signed copies of his autobiography had snaked pleasingly out of and all around the huge white tent. Knowing his fondness for interesting gins, several of his admirers had brought bottles along with them to give him; these were currently clanking around in a bag on the back seat of the car while he took sips from a miniature and regaled Lainey with stories the publisher hadn't dared to let him include in the book.

They were certainly making the journey fly by.

"But you said there was a paparazzo taking photos, so what happened next?" She was intrigued.

"Alicia beckoned him over and offered him a swig of champagne from the bottle she was holding. Couldn't resist it, could he? I mean, who could? She was a goddess." Richard chuckled at the memory. "When he reached the side of the fountain, she pretended to lose her balance and grabbed hold of his arm. Clever girl," he said happily. "She managed to pull him and his camera into the water with her. I opened the back of the camera and exposed the film, all sorted. Alicia gave him a kiss he wouldn't forget in a hurry to make up for it, and we all lived happily ever after. Ah, they were the good old days when you could get away with anything. Well, pretty much."

Lainey checked the fuel gauge. "I need to stop for petrol."

"No problem. I'll grab us a couple of coffees to keep us going. Did I ever tell you about the time I had coffee with Peter O'Toole at the casino in Monte Carlo? Well, we'd *planned* to stick to coffee, but somehow we managed to end up on a yacht that was heading down to Morocco, and the owner had a pair of lion cubs on board . . ."

By the time Lainey had finished filling up the car, Richard had collected the coffees and was back in the passenger seat, resting the drinks on a copy of his book and waving at an enthralled couple in a Fiat Punto who'd pulled up at the next pump.

It wasn't until they were several miles down the road that Lainey looked in the rearview mirror. "Richard, what happened to the other bag on the back seat?"

"The bottles of gin? They're still there."

"Not that bag. The one containing the cards."

"Ah, those." His careless shrug told her what was about to come. "I checked through them, then disposed of them responsibly in the bin back at the petrol station."

"Oh, Richard!"

"Now listen, darling, isn't it better than putting things into recycling boxes if people are going to go through them? This way, the bag's stuffed into the bottom of a bin miles from home. I thought you'd be delighted with me for being so thoughtful. I took notice of what you said!"

Lainey sighed, because he was making himself sound so reasonable. The other morning, as she'd been driving out through the gates of Menhenick House to take India and Violet to school, they'd spotted Pauline lurking near the recycling boxes waiting on the pavement for garbage collection. Lainey herself was the one who'd mentioned it to Richard, warning him that he probably shouldn't put personal items in the boxes.

So he'd done as he was told, which meant she wasn't allowed to be cross with him now.

Oh, but she just knew he'd used it as an excuse not to reply to anything that might need replying to.

"Did you read all the cards?"

"Yes."

"Are you sure?"

"Of course." He looked outraged at the very idea that he might not have done.

Which of course meant he hadn't.

"What about the one Pauline gave you?" It had had *Top Secret* written on the outside of the envelope, and Pauline had explained that she was passing it on for a friend who'd been unable to make it along to today's event but had gone on to stress how vitally important it was that Richard read it.

"It was probably a letter to let me know that today is the anniversary of the first time she bought a copy of the *Radio Times* with a photo of me on the cover."

"So you've binned it." Lainey tutted.

"But in a thoughtful way, in a petrol station sixty miles from St. Carys, so Pauline will never know." In Richard's eyes, he was a paragon of virtue, an absolute hero.

"You're a bad man."

He laughed. "If you think I'm bad now, you should have seen me when I was thirty."

Silence fell for a few minutes and Lainey assumed he'd dozed off, but when she glanced over, she saw that he was looking at the copy of his autobiography on his lap, lying open now at the page containing a glossy photograph of himself with his late son. The photo had been taken in a garden somewhere Lainey didn't recognize, back when Tony was in his late thirties and still healthy, and the connection between the two handsome men was striking. They were laughing together, clearly reveling in each other's company, and the camera had caught them just as Richard was gesturing toward Tony with his hand, as if to say *Look at you, aren't you amazing? I'm your father and I couldn't be prouder of you if I tried.*

Now, as Richard gently stroked his fingertips over his son's photograph, she glimpsed another side of the ever-cheerful actor. Quietly she said, "You must miss him so much."

Richard nodded. "Oh yes. Every hour of every day." He paused. "I still can't believe an old bastard like me managed to produce such a wonderful human being. I know he's gone, but sometimes I dream that he's still alive, you know?"

Lainey murmured, "I know." It had happened to her, too, in the first years after losing her mum.

"Sorry, of course you do. Isn't it incredible when it happens? It's like he's come back to me, and it's the best feeling in the world." Another pause. "And then you wake up and *bam,* it hits you all over again that he's gone. My beautiful boy. I loved him more than life itself. If I'd had the chance, I would've swapped places with him in an instant."

"Grief is the price we pay for love," said Lainey, blinking away a tear.

"It certainly is. Sorry, darling, this won't do at all, will it?" Gathering himself, Richard whisked a yellow silk handkerchief out of his jacket pocket and handed it to her. "Let's talk about something more cheerful. If you're crying too much to see where you're driving, we're both going to end up dead." A glimmer of the old irreverent smile lifted the corners of his mouth. "And if that happens, an awful lot of women are going to be absolutely furious with you."

They were almost home when Lainey's phone beeped with a text. "Can you read it for me?" she said.

"Sure it isn't going to be saucy?"

"I'm completely sure." Such was the current absence of opportunities for sauciness in her life.

"It's from Kit." He took his reading spectacles out of the top pocket of his blue blazer. "Sure he isn't going to be saying something terrible about me?"

"Actually, he might. Brace yourself."

But the text was brief and to the point. In Shakespearean tones, Richard read aloud: " 'I've volunteered you for a job, because you'll be better at it than me. Don't be cross; it'll be fun! And Seth says thanks, you're a lifesaver. AGAIN.' "

"Cryptic," said Lainey.

"Want to stop and call him, find out what's going on?"

"No, we're nearly there." She didn't want Richard to be watching her this closely while she found out just how she was going to be saving Seth's life.

Although there probably wasn't going to be actual mouth-to-mouth resuscitation involved.

"Thanks for helping out," said Seth when they entered the kitchen. "I wouldn't have asked if I hadn't been desperate."

"I don't know what I've agreed to yet."

Lainey couldn't help it; the sight of him looking so frazzled, with that lock of dark hair falling over his forehead and his white shirt untucked, was having a bit of an effect on her.

"Two helpers were on their way to start working for one of our clients this afternoon when they came off their motorbike. They called me from the hospital two hours ago; between them they have a fractured femur, seven broken ribs, a snapped collarbone, three broken fingers, and one dislocated ankle."

"Oh, what? That's *awful.* Poor things!"

"Well, yes." Seth raked back his ruffled hair. "And obviously I'm glad they're still alive, but I then spent the next hour on the phone trying to book last-minute replacements, and it was completely impossible. I thought I was going to have to call Grace and tell her the holiday was canceled, then Kit overheard me on the phone and suggested you for the job."

"What kind of job?" Maybe it was something fantastic, a once-in-a-lifetime experience. A luxurious world cruise, perhaps, or a visit to all the best theme parks in Florida, or a month on the beach in Bali . . .

"It's four days in a house on the outskirts of Bristol," said Seth.

Lainey blinked. Not quite the glamour quotient she'd been anticipating. "Grace is a single mother of three young autistic boys," he continued. "She takes them for four days every year to stay in her sister's house while her sister goes to visit a friend in London. The boys have their particular routines and need careful handling, and they've spent months looking forward to this break. But Grace can't manage them on her own; it's too much for her. She has a bit of help at home, but the trip to Bristol was arranged to happen while the helper's away on holiday in Ibiza. Every last detail has been planned. You have an enhanced DBS, yes?"

He was referring to the Disclosure and Barring Service certificate; the enhanced version was a requirement when working with vulnerable adults and all children. Lainey nodded and glanced across at Kit, who'd just appeared in the kitchen doorway; he was looking shamefaced.

"We both have them," she told Seth.

"But you're so much better at that stuff than me," Kit said. "You can deal with anything, nothing bothers you."

Diapers were what he was talking about. Diaper changing and bottom wiping and poo. Kit was more the sporty, activity type.

Lainey raised an eyebrow to let him know she knew exactly why he hadn't volunteered himself for the job.

On the defensive now, Kit said, "I know, but it's *true.* You're brilliant with kids."

Seth turned back to Lainey. "You will do it, won't you? You're not going to refuse?"

Did she have a choice? No. Was she looking forward to it? Not really. Would she make sure Kit understood that he owed her a massive favor in return for having thrown her under this metaphorical bus? Oh, definitely.

And the more poo she had to clean up, the bigger the favor was going to be. "Of course I'm not going to refuse. It's fine. When do I have to go? Tonight?"

Seth was visibly relieved. "Thanks. And no, you can relax for the rest of this evening. We'll leave here first thing tomorrow."

"We?"

The way Seth looked at her caused her chest to start thudding suddenly, like horses' hooves racing across wet sand.

"Sorry, didn't I say? I'll be coming along too."

CHAPTER 18

"Look at him. Can you believe the favors that man's done for me over the years?" Grace was watching as Seth loaded the motley collection of cases into the rented van at just after six the following morning. "God knows he doesn't make any money out of us, but he still insists on arranging everything. And we love him for it, don't we, boys?"

Lainey, next to her, saw the two older boys nod automatically because it was expected of them. Bay, the youngest at five years old, was nonverbal and sucking the corner of a faded blue blanket. Stevie, age eight, clutched a shopping bag filled with receipts. Ned, the eldest, was ten years old and busy scribbling with a blue felt-tip pen in an exercise book. All three boys were tall for their age, with white-blond hair and brown eyes.

"Are we going now?" said Ned.

"Very soon, darling."

"Is *she* coming with us?"

"Yes, I explained that. Her name's Lainey, remember? And she and Seth are going to be helping me look after you so we can all have a fantastic time."

Ned shook his head. "I don't want her looking after us."

"But we can't manage on our own, can we?" Grace indicated her bad leg and her walking stick. "So we need someone else, and Seth found Lainey, and she's wearing blue because that's your favorite color."

"Not that kind of blue." Ned turned away, distinctly unimpressed.

"Well, if Lainey doesn't come with us, we'll all have to stay at home. And that would be a shame because this is our lovely holiday and we've all been looking forward to it, haven't we?"

Ned rolled his eyes. "Fine. So can we go now?"

"As soon as you've had a wee, darling."

He addressed Lainey without making eye contact. "What happened to the other people who were coming with us?"

"They had an accident," Lainey reminded him.

"Like when we don't go for a wee before getting in the car?"

"Not that kind of accident. They came off their motorbike and now they're in the hospital, but they'll be better soon."

"Soon? So they can still come with us to Bristol?"

"No." She shook her head firmly. "They can't."

"Was there a lot of blood when they had the accident?"

"Do you like blood?"

"No, I hate it. It's too red."

"They were lucky. There wasn't any blood at all," said Lainey. "Just a few broken bones."

"Did their bones make a noise when they broke? Like, did they go *craaack*?"

"Well, maybe a tiny crack."

"I like that kind of sound," said Ned. *"Craaack!"*

Lainey smiled. It was going to be an interesting trip.

Oh, but so much more interesting for having Seth with her. She watched as he finished loading up the vehicle and signaled across to them that he was ready to leave. He was wearing a navy polo shirt and jeans and looking — let's face it — pretty damn gorgeous.

Next to her, clearly having noticed this too, Grace said quietly, "When I was young and painfully shy, I spent years getting picked on at school because I was so quiet and easy to make fun of. Then, when I was seventeen, I took a job during the summer holidays working in an ice cream booth on Menhenick Beach. That was the year Sir Richard bought the big house there and brought his family down to St. Carys for the summer. All the girls in my class fell in love with Seth, and wherever he went, they followed like geese. That's how he found out they were being mean to me. I mean, he could have had anyone he wanted, and *obviously* he didn't fancy me or anything like that, but he spent time chatting to me and just being friendly. And then he started inviting me to join them after I'd finished work . . . even though I didn't want to at first. But he wouldn't take no for an answer, so I started going along with him to the parties that were being held on the beach. And the fact that Seth was so kind meant the girls had to be nice to me too, because they were so desperate for him to like them. But eventually we all got used to each other, I stopped being terrified of them, we ended up becoming friends, and the teasing became a thing of the past."

She shook her head as if still marveling at what Seth had achieved during the space of one summer. "You can't imagine the difference he made to my life. He returned to London, but we always knew he could be back at any time. School stopped being an ordeal and I had some friends of my own at last. I actually began to enjoy getting up in the mornings, and that was all thanks to him. He didn't need to do any of it, but he did."

"That's fantastic." Lainey was moved to hear about Seth's kindness as a schoolboy.

"If this was all happening in a book or a film, years would pass, Seth would fall on hard times and everything would go wrong in his life, while I'd miraculously find myself in a position to return the favor and do something wonderful for him." Grace looked rueful. "Except that hasn't happened, has it? Here we are, fifteen years on, and he's still the one helping me."

"He doesn't have to, though," said Lainey. "He's doing it because he wants to, because you're friends."

"I know, I do know that. I just don't like feeling beholden. If only I could repay him in some way."

"We never know what's going to happen." Lainey shrugged. "Maybe one day you'll get your chance."

Ned was back from the bathroom. "You

could bake him a cake."

"With my cooking? Oh, poor Seth, that would be too cruel." Grace smiled at her eldest son.

But Ned was heading impatiently for the front door. "Come on, hurry up. Let's go."

The early start enabled a speedy, relatively traffic-free journey across Bodmin Moor and up the M5. Ned, using a variety of blue felt-tip pens, carefully filled pages of his exercise book with the registration numbers of vehicles they passed along the way. Bay listened to children's stories through headphones and let out intermittent shrieks. Stevie, clutching his bag of shopping receipts, unfurled them one by one and read the lists of items and their prices aloud. After pointedly ignoring Lainey for the first hour, he eventually gave in and passed her one of the long receipts. Still gazing out of the window on his side of the people carrier, he said, "Now you read them."

"OK." Touched by the tiny breakthrough, Lainey said, "Jersey Royal potatoes —"

"Not *potatoes*. You have to say it like it's written."

"Sorry. Jersey Royal pots, one pound fifty —"

"No! You don't say the prices." Stevie shook his head wildly at her faux pas. "You say what the things are, then I say how much they cost."

"Right, got it." Impressed, Lainey said, "And do you know all the prices?"

"Yes."

"That's amazing." She knew that only a tiny percentage of people on the autism spectrum possessed rare talents, but Stevie was evidently one of them. "Right, here we go. Jersey Royal pots . . ."

"Seven."

Meeting Seth's gaze in the rearview mirror for a split second, she saw him nod, encouraging her to continue. "Chantenay cars."

"Eleven."

"Toms."

"Waaahhh!" Securely strapped in next to his mother, Bay began kicking the back of the seat in front of him.

When he'd finished, Stevie said, "Three hundred and twenty-six."

They reached their destination at nine in the morning. Situated away from any other houses on the very edge of a village called Easter Compton, it was a rundown-looking property surrounded by an overgrown garden.

"I know it's not Buckingham Palace."

Grace was apologetic. "But my sister's never been house-proud. On the upside, it means she's not going to mind if a wall gets scribbled on or a couple of mugs are broken. If we rented somewhere from a stranger, I wouldn't be able to relax for a second."

Once the car was unpacked, they let themselves into the empty house, which was dusty and cluttered but clean enough.

"Now we have bacon sandwiches with tomato ketchup," Ned announced, because this was what they always did upon arrival.

"Coming up," said Grace, but Lainey gestured for her to sit down.

"Relax. It's your holiday too." Well, inasmuch as any kind of relaxation was possible under the circumstances. "I'll put the kettle on and make the sandwiches."

"And I'll take the boys outside." Seth scooped Bay up. "Let's explore the garden, shall we?"

"Can we climb trees?" said Ned.

Seth shook his head. "No, remember what your mum told you. Not until you're older."

Through the kitchen window, they watched Seth outside with the boys. Grace said, "Ned broke his arm last year jumping out of a tree. He does things without thinking they might not be a good idea."

"I did something like that once; lucky I

didn't break my neck." Lainey winced at the memory. "I was staying at my gran's house, got one of my flying fairy dolls caught in the top branches of the tree outside my bedroom window and thought I could climb out and reach it. But then I got stuck and couldn't climb back inside or get down the tree."

"Oh my word! What did your gran do?"

"Nothing, she was having a nap and had taken her hearing aid out. She lived on the outskirts of a village, so no one would have heard me if I'd yelled for help. I honestly thought I was going to fall trying to get down and probably die."

"And yet here you are." Grace smiled. "Still alive. How did you manage it?"

"A boy saw me from the field behind my gran's house. He came running across, jumped over the wall into her garden, and climbed up the tree. He was older and taller than me and he helped me down. I was so relieved to reach the ground I almost burst into tears. I wanted to hug him because he'd saved my life! But I didn't," Lainey said wryly. "Which was just as well because he called me an idiot. Then he turned and jumped over the wall again and ran back across the field that led down to Goose-brook, and I never saw him again." She laughed. "Thank *God.* I spent the rest of the week absolutely terrified he was going to turn up and tell Gran what I'd done, then she'd have told Mum and I'd never have been allowed to stay with my gran again!"

"Ha, bet it put you off climbing trees for life," said Grace. "That's the trouble with Ned — it wouldn't occur to him to stop doing things that might hurt him. Like that." She pointed through the window, where her oldest son, blond hair gleaming in the sunlight, was now clambering onto the wooden garden table. Lowering Bay to the ground, Seth swiftly retrieved Ned before he was able to launch himself like Spider-Man at the washing line six feet away. "They really like him," she continued fondly. "He has the magic touch."

"He's so good with them," Lainey agreed.

"He always has been. When the time comes, he's going to make a brilliant father." After a pause, Grace said drily, "Unlike my ex-husband, who couldn't have been more rubbish if he'd tried."

"What happened to him? Sorry, you don't have to tell me."

"Oh, no worries. It's one of the great love stories of our time." Half laughing, Grace took a gulp of hot tea. "I met Pete when I was working in the co-op. We got chatting and he started coming into the shop more and more often. It kind of became a standing joke. He'd be popping in three or four times a day, and everyone at work thought it was so romantic. Then he invited me out and we started seeing each other, and the next thing you know, I was pregnant. Everything was OK for a year or two; it was all a bit sudden, but we loved each other and thought we could make it work . . . except Ned screamed nonstop and never slept, and I thought it had to be my fault, that I must be a terrible mother. Then Pete's mum told me the reason he was so difficult was because I was making too much of a fuss of him, and the best thing I could do was have another baby, then I wouldn't have time to be so neurotic."

"Ouch." Lainey turned back from frying the bacon, appalled.

"And Pete always did what his mum told him to do, so a year later, Stevie came along. We did still love each other, you see. All we wanted was to make our marriage as happy as possible. But it just got more and more difficult, and we couldn't understand why our children were so much harder to cope with than other people's, and finally they were referred to a specialist and were both diagnosed. It was almost a relief for me in a way, because at least we had an answer at last, but Pete found it harder to accept. He couldn't cope. We struggled on for a while, because what else could we do? But he was becoming more and more stressed and withdrawn. Then one day he just said he couldn't handle it anymore and walked out."

"Oh, Grace." The determinedly brave face she was putting on made the story all the more heartbreaking.

"And a week later, I found out I was expecting again." A wry smile.

"What did he say when you told him?"

"He said I always did have a rubbish sense of timing. Then he told me he'd moved in with the barmaid from the Crown because she wasn't always nagging and she understood him. Which was nice."

"I don't know how you get through something like that," Lainey marveled.

"It wasn't the best time of my life, I'll give you that. But I had my boys," Grace said simply. "And I still have them, and I love them to bits. They're my world."

"Of course they are." A lump sprang into Lainey's throat; she had to concentrate on turning the strips of bacon in order to get herself back under control.

"Not saying they're not hard work, because they are, obviously. But they mean everything to me. I'm lucky to have them, and Pete's the one who's missing out."

"He doesn't see them?"

"No. Then again, lots of friends have melted away over the years. Especially the ones with so-called *normal* children."

From the garden, through the open window, came one of Bay's earsplitting shrieks, followed by the sound of Seth saying, "Don't worry, it's just a butterfly. It won't hurt you."

"In fact, pretty much the only person who doesn't steer well clear of us is Seth. He's our knight in shining armor." Draining her mug, Grace rose to her feet to start buttering slices of bread. "He was telling me last week that he has a new girlfriend."

"He does."

"Dawn, he said her name was. Isn't that a beautiful name? Have you met her?"

"I have." Lainey nodded, wishing she had the kind of name that people thought was beautiful.

"Oh, he deserves the best. She must be absolutely stunning." Grace gave a happy sigh. "And I bet she's lovely too."

What else could she say? Lainey drained the strips of crispy bacon on a sheet of kitchen paper and summoned a bright smile. "She is!"

CHAPTER 19

Fourteen hours later, the boys and their mum were asleep upstairs in their rooms and the house was quiet — for now at least.

Seth came down the staircase with an armful of bedding. "How are you doing? Shattered?"

"It's been an experience." Lainey watched him dump the duvet and pillows on the sofa; she had a narrow single bed up in the converted attic, but Seth would be sleeping down here in case Stevie or Ned woke up and started wandering around the house. "Are you ready to go to sleep? Because I can leave you to it . . ."

"No, no, it's not even midnight yet. Want a drink? Red wine?"

"Are you having one?"

"Better not." He shook his head. "I'm on child-wrangling duty, so I'll stick to water."

"I will too." After all, this wasn't a holiday; they were here to work.

Seth returned from the kitchen with two glasses of cold water from the tap.

Once he was sitting next to her on the sofa, they solemnly clinked their drinks together.

"Thanks again. Now you know why I didn't want to cancel."

Lainey nodded. "I do."

"They're good kids. It just breaks my heart to see what Grace has to go through. Has had to go through," he amended, "practically her whole adult life."

"But you've stuck by her. She appreciates that so much," Lainey told him, "and she loves you for it. Not *love* loves you." It was her turn to correct herself. "She's just so grateful for everything you've done to help her."

"Who wouldn't want to help?"

"Well, lots of people."

Seth tilted his head sideways. "What are you looking at?"

Whoops, the honest answer was that she'd been studying his profile, the line of his jaw, the curve of his neck, and the way his dark hair curled over the collar of his polo shirt. But since she wasn't about to give him the honest answer, Lainey said, "You've got some dried drool and tomato ketchup on your shirt." She patted her own shoulder to show him where it was.

He pointed. "And you've got chocolate in your hair."

"Let's hope it is chocolate."

Seth leaned across, lifted the section of hair, and inhaled. "It's OK, you're safe."

Which shouldn't have sounded seductive, but somehow did. Flustered by his proximity, Lainey jumped up. "I'm going to get some chips."

In the kitchen, she bent over the sink and squirted soap onto the glued-together strands. When the chocolate had been rinsed away, she grabbed a bag of chips from the cupboard and called out, "How about some Brie and crackers?"

But when she returned to the living room, he was on his phone. "No, Grace has gone to bed. That was Lainey."

Lainey stopped dead in her tracks; Seth was on his feet now, facing away from her.

"I couldn't get anyone else at such short notice. She has an enhanced DBS and agreed to help out."

She silently reversed into the kitchen, her ears on stalks. After several seconds of listening to whoever was on the other end of the phone, Seth said, "We've been busy. I didn't have time to call. I wasn't deliberately not telling you."

Yeesh. She slid farther back across the kitchen, opened and closed a couple of cupboard doors for effect, and gave her bag of chips a rustle and shake for added authenticity. When it was safe, she returned to the living room. Seth, no longer on the phone, was studying the sheet of paper printed with tomorrow's schedule of activities, clearly laid out so the boys knew what would be happening and could be reassured there'd be no surprises.

"We need to be at the shopping mall as soon as it opens, so they can see the fountain while the place is still practically empty."

Lainey nodded; Ned and Stevie were evidently enthralled by the spectacular indoor fountain that intermittently sent a jet of water shooting high into the air.

"And then at nine thirty, we'll leave there and head to the zoo." Again, before too many other people arrived, because crowds and noise were what most unsettled them. She'd already learned today that if Ned didn't want to go where you wanted him to go, he was apt to leg it in the opposite direction, whereas Bay threw himself to the ground and wailed inconsolably. On the upside, she'd discovered that if Stevie was growing anxious, he could be calmed by having items from his shopping lists read aloud to him.

"That was Dawn on the phone," said Seth when she'd sat back down and ripped open the packet of chips.

"Oh?"

"Did you hear what I was saying?"

"No." Lainey caught his raised eyebrow. "OK, yes."

"She's a bit put out. About you being here."

"Sorry."

The corners of his mouth twitched with amusement. "You don't have to apologize."

"I know I don't. But there's no reason for her to be put out, is there? I can't believe she is." Lainey realized she was burbling. "I mean, what's the point? This is Dawn we're talking about! Why would she ever need to worry about anyone else?" It didn't help that Seth was watching her intently, the expression in his dark eyes unreadable. Panicking, she thrust the bag of chips at his chest. "Here, grab yourself a handful."

Seth did the world's tiniest double take, and she felt her cheeks heat up as realization belatedly dawned. Because this, *this* was the effect he had on her.

It was also the reason she could never aspire to be as irresistible to the opposite sex as Dawn, who as well as being absolutely stunning to look at was dignified and in control at all times and would *never* inadvertently say something so ridiculous.

Flustered, Lainey said, "OK, can we delete that? Pretend I didn't say it?"

"We can pretend." Seth was making heroic attempts to keep a straight face. "But I'm not going to be able to forget it."

Ned was muttering "pig" under his breath.

Seth reached for his hand, just in case he was about to rush up to someone and start saying it to their face. He gave Ned's fingers a reassuring squeeze. "They don't have any pigs here at the zoo. We're seeing them tomorrow, remember? At the farm."

"I like pigs. What time tomorrow?"

"Two o'clock. It's on the list."

But Ned had stopped walking; he pulled his hand free, took the notebook out of his pocket, and carefully wrote down the time to make completely sure he didn't forget. As a well-built couple walked past, each enjoying an ice cream, he put away the notebook and said in a loud voice, "Pigs at two o'clock."

Forty minutes later, it was Stevie's turn to be the center of attention. Watching impassively as his younger brother threw himself to the ground and kicked over one of the chairs outside the café, Ned said, "Every-one's looking at him."

Seth nodded; Ned wasn't wrong. Stevie was having one of his dramatic out-of-the-blue meltdowns, yelling at the top of his voice and hammering his heels against the tarmac. Lainey was kneeling at his side, speaking gently to him and making sure he didn't injure himself. As she smoothed Stevie's hair back from his forehead, Seth marveled at the instinctive way she dealt with him and found himself slightly wishing he could know how that felt.

The next moment, she raised her head, eyes narrowed. Turning and following the direction of her gaze, Seth saw a group of three young teenage girls mocking Stevie, laughing and mimicking his flailing arms.

Grace had taken Bay to the disabled bathroom to change his diaper. Seth, still holding Ned's arm, was in no position to intervene. Lainey was unable to respond either, though she clearly wanted to. Mean-while, the teenagers were egging each other on, getting carried away.

"Now, now, girls." A young lad wearing the bottle-green uniform of a zoo employee approached them. "If you had autism and were that upset about something, you wouldn't want people making fun of you, would you? It doesn't cost anything to be kind."

Shamefaced, the girls instantly stopped their messing around and sloped off.

Seth guessed that a comment from a middle-aged employee wouldn't have been nearly as effective at silencing them as a comment from a good-looking lad not much older than themselves.

Still stroking Stevie's forehead, Lainey said to him, "Thanks so much."

"S'alright. They're just a bit immature." The boy had bright eyes and a beaming smile. Crouching down a few feet away from Stevie, so as not to scare him, he said, "Hey, d'you want to see my favorite animal in the whole world?"

He waited patiently until Stevie ran out of screams and said, "What kind of animal?"

"Baby giraffe. Honestly, mate, he's amazing. Only born last week and he's a right character. You should see him! Have you been over to our giraffe house yet?"

Slowly, Stevie shook his head.

"Well, d'you want to visit the giraffes? You're gonna love them, I'm telling you. And the new baby one's the absolute best."

Stevie sat up, got to his feet, and nodded. "OK."

"Great! Follow me, mate. I'll show you

where they are."

How old was this cheerful, skinny boy with effortless empathy? No more than eighteen, Seth estimated, but his easy manner and enthusiasm were a joy to behold.

As they made their way across the grass in the direction of the giraffe house, Seth heard Lainey say to him, "If only there were more people like you."

"Hey, I'm just lucky." The boy shrugged off the compliment and grinned at her. "I've got the best job in the world."

CHAPTER 20

And now, following another full day, it was almost midnight once more.

Almost silent, too, Seth noted, apart from the occasional muffled cry of *"Pig!"* filtering downstairs from Ned's room.

"Ah, wasn't the zoo great? Look at this one." As he carried the tray of cheese and grapes through from the kitchen, he saw Lainey holding up her phone to show him one of the very many photos she'd taken.

He put the tray down and sat beside her, breathing in the scent of her shampoo as he studied the photo. It was of Bay, Stevie, and Ned all gazing up in wonder and delight as the baby giraffe's mother curved her long neck and gazed down at them like a benign sunflower.

"And this one." She scrolled through a dozen or more unsuccessful attempts before finding one of Bay transfixed by the sight of an orangutan effortlessly swinging from branch to branch in front of him. "I'm going to get the best ones printed out and send them to Grace as soon as we're home." She pointed to Seth's phone, lying facedown on the coffee table next to the tray. "You haven't shown me yours yet. Did you manage to get the penguins swimming over our heads in the underwater tunnel?"

"They were too fast. But I managed a couple of good ones with Ned and the seals." Seth picked up his mobile and leaned back again, aware of Lainey's arm brushing against his shoulder as she reached for a grape. Instantly he wanted it to happen again. Watching her today, observing the humor and patience with which she handled the boys, had done nothing to dampen his feelings for her. Which obviously wasn't ideal, but was making this time away much more enjoyable than it would have been otherwise.

So long as nothing happened, where was the harm?

"Let me see." As he began scrolling through his own photos, Lainey leaned in to get a better view.

"Oh, that's brilliant." She pointed to a moment he'd captured of Grace and Ned laughing together at the antics of a family of meerkats. "They both look so happy!"

Then she clapped her hands at the sight of the next photo, of herself and Stevie pulling the ugliest faces they could manage. "And there's us, looking terrifying. Ha, scary creatures."

Seth loved the fact that she'd gone for it, unselfconsciously making her face as contorted as possible; so many girls wouldn't dream of allowing themselves to be captured in hideous mode. But all Lainey had cared about was making the moment fun for Stevie.

Sliding his finger across the screen, he sent a kaleidoscope of pictures whizzing past at dizzying speed until it landed on one of Dawn from last week. She'd asked him to take a photo of her and had perched prettily on the arm of the bench in her tiny back garden, posing like a professional with her shoulders back and her head tilted at the optimum angle to show off her cheekbones and neat jawline. He'd taken the required photo, but it hadn't met with her approval and she'd requested several more before deleting the less-pleasing efforts and expertly setting about the remaining one with a variety of filters.

"Gosh, look at Dawn. Isn't she just stunning?" Lainey's hand instinctively lifted to smooth down her own tangled curls. "I bet she's never had a bad hair day in her life."

"There's more to life than having great hair." Seth felt the urge to tell her that the other evening he'd watched Dawn spend the best part of an hour painstakingly blow-drying her hair until every last inch of it was immaculate.

"Oh, I know, there's also having a face like a film star, and a flawless figure, and fabulous clothes." Lainey showed him another photo on her phone. "See? There's you and your perfect girlfriend . . . and here's me and my idiot fake boyfriend!"

He studied the photo of Kit, dressed in a Spider-Man costume and captured in mid-leap as he launched himself from a diving board into an open-air swimming pool, while Lainey, wearing emerald-green face paint, a witch's hat, and a huge false nose, bobbed around in the water brandishing a broomstick.

She laughed at the memory. "We had a fancy dress party at the chateau to celebrate Biddy's birthday. See my face? That was Kit's idea."

"Suits you," said Seth.

"Except he promised me it would wash off and it didn't. My face was pale green for a week." She expanded the photo so he could see her in greater detail. "How about those teeth too? Look at me. What a state!"

Her lack of ego was what charmed him. "But you had a good time."

"Of course! And that's Anton over there." Lainey indicated a lithe, dark-haired male wearing a chef's apron and seemingly nothing else. "He went as the Naked Chef."

Seth nodded. "Who's Anton?"

"Oh, I forgot you didn't know." She pulled a *bleurgh* face. "Anton worked at the chateau too; he was the one I was kind of seeing before we all lost our jobs. When he told me he was moving on down to Saint-Tropez, I thought we might go together. But that was more commitment than Anton wanted, so he headed off there on his own and I came back to the UK with Kit. God, that makes me sound like such a loser. I wish I hadn't said it now. Anton was always a bit of a player, and he just wasn't interested in settling down with one person. But that's fair enough; he's only twenty-six, plenty of time before he needs to think about —"

As if on cue, the phone in Seth's hand burst into life and Dawn's name flashed up on the screen.

He waited.

"Aren't you going to answer that?"

He waited some more, until the ringing

242

stopped.

"Naughty," Lainey chided, helping herself to another grape.

"It's late. I'll say I was asleep."

"Why don't you want to speak to her?" She was looking at him with concern.

His phone chimed as a text came through: You can't be asleep yet, it's too early. Why aren't you picking up?

Seth angled the screen to show Lainey. "Now I'm definitely not answering."

"I thought it was all going so well for you two. You seem perfectly matched."

How much was it fair to tell her? More than anything, Seth longed to kiss her, wanted to know how that would feel. But that couldn't happen, which left talking to her as the next best thing. He sat back against the sofa cushions. "We've only been seeing each other for a few weeks. But right from the word *go,* it felt as if it was all happening too fast."

"Oh." She nodded in sympathy, tucking her bare feet beneath her and shifting sideways in order to be able to see him more easily without straining her neck.

"You know how you just said about Anton only being twenty-six, so of course he wasn't ready to settle down yet? Well, with Dawn it's kind of the opposite."

"Oh . . ." Lainey looked intrigued. "How old is she then? I'd have said thirty-one, thirty-two."

"So would I." Seth paused, wondering if he should be sharing this. Then again, why not? "She told me she was thirty-four."

"Well, she's looking fantastic for her age."

It was as if Lainey was on Dawn's side. Which was admirably loyal of her, but . . .

"Then she dropped her purse on Thursday evening and a couple of cards slid out. One of them was her driver's license. It landed under the coffee table and I fished it out for her. I wasn't looking for her date of birth, but it kind of jumped out at me." Drily, he added, "That was when I discovered she's actually thirty-seven."

Lainey's eyes widened. "Wow, she *really* looks fantastic for her age."

"Yes." But she'd lied to him, which was never great news.

"Does she use superexpensive moisturizer? I always wondered if it actually makes a difference."

"The bottles do look expensive, yes."

"So." She paused, reaching across for yet another grape. "How d'you feel about that?"

"The hundreds of pounds she spends on moisturizer? Sorry." Seth smiled, because Lainey was cutting to the chase; she knew perfectly well why the fact that Dawn was thirty-seven made a difference. He was able to sympathize with Dawn's situation, but she hadn't been honest with him, and it had been for her own purposes. The last thing he wanted was to be hustled into a relationship he wasn't ready for simply because her biological clock was clanging away. "Let's say it explains a lot."

"And does she know you know?"

"Oh yes." He recalled the moment Dawn had snatched the driver's license from him, her cheeks coloring at the realization that it was already too late. "She told me the reason she'd fibbed about her age was because of the Chinese zodiac. Apparently she didn't want her sign to be the year of the pig."

"Right." Lainey nodded, understanding now that Ned's cries drifting down the stairs were what had prompted the story. "But she shaved off three years, not just one."

"The next two were rat and ox; apparently she didn't fancy being those either." They both knew the excuse was as flimsy as tissue paper and that the real reason was because, for superorganized Dawn, time was running out.

"She'd have had to come clean sooner or later," said Lainey.

"I know." With the emphasis on *later.*

"When you said it explains a lot, in what way?"

Was it wrong to be discussing his and Dawn's relationship with someone else, particularly when the someone else was Lainey? But he knew he could trust her not to gossip. Furthermore, deep down, he was already pretty sure he knew what he needed to do.

"You know what Dawn's like." He shrugged. "She's up-front and superconfident. Knows her own mind and never has any doubts."

"Sounds like you." Lainey looked amused. "That's why I thought you were so good together."

"Except it just felt from the beginning as if she'd pressed the fast-forward button, as if she had her checklist and I ticked all the boxes, so we didn't need to take things slowly. It was like a done deal; we'd found each other and that was that. Even when Richard made jokes about my short attention span, she just said everything was going to be different now; all those years of playing the field had just been practice runs, but since meeting her, I didn't need to bother with that sort of thing anymore."

"That *is* confident." Carefully Lainey said,

246

"And was there any mention of having children?"

"Not directly." But then Dawn was far too smart for that, wasn't she? "Just the occasional jokey comment about it happening at some stage in the future. Except that was when I still thought she was thirty-four."

"So you think time's running out and she's chosen you for the job. Sorry, that sounds awful. I feel bad saying it . . ."

Seth nodded. "But yes, that's exactly what I think."

"She can't force you to have children with her. Not if you don't want it to happen."

"I know."

"Are you worried that she's going to try to talk you into it?"

"I'm just wondering if it's right to carry on. Because it feels as if she has a lot more invested in this relationship than I do. Maybe I should call it a day."

Lainey started as the phone gave another *ting*. "Oh God, it's like she's *listening* to us!"

Seth didn't move. "It's OK. I'm not going to answer it."

"How can you not even look, though?"

"Easily." He inclined his head. "You can if you like."

Lainey turned the phone over, visibly

flinched, and put it back down. "What does it say?"

"It says: 'Are you shagging Lainey?' "

Oh. Seth pulled a face. "Sorry about that. I'll have a word with her. Dawn has trust issues."

"But she's so confident! How can she be confident *and* insecure?"

"As soon as we get back, I'm going to tell her it's over. It hasn't worked out."

Lainey said, "That means she'll really think something happened."

And Seth discovered that the flippant response on the tip of his tongue was refusing to come out. In that moment, he looked at Lainey and realized that her words were truer than she could ever know, because something *had* happened over the course of the last two days, something that was extraordinary and wonderful, confusing and agonizing.

It wasn't an emotion he'd ever experienced before, but he thought he might be in love.

Which was crazy, because was it really possible to fall in love with someone when you'd never even held their hand, touched their face, or kissed them?

These thoughts had crossed his mind before, of course, but all of a sudden the emotions were coming together, coalescing and intensifying inside his chest, becoming weighty and more real.

The hairs on the back of his neck were standing at attention; it was one of those moments he knew would remain with him for the rest of his life. Here they were in this dusty, cluttered, dimly lit room, and here he was experiencing a revelation: from her quick wit, empathy, and kindness, to the way her eyes danced and her head tilted back when she laughed, he quite simply adored every single thing about the girl sitting next to him on this blue corduroy sofa.

Oh God. Now what?

Chapter 21

"I know what you're thinking," said Lainey. Did she?

He raised an eyebrow. "Oh?"

"It's an awkward situation. I mean, *really* awkward." She reached for the cheese knife and helped herself to a slice of softened Cambozola.

Seth's mouth was dry; he had no idea what could be about to happen.

"You're going to have to tell her." She popped the melting cheese into her own mouth, savored the taste, and did a little swoon. "God, this stuff is *heaven.* No, look, poor Dawn, you have to make sure she completely understands. Because if I thought she was still thinking it, I'd just die."

Half of Seth was hearing what she was saying; the other half was imagining what Lainey *might* have been about to say when she'd told him she knew what he was thinking. Except that hadn't happened and nor could it happen, no matter how much he wanted it to.

"I'll make sure she understands. Don't worry."

"And when you break up with her, do it nicely. Be sensitive. She's going to be so upset."

"I thought I'd do it by text." Seth kept a straight face as Lainey's mouth dropped open in dismay. "That was a joke, by the way."

Miraculously on cue, they heard Ned, upstairs in his bedroom, chanting "Pig pig pig" to himself.

"And that's for trying to be funny." Smiling, Lainey shook her head at him. "Poor Dawn, you have to be kind to her. Being dumped is always horrible, and it's probably her first time."

"Why would it be her first time?"

"Oh come on, look at her — beauty and brains, she's the whole package! Who in their right mind would ever want to dump someone like that? Apart from you, of course."

Talk about a surreal situation. "Are you saying you think we should stay together?" He had no intention of doing it, but he asked the question anyway.

"No, no . . . this is your life and it's none

of my business who you see." Lainey shook her head. "I'm just saying if you're going to do it, you need to be gentle with her, because it's no fun being on the receiving end." She looked at him, and for a split second, Seth thought he glimpsed emotion of another kind.

Thought or hoped?

He said, "I'll be gentle," and experienced once more the sensation of two conversations, one of them unspoken, running concurrently.

"I've just realized something. You've never been dumped!" Lainey's eyes widened and she pointed an accusing finger at him. "You haven't, have you? Oh my God!"

"Let me just . . ." Seth already knew the answer, obviously, but he pretended to give the question consideration. At last he said, "No, don't think I have."

"No one's ever said they didn't want to see you anymore. You have no idea what it feels like!" She started to laugh. "That's amazing. What's it like to be you?"

"Well, I would have said it was great, up until tonight. But you're starting to make me feel like I've been missing out."

Lainey popped another grape into her mouth and crunched it between her teeth; she was still laughing and shaking her head.

"So you've never been rejected? *Ever?*"

"Now you're just making fun of me."

"Ask me out."

"Sorry?"

She gave him an encouraging nod. "Go on, do it now."

"OK, would you like to go out with me on a date?" He knew, of course, what she was going to say.

"Why thank you, Seth, I'd love to."

A zing of adrenaline shot through his body, because she looked and sounded as if she truly meant it.

Then she made a sound like a reverse record scratch and said, "Only joking! No thanks, no way." She beamed at him and gave the side of his knee a playful nudge with her toes. "There you go, that's rejection. How does it feel?"

"I'm devastated, obviously."

Her eyes danced. "Try not to cry."

He didn't want to cry. More than ever now, he wanted to kiss her. Upstairs, a bed creaked and he prepared himself for another cry of *"Pig!"* from Ned. Except it was coming from a bedroom on the other side of the house and the voice calling "Mum!" belonged to Stevie. But it was Grace's holiday, and tonight she was wearing the earplugs she so rarely got to wear. Getting to his feet,

Seth said, "He probably just needs taking to the bathroom. I'll be back in two minutes."

In addition to the bathroom visit, however, Stevie had been spooked by the sound of an owl hooting in the tree just outside and needed reassurance that it wasn't a pterodactyl intent on bursting in through the window. Seth had to read him a story and spend a further fifteen minutes explaining to him that owls couldn't fly through glass before Stevie was able to settle down and go back to sleep.

By the time he returned downstairs, he saw that Lainey had beaten Stevie to it.

She was still stretched out where he'd left her, and her head had fallen to the right.

Her breathing was slow and even, her left hand rested across her stomach and the amber glow from the table lamp was throwing shadows across her face.

Seth hesitated, then sat back down on the sofa, half expecting the movement to wake her up so they could carry on their conversation. But she didn't stir — even her lashes hadn't flickered — and now he was faced with a dilemma, because on the one hand he didn't want to shake her awake, but on the other hand, this was his bed. If she were to wake up an hour from now and stumble upstairs, how would she feel if she pushed open the door to her room and found him fast asleep in her bed?

He weighed up his options. It had been a long and tiring day. She was exhausted and so was he. The evening had come to an end, which was obviously a shame, but maybe it was just as well. Resting against the squashy sofa cushions, Seth tilted his head sideways and studied Lainey. A strand of hair had fallen across her cheek and his fingers itched to move it away, but that would be wrong, if not downright creepy. He watched her rib cage rise and fall and found his own breathing slowing to match hers. Outside in the darkness the owl hooted again, but the house thankfully remained silent. He felt his limbs grow heavy and his own eyelids begin to close . . .

Lainey stirred; someone was touching her face. A finger was prodding her cheek and warm breath was landing on her temple. Her eyes snapped open and she almost let out a yelp, because Ned's face was completely filling her field of vision, his eyes less than four inches from her own.

An unnerving sight, to say the least. "Are you awake?" he said.

"I am now." At least he'd stopped repeatedly poking her cheek with his index finger.

"Pigs."

She swallowed, still in the process of gathering her thoughts and discovering that she was downstairs lying on the sofa.

More to the point, she was not its only occupant. Anyway, pigs. "What about them?"

"When are we going to see them? Is it still two o'clock?"

She nodded. "Yes."

"Definite, though? Definitely two o'clock?"

"Yes."

"OK." Ned, who'd been kneeling in front of her, wrote the information down in his notebook, then clambered laboriously to his feet. "You can go back to sleep now. Good night."

He left the living room and made his way upstairs. She heard the bedroom door close, then the creaking of floorboards as he climbed back into his bed.

She silently exhaled. By this time, every inch of her body was prickling with the awareness that she was lying on her side along the length of the sofa . . . and behind her was Seth. Her bare feet were entwined with his, she could feel his left hand resting on the dip of her waist, and the back of her head was nestled into the curved space between his arm and his chest.

It was simultaneously the most thrilling experience in the world and the most mortifying, because how embarrassing was it to have fallen asleep on what was effectively Seth's bed? He was her boss, she was his employee, and now here they were practically wrapped around each other, albeit fully clothed. But she could feel his warm breath on the back of her neck, and the intimacy of it was causing her stomach to squirm with anticipation, because if he were to move his head just the tiniest bit closer, his lips could be brushing against her hypersensitive skin, dropping light, languorous kisses . . . Oh crikey, and now she could feel the microscopic hairs on her neck standing on end, as if they were reaching out to him, clamoring and *yearning* to be kissed.

The downside was, no way could she stay here. It was all very well innocently falling asleep and staying asleep, but Ned would be bound to mention at some stage tomorrow that he'd woken her up and they'd had a conversation. Which would make it odd — if not downright suspicious — if it then came out that she'd stayed down here in Seth's arms.

She remained where she was for one

minute more, silently committing each blissful moment and sensation to memory. Then, muscle by muscle, she carefully removed herself from the situation, breaking the connection between Seth's body and her own. His breathing didn't alter; he was clearly out for the count.

Finally off the sofa, she turned and gazed down at him. He looked almost irresistible lying there on his own, with the shadows from his dark lashes falling across his cheekbones, and his lips fractionally parted. Poor Dawn, if he went ahead and finished with her; it couldn't be easy to love and lose a boyfriend, especially when you'd already decided he was going to be yours for good.

Night. Lainey mouthed the word rather than said it, then puckered up her lips and blew Seth a kiss, purely because it was three in the morning and there was no one there to see her do it.

As she left the living room, she let out another squeak, because Ned was making his way silently down the stairs again, still clutching his notebook and pen.

"Pigs at two o'clock," she whispered.

"I know that. You already told me. But what time do we have to leave this house to get there?"

"It's ten minutes away. So we'll leave here

at ten to two."

He wrote this information in his note-book, then lifted his head. "Are you Seth's girlfriend?"

Lainey's heart thudded. *I wish.* "No, sweetheart. I'm not. Shall we go back up the stairs now?"

"OK. Can I have toast for breakfast with strawberry jam? Cut into squares?"

"Of course you can."

He blinked. "But they have to be the right kind of squares."

"They will be," said Lainey. "I promise."

CHAPTER 22

The visit to the pigs had been a great success. Every year the farmer, who was an old friend of the boys' aunt, invited them to his farm, and every year it was the highlight of their holiday. Dozens of photos were taken. In the barn, Ned and Stevie were allowed to hold the pink, wriggling piglets. Outside, they'd watched the older pigs rolling around like happy hippos in the mud. Stevie had wanted to take one home with him and went into a meltdown when Grace explained that he couldn't. And when Ned had presented Lainey with a picture he'd drawn of a beaming cross-eyed piglet covered with a tartan blanket, he'd said, "This is for you because I heard you tell Mum that you love pigs in blankets."

Next, it was time for their visit to Clifton. Seth pulled the van into a private parking bay outside the travel agency and smiled at the sight of a large black cat stretched out on the mat outside the front door.

As they climbed out, he said, "This is my agency. And see up there? That's my flat. We can go inside and have a look around if you want."

It was clearly an offer they could refuse. Stevie didn't even bother to reply.

Bay let out a wail. Ned said, "No, that would be boring. Is this your cat?"

Seth shook his head. "His name's Jeremy. He belongs to my friend Flo, who lives around the corner, but he likes to spend a lot of his time on our doormat. Don't you, Jeremy?"

The cat slowly blinked, eyeing Seth with an air of superiority followed by a dismissive swish of his tail.

"Jeremy's a stupid name for a cat," said Stevie. "Come on, we need to go to the bridge. Hurry up."

"Kkkhhheeeiiishhh," hissed Jeremy.

Together they made their way across Clifton until they came to the iconic suspension bridge stretched across the rocky sides of the Avon Gorge. High in the almost cloudless sky above them, two hot-air balloons drifted across in silence from the other side. All around them people were gazing up at the balloons, captivated and enthralled by the magical sight of their stately progress.

Apart from Stevie and Ned, who couldn't have been less interested and cared only about getting to the bridge, with its geometric lines, graceful swooping curves, and pleasingly parallel rows of metal struts.

"This is my favorite bridge in the world," Ned announced.

Lainey gave his hand a squeeze. "I can see why. It's amazing."

Far below them, the River Avon glinted gunmetal gray in the sunshine. The six of them made their way along the pedestrian walkway, crossing the bridge, until Ned said, "Is this the middle? OK, everyone stop now so I can take photos. Out of the way."

They obediently waited to one side while he took a dozen or so photographs of the bridge itself and the view toward the center of Bristol. Then he gestured for them to take up position at the central point. "Come on, stand in a line. Mum, you and Bay next to Lainey, then Seth and Stevie. That's it, all in a row. Now hold hands." He eyed them beadily, sensing reluctance. "Everyone has to hold hands."

Lainey felt her bare shoulders prickle with embarrassment. It was all very well waking up in the middle of the night to discover you'd fallen asleep on the sofa next to someone you found wildly attractive and had managed to get your legs a tiny bit entwined with theirs. But being fully conscious and actually holding hands with them in broad daylight was altogether more personal.

Inspiration struck and she said brightly, "Let's not have Stevie on the end. It's better if he stands between me and Seth so that —"

"No." Ned was already shaking his head in don't-mess-with-me fashion. "You can't do it that way; it wouldn't make the right shape. You all have to stay where you are."

Next to her, Lainey felt Seth move closer and realized he was uncomfortable too. But if there was no gap between them, the fact that they weren't holding hands wouldn't be apparent.

"You're doing it all *wrong*!" Ned shouted like a frustrated film director. "You all need to be *this* far apart so I can see the shape of your arms and your hands holding each other, like when you showed me last night how to make paper dolls. It has to be the *proper* way or the pictures won't be any good!"

Well, she'd tried. And it was clearly her own fault for teaching him how to make strings of paper dolls in the first place.

Catching Seth's eye, she mouthed *Let's do it* and held out her hand.

The next moment, his warm fingers closed around hers and her rib cage expanded to make room for a juddery intake of breath. She had to pretend to cough to disguise it, prompting Ned to say bossily, "Don't cough. Just stand still and look *happy.*"

Happy. Lainey gazed directly into the lens of his camera and did her best to ignore the zings of sensation caused by physical contact, because feeling as if she might be about to spontaneously combust was hardly restful. And Ned the perfectionist wouldn't be happy until he'd taken at least ten more photos.

"No, don't look that happy," he ordered. "That's too much."

In accordance with the final items on Sunday's list, takeout pizzas were collected from their favorite Italian restaurant on Whiteladies Road, then eaten with relish back at the cottage before cases were repacked and order restored. A note for Grace's sister, apologizing for the broken plant pot out on the patio, was left on the kitchen table alongside its brand-new replacement.

At six o'clock, they piled once more into the van and set off home.

The Sunday-evening holiday exodus from Devon and Cornwall meant traffic was heavy heading north but light on their side of the motorway.

"Don't look," Ned instructed as they whizzed past the exit to Weston-super-Mare. "I'm going to draw you a picture."

"For me? Fantastic," said Lainey.

"You have to turn away properly or you'll see it."

The *scritch-scratch* of pencil against paper began. Ned was a painstaking artist, carefully adding details and coloring in the drawing with shades of light and dark blue. Lainey's neck began to ache as they passed the turnoffs to Burnham-on-Sea, then Bridgwater, then Cullompton. Finally, as they were approaching Exeter, he tipped the colored pencils back into his pencil case and said, "Finished."

They were sitting on opposite sides of the car, both strapped in by their seat belts. When she tried and failed to reach across, he said, "I'll just show it to you."

"Ned, that's fantastic," she exclaimed when he held up his opened notebook, and she meant it too. The amount of detail in the drawing was impressive; there they all were, lined up along the walkway of the suspension bridge with the spectacular view

265

of the gorge behind them. OK, so their faces weren't recognizable, but their hair and clothing was accurately depicted, and the details of the bridge had been captured right down to the shading on the metal struts behind them. Lainey shook her head in admiration. "You're so clever. Your drawings really are brilliant."

Ned snapped shut the notebook and opened his comic. "I know."

They arrived back in St. Carys at 8:15 and carried all the cases into Grace's house. "Thank you so much." Leaning heavily on her stick, Grace gave first Seth, then Lainey a hug. "Honestly, it might not have seemed like much of a holiday to you, but it's been wonderful." Tears of gratitude swam in her eyes. "And I promise you, the boys have had the best time. They won't stop talking about it for weeks."

"We've loved being with you. It's been great," Lainey told her.

Ned poked his head around the door. "What are we having to eat?"

"Darling, are you going to say goodbye?"

"I already did." He turned to Lainey. "Goodbye again. I put your drawing in the picnic basket, inside the atlas, so it doesn't get crumpled. When you get home, you can put it in a frame and hang it on your wall."

Ned didn't do hugs, but this was his version of one. Deeply touched, she said, "Thank you, darling. I'll definitely do that."

She also knew that each time she looked at the drawing, she would remember the sensation that had rushed through her body when Seth, standing beside her on the suspension bridge, had taken her hand in his.

They arrived back at Menhenick House to find prosecco being drunk around the kitchen table.

"Here they are," said Richard, breaking off from relaying one of his scurrilous Hollywood stories.

"Hello, darling!" Putting down her glass, Dawn rose to her feet and greeted Seth with a kiss. "I sent you a few texts, but you didn't reply."

Slightly surprised to see her there, he shrugged. "Sorry, I've been driving for the last few hours. My phone was switched off."

"I guessed as much. So I dropped by to see if anyone here knew when you'd be home." Her eyes sparkled as her fingertips lightly caressed his forearm. "That was when this terrible pair of enablers said you wouldn't be long and persuaded me to stay for a drink."

She'd met the family a couple of times before now, and they'd all got on well together. The thing about Majella and Richard was that their hospitality knew no bounds. As he dumped the picnic basket on the table, Seth said, "And how many drinks ago was that?"

"Just a few." Richard's wink encompassed Majella and Dawn. "Don't worry, we can open another bottle now you're back."

"I'll leave you to it," said Lainey. "It's been a busy few days and I'm pretty shattered."

"Oh no, you can't go yet," Dawn protested. "Stay for one drink at least. Come on, sit down next to me. How did everything go?" She was looking sleek and lovely in a sleeveless amber slip dress and elegant tan sandals that Lainey had seen online as worn by celebrities. They cost over three hundred pounds.

Richard, who could move with alacrity when he wanted to, had already poured out a fizzing glass of prosecco and was pressing it into Lainey's hand. "There you are, my angel. Get that down you."

"And have some of these." On her feet now, Majella slid a dish of tortilla chips and dips across the table. "Were the boys OK? I hope you didn't have any trouble."

"They were fine. Bit lively," said Lainey with a smile, "but nothing we couldn't handle."

"Does anything in here need to go in the fridge?" Majella started to unpack the picnic bag. "Ooh, flapjacks, my favorite." She tipped them onto a plate, then lifted out a bottle of orange juice. "And what's this?"

As she'd reached for the road map, pushed down one side of the bag, it had fallen open to reveal Ned's drawing. Lainey's heart skipped a beat, because Dawn was sitting next to her, leaning in and giving her a nudge.

"Listen." Dawn's mouth was close to her ear, her voice a discreet whisper. "Seth told me you overheard a bit of our phone conversation on Friday, and I just wanted to apologize. I was being ridiculous. Of course I don't think anything would ever happen between the two of you. I'm so sorry if you were embarrassed."

"I wasn't," Lainey murmured while Richard launched into a picnic-related story involving Jack Nicholson and a squirrel. Poor Dawn, she was a lovely woman who had no idea that by next weekend her plans of a future with Seth would lie in tatters. "Honestly, don't worry. It's fine."

"This is so *sweet*," Majella exclaimed,

gazing at the drawing that Ned had torn out of his notebook.

"What is it?" said Dawn. "Let's have a look."

Richard continued blithely. "And when he woke up, there was the squirrel, sitting on his chest —"

"The last time you told us this story," said Seth, "it was an iguana."

Without missing a beat, Richard waved his glass. "No, no, the iguana situation was with Roger Moore."

"Oh, *so* sweet." Dawn's voice was extra bright as she took in the details of Ned's drawing, passed over to her by Majella. "Look at that, all five of you together!"

"Ned made us hold hands like that," Lainey blurted out. "We didn't want to, but he forced us to, didn't he?" She turned to Seth and nodded vigorously. "Trust me, once Ned's made up his mind about something, there's no arguing with him."

"It's OK." Next to her, Dawn smiled and gave her arm a reassuring pat. "No need to panic, I believe you. Please don't think you have to explain everything."

"Lainey taught him how to make paper dolls," Seth said easily. "That's why he wanted us holding hands like that."

"Really, don't worry." Dawn beamed up

at him. "It's a lovely drawing. He's so talented."

"I haven't seen it properly yet." Seth held out his hand and Dawn picked the sheet of paper up to pass it over to him. Noticing something written on the other side, she paused to read it.

"Let me guess, one of his lists," Lainey said with a grin. "Ned *really* loves a list!"

Then her grin faded, because Dawn was holding the torn-out sheet of paper in front of her. And there, in Ned's slow, deliberate handwriting, were the words:

1. Pigs at two o'clock.
2. Leave the house at ten to two o'clock.
3. Lainey isn't Seth's girlfriend, they just sleep together.

Lainey's blood ran cold. "Oh, but —"

"No, really, no need to say a word." Dawn's voice was brittle and almost painfully high-pitched. "It's *fine.*"

CHAPTER 23

Seth was seconds away from finishing with Dawn when his mobile beeped, signaling the arrival of a text from his mother: I need to speak to you about something very important. Call me ASAP, PLEASE.

This was because he'd switched his phone off earlier and hadn't replied to her voice-mail, left while she'd been enjoying lunch at a restaurant on the beach in Marbella. Clearly having a good time and with the sounds of chattering voices and clinking glasses in the background, she had launched into a rambling story about how she'd just bumped into an old friend and it was the biggest coincidence and honestly, wasn't it incredible that there were, like, billions and billions of people in the world but here they were sitting on a restaurant balcony and who should be walking past but Shelley, who used to go out with this crazy Greek guy back when they'd shared a flat together, across from the Blackjack Club on Wardour Street, remember?

Which was why Seth hadn't bothered returning the call, what with the infamous Blackjack Club having been closed down before he was born.

He turned his phone off again, because the something very important his mother was bursting to tell him was most likely that allegedly hilarious story about the time she and Shelley had swum naked in a hotel pool in Antibes, gotten into a drunken row with the unamused owner of the hotel, and ended up getting themselves arrested. Basically, Seth had heard it all before.

And at that moment, he had a rather more pressing situation to deal with. It wasn't something he was looking forward to, but it had to be done.

They'd walked back to Dawn's cottage together in silence; this was a task that couldn't be carried out amid the chaos of Menhenick House. Now she passed him a coffee and said, "You've still got your shoes on. Aren't you going to take them off?"

Seth shook his head. "I'm not staying."

"But I want you to stay."

"We need to talk." Such a cliché.

Her eyes pleaded with him. "Have I said anything about what was written on the back of that drawing? No, I haven't, even though I could."

"Nothing happened," Seth reiterated. "We explained what Ned meant when he wrote it."

"And I said I believed you," Dawn replied, despite patently not believing him for a second.

"Anyway. None of that has anything to do with what I need to say now. I just feel we should cool things off." He stirred his coffee, even though she'd already stirred it for him. "It's been great, and you're great, but I think we'd be better off as friends."

A muscle was twitching in her temple. "Do you? Why, though?" She spread her hands. "What have I done *wrong*?"

Seth exhaled; how he hated it when this happened. It was so much easier when the hint was gracefully taken. Then again, lawyers liked to argue; it was in their nature not to give up without a fight.

"You haven't done anything wrong. I just feel as if . . . something's missing."

"Nothing," Dawn said slowly, "is missing. Trust me."

"It's not you."

"And it's not you either. We're perfect together and you know it. *Everyone* knows it." Her gaze was unwavering. "They keep

274

telling me."

"But —"

"I suppose Lainey threw herself at you. That's the thanks I get for trying to help her out."

"She didn't throw herself at me," said Seth. "She fell asleep on the sofa."

"Oh, of course she did, of course it wasn't all part of her carefully laid plan."

"There was no plan; there was no throwing involved. And this isn't helping. Look, it's entirely my fault. I told you before, I don't have much of an attention span when it comes to relationships ... . It's just the way I am."

"But I *love* you." A trace of desperation was creeping into her voice now.

He shook his head. "I think you loved the idea of me. I seemed to fit the bill, that's all."

"Is it because I'm too old for you?"

"No, it's not that at all. Your age isn't an issue for me." And it wasn't, he genuinely meant that. "But you talked about wanting children. You clearly do want them. Children are great," he added, "but I'm not ready for them yet."

"Men think that all the time, but when the babies come along, they fall in love with them."

"I need to concentrate on building up the business."

"For how many years?"

"I don't know how many years."

"And by the time you're ready to think about babies, I'll be too old to give them to you."

Seth felt sorry for her; it couldn't be easy for any woman in her situation.

"Oh *God*." Dawn sat back and gestured impatiently at the carpet beneath the coffee table. "I wish you'd never picked up my driver's license."

"I'd have found out eventually," said Seth.

For the first time, even as tears swam in her eyes, she managed a wry smile. "I was kind of hoping that by the time you found out, you'd be so in love with me it'd be too late." As she showed him to the front door, she added sadly, "We'd have had beautiful babies."

"That's true, especially if they looked like you."

Her gaze searched his face. "How about if I freeze my eggs?"

What could he do? What could he say? He looked at her and shook his head fractionally.

"OK, forget I said that; it was just a joke. The fact remains that you aren't going to find anyone better than me." She straightened her spine and gave him one of her confident smiles. "You might think you can, but you really can't. Then again, maybe you just need a bit of space to get your thoughts in order."

"Maybe." Seth let this go; it clearly hadn't been a joke, but he was also keen to make his escape.

"And maybe you also need a few weeks to get . . . *her* out of your system. And yes" — she nodded calmly — "I'm talking about Lainey."

Seth said, "You've got it wrong."

"Come on, I'm not an idiot. I can read you like a book. But if stepping back and letting it happen is what it takes, I'm happy to go along with that." Reaching up, she planted a fleeting kiss on his cheek an inch from his mouth. "Then once it's over and you realize she was just another run-of-the-mill fling after all, you'll know you can come back to me."

Lainey was standing on a stool, energetically cleaning the kitchen windows from the outside, when she heard footsteps crunching across the gravel behind her.

"Hello again," said Christina. "How are you? So sorry, I've forgotten your name.

277

I'm here to see Seth."

"It's Lainey. And I'm good, thanks." She hesitated. "But Seth isn't here. He's gone to see a client in Truro."

"Has he? Oh, what a pain! Never mind, I'll just hang around until he turns up. Who else is here at the moment?"

"No one, I'm afraid. Well, Majella's up in the office, but she's pretty busy." Lainey felt the need to say it before Christina could insist on whisking Majella off somewhere for lunch. "The kids are at school, and Kit's driven Richard up to an event in Oxford."

"Ah, well. No worries. I can keep myself occupied." Christina beamed at her. "What time will Seth be back?"

Lainey checked her watch. "Well, it's midday now and he left at ten, so he'll probably be another hour or so. Would you like me to call and let him know you're here?"

Was there a reason for Christina's confusion? Because while Lainey had been clearing away the breakfast things this morning, she'd heard Seth take the call from his mother and he'd definitely told her he had a meeting in Truro at eleven.

"No need. It's fine. I'm happy to wait."

Lainey said, "I think he was expecting to see you a bit later this afternoon. He mentioned you'd be here around three."

"Did he?" Christina shrugged. "Maybe he did say three and I forgot. Anyway, what could be nicer than sitting out in the garden with a glass of wine? Don't worry about me. You just carry on with your work. I know my way to the fridge!"

By half past one, Lainey had finished the windows, made a chicken and ham pie, and put it in the oven to bake. Glancing outside every so often, she saw Christina stretched out on Majella's favorite chaise longue on the back lawn, spending a rather more relaxing ninety minutes deepening her already impressive tan, playing on her phone, and steadily making her way through a bottle of pinot gris.

Ah well, all right for some.

Remembering that she was yet to tackle the poster-paint stain on the pale-green carpet in Harry's bedroom, she headed upstairs with an armful of cleaning tools and prepared to do battle with the mess that had only worsened after Harry had attempted to clean it up himself. His room smelled of chocolate, dried mud, and small boy, and when she knelt down, she spotted odd socks and discarded candy wrappers stuffed under the bed along with cricket pads, toast crusts, a table tennis paddle, and a broken snorkel.

The task wasn't an easy one, and she spent some time loosening the stain before soaking up as much of the bright-blue paint as possible with damp kitchen towels. At one stage, she heard what sounded like India's bedroom door being opened, but India was at school, so it had to be one of the dogs.

It wasn't until several minutes later, upon hearing a clatter and a muffled curse, that Lainey rose to her feet and peered out of Harry's window. Both the chaise longue and the wine bottle — upturned in its ice bucket — were empty.

Was Christina all right? Had she fallen somewhere in the house and hurt herself? Leaving the bedroom, Lainey made her way barefoot along the landing and heard more noises coming from the bathroom farther down on the right: a persistently creaking floorboard followed seconds later by a loud plasticky clunk.

Lainey paused. OK, this was awkward. The bathroom door was mostly but not completely closed. If she called out and Christina was sitting on the toilet having a wee, it would be embarrassing. But she couldn't creep away, because what if the woman was unwell and in need of help?

Moving silently closer, she reluctantly

looked through the gap in the doorway, then did a double take. Because there was Christina leaning against the marble-topped sink, wrestling to get the brush off Violet's electric toothbrush.

Lainey blinked. Why on earth was she doing that? Surely she hadn't been using the toothbrush; if she had, the sound of it would have been audible.

The brush head came off at last, and Christina pulled a plastic sandwich bag from her jeans pocket and dropped it inside, which made even *less* sense than —

"Wah!" Lainey let out a squeal of shock as something brushed against her heel.

The next moment, a furry body slid past her bare ankle, and she realized that while she'd been spying on Christina, Radley the silent assassin had been spying on *her.*

Thanks a lot, cat.

CHAPTER 24

"Who's there? What's going on?" Equally startled, Christina dropped the sandwich bag into the sink as she spun around.

Lainey clutched her chest. "I didn't know Radley was behind me and he caught me by surprise. I came to see if you were OK. I was worried about you." She flushed at the semi-lie, then looked from the headless electric toothbrush to the transparent plastic bag in the sink. "What are you doing?"

Because there were some questions you just had to ask.

Christina was shaking her head, casting around for inspiration. Finally, she swallowed and said accusingly, "You aren't a mother. You don't know how it feels. Wait till you have children, then you'll understand."

Lainey stared at her. "I don't even know what that's supposed to mean."

"I miss Seth! How often do I get to see

my son? Not very often at all. And I miss him so much . . . so I just thought it would be nice to have his toothbrush as a keepsake, to remind me of him when we're apart."

It was the worst lie in the history of lies, which kind of went to show the nonsense you could come up with when you had an entire bottle of wine inside you. Even Christina had the grace to look ashamed. Lainey glanced at the unzipped quilted leather shoulder bag sitting on the window ledge and saw something poking out of it. She pointed. "What's that?"

"Nothing."

But she was already crossing the bathroom, beating Christina to it and plucking out a second sandwich bag. Inside this one, a small bird's nest of hair was clearly visible.

"You went into India's room. That's her hair, taken from her hairbrush."

"I . . . I thought it was Seth's."

"It's purple," said Lainey.

"Well, keep it, then. I didn't realize. You can have it back."

Lainey looked at the two electric toothbrushes lined up next to the sink, the bright-pink one on the left and the headless black one on the right.

"Seth has an en suite bathroom," she said.

"He doesn't use this one. That black tooth-brush belongs to Violet."

Christina's narrow shoulders slumped. "Oh for fuck's sake. Why can't anything ever go to plan?"

"Let's go downstairs." Lainey gestured to the bathroom door. "Come on, I'll make you a coffee."

"Don't bother. I may as well just leave." Christina picked up her shoulder bag and took out her phone. "I'll call a taxi."

Downstairs, the front door opened and slammed shut, and they heard a volley of barks as the dogs greeted the latest arrival with delight.

"That's Seth," said Lainey.

"OK, this is important." Christina clutched her arm. "Can you *please* not tell him about this?"

Lainey fitted the head back onto Violet's toothbrush, then dropped the bundle of purple hair into the toilet and pulled the flush. She followed Christina down the staircase and they found Seth in the kitchen, taking a fresh box of coffee pods out of the cupboard.

"Mum, you're early." He greeted Christina with a kiss. "What time did you get here?"

"I'll make the coffee." Lainey began lay-

284

ing out cups and saucers, aware that Seth was giving her a quizzical look.

He studied his mother. "Is everything OK?"

"Yes, yes, of course everything's OK. Why wouldn't it be? I got the time wrong, that's all!"

Lainey took the coffee pods from Seth, who said, "What were you both doing upstairs?"

"I was cleaning the carpet in Harry's room." She hesitated. "And your mum was —"

"Admiring the view," Christina blurted out. "From the window on the landing. It's . . . such a great view from up there."

Lainey busied herself with the coffee machine, paying extra close attention to the pods.

Seth said, "Is something going on here that I should know about? Mum?"

"No!"

Lainey saw him glance through the kitchen window, clocking the upturned wine bottle in the ice bucket next to the chaise longue. He turned to look at her. "Can we just have a quick word outside?"

"Oh, for God's sake. *Fine,*" Christina almost shouted. "I'm going to have to tell you now, aren't I? Because if I don't, *she* will. And it's so unfair, because I'm not even *ready.*"

A muscle was jumping in Seth's jaw. "Not even ready to tell me what?"

Lainey had made the coffee and left them to it. Having carried the drinks through to the living room and closed the door, Seth sat down opposite his mother.

"Right, first things first. Where's the boyfriend?" For a second he struggled to recall the name of his future stepfather. "Laszlo."

"We broke up." She wrinkled her nose at the cup in front of her. "Do we have to drink this? I'd rather have wine."

"I think you've had plenty." As long as he could remember, his mother had been an overenthusiastic drinker; he was used to it. "So that means the wedding's off?"

Her shrug was dismissive. "He was a lying toad who only cared about himself. And don't say you told me so, because you didn't."

"Is he the reason for this visit?"

She shook her head. "No."

"So why are you here?"

"Darling, you know I love you. With all my heart."

Of course she did, in her own chaotic way.

Seth nodded. "Just tell me what's going on."

"Well, remember I called and told you about bumping into Shelley in Marbella? So she joined us for lunch, and we had a wonderful afternoon catching up, talking about the old days and all the people we'd known back then . . . you know how it is, such fun hearing all the gossip about old friends . . ." She paused to lean forward and take a gulp of the unwanted coffee, and Seth said nothing, because he could sense she was building up to the important bit.

The cup clattered back into the saucer and she began fiddling with the many bracelets on her thin wrist. "And then Shelley told me she'd heard some news about someone we'd both known a long time ago. He was Italian . . . a bit of a playboy type . . . great fun, you know what I'm saying. Anyway, apparently he's really ill now, doesn't have long left to live. And you know what it's like when you suddenly discover that someone you care about is about to die . . . it gets you thinking about the past. Because I liked him a lot, I really did. And apparently he never went on to have children. The thing is, according to Shelley he's practically a billionaire and a total recluse. He lives in a massive villa on the shore of Lake Como. And I just thought it might be a nice idea to pay him a visit."

Seth frowned, because this was a bizarre idea even by his mother's standards. "You mean he's incredibly wealthy and doesn't have anyone better to leave his money to, so maybe he'll take one look at you, decide to change his will, and bequeath you all his worldly goods?"

For a long moment, Christina stared out of the window as seagulls wheeled like kites overhead. Finally, she turned back to him. "You do have a low opinion of me, don't you? But maybe I'm not as selfish as you like to make out. And remember, when I came here today I didn't want to tell you any of this, but now you're forcing me to do it." She paused once more, preparing herself, and in that split second, he knew. "You're the reason I want to see him, Seth. Because there's a good chance he does have a child he could leave his money to."

And there it was. Almost, but not quite, a complete bombshell of a surprise. "Me." He sat back and shook his head.

"Possibly. It's not definite."

"If you didn't come here to tell me this, why did you come here?"

"To find out," said Christina. "Without you knowing about it. This is all Lainey's fault — she caught me in the bathroom trying to take your toothbrush." Impatiently, she added, "Except it was the wrong bathroom and it wasn't your toothbrush."

"So you were going to try to match my DNA with . . . ?"

"The hair from India's brush. Well, that was plan A. But it was purple, wasn't it, so goodness knows if it would even still work anyway. Then I tried to get your toothbrush. I just wanted to find out the truth," she blurted out. "After all these years of deliberately not thinking about it, all of a sudden I needed to know. And it's dead easy for the testing people to see if two samples belong to half siblings. So if the test proved that you were Tony's all along, I could stop wondering!"

Seth marveled at the way his mother's mind worked. He strongly suspected the large-amount-of-money situation had been the deciding factor.

Christina was frowning now, studying him closely. "I have to say, you don't seem that surprised."

"Don't I?" Seth finished his coffee and summoned a brief smile. "Maybe that's because I'm not."

"Oh no." Lainey covered her mouth and gazed at Seth sitting next to her on the dry

289

sand. "I mean, I'd kind of figured it out, but how awful for you. I'm so sorry."

She'd known as soon as he'd asked her to come down to the beach with him that her guess had been right and also that he didn't want to confide in Majella, who would be devastated by the news.

"Thanks." Ruefully, Seth added, "Funny how it didn't occur to my mother to say sorry. There again, I've known her long enough not to expect too much."

"How are you feeling?"

"I'm OK. I'm fine."

"Really?" How could he be?

He scooped up a handful of dry sand and let it sift through his fingers. "When I was seventeen, my mum called me on the afternoon of the last day of school before the Christmas holidays. She wanted me to fly out to Barbados and spend Christmas and New Year's with her and a bunch of her posh, druggy friends in a five-star hotel. Which wasn't my idea of fun. So I asked if I could stay in London with Dad and Majella instead. The girls were two years old," he explained. "I just loved spending time with them. But of course it hurt my mother's feelings; she was offended that I'd want to be with Dad rather than with her. And that was when she told me the chances were he probably wasn't my real father anyway."

"Oh *no.*"

Seth shrugged. "She was upset, and I'm sure drinking was involved. She just lashed out."

What must it have been like, growing up with a mother like that? "Did she apologize afterward?"

"She didn't even remember saying it." He glanced sideways at her, smiled briefly. "And I only found that out this afternoon. After the phone call, I never mentioned it again, and neither did she. Today, she told me Tony might not be my biological father and couldn't understand why I wasn't surprised."

"But what made her tell you today?"

His eyes glinted with amusement. "Ah, well, she's just found out the other contender is about to die. He's absolutely loaded, it turns out, and doesn't have any other children, so Mum thought I might want to pay him a quick visit and introduce myself."

He was calm on the outside, but Lainey wondered what he must be feeling.

Cautiously she said, "And . . . will you?"

"No." Seth shook his head. "Really no. I don't see the point. He's just someone who had a one-night stand thirty-three years ago with my mother. Poor guy. Imagine being on your deathbed and a complete stranger turns up waving a Father's Day card."

"Some people would want to do that."

"I'm sure they would. But I'm not one of them."

"Have you Googled him?"

Another shake. "I don't know his surname, and I don't even want to know it. That's how uninterested I am. Because I already have a father. Dad might not be around anymore, but he was the one who brought me up. I loved him and he loved me. And I love the rest of my family too." He paused to watch the frilly-edged waves roll in, ghostly white in the moonlight. "I don't want them to find out about any of this, by the way."

"Oh God, of *course* not." Lainey barely had time to feel offended before his hand came to rest on her arm.

"Sorry, I didn't mean it to sound like that. I completely trust you. I just meant there's no need for them to know, because it's all so irrelevant. Apart from anything else, this guy might not even be related to me."

"You don't want to do the DNA test to find out?"

"No." He moved his hand away and Lainey's arm felt suddenly naked; she tried not to feel bereft.

"OK."

"As far as I'm concerned, Tony's my father and that's that. End of."

"Well, good."

"Are you shivering?"

The physical contact had caused the fine hairs to stand up on her forearm, and he must have felt them. Lainey, not cold at all, said, "Yes, getting a bit chilly now." In her head, floozy Lainey added, *But if you put your arms around me, that'll warm me up.*

Luckily, floozy Lainey didn't say this out loud.

"Come on, let's get you inside." Already on his feet, Seth reached for her hand and hauled her upright. "Kit's going to be wondering where you've gotten to."

The soft sand shifted beneath her and Lainey, caught off balance, stumbled against him. For a moment their eyes met and time stood still, adrenaline surging through her bloodstream. The impulse to lean in and feel his body against hers was almost overwhelming. What if she were to give in to temptation and actually do it?

It was one of those sliding-doors moments. Oh, but she was the employee here, working for Seth's family; how could she be the one to make the first move? What if he were to pull away in horror, saying, *God, what are you playing at? You can't do that — have you lost your* mind?

"Sorry, my flip-flop went sideways." Breaking contact, she made an exaggerated point of wriggling it back into place on her foot. "And I do need to catch up with Kit, because tonight was his first date in months, so he's going to want to tell me how it went."

"We'd better get you back for the debrief then." As they made their way up the narrow path to the bottom of the garden, Seth said, "Who's he seeing, anyone we know?"

"His name's Tom, and he runs that bar on the harbor; he's got white-blond hair and —"

"It's OK. Everyone knows Tom. He's a . . . character." Seth held the gate open for her to go through ahead of him.

"You hesitated," said Lainey. "What does that mean?" Because hesitation was never good news.

"Sorry, they might hit it off and everything'll be great."

"But?"

"Well, he has a reputation as a bit of a heartbreaker."

"I guessed he might. He looks the type." Who'd have thought it? Two in the same small town. "But what can you do? Luckily Kit's used to being dumped and having his heart broken."

"It'll all come good in the end. He'll meet the right guy one day." As he said it, they both heard the rhythmic *rib-ribbit* sound of a frog in the garden pond over to their left.

"Let's hope so." Lainey nodded in the direction of the frog. "I suppose we all have to kiss a few of those first."

"And hope they aren't poisonous," Seth said with a grin.

CHAPTER 25

It was about the least romantic place for a reunion, but that didn't matter at all. The sky was gray, rain was falling steadily over Bristol Parkway, and the parking lot was full of grim-faced people hurrying from their cars into the shelter of the station. But when Wyatt caught sight of Penny, he felt his heart lift like a helium balloon. There she was, wearing a lemon-yellow raincoat and pale-pink pumps, and carrying a navy umbrella covered in multicolored cats and dogs. It was like one of those Disney moments when the sun comes out, flowers open, and woodland creatures burst into song.

Oh, it was *so* good to see her again.

He waved and pulled into the short-stay section of the parking lot, and Penny splashed her way through the puddles, hauling her purple overnight case behind her. She'd caught the train from Walsall to

Bristol, he'd driven here from London, and now they'd be making the rest of the journey down to Cornwall together.

Wyatt jumped out of the car. For a split second, they both hesitated, then Penny threw herself into his arms and he swung her around. "Look at you," he cried. "It's so good to see you again!"

"Same! I can't believe it!" She was beaming, her umbrella tumbling to the wet tarmac. "I did wonder if it'd feel weird or awkward, even just for a few seconds, but it doesn't at all. Not even a tiny bit."

"It doesn't feel awkward." Wyatt agreed. "It feels right."

And it did. He thought he must be the happiest man at this train station. When they'd finally stopped grinning at each other like idiots, he reached for her case and lifted it into the trunk of the car alongside his own.

"Louis Vuitton." Penny nodded at his case, then pointed to hers. "Discount store."

"Yours looks fine." He rolled up her umbrella. "I like this too."

"So do I. It makes people smile."

As did she. Wyatt said, "Hopefully we won't need it for the wedding."

"We won't. The weather's clearing from the west. By the time we reach Cornwall, it's going to be sunny and fabulous."

"And did you bring along your CDs?""

Penny gave him a *How could you?* look and pulled them out of her shoulder bag. "Of course! I'll even let you choose the first one."

Whenever they'd traveled by car, they had loved to sing along to Penny's music collection.

"Well, why don't we start with *Les Misérables*?" Wyatt opened the passenger door for her with a flourish. "Seeing as it's your favorite."

They chatted and sang their way down the motorway. The rain stopped, and as Penny had promised, the sun came out. By 4:30, they'd reached St. Carys and were checking into the Mariscombe House Hotel, which was thankfully living up to its excellent online reputation.

"I've never been here before." Penny was gazing at the view. "But I love it already."

A passing waitress said cheerfully, "Ah, this place has magical powers. Once you're under its spell, you'll never want to leave."

They unpacked in their separate rooms and met up again downstairs.

"I've already taken a million photos from my bedroom window." Penny's eyes were sparkling. "Seriously, it's just so gorgeous."

"Don't get too settled; we're leaving in the morning. But you might like the hotel in Saint Ives even more. You look lovely, by the way." Wyatt stepped back to admire her; she'd changed into a lime-green sundress and ribbon-tied lilac sandals, and given herself another spritz of perfume.

"Thank you. So do you. Hang on, let me just . . ." Reaching over, she straightened the collar of his favorite polo shirt. "There, that's better. What time are they expecting us?"

"I said we'd be with them at five thirty, so we should probably head over there now."

"I just heard the gate open." In the kitchen at Menhenick House, Kit said, "Sounds like Jilted John's turned up."

"Don't call him that." Lainey flicked a tea towel at him. "Poor Wyatt. And he wasn't jilted."

"Because you have to be engaged before jilting can happen, and he didn't even manage to get that far."

"He must still be heartbroken. We'll have to be really nice to him."

"Hang on, there are two sets of footsteps." As Kit said it, they both heard the sound of female laughter outside and looked at each other, eyebrows raised.

"Maybe he's got himself a new girlfriend," said Kit, "and now he's here to pick up the ring so he can try proposing to her instead."

But when Lainey flung open the door, there was Wyatt with Penny at his side, and they were both looking so *happy* together.

"Lainey? Hello again! I didn't know if I'd recognize you, but I do. Plus, I cheated and looked you up on Facebook." Wyatt thrust a huge and fancy bouquet of roses into her unsuspecting arms, then tried to give her a hug, which didn't quite work, what with the flowers getting squashed between them.

"It's lovely to see you. Both of you." Turning to Penny, Lainey said, "We didn't know you were coming too . . . Does this mean you're back together?"

Oh wow, as soon as he got the ring back, was he about to go down on one knee and propose all over again?

"We aren't back together," said Penny. "Not in that way, at least."

"We just missed each other," Wyatt chimed in. "As friends."

"Best friends." Penny nodded. "We love spending time together."

"She agreed to come down here with me this weekend, so we could go to the wedding together and I wouldn't have to feel like a third wheel."

"I didn't *agree* to come along," said Penny. "I *offered.* And I'm so glad he said yes. We're having the best time," she went on happily. "Even the journey down here was great. We sang all the way!"

"Well, that's fantastic. And you didn't have to do this." Lainey indicated the flowers, which bore the name of a London florist so famous even she'd heard of them.

"This is for you too." Wyatt produced a bottle of Cristal. "And if you're free, we'd love you to join us this evening for dinner at Mariscombe House."

"Dinner this evening?" The half-open kitchen door was pushed fully open and Richard came in, his eyes lighting up at the sight of the champagne. "Am I invited?"

Wyatt and Penny visibly boggled at the unexpected arrival of an ancient Hollywood icon in a battered straw hat, checked shirt, and crumpled trousers. Wyatt swallowed and attempted to gather his wits. "By all means, Lord . . . Sir . . . Of course, it'd be an honor."

"If that's chilled" — Richard indicated the bottle — "it seems a shame not to open it. So you're the fellow who lost the ring, are you?" He nodded at Penny. "And you're the one who turned him down and did a runner?"

"Well, kind of," said Penny. "Sorry if I look a bit shell-shocked, but you're my gran's favorite actor."

"Always the grans." Richard looked mournful. "Nature's way of reminding me how ancient and decrepit I am. You've come along with him to collect the ring, then? Had second thoughts about turning him down?"

Penny smiled and shook her head. "Nothing like that. We've decided we're better off as friends."

"Oh dear, was he rubbish in bed?"

"Richard!" Mortified on their behalf, Lainey shot him a warning look. "Stop it, that's *rude.*"

Renowned for the impulsive remarks that had made him such a hit on chat shows over the decades, Richard said, "I think it's a perfectly reasonable question."

"It's definitely a great way not to get invited out to dinner," said Lainey.

Wyatt turned to her. "Hey, we had no idea this was who you were working for now. It's fine. No worries. It's an honor to be made fun of by Sir Richard Myles."

Richard rummaged in the deep pocket of his cream linen trousers and pulled out the diamond ring that had spent the last three weeks locked in his safe. Holding it toward

Wyatt, he said, "So does this mean I'm still invited to join you?"

"Of course you're invited, Sir . . . M'lord . . . Of course you are." Wyatt turned as the kitchen door opened once more and Majella popped her head round. His ears turning pink, he gestured expansively. "Everyone's welcome to join us. The more the merrier!"

Seth was still up in Bristol, and the twins stayed at home with Harry and the dogs, so there were six of them in the end, occupying a corner table in the hotel's busy restaurant. Richard sat with his back to the other diners, to avoid their endless glances in his direction. Champagne was poured, toasts were made, and the conversation flowed. Lainey, having privately had her doubts about how well Wyatt and Penny's just-good-friends plan would work out, began to think it might stand a chance after all.

And how lovely it was to see him happy again, cheerfully admitting that the surprise wedding proposal had been a terrible idea in the first place.

"Although the chateau was great," he continued. "Couldn't fault it. Mom was talking about it just the other day, saying what a fantastic place it was. Dad said he'd take her back there for a holiday in September if she wants."

"Except they aren't taking any more bookings," said Kit.

"You mean it's full?" Wyatt looked alarmed. "Booked up for the rest of the season?"

Lainey shook her head. "Kind of the opposite. They couldn't manage to keep the business running. The place is up for sale now."

"Oh no, I had no idea. That's awful!" Wyatt sat back in dismay. "Couldn't they just, like, borrow some money to get them through?"

"They'd already done that," said Kit. "All their savings were gone, and the bank wouldn't lend them any more. That's the reason we came here," he explained. "Biddy and Bill had to let us go."

"Well, that's a crying shame. Mom and Dad'll be so disappointed. They were looking forward to staying there again. So what are Biddy and Bill doing now? Did they move back to the UK too?"

"They're still there," Lainey explained. "Trying their best to persuade someone else to buy the chateau. It's OK. It'll happen eventually. I called Biddy last night and told her you were coming down today. She sends her love and says she hopes you're feeling a bit better now."

Wyatt exchanged a smile with Penny. "You can tell her I am."

"We both are," said Penny. "Oh, is everything OK?"

"Everything's fine." As soon as she'd said it, Lainey realized that Penny hadn't been addressing her. To her left, Kit had frozen with his glass halfway to his lips and was staring across the room.

Following the direction of his gaze, Lainey observed two men leaving the outside terraced area, making their way through reception. The man closest to them was tall, dark, and built like a rugby player, while the other, largely hidden from view, was shorter and slimmer. The next moment, she caught a glimpse of spiky white-blond hair and realization dawned.

The *next* next moment, as they came into full view, they stopped walking and turned to face each other. The dark-haired man said something to Tom, who replied with a playful smile and slid his arm around his companion's waist. They leaned closer, words were exchanged, and Tom reached up affectionately to stroke the side of the other man's jaw. Then they made their way across the hall, ascended the staircase together, and disappeared from view.

Lainey heard Kit exhale. Under cover of the table, she gave his knee a consoling squeeze. His first date with Tom had gone brilliantly. At the end of the evening, Tom had promised to be in touch soon but had warned Kit that, for the next couple of weeks, the bar was crazy busy and he might not be able to spare the time to get away.

In a low voice, Kit murmured, "When he said he was going to be rushed off his feet, I didn't realize he meant by a fullback."

"Sorry." Lainey felt for him. It wasn't her fault, but what else could she say?

She'd tried to gently warn him about Tom's reputation, but it was one of those situations where, if you were the besotted one, you really needed to learn about it for yourself.

And she knew only too well how that felt; hadn't she been gullible enough to believe that Anton would want to keep her in his life when they left the chateau?

She dismissed the memory; time had swiftly healed that small wound, thankfully, and she barely thought of Anton now. When she came across his updates on Facebook, she no longer harbored any desire to be the girl at his side.

Hopefully Kit would make a similarly

speedy recovery.

"Tom doesn't deserve you," Lainey whispered in his ear. "You can do so much better."

Across the table, Wyatt was looking concerned because Kit was still holding his glass without taking a drink. "Is there something wrong with the Laurent-Perrier?"

Recovering himself, Kit looked at the glass and grinned. "Are you kidding? I've never met a champagne I didn't like."

Once dinner was over, they headed out onto the terrace. Stars twinkled like sequins in the navy-blue sky and the trees on the grounds were strung with fairy lights. Dot Strachan, one of the owners of the hotel, showed them to another discreetly positioned table where Richard wouldn't be bothered by tourists, and Richard promptly swept Dot — who was glamorous and in her seventies — into a bit of a waltz that instantly caught the attention of everyone on the terrace.

"I don't know why we bother trying to look after him," Dot laughed once he'd twirled her around the tables and back again.

"Because you adore me," said Richard. "Almost as much as you adore that lucky husband of yours."

Dot's eyes sparkled. "Ah, that's probably why."

More drinks arrived, the conversation continued to flow, and when someone approached their table twenty minutes later, it took Lainey a couple of seconds to recognize who it was.

Normally the woman's hair was loose and windblown and her clothes and footwear were on the frumpy side. This evening, by contrast, she was wearing what looked like her very best dress, with medium-heeled patent shoes, and her hair was fastened up in a bun. She was even wearing blue eye-shadow and peach lipstick.

"Oh my word, Sir Richard, how lovely to bump into you here!" Pauline came to a halt in front of him, her face lighting up. "My goodness, look at you all, drinking champagne!"

Wyatt, the hospitable host, said at once, "If you're a friend of Sir Richard's, let me pour you a glass," and reached for the bottle in the ice bucket.

"Oh, no, no, I couldn't. That's very kind but I'm more a fan than a friend . . . well, just a fan really . . . and I have my water." Pauline held up her own half-full glass. "I can't believe how expensive the drinks are here! I asked for a mineral water, but even that was quite pricey, so I got them to give me normal water from the tap. And that was free!"

"Well, good. And so it should be." Next to Wyatt, Penny gave Pauline a warm smile. "And are you here with friends?"

"No, I'm on my own. My next-door neighbor knows I'm a fan of Sir Richard, and she told me she'd seen him coming into the restaurant earlier, so I put on my best clothes and did myself up so they couldn't refuse to serve me at the bar. I hardly recognized myself when I looked in the mirror, I can tell you!" Pauline smacked her lips together and beamed. "It's been a few years since I last wore lipstick!"

"You look lovely," Penny assured her. "My gran's a big fan of Sir Richard too. I can't wait to see her face when I show her the photo we took earlier of the two of us together!"

"Oh . . ." Pauline's look of longing was enough to melt the hardest of hearts.

Lainey watched as Penny jumped up.

"Here, give me your phone," she urged the older woman. "I'll take one of you with Sir Richard, shall I? It's better than doing a selfie and trying to fit both of you into the frame."

Majella was biting her lip, doing her best not to laugh, because Penny was a kind and lovely person who was just being helpful, which meant that Richard was now unable to refuse. Forced to get to his feet, he smiled for the camera with Pauline beaming like a lottery winner at his side, while Penny moved around them saying brightly, "There . . . oops, no. You blinked, let's just do another one . . . and a couple more to make sure."

"Thank you, thank you so much." There were tears of joy in Pauline's eyes as she turned to gaze up at her idol. "This is the best day of my life. I never thought I'd get my picture taken with you . . . You don't know how much this means to me."

"That's fine," said Richard, clearly uncomfortable and eager for her to leave them in peace.

"It's not as if he'd ever say no, is it? Gosh," Penny exclaimed. "How long does it take to have a selfie done? I mean, he's such a kind person, he's always going to be nice to his fans, isn't he? Especially when he knows how much it means to them."

Even Richard had the grace to look embarrassed at this. Lainey and Majella exchanged a glance and struggled to look as if it were an entirely plausible description of his character.

"I know," said Pauline, "and I'm sure he *is* nice. But it's such a shame he never replies to letters. It would mean so much to the people who've sent them to him."

"Does he never reply?" Penny looked surprised. "Oh, I'm sure he must do sometimes! Once in a while, at least!"

Shamefaced, Richard cleared his throat. "Well, I do my best, but I can't always manage it. There are just, you know, too many."

"But I belong to your online fan club and there are hundreds of us who've sent you cards and letters and presents." Emboldened, Pauline continued, "And none of us has ever had a reply. Not that it stops us from writing to you," she added hastily. "I'm just saying, it would be so nice if occasionally it could happen. Because then at least we'd know you'd seen what we'd written."

"Of course," agreed Penny. "That would make a world of difference, I can completely understand that."

"Well . . ." Increasingly discomfited, Richard said, "I'll see what I can do."

"That would be wonderful. You don't have to write to me," added Pauline, "but a friend of mine has written to you three times now, and she was so disappointed when you didn't reply. Her name's Nerys, and she sent the last one two weeks ago in a turquoise envelope because I told her you once said in an interview that turquoise was your favorite color. It would mean the world to her —"

"Everything OK here?" Dot Strachan was back, having spotted that Pauline was outstaying her welcome. With a charming smile, she rested a hand in the small of Pauline's back and said amiably, "Shall we leave these people to enjoy their drinks in peace?"

"Of course. Sorry. But it's been lovely to have the chance to say hello. And thanks for the photos. Thank you *so* much."

Penny nodded enthusiastically. "No trouble at all. It's been lovely to meet you too!"

When Dot had guided Pauline back into the hotel, Majella said playfully, "So that's you told."

Richard tipped his head back and took a hefty glug of brandy. "Bloody hell. I don't have many years left. I can't spend the rest of my life writing back to people I don't even know." He turned to Penny. "I mean, as much as I'd like to."

Which was a massive fib, obviously.

Lainey said, "Look, I know Pauline's a bit over-the-top, but she does have a point. Why don't you let me open the fan mail from now on and go through it, just to see what's there? We could send out some signed photos every week, maybe answer a few questions. And I'll do it all in my own time," she blurted out before Richard could come up with some reason to object. "You'd hardly have to do anything at all. Five minutes a day, maximum. Shall we do that?"

Across the table, Penny and Wyatt were looking expectant. Next to Lainey, Kit was quietly snorting with laughter at Richard being backed into a corner and getting his comeuppance at last.

"Fine, OK, we'll do it. Five minutes a day."

Hooray!

"Great." Lainey beamed at him. "Five, maybe ten minutes. Definitely no more than ten."

CHAPTER 26

The view from his room on the second floor of the hotel was the kind that couldn't fail to lift the spirits. Wyatt took in the sweep of Mariscombe Bay, the crescent of pale-yellow sand, the early-morning swimmers and joggers, and the seagulls soaring overhead in a pale-blue, nearly cloudless sky.

Penny, who was in no way an early riser, was still asleep in her own room; they'd made plans to meet downstairs for breakfast at 9:30, which was two hours from now. Picking up his phone, Wyatt took several photos of the beach to show her later — what a beautiful morning, and hopefully the weather would hold for tomorrow's wedding in Saint Ives. His attention was caught by two dogs cavorting together on the beach, launching themselves into the waves in pursuit of a yellow ball that had been thrown by their owner. The larger of the dogs managed to reach it first and swam back to shore, its tail wagging triumphantly as it dropped the ball at the feet of . . .

Wyatt picked up the pair of binoculars on the window ledge and brought them into focus. Yes, it was Lainey's coworker, Kit. Wearing rather fewer clothes than he'd had on during dinner last night.

And now he was hurling the ball back into the sea, this time racing after the two dogs into the water. As he watched them, Wyatt found himself smiling; he hadn't seen his parents' dogs for a few days and was missing them. He put down the binoculars, pulled on a shirt and board shorts, and picked up his room key.

Down the stairs he went, out of the hotel, and across the sloping lawn, still damp with dew where the sun's rays hadn't reached it yet. He made his way down the path to the stone steps and began his descent.

It was stumbling on a stray pebble that caused him to miss a step, lose his balance, and go careering down the rest of them with an undignified shout. He braced himself in anticipation of the pain when he reached the bottom, but the worst had already happened. Landing on the sand with a thud caused no further damage, apart from to his pride.

"Oh great," he muttered to himself as

heads turned in his direction and a young blond woman came hurrying across the beach toward him.

"You poor thing! Are you hurt?"

"Nothing too terrible." The pain in his ankle was as breath-catching as it was familiar. "Just give me a minute . . ."

"The same thing happened to me once. Right here." The blond indicated the steps. "I tried to catch a runaway stroller and it landed on me, sent me flying. My back was in agony and I could hardly walk for days! Although, on the bright side, it's kind of how me and my husband ended up getting together, so —"

"Wyatt, it *is* you. Oh God, are you OK?" It was Kit, dripping with seawater and clearly concerned, the two dogs at his heels. He knelt beside him. "Did you hit your head? How's your back? Glenda, stop it, don't lick his toes."

"I didn't hit my head. My back's fine." Despite the waves of pain, Wyatt couldn't help gasping with laughter. "But could you get the dog away from me? My feet are really ticklish. It's my right ankle that's the problem," he went on as the blond woman gently scooped Glenda into her arms. "I broke it last Christmas and it felt exactly like this. And I wasn't watching where I was going, so it looks like I've just done the same thing again."

"Oh, Wyatt, that's terrible," said Kit.

"They did warn me the break might be weaker and more vulnerable. I went over on a pebble and missed the step. I'm an idiot." Wyatt sighed, because his ankle was already beginning to balloon. "I just wish it weren't my right foot. Means I'm not going to be able to drive."

The blond woman took control of both dogs while Kit helped Wyatt to his feet. Well, foot. Attempting to put any weight on the bad ankle made him gasp, and he had to lean heavily on Kit in order to stay upright.

"This isn't great timing." Kit was sympathetic.

"I know. Can't see me dancing at the wedding." Wyatt grimaced with pain; it was also hard to concentrate when you were being supported by a dripping-wet male wearing nothing but a pair of shorts. His own arm was slung across Kit's broad shoulders and Kit's arm was firmly grasping him around the waist. Never having been the rugby- or football-playing type, close physical contact with another man wasn't something he was remotely familiar with. *"Owww,"* he hissed through gritted teeth, having accidentally put pressure on his right foot.

"It's OK, I've got you," said Kit. "Just relax and lean on me. I'm stronger than I look."

It took a while to reach the hotel. The blond woman's name was Sophie, Wyatt discovered, and she was married to the man who ran the place alongside his grandmother, the glamorous Dot. She volunteered to take the dogs back to Menhenick House, and Kit raced upstairs with the key to let himself into Wyatt's room, collect his car keys, and borrow a shirt. Having called Lainey to let her know what was happening, he then helped Wyatt out to the car and drove him to the local hospital.

Hopefully they wouldn't have to sit in the emergency room for seven hours surrounded by drunks and full-on gang warfare, which had been Wyatt's experience last time.

"Oh my God!" Coming down the staircase on her way to the hotel's breakfast room at 9:30, Penny stopped dead in her tracks. "What's been going on?"

The answer to that was: quite a lot. But Wyatt, levering himself to his feet, said, "You see, this is what happens when you stay in bed half the morning; you miss out on all the fun."

"If that's what you call fun, I'm glad I stayed in bed. But where have you been? What happened?" Her eyes widened. "Were you sleepwalking? Did you jump out of your window?"

"Nothing so dramatic. I was heading down to the beach and went over on my bad ankle. Kit was there, thank goodness. He helped me up and drove me to the local hospital. They were brilliant." And it was true; each time they had tried to resume their conversation about Kit's year at the chateau, they'd been interrupted, first by the triage nurse, then the doctor, then the trip to the X-ray department and finally the second meeting with the doctor. Wyatt had scarcely been able to believe the speediness of it all; within an hour, he'd been fitted with a heavy surgical boot and a crutch and sent on his way.

"Same ankle as before?" Penny winced at the thought.

"It's the same break, just cracked open again. But it's stable and it'll mend, no need for surgery." He indicated the cumbersome boot. "I have to wear this for as long as I need it. And I can't drive, obviously, but if we want to stay here for an extra night, it's Kit's day off tomorrow and he's happy to take us down to Saint Ives and bring us back again after the wedding."

"Oh, but we could get a taxi." Penny looked worried. "Although it'd cost a fortune."

Wyatt was touched; despite his family's wealth, she was always trying to save money on his behalf. "That doesn't matter. But Kit offered and I've already accepted. It'd be rude to change the arrangements now."

"Poor you." She gave him a consoling hug. "You aren't going to be able to dance!"

"I'm beginning to think I'm a bit jinxed when it comes to weddings." Wyatt broke into a grin. "Never mind. I have my boot and my crutch. I'm sure I can manage to hobble in time with the music."

"Your eyes are all sparkly." She studied his face. "You look so happy."

"Possibly because I've been up for hours," Wyatt told her, "and I'm finally going to get some breakfast."

"You've got that look in your eyes," said Richard.

"I have." Lainey nodded. "Well spotted."

He put down his coffee. "You're going to make me *do* something, aren't you?"

She shook her head. "Not yet. I'm just asking for permission to open any letters addressed to you."

"Of course, fire away." Evidently relieved, he gestured around the cluttered study. "Help yourself, do your thing, answer as many letters as you like."

"And when I've typed them, you can sign them."

"Yes, yes. Whatever."

Lainey felt all-powerful; Richard's conscience had clearly been pricked by last night's encounter with well-meaning Penny and über-grateful Pauline. "Thanks. You'll make a lot of old ladies very happy."

He looked rueful. "You're enjoying this, aren't you? I can tell."

"I am a bit. Smile."

"What?"

He was sitting in his favorite armchair with a fountain pen in one hand and the newspaper open to the daily crossword. He flashed a professional smile, allowing her to take a few nicely informal photos, then said, "I suppose you're going to send them pictures of me looking ancient and knackered."

"You're older than the Rolling Stones," Lainey reminded him. "You're allowed to look ancient and knackered."

Richard wagged a finger at her. "Now you're pushing your luck."

"Hey, you're lucky, these women love you

for who you are. I'm just saying a little bit of interaction goes a long way." Lainey was already busy rummaging among the clutter of magazines and newspapers on the desk, picking out unopened letters that were only still there because he was too lazy to throw them away. "Right, I'll make a start with these. From now on, give them to me instead of leaving them in random places. And well done," she added, because one thing she'd learned while running the children's club at the chateau was that praise was important. "You're doing a good thing."

Richard's shrug was good-natured as he returned his attention to the crossword. "You're the one doing it." She was about to leave the sunny study when he added, "You forgot to look in the wastepaper bin. There're probably a few more in there."

It was seven in the evening, and Kit had headed off to the gym. Lainey was sitting cross-legged on the pull-out bed in the flat above the garage, surrounded by opened letters and cards, compiling a list of people to reply to. She'd already printed off a hundred of the photos and stood over Richard making sure he signed them himself, rather than outsourcing the dreary task to a passing grandchild.

Reaching across now, she picked up one of the last remaining envelopes, the turquoise one with the neatly handwritten address that had to have been sent by Pauline's friend Nerys. OK, this was one letter she was definitely going to reply to.

She unfolded the two sheets of matching turquoise writing paper and began to read.

Dear Sir Richard,

This is the third and final time I shall be writing to you. I know you don't reply to letters as a rule, but I do wish there was a way of finding out whether or not you've read the previous two I sent you.

Anyway, I hope you're keeping well. I've enjoyed following your career over the years. The reason I'm contacting you is because I'd love to know if you remember my mum, Alexandra Davies. She met you while she was working as a secretary in your agent's offices in Los Angeles. I'm afraid Mum died a few years ago, but she always loved watching you on TV. After returning from LA, she settled back into life in Cardiff. I would love to hear if you have any happy memories of her and wanted to tell you that she thought you were a wonderful man and remembered you fondly for the rest of her life.

That's all. It would be lovely to hear from you, although I've learned that it's highly unlikely to happen. Still, you never know, which is why I'm giving this one last try.

Respectfully yours,
Nerys Davies

P.S. Mum's favorite of all your films was *The Unsent Letter.* It always made her cry.

Lainey refolded the sheets of writing paper, picked up her phone, and called Richard's number. Not that he often bothered to charge it up, but it was worth a try.

"Hello, what now?" By some miracle, he'd actually answered the call.

"Richard, that letter in the turquoise envelope from Pauline's friend Nerys. She's the daughter of Alexandra Davies, who knew you years ago in LA."

"Who?"

"Alexandra Davies. She was a secretary at your agent's offices."

"You know what I'm like with names," Richard grumbled. "And have you any idea how many people worked in those offices?"

"I just thought you might remember her."

"Well, I don't," said Richard. "Hollywood's full of people who think actors will remember them when all they did was say hello to them once in the street. Can I get back to my snooze now?" Signing those photos had evidently exceeded his being-nice-to-the-fans capacity for the day.

"Of course you can. I'll write a nice letter back to Nerys apologizing for your terrible memory. You enjoy your snooze."

He chuckled. "Thanks, boss."

"And you can sign the letter before I post it tomorrow."

"You're a hard taskmaster," said Richard.

Sunshine was dappling the surface of the Pacific Ocean, Venice Beach was dotted with people enjoying the weather, and Richard was wondering if he'd ever felt this happy. There she was, making her way up the beach toward him in her modest dark-blue one-piece swimsuit. As she reached him, her pale skin glimmered with droplets of water and the look on her face was one of sheer joy.

"You're back." He was scarcely able to believe it. "I thought I was never going to see you again!"

"I had to come back. I missed you so

much." As she fell into his arms, her warm breath mingled with his, and he felt the seawater from her swimsuit sinking into the sweater he hadn't even known he was wearing.

"I've missed you too. But how did you get here?"

"I swam here." Sandy stroked his face lovingly. "All the way from Cardiff."

Richard opened his eyes and stared up at the ceiling, his heart clamoring in his chest. For some reason, it wasn't the fact that she'd swum from Cardiff that had done it; it was the discovery that his body was tanned and taut, as athletic as it had been in his twenties, that had jolted him into realizing this was a dream.

But a dream that just went to show that his subconscious had been working away during the night, solving the conundrum he hadn't managed to work out for himself.

He'd only known her as Sandy — they'd all called her that at the agency. But of course it was short for Alexandra. Sandy's shyness, her pale skin, and her soft Welsh accent had marked her out among all the tanned, confident California girls. And it was that unprepossessing manner that had charmed him when he'd gotten to know her.

Having been able to identify Alexandra

Davies as Sandy, Richard felt as if the last piece of a jigsaw had just slotted satisfyingly into place. And now her daughter had written to him asking if he remembered her mother, which meant Sandy wanted to see him again and was wondering, in her characteristically shy way, if he would be interested in meeting up with her.

He checked his bedside clock and tried to decide whether it would be OK to wake Lainey at 5:23 in the morning.

Because the answer to Sandy's question was yes, yes he definitely would.

CHAPTER 27

Hurrying to answer the hammering at the door at 6:30, a dozen possibilities as to what could be wrong flashed through Lainey's mind, the most likely among them being that something bad had happened to Richard.

Well, he was eighty; sooner or later it was going to come to them all.

But when she unlocked the door, there he was on the top step outside the flat, fully dressed and completely alive.

"What's happened?" said Lainey. "Is someone ill?"

"No. I've remembered who she is. I do know her!"

For heaven's sake, was he drunk? "Who do you know?"

"Alexandra. Sandy!"

She leaned against the door. "Richard, it's half past six in the morning."

"I know! I waited a whole hour before I

came over. Are you going to let me in? I'll make you a cup of tea if you want. We went out together for a few weeks . . . well, not *out* out, because it needed to be under the radar." Having followed her inside, he watched as she swept the sheets and pillows off the bed and expertly folded it back into its day job as a sofa. "Well, will you look at that? Marvelous what they can do these days."

"Why did you have to be under the radar?"

"It was when I was meant to be having a passionate affair with Lara O'Leary. I wasn't, because she was a lesbian, but our studios needed the public to think we were a couple. Right, where d'you keep the tea bags? And the milk? And the cups?"

"Sit down." Lainey indicated the sofa. "I'll make the tea."

"I bumped into her in a coffee shop one evening, close to my agent's offices. Literally bumped into her," Richard went on. "She dropped her doughnut on the floor, so I bought her another. She was the loveliest thing, unlike anyone I'd ever met before. We started seeing each other, and it was such a breath of fresh air . . . She used to wear dark glasses and a head scarf, and slip into my apartment building so no one knew what was going on. And she was happy for us to be a secret too, unlike all the other girls over there, who only ever wanted us to be seen out together in public."

"I like this story." Lainey's voice softened, because he was so clearly picturing his young girlfriend in his mind's eye.

"I dreamed about her last night. Isn't that amazing? It was like we were there, together again on Venice Beach . . ."

"So what happened? Back then, I mean. Not in the dream." She finished stirring sugar into his tea and passed the mug to him. "What went wrong?"

"Nothing went wrong between *us*. Her father was taken ill and needed looking after, I heard, back in Wales. I was in Rome for a few weeks, shooting a movie. By the time I got back, Sandy was gone. Left her apartment, left the agency, left LA. She didn't leave any kind of message or write to me and I had no way of getting in touch with her. It was fifty-odd years ago," Richard said defensively when Lainey frowned. "Not like these days."

"But surely —"

"She was the one who left. It was her decision to break contact. So why would I knock myself out trying to track her down? I wasn't going to *beg*."

"OK." Lainey sat at the little dining table

opposite him. That made sense.

Richard was unaccustomed to rejection in any form, and his pride had been dented. And presumably there would have been plenty of beautiful, aspiring actresses only too eager to take his mind off the shy Welsh girl who'd left LA without saying goodbye.

"But that was then." Richard's eyes were bright. "And this is now. If asking her daughter to write to me is Sandy's way of getting back in touch . . . well, why not? I'm up for that. It's not as if I'm going to bear a grudge. That's why I'm here, to stop you sending off the letter saying I don't remember her. I know you said you'd make me sign it, but then I thought maybe you'd forge my signature to get it in the post —"

"Richard, you haven't read the letter from Nerys yet." Yeesh, this was awful; how was she to know he'd not only suddenly remember who Alexandra was but would turn out to have a belated yearning to see her again?

"Well, show it to me then! Is there a phone number? I'm going to give her a call, suggest we meet up and —"

"OK, stop." Lainey held up her hands and crossed to the cupboard containing the file she'd put together last night. Rustling through the many letters, she found the one from Nerys, hesitating before passing it over to him. "Richard, I'm so sorry, Sandy isn't with us anymore. She died a few years ago."

As he searched her face, the light faded from his eyes. He sat back against the sofa and his shoulders sagged. "Oh. Fuck. Are you sure?" But it was said with resignation rather than despair. Once you reached eighty, the death of your contemporaries no longer came as a massive surprise.

"I really am sorry," Lainey said, and gave him the letter.

Richard read it in silence, then heaved a sigh and shook his head. "Well, that's that. What a shame."

"I'll throw away the letter I wrote to her from you."

"What did it say?"

"Just that you were so sorry you couldn't quite remember Alexandra, but your memory for names wasn't great these days, and that those had been happy times and you were sorry to hear of her death. I also said you were delighted to hear that her mum had enjoyed watching *The Unsent Letter* because although it hadn't been one of your more successful films, it was always one of your personal favorites." Lainey opened a second folder and took out the typed letter. "Here, you can borrow bits of it."

"Bits of it? Why would I want to borrow them?"

"So you can write back to Nerys."

Richard looked baffled. "Can't we just send her that one?"

"But you've remembered Sandy now! You know who she was . . . You were a couple! It was a lovely, romantic story, and you were desperate to meet up with her again, so you need to tell Nerys that. She'll be thrilled!"

"I did want to meet up with her. But I can't, can I? Because she's dead." His disappointment was palpable.

"I know, and it's sad. But don't you want to write to Nerys anyway? She'll be able to tell you more about her mum, won't she?"

Richard shrugged. "She's still going to be dead, though."

"I'll write it if you want. But it'd be so much better coming from you. And look, there's an email address; you could send her a quick message this morning."

He frowned. "If there was an email address, why were we going to post a letter back to her?"

"Because people prefer proper letters, that's why. They can show them off to their friends. But email's quicker and easier, obviously, and it's not as if Nerys is one of those fans who's desperate for a handwritten signature."

Richard rose to his feet. "I can't believe I was stupid enough to believe you when you said none of this was going to take more than ten minutes."

For the next couple of hours, he sat in a garden chair overlooking the bay and allowed his mind to drift back to the time he and Sandy had spent together. Part of him couldn't see the point in making contact with her daughter, but part of him did want to hear more.

Finally, he headed back to the office, sat down with his iPad, and began to compose an email.

Dear Nerys,
Thank you for your letter. Sorry about not reading the previous ones you sent. Of course I remember your mother, Sandy. She was a lovely girl and I'm so sorry to hear she's no longer with us. We shared such happy times together, and I remember how sad I was when she left to look after her father. I hope her life was happy after she returned to the UK.

Sorry, I'm not very good at writing. Not my greatest skill. If you have any photos of Sandy, I'd like to see them.

Best wishes,
Richard

It was a stilted, poorly constructed effort, he knew that. With the endless alterations, it had taken him the better part of an hour to write those few lines. Lainey could have managed it in two minutes, but he was determined to do it himself, without the help of a ghostwriter. He pressed Send, then sat back and closed his eyes, feeling the warmth of the sun on his eyelids. How long would it be before he heard back?

All of a sudden, he couldn't bear the fact that he was now the one having to wait. The words *Always so impatient!* sang through his mind, and he looked at the framed photo on his desk of his beloved lost son, remembering how Tony had always teased him for his inability to allow things to happen in their own good time.

He felt the familiar cavernous ache of loss for the boy he'd loved so much. *Oh, Tony, is that really you talking to me? How I wish you were still here.*

"Well?" said Lainey when he found her in the kitchen energetically scrubbing the floor.

"I've sent her an email, asked if she has

any photos of Sandy."

"That's great!"

"But that was ten minutes ago and she hasn't got back to me yet."

"Pot, kettle," said Lainey.

"I know, I know. Feel free to gloat."

"Want me to make you a coffee?"

"I can make my own." He found the pods and took a mug down from the cupboard; if it hadn't been still early, a proper drink would have gone down nicely and settled the butterflies in his chest. God, waiting for something important to happen was just the pits; how he hated the way it made him feel.

Ting sang the iPad he'd carried in and left on the kitchen table, and his pulse rate doubled.

"Is it her?" Lainey stopped scrubbing and sat back on her heels.

"Yes." Richard nodded and opened the email. It took a few seconds for the attached photos to download, and as soon as he saw them, a lump expanded in his throat.

He should have known this would be a mistake. "Are you OK?" Lainey sounded concerned.

It came out as a croak. "When I asked to see photos, I wasn't expecting her to send me these."

There were three, and the sight of them

had sent him hurtling back in time to a lazy summer's afternoon in his apartment. He'd brought home a camera with a self-timer, and they'd been able to take photos of the two of them together. Nothing seedy, just normal happy snaps, with Sandy wearing a pink-and-white-gingham dress and the biggest smile, and himself in a white shirt and dark-gray high-waisted trousers, with his arms around her waist and their heads close together. In the third photo, they were kissing, and he could remember it as clearly as if it had happened yesterday: the feel of her skin, the smell of her neck, the sound of her laughter . . .

He swallowed the lump in his throat. "She could have sold these to the movie magazines, made some money. But she didn't."

"Because she was a good person." Lainey was at his side now, studying the photos. "She looks lovely."

"She was." He scrolled up to read what Nerys had written above them: *These are the ones she especially treasured. Did you want me to send you a couple of more recent pics?*

He hesitated. Did he?

Oh, who was he kidding?

Yes please.

CHAPTER 28

This time, Richard had to wait less than a minute. When the next email dropped into his inbox, there was a photo of Sandy smiling for the camera, looking contented and cheerful in a lilac dress, her creamy-white hair swept back and tucked behind her ears. She looked exactly as she'd always looked, just fifty years older.

While he'd been studying every last detail of her, a second photograph had downloaded. This time Sandy was sitting on a sofa next to a younger woman who had to be Nerys, because the likeness was so strong. Her hair was blond, and she was wearing a stripy cardigan and jeans. But the sparkling eyes and shy smile were the same as her mother's, and he sensed at once that she shared Sandy's kind nature and absolute trustworthiness.

His attention shifted back to what she had written above the photos:

Here you are. Mum still looked wonderful, didn't she? I loved her so much, and of course still miss her dreadfully. As you can imagine, I was surprised when she first told me about you and her. Don't worry, though, she never did tell anyone else — only my grandmother, and then me, once I'd turned twenty-one and could be trusted to keep the story to myself. She did what you wanted and kept everything a secret until the day she died. And I've never told anyone either.

Richard finished reading. Then he reread the words. The blood in his veins seemed to heat up by a degree or two. He leaned over the iPad screen and typed: Told anyone what?

The reply this time was almost instantaneous: You know what. Don't you?

He didn't know, but a part of him was beginning to wonder. Unless he was reading into the words a meaning that hadn't been implied.

Or . . . or this was all some kind of elaborate double bluff.

Clumsily, with fingers that suddenly felt too big for the keys on the screen, he typed: What's your telephone number?

No reply. No reply. No reply.

Finally: Sorry, minor panic attack, needed a few minutes to prepare myself.

This is my number . . .

Having retreated to his office and closed the door firmly, Richard called the number. The phone was picked up on the fifth ring and he knew Nerys had been psyching herself up to answer it.

"Hello." She sounded breathless. "Sorry if I muddle my words. I'm a bit nervous. Well, a lot nervous."

And there it was, the soft voice with the Welsh accent he'd always loved, followed by the shy laugh he remembered so well.

"You sound just like her."

"You remember her voice?"

"Of course I do." He knew the answer already, but the question needed to be asked. Bracing himself, he said, "Why did she disappear?"

"She didn't disappear. She came home, to Cardiff."

His fingers tightened around the phone that was pressed to his ear. "Why?"

"Because she was pregnant."

There it was. Oh God.

He gathered himself. "Pregnant with you?"

"Yes."

"Why didn't she tell me?"

There was a pause, then Nerys said, "Look, I don't want anything from you, cross my heart, so you don't have to pretend that you didn't know —"

"*What?* But I really *didn't* know," Richard blurted out. "I had no idea. She didn't tell me, I swear."

"You sound as if you're telling the truth," said Nerys, "but that's the trouble with you being an actor. How do I know?"

"I'll take a lie detector test. I swear on the life of my grandchildren. I was pretty broken up when she left because I had no idea why she'd gone. She didn't even say goodbye."

"OK, OK, I believe you. And if I'm honest, I did always kind of wonder, but Mum never wanted to rock the boat in case it caused upset. She was so worried you might be angry with her or that it could damage your career."

"I was away filming on location." Suspicions were beginning to unfurl in Richard's mind. "When I got back, Mickey, my agent, told me she'd left. He said her father was ill and needed looking after, so she'd gone home to Cardiff. Well, she knew my address and phone number, so I waited to hear from her. But I never did."

"Mum told me that she'd started feeling really sick in the mornings and Mickey caught her at work one day heaving at the smell of his cigar. When she asked to leave the office, he wouldn't let her, so she ended up puking into his wastepaper basket."

"Oh God," said Richard. "Poor girl." Mickey Hartnett had been one of the most ruthless and successful agents in Hollywood, not to mention one of the most eagle-eyed. On one occasion when he'd been flirting with Sandy in reception, Mickey had spotted them together and had later jokingly warned him to keep away from his staff.

"Well, it was a bit of a giveaway," Nerys continued. "And when Mum broke down in his office, it didn't take Mickey long to find out who was responsible. He told her he'd get in touch with you."

"But he didn't."

"Two days later, he called her into his office. He explained that you were sorry, but it would spell disaster for your career, and it was never meant to be more than a bit of harmless fun in the sun. He said you felt it was all a bit embarrassing and that all you could offer her was money."

It was Richard's turn to feel sick. "He never breathed a word about any of this."

"Mickey took care of everything. Mum said he was very kind to her. He drew up a contract and she signed it, promising to never contact you again. Because she thought that was what you wanted. Then he arranged her flight home and that was it; she came back to Cardiff."

"How much did he pay her to leave?" Richard scarcely recognized his own voice.

"Oh, you were generous. Ten thousand dollars. Mum bought this house with the money. Two-bedroom terrace, little garden at the back, even an inside toilet. Everything a heartbroken single mother could wish for."

Ten thousand dollars for Mickey Hartnett to avoid a scandal. Small change compared to the money he was demanding from the studios if they wanted Richard Myles to star in their next blockbuster movie. He'd been aware, of course, that such negotiations went on within the industry — it was just the way things had worked back then — but it had never even occurred to him that he himself might have been involved in one.

"I feel terrible about this. If I'd known, it could all have been handled differently."

"It's a shame Mum isn't still here. This would have made her so happy."

"What can I say? Mickey Hartnett was a ruthless bastard. It kills me that he knew the truth and never told me."

"But Mum was realistic. She was a nobody

from Wales, and you were a Hollywood star. She loved you till the day she died," Nerys continued softly, "and she loved me too. That was enough for her."

"I'm still sorry, though. God, I wish you'd contacted me before."

Her laugh was so like Sandy's. "I did try, but you didn't see the letters."

"I meant before she died."

"Ah, she always said we must never get in touch, not while she was alive. But afterward . . . well, I suppose the internet made it possible. I bought my first computer two years ago, and suddenly I was able to learn so much more about you. I found a Facebook group online for fans of Sir Richard Myles, and that was an eye-opener, I can tell you."

"Oh crikey. What were they saying about me?"

Drily, Nerys said, "That you never reply to their letters. But they love you anyway."

Richard half laughed, still unaccustomed to feeling guilty. "No accounting for taste."

"It's a friendly group. They made me welcome. We even had a get-together last Christmas to celebrate your birthday. About twenty of us had lunch in a smart restaurant in Swindon. It's mainly run by Pauline, of course. She's a nice lady, a bit over-the-top and completely besotted with you, but she means well. Last night she wrote on there about getting to meet you when you were out having dinner with friends at one of the local hotels, and it was like the highlight of her entire life because you never usually speak to her at all!"

He winced. "Sometimes it's too much. It gets embarrassing."

"But Pauline did say she'd told you off for not answering our messages."

"She did." He nodded in agreement. "And she mentioned yours, in the turquoise envelope."

"I know, she told me that too. Wasn't that kind of her? She's always inviting us to go and stay with her so we can walk around St. Carys and maybe catch a glimpse of you. Not that I'd ever do that," Nerys added hastily. "It sounds a bit stalkerish to me . . . Oh goodness, is that the time? I'm so sorry, I promised to take my neighbor to visit her husband in hospital. She'll be wondering where I've gotten to!"

Five minutes later, wandering outside, Richard found Majella working on her laptop in the garden while Lainey hung a basket of laundry out to dry on the line.

"How did it go?" said Lainey. "Are you

BFFs now?"

"Am I what?"

"You and Nerys, BFFs. It stands for best friends forever." She turned to Majella. "You aren't going to believe this. Richard replied to one of his fans today! We actually shamed him into it. Turns out she's the daughter of someone he knew in his Hollywood days, isn't that brilliant? So he emailed her, then she emailed him back, and then he emailed her again!"

"Wow." Majella looked up from her laptop. "That's what I call a double first."

"She sounded nice in her letter. *Was* she nice?"

"Er . . . yes. Fine." Nerys was his daughter, and she had ended their phone call because she was anxious not to keep her elderly neighbor waiting. After she'd hung up, Richard had found himself feeling . . . well, rejected.

"Isn't that great? I told you it'd be worth the effort — can you imagine how thrilled she must have been to hear from you?" Evidently delighted with herself, Lainey went on, "Now, one of the other letters was from a man in Edinburgh whose sister's having her seventieth birthday next week. So I think I'm going to buy some cards, then you can send her one and wish her a happy birthday."

"OK."

"See?" She beamed at him as she hung up one of Harry's school shirts. "It's nice to be nice, isn't it?"

"Oh, it's the best." Richard checked his watch; was it midday yet? He'd just spoken to someone who was either a genius hoaxer or his daughter, and his emotions were all over the place. He could really do with a drink.

One thing he did know, though: it was a good job Mickey the bastard Hartnett was no longer around. Because if the man hadn't snorted that bucketful of cocaine and drowned in his mistress's hot tub twenty years ago, Richard would definitely kill him.

CHAPTER 29

"OK, bit of an emergency. Who's in the house right now? I need help and it needs to be fast."

It was Seth at the other end of the phone. Lainey blinked, because he was in Bristol. She put down the bag of rice and did a quick mental check. "Kit's driving Wyatt and Penny down to Saint Ives, Harry and Violet are both out with friends, Majella's getting ready for someone's birthday lunch at the Italian place on Silver Street and Richard's drinking gin in the garden. India's upstairs in the bath, and I've just started making a risotto."

"Perfect. Now listen: get India out of the bath. The two of you need to head over to Bude in no time flat and break into a house. I'll text you the address."

It sounded horribly like the opening segment of an episode of *CSI*. "Why, what's happened, has there been an accident? Oh

God, is someone dead?" Alarmed, Lainey said, "Shouldn't you call the police?"

"It's not that kind of emergency. My clients drove down from Bude to Southampton this morning to set out on their cruise, and they've forgotten their passports."

"Oh *no.*"

"Tell me about it. I even made them stick a Post-it Note to the front door, but it still happened. When you get to the address, you're going to have to smash the window of the downstairs bathroom and climb in that way, because everything else is double-glazed. Then as soon as you've found the passports, you need to drive down to Southampton, so the Gardners can get on board before the ship sets sail for New York at four thirty."

Was it even possible, time-wise? Just about. "And why do I need India with me?"

"The broken window will be visible from the road, so she'll have to stay at the house until a glazier can get there and make it secure. Because on top of everything else, they don't need a burglary."

"Um . . . actually, I think India might be busy."

"This is an emergency. Tell her she has to do it."

Lainey's mind was racing. "Maybe I could ask a neighbor to wait there until it's fixed."

"And what if they can't? Just take India, OK? You need to get a move on; there's no time to waste."

As Lainey hung up, India wandered into the kitchen carrying a magazine, a packet of Jaffa Cakes, and a Diet Coke. "You're looking a bit panicky. Problem?"

"No problem at all." Lainey switched off the heat beneath the diced onions gently sizzling in the pan.

"That smells fantastic! What's for lunch?"

"Toast."

As they raced along narrow, twisting country lanes, Lainey said, "Look, I'm really sorry about this."

"Well, I can't say it's how I was expecting to spend my Saturday afternoon. But never mind, can't be helped. These things happen."

"I don't think you should be doing that, though."

"Doing what? *Waaah!*" Majella let out a yelp as the car hit a pothole.

"Plucking your eyebrows at thirty miles an hour. It's asking for trouble."

"I'm only plucking one eyebrow. I'd just finished the first one when you dragged me downstairs. I can't go out with uneven eyebrows," Majella protested. "It's embarrassing."

"Not as embarrassing as losing an eye and having to spend the rest of your life telling people how it happened. Please, put the tweezers *down.*"

Her phone beeped with a text from Seth, and Majella looked at it. "He's sent the address of the house. I'll put it into the GPS. God, I hope you can get the passports down there in time."

"So do I." Still feeling guilty about dragging Majella away from the birthday lunch she'd been so looking forward to, Lainey said, "If the window's fixed quickly, maybe you'll be able to get back in time to catch up."

"Except look at me. What a mess." Ruefully Majella indicated her barely combed hair, makeup-free face, asymmetrical eyebrows, and denim button-down dress with two buttons missing. "I thought I had another hour to get ready. Never mind, I'll survive."

"But weren't you being set up to meet someone? Violet mentioned it last night."

"I was. One of my friend Judi's cousins. His name's Oliver and he's supposed to be lovely. Here, I'll show you, she sent me a pic." Skimming through the texts on her own phone, Majella found what she was looking for and briefly waved the photo in front of Lainey so she could get the gist.

"Oh, *handsome.*"

"I know!"

"Sorry." Would this guilt never end?

"It's OK. Can't have the Gardners getting home from their cruise of a lifetime to find a ransacked house."

They reached Bude twenty minutes later and found the address. Lainey screeched to a halt half-on and half-off the pavement, then they leaped out of the car together like cops in a movie and raced to the right-hand side of the smartly decorated detached house. There was the narrow window, as promised. Lainey took off her cardigan and wrapped it around her right hand, then closed her eyes and punched the glass as hard as she could. "I've always wanted to do that!" she said with satisfaction.

Luckily there was no burglar alarm to contend with. Having knocked the remaining shards of glass out from around the window frame, she clambered up onto the ledge and squeezed her way through, sending soap dispensers, jars, and aerosol cans flying as she stepped over the shelf and into the sink.

"The spare key to the front door is in the kitchen, in the cookie tin in the left-hand cupboard above the dishwasher," Majella called out as Lainey lowered herself to the floor and crunched over the broken glass.

"Right." She made her way through the house to the kitchen and found the key in the tin, hidden beneath the chocolate cookies. Although really, what if a burglar saw the tin and fancied a few cookies? Surely it would make more sense to hide the key in among the dusters and tins of polish.

She turned and surveyed the kitchen, scanning the counters for the forgotten passports. Not in here. She checked the hallway — no sign of them — then unlocked the front door and let Majella in.

"Found them?"

"Not yet."

"Bugger."

They split up. Lainey searched the rest of the ground floor while Majella ran upstairs. After five minutes, they switched in case all that was needed was a fresh pair of eyes.

"Oh for God's *sake,*" Majella cried out in frustration from the living room. "This is ridiculous. According to Seth, Mrs. Gardner had the passports in her hand; all she did was put them down somewhere and forget to pick them back up again."

"How can they just disappear?" Lainey yelled back, throwing aside the duvet in the Gardners' bedroom and checking the pillows. "What if we can't find them?"

"Well, on the bright side, you can stay here and deal with the glazier, and I'll be able to get home in time to make myself beautiful and persuade Judi's handsome cousin that I'm the woman of his dreams."

"You might not like him. He might be awful."

"Come on, you saw the photo. He looks like Pierce Brosnan." Emerging from the living room as Lainey gave up on the search upstairs, Majella said, "I'll make allowances."

"One of us is going to have to call Seth and tell him we can't find them." Lainey couldn't bear it; more than anything, she'd longed to be able to rise to the occasion, solve the problem, and earn Seth's undying gratitude, because . . . well, because as she'd told Richard this morning, it was nice to be nice. And it would make Seth happy, almost as happy as the Gardners would be when she arrived at the departure terminal at Southampton and presented them with the passports they'd so carelessly mislaid.

Except she'd failed. They hadn't been able to find the damn things, which meant there were would be no ecstatic reunion for the Gardners and their lost passports . . .

Or for herself and Seth.

"Look, we've done our best," said Majella. "And it's a shame, but it's really not our fault they left them somewhere ridiculous. You can tell Seth, and I'll call the glazier. And I'll take a cab back to St. Carys if you're happy to stay here and get this place sorted out." She waved an invisible magic wand around her own head and broke into a huge smile. "Looks like Cinderella is going to make it to the ball after all!"

Lainey nodded, because it was good news for Majella. "That's fine. Of course I'll stay here." She took out her phone, mentally bracing herself for Seth's disappointment, and scrolled to his name.

Bing-bong-bing-bong chimed the 1970s doorbell.

"Oh God, what now?" said Majella.

"Maybe someone heard us smash the window and called the police."

"Great, so now they'll arrest us and I'll never get to meet my perfect man."

Majella pulled open the front door. "Hi, hello. We're not burglars, I absolutely promise."

Lainey, behind her, saw a startled-looking man with sandy hair, sunglasses perched on top of his head, and a blue-and-white-striped beach bag slung over his shoulder. He was wearing a bright-purple T-shirt with a photo of a kitten on the front, red knee-length shorts, and bright-green espadrilles.

"Right, OK, I believe you. But I was actually looking for the Gardners." His gaze flickered from Majella to Lainey. "And you aren't them."

"They're not here," said Majella. "But we can pass on a message if you want."

"But this is their house?"

"It is." It crossed Lainey's mind that despite the outlandish outfit, this man could in fact be a burglar himself, disguised as a harmless tourist in order to break into a house whose owners were away. She added hastily, "They just popped out. They'll be back soon."

He hesitated. "Oh, OK. Well, don't worry then. I'll call back later."

And now he was looking at Majella oddly, as if it had just occurred to him that her announcement that she wasn't a burglar might in fact have been a clever double bluff.

For a couple of seconds, they stood there gazing at each other with mutual suspicion. At length, Lainey said, "Can I ask why you want to speak to them?"

The man hesitated, then reached into his

beach bag. "Well, I was just walking up the hill and I found their passports lying in the gutter, so —"

"Oh my God!" Launching herself at him, Lainey grabbed the passports out of his hand and yelled, "You're amazing! That's what we've been looking for! I need to take them . . . What were they doing in the gutter?"

"It was three doors up from here, so I'm guessing one of the Gardners put them on the roof of their car as they were getting in, then forgot they were there and just drove off."

Of course, of *course* that was how it had happened. Lainey said, "You're a lifesaver and I could kiss you, but I really have to go."

CHAPTER 30

"Wow," said the man as they watched Lainey do an expert three-point turn and roar off up the road with a cheery wave out of the sunroof.

"You have no idea how grateful we are. You've saved the Gardners' vacation." Gratitude wasn't exactly the emotion Majella was feeling, because now she was definitely going to miss the birthday lunch, but it was brilliant news for the Gardners. Having seen the hospital letters and appointments pinned up on the corkboard in the kitchen, she now knew that Mr. Gardner was suffering from Parkinson's, so to have missed the cruise would have been a crushing disappointment for both him and his wife, who cared for him and had presumably been preoccupied with helping him into the car when she'd left the passports on the roof.

"Well, I'm glad I was able to help. Look,

don't panic, but can I just get something out of your hair?"

"What is it?"

"It's OK, nothing bad . . ." He put down his bag and approached her, carefully gathering something into his cupped hands.

"Oh God!" She let out a yelp as he stepped back and swiftly threw the massive spider into the front yard. "It's a monster! You said it was nothing bad."

He grinned. "Sorry. It seemed safer than telling you what it was."

Majella took steadying gulps of air and pressed her hand to her frantically thudding chest. "We were ransacking the house looking for the passports. It must have happened when I was searching the cupboard under the stairs. Well, thanks. I suppose I'd better call a glazier." The man looked surprised, and she explained, "The Gardners are down at Southampton, waiting to get on their cruise ship. We had orders to break in and find the passports. But now I need to make sure the house is secure."

"Of course. Am I allowed to ask another question?"

"Feel free."

He pointed tentatively. "Why are your eyebrows like that?"

An hour later, they were sitting at the

kitchen table, still talking. His name was Dan, Majella had discovered, and he was down here on vacation with his wife and two children. She'd called Seth to let him know that Lainey and the passports were on their way to Southampton. She'd also contacted the emergency glazier, who said he was busy on a couple of other calls but would get to her as soon as he could.

Having swept up the broken glass and tidied the house, they were now waiting for him to turn up. And since there was no milk in the house because the fridge had had a pre-vacation clear out, Dan had zipped back to the house he was renting farther up the hill and returned with two coffees.

Somehow the humiliating eyebrow situation had broken down any remaining barriers, and since then they'd been chatting nonstop.

"You don't have to stay," said Majella when the coffee had been drunk.

Dan shrugged easily. "If you'd rather be on your own, that's fine. But if you're happy for me to stay and keep you company . . . well, that's good too. Like I said, Sara and the girls have gone off on a girlie shopping trip, so I don't have anything else to do." His eyes crinkled at the corners. "I'm banned from going along with them. Thank God."

Majella laughed. "I have girls and my husband used to be banned too. Trust me, it's the best way. How long have you been married?"

Dan sat back and counted on his fingers. "Well, we *got* married sixteen years ago. But we broke up five years ago and now we're divorced."

"Really? Oh sorry, I didn't realize. But you called her your wife."

He shrugged. "It's not the first thing you tend to blurt out when you meet someone. We had an amicable divorce and we've stayed friends for the sake of the girls. We come down here every summer for a week's vacation. *En famille,*" he added wryly. "Apart from those hours-long shopping expeditions."

"Ah, but it's nice that you can go away together."

"How about you and your husband? All good?"

"Well, it *was* good. He died a few years ago." There it was, the habitual stab of pain as she uttered the words. But it was lessening, and it was becoming easier to say.

"I'm so sorry. How awful for you."

"It was. But we're getting there." To

lighten the mood, Majella said, "I've just started dating again."

"Oh, well done. And how's that going?"

"Funny you should ask. Absolutely dreadful." She laughed. "Diabolical, in fact. I was looking forward to meeting someone at a lunch party today, but all this happened instead. Which is why I'm stuck here with my wonky eyebrows, no makeup on, and terrible clothes. Instead of there, dolled up to the nines, and making a drop-dead-gorgeous man fall in love with me at first sight."

"Well, that's a shame. I mean, I'd offer to stay here and wait for the glazier so you can get to your party, but I'm a stranger . . ."

"Thank you." Majella nodded, grateful to him for understanding. "I've met you, so I do trust you, but this is my responsibility."

"If he does turn up soon, I can definitely drive you back to St. Carys, if that would help."

"You're so kind. I don't think he's going to get here in time, but thanks for the offer."

"You should pluck your other eyebrow, though," said Dan. "Just in case."

"I shall. Can it be my turn to ask you another question now?"

"Anything you like."

"The kitten T-shirt?"

"Ah, of course. A Father's Day present from my daughters. They forced me to put it on this morning." Mournfully he added, "I think it might be their way of ensuring I never get another girlfriend."

Majella grinned. "It means you're a great dad."

"Either that or a soft touch."

The next second, they both jumped as the doorbell did its *bing-bong* thing again.

"All right, love?" It was the emergency glazier. "You sounded so desperate earlier, I decided to bump you up the list. Where's this broken window, then? Let's get it sorted for you."

"Brilliant," said Dan. "You're her knight in shining armor."

And Majella's heart did a tiny skip-and-a-jump because maybe this was fate, it was meant to be, and thirty years from now, she and Oliver would laugh and tell friends the story of how, if it hadn't been for a kind-hearted glazier, they would never have met at Oliver's cousin's lunch party.

The replacement window was installed in record time, while Majella frantically plucked the scary eyebrow. Once the glazier and his frankly extortionate weekend call fee had been paid and the house secured, she jumped into the passenger seat of Dan's Toyota.

"This is so kind of you." She checked her freshly plucked eyebrow in the rearview mirror — still bright red, but it would die down soon enough.

"My pleasure." They left Bude and headed toward St. Carys. "Should you make a call and let them know you'll be there in an hour?"

He was right. Majella rang Judi to update her on the situation and explain that — *hooray* — she'd be joining them after all. Then Dan's ex-wife called him and he told her on hands-free about the unexpected turn his own day had taken.

"She sounds lovely," said Majella when the call was over and Dan's ex-wife had wished her good luck with the potential new man.

"She is lovely. We get on so much better now we aren't married."

Twenty-five minutes later, they reached Menhenick House and he pulled up opposite the open gates. Majella said, "Thank you so much. Can I at least give you some money for the petrol?"

"Don't even think of it. Happy to help." Dan frowned, gazing through the open gates. "Who's that over there, the chap in the hat? You know who he reminds me of? That old actor . . . the one with all the ex-wives . . ."

"Sir Richard Myles, you mean? That's my father-in-law."

"You must hear it all the time then," said Dan. "I bet people are always saying it. Your father-in-law looks just like him."

Time was of the essence. Majella opened the passenger door. "You've been brilliant. Thanks for finding the passports, and for the lift . . ."

Jokingly he shooed her away. "Off you go. Get yourself done up and knock this guy's socks off. I hope it goes well for you."

Majella ran a hand over her hair to smooth it down, which was especially pointless seeing as she was about to jump in the shower. "Me too. I'm starting to get nervous now."

"Hey, just relax and enjoy yourself." Dan's smile was reassuring as he knocked the car into gear. "No need to be nervous. Remember, he's the lucky one."

As soon as it was safe to pull up at the side of the road, Lainey stopped and called Seth's number.

He picked up on the second ring. "It's OK if you missed it, you did your best."

"No, I got there just in time."

"Oh thank *God.*" She heard him exhale with relief.

"Poor Mrs. Gardner. She and her husband were waiting in the taxi at the entrance to the main gate. She burst into tears when she saw me with the passports. Honestly, it was worth all the agony."

"Thanks so much for doing it. You're a star."

His words made her flush with joy. "Two minutes to spare — I bet the taxi driver had to actually drive up the gangplank and fling them onto the ship — *Aargh!*" Lainey jumped in her seat as the earth-shaking blast of the ship's horn sounded behind her.

When it had finished, Seth said, "And off they go. All thanks to you. Go and get something to eat now."

"I will. I'm going to treat myself," said Lainey, "to a convenience store sausage roll."

"Oh, here she is at last," Judi exclaimed, greeting Majella with open arms and an enthusiastic hug. "And look at her, doesn't she look fabulous?"

And Majella smiled, because she actually did feel fabulous. Having gotten herself showered and ready faster than the speed of light, for once all the preparations had gone well and it felt like an omen. Her makeup was just right, she'd put her freshly washed hair up in a casual topknot, and the loose fronds had curled fetchingly around her face, and her white sundress was the nicest thing she'd bought in years. Glancing around the restaurant, she nodded and waved at several people she knew and took note of those she hadn't met before, searching for Oliver.

Oh no, don't say he was one of those people who put up photos of himself that had been taken thirty years ago. Unable to spot him anywhere, Majella said, "So where's this cousin you were telling me about?"

"Ollie? Oh, he's not here yet. Something came up, but he's going to try to get along later."

Which felt like nature's way of letting you know what an idiot you'd been for thinking your own better-than-expected preparations might have been an omen.

But when at last Oliver did arrive, Majella sent up a silent prayer of thanks, because he was even better looking in real life. Maybe today wasn't going to turn out to be a disaster after all. Then again, mustn't look too keen. Spotting a couple of friends in the open-air section of the restaurant, she made her way over to chat to them, because that was what you were meant to do, wasn't it? At least it had been once, back in the olden days, when she'd last been single and in the market for a man.

Twenty minutes later, a hand came to rest on her hip and a voice murmured in her ear, "Are you playing hard to get?"

Turning, she saw his navy-blue eyes and intimate smile. "Sorry?"

"Come on, my cousin told me I needed to meet you. She also told you that you should meet me. I know, because she told me that too. Yet here you are, completely ignoring me. Hi, I'm Oliver. And you're Majella."

"Hello." She tried to shake his hand, but he was already leaning in to give her a kiss on each cheek. "Sorry, I was just chatting to —"

"I know, I saw. But I'm here now, so you can chat to me instead." Guiding her over to a quieter section of the garden, he said, "So where are we staying tonight? Your place? Because that'd be easier than me having to book a hotel."

Majella said, "Are you joking?"

"Hahaha, of course I'm joking." He pinched the bridge of his nose between his thumb and index finger, then burst out laughing so wildly that everyone turned to see what was going on. "No, really, you're gorgeous. Judi said you lost your husband a while back. So that was careless!"

Viewing him from this angle, Majella saw the distracted look in his beautiful eyes, and the faint dusting of white at the entrance to his left nostril. Pointing from a safe distance, she said, "You've got a bit of powder . . ."

"Oh, thanks!" He sniffed again and vigorously wiped his nose with the back of his hand. "Bloody good stuff, this. Got a few spare wraps if you want some. Have to sell it, mind — can't give it away, no offense. So, you interested?"

To think that she'd been looking forward to meeting him for days. Judi had described her cousin as a lovely guy, great fun and a real extrovert. What a shame she'd forgotten to mention that he was also a drug dealer and a prat.

Oh well, at least she was getting used to being disappointed. "Thanks," she said, "but no thanks."

"Oh whoa, and now you're giving me one of those looks that tells me you've never tried it!" He raised his hands in mock surrender, then leaned in conspiratorially. "Which means you don't know what you're missing. Lighten up, Mary Poppins! Tell you what, I'll do you a couple of wraps half price as a special treat, what d'you say to that?"

He was drinking red wine and had evidently managed to spill some on his left hand. Majella belatedly noticed the stain on the side of her favorite new dress where he'd rested his hand on her hip.

"I say, see that guy over there?" She pointed to a fiftysomething man she'd never seen before in her life. "He's a good friend of mine and he's also a detective inspector with the Devon and Cornwall Police."

CHAPTER 31

The sun had been shining all day in Saint Ives and the temperature was perfect. Against all the odds, it had also turned out to be one of the best weddings Wyatt had ever attended.

His ankle, snugly encased in the stormtrooperish surgical boot, was still swollen but no longer too painful to stand on, though the narrow, winding staircases and lack of an elevator at this hotel would have made it tricky to navigate his way up to the fourth floor, which was why it made sense to travel back to Mariscombe House tonight. Having driven them down here at lunchtime, Kit had spent the afternoon exploring Saint Ives. When Bella, the bride, had heard that he would be driving them home to St. Carys later, she'd promptly insisted that he join them for the evening party.

"Is he good-looking?" she said.

When Wyatt had hesitated, wondering how he was meant to reply to that, Penny had exclaimed, "Oh, wait till you see him. He's gorgeous! And so lovely too!"

"In that case, tell him to get himself over here." Bella beamed. "I've got three single bridesmaids all gagging to meet the man of their dreams!"

Whereupon Penny, her eyes sparkling after three glasses of prosecco, replied playfully, "They might have to get past me first."

The bride had laughed before casting a quick glance in Wyatt's direction to check that laughing was allowed.

And Wyatt had pretended he was fine with it, but deep down he experienced a brief sharp pang of envy. Or was it jealousy? He couldn't tell which.

Oh well.

The band was good, though. Since the floor was shiny and attempting to dance would be playing with fire, he sat, temporarily alone, at one of the tables dotted around the perimeter of the function room and tapped his good foot along with the music. They were belting out a song by Take That and the dance floor was full of people giving it all they had, but there was only one couple whose progress Wyatt was following.

Penny's fine golden hair swung around her

shoulders and her face was a picture of joy as Kit twirled her in a circle and did a bit of fancy footwork that made her laugh before reaching for her waist and pulling her into a reverse twirl. She had perfect timing, loved to dance, and was more than a match for him. Others were noticing them too and casting admiring glances in their direction, because they were such a great pairing and were so obviously having a ball.

Wyatt took a swallow of Bacardi and Coke and carried on tapping his foot, wishing he hadn't broken his ankle. What he wouldn't give for it to be him out there.

"You want to keep an eye on her," Baz, one of his friends, called out jokingly as he made his way past with a tray of drinks. "Or who knows what might happen?"

"If you want to be helpful," said Wyatt, "you could ask her to join you for the next dance."

The music ended, and with a wink, Baz made his way over and succeeded in breaking up the pairing. Although how thrilled Penny would be when she discovered he danced like a giraffe was anyone's guess.

Kit returned to their table and thirstily glugged down half a pint of water.

"It is hot in here," Wyatt said. "I was about to head outside for some fresh air."

"Good idea. I'll join you."

Out on the terrace, they found a wooden bench away from two groups of wedding guests competing to see who could be the noisiest.

"This must be boring for you," said Wyatt as Kit took another swallow of water. "Not knowing anyone and not even able to have a drink to take the edge off."

"It's fine. Don't worry. I've never been much of a drinker anyway."

"You must let me pay you for doing this. You gave up your day off."

"Hey, it's not a problem. I didn't have any other plans." His smile wry, Kit added, "If anything, you've taken my mind off someone who isn't interested in me, so that's a good thing." He craned his neck, checking that Penny was OK inside. "That guy's a terrible dancer."

"I know."

"Does it bother you, seeing her dancing with someone else?"

"What, with Baz? Not at all." Wyatt brushed aside a fluttering moth. "So, who wasn't interested in you?"

"Oh, I'm not heartbroken. Lainey warned me it wasn't likely to pan out." Kit shrugged. "But you know what it's like, sometimes you can't help thinking that maybe you could be the one they've been waiting for all their lives."

Wyatt nodded slowly. For the moment, he couldn't think of what to say.

Kit said, "Sorry, am I being insensitive? I mean, it's great that you and Penny are still able to be friends, but it can't be easy. Especially for you."

"It isn't a problem." If only he knew. Wyatt took a sip of his Bacardi, keen to change the subject. "Where'd you meet this girl then?"

"What girl?"

"The one who wasn't interested in you."

"Oh!" Kit looked amused. "It wasn't a girl; it was a guy. Sorry, didn't you know? I thought someone might have mentioned it."

Across the terrace, a girl shrieked with laughter, having fallen off her high heels while trying to twerk energetically like Beyoncé. Wyatt used the distraction to gather his thoughts, but it was hard to concentrate when your mouth had gone dry and your heart was suddenly hammering against your ribs. After a few seconds, once the girl had been hauled out of the flower bed by her friends, he said, "No, I didn't know. I'm not very good at figuring out that kind of thing."

"No reason why you should be. I suppose I just imagined Lainey or Majella might have said something. Sometimes it crops up in conversation; sometimes it doesn't."

He sounded so relaxed. Wyatt waved away an invisible insect and took another gulp of his drink in an effort to get his breathing back under control. He was remembering yesterday's fall on the path leading down to Mariscombe beach, and Kit helping him to his feet, and the way his skin had reacted to the sensation of Kit's bare arm around his waist as he'd supported him all the way back to the hotel.

"What was it like?" He heard the words escaping from his mouth as if someone else were saying them. "Coming out?"

Kit looked at him. Then his mouth softened into an almost-smile. "To my mum, you mean? An awful lot easier than I expected it to be, if I'm honest. Same as with the rest of my family and friends. Compared with all those months and years of endlessly worrying about how everyone was going to react, the relief once it was out there was just incredible."

"Right." Wyatt swallowed and nodded slowly.

"That was a while back now. Best thing I ever did."

"That's good." Wyatt cleared his throat.

"Easier for some people than others, of

course," Kit said gently.

"Yes."

"Have you ever told anyone?"

"No." Wyatt shook his head. "I never have."

Kit's voice remained calm. "You can practice saying it to me if you like."

How many times had he looked at his reflection in the mirror and uttered the words? Dozens, maybe even hundreds of times. But only ever when he'd been alone, never when another person had been present.

Well, apart from the time he'd gone to view his grandmother in the funeral home, but no one who was still breathing.

He looked up at Kit, who gave him an encouraging nod. "I'm gay," said Wyatt.

"There. Well done."

Inside, the music had stopped for a few moments and through the windows, they saw Penny making her way out onto the terrace. As she came over to join them, she was fanning herself. "Phew, it's cooler out here! And that was an experience I won't forget in a hurry — Baz is great, but he's a shocking dancer."

"I've got something to tell you," said Wyatt. "I'm gay."

For a second, silence shimmered in the

honeysuckle-scented night air. Then, Penny leaned across to take his hand and gave it a squeeze. "Oh, darling. Thank you for telling me. I love you."

She didn't sound very surprised. Then again, Wyatt supposed, she had less reason to be than most.

"Did you know?"

She smiled, reached sideways, and planted a fond kiss on his cheek. "It crossed my mind. I had an inkling, let's say."

"Because we didn't sleep together."

"Pretty much." Another compression of his hand in her smaller one.

"I'm sorry."

"Don't you dare apologize. Everything's going to be fine."

"It's the family," said Wyatt. "They never stopped talking about how I needed to find myself a nice girl, settle down, and start having kids." He looked at her, willing her to understand.

"And I was the nice girl," said Penny.

"I thought I could change. I really wanted it to work out for us. My brothers . . . they always teased me because I wasn't going out to clubs and bars, putting myself out there like all the other guys and sleeping with . . . well, anything in a skirt. And Mom would tell them off, which just made it a hundred times worse because then they teased me more."

"Maybe she was defending you because she knew."

"I don't think so. She used to tell me privately not to worry, the right girl was out there somewhere and I'd get there in the end. And the thing is, how *could* she know, when I wasn't even sure myself? I didn't know *what* I was feeling. I was confused, and the thought of upsetting Mom and Dad was just unbearable . . . I couldn't do it to them."

"Would they be upset, though?" said Penny. "Really?"

Wyatt spread his arms in defeat. "Who knows? You never can tell."

"They're lovely people. I think they'd be fine."

"But what if they aren't?"

"I know how you're feeling," said Kit. "I was worried too. And my mum's fantastic," he added, "but there was always the creeping fear that she might be disappointed."

Penny said, "And was she?"

"No, she was brilliant. I was lucky. But I already knew that."

"My brothers will be unbearable." Wyatt's forehead creased. "They'll tease me like you wouldn't believe."

"I'll teach you some killer one-liners to knock them flat," said Kit. "And don't worry, I went through all that with some of my mates from school. The novelty soon wears off, I promise."

The future was beginning to sound less daunting already. Wyatt felt his spirits lift a notch. Because he'd enjoyed saying it before, he announced it again.

"I'm gay." Emboldened, he addressed his imaginary brothers. "Get used to it."

Penny clapped her hands. "Bravo. Brilliant."

"So this is where you've been hiding! I wondered where you'd all gotten to," bellowed Baz, heading toward them with a sloshing pint of lager in each hand. "Bloody hot in there, isn't it? Everyone all right?" He paused, surveying the three of them. "Not interrupting anything, am I?"

Wyatt looked at Baz; the two of them had worked together for the last three years. Baz was a blokey bloke, a relentless skirt-chaser, like most of the twentysomething males at their company and not unlike Wyatt's own brothers. Wyatt smiled up at him. "Not at all. We were just chatting about what it's like to be gay."

Baz did a snort and a comedy double take. "Why'd you want to talk about that?"

"Because I'm gay."

"You? No you're not."

"Yes, I am."

"Seriously?"

"Yes."

"Wow."

"No big deal." As he said it, Wyatt felt himself growing braver; he'd started, so he'd finish. "And you don't have to worry — I don't secretly fancy you. You're not my type."

"Well, that's . . . I don't know what to say." Baz spread his hands. "That's . . . great." He hesitated, at a loss, and cast a cautious glance in Penny's direction. "I mean, I'm guessing. Is it great?"

"It is." Happiness swelled in Wyatt's chest; it was like jumping off a cliff and discovering you could fly.

"It's definitely great." Penny patted his arm.

"Right. If everyone's OK with it, that's cool." Still adjusting to the news, Baz said, "Does everyone at work know? Am I, like, the last one to find out?"

Still beaming, Wyatt shook his head. "Nope, quite the opposite. You're the first."

"Oh wow, that *is* cool. Thanks, man. I'm . . . honored. Sorry, does that sound weird?"

"It doesn't sound weird. It sounds fantastic." And now Wyatt could feel his throat tightening with emotion, because he'd been too scared to admit the truth for years, and now his clumsy, well-meaning, ultra-macho work colleague was the one who was anxious not to say the wrong thing.

"Oh, phew." Visibly relieved, Baz grinned and held out his arms, splashing yet more lager onto the flagstones. "Come here, mate, give us a hug."

When they broke apart, after much mutual and only semi-awkward back slapping, they heard the sound of the band inside striking up the opening bars of Elton John's "I'm Still Standing."

Baz's eyes lit up. "I bloody love this song. Shall we get back inside now?" He looked at Penny and Wyatt. "Hit that dance floor?"

Wyatt hesitated. Baz was already making enthusiastic giraffey neck movements and waggling his hips as if swishing an imaginary tail.

"Thanks, but you're all right." He indicated his crutch and his surgical boot. "Floor's a bit slippery. Better not."

Sometimes a broken ankle came in handy after all.

CHAPTER 32

Having collected Harry from his after-school karate club on Monday evening, Lainey arrived back at Menhenick House to find Seth's car on the driveway and Seth unloading bags from the trunk. Her heart did a little jiggle at the sight of him leaning forward to haul out the black case that had been pushed to the back, and not only because the view from where she was standing was pretty amazing, what with his long legs in faded jeans, those finely muscled arms, and that section of taut, tanned stomach revealing itself for a second as he reached up to close the trunk.

She breathed out slowly; she wouldn't admit it to anyone else, least of all Seth, but she missed him when he was away. Like, missed him a *lot*. For the last few days, while he'd been working in Bristol, it just hadn't been the same. She looked forward to being able to see him, to talk to him and make him smile, because that in turn made *her* feel zingy and alive.

All the symptoms of a massive crush, obviously. But that was OK. So long as she kept it to herself, where was the harm?

"Here, you can make yourself useful." He held out one of the big canvas bags. "Give me a hand getting these into the house, will you?"

And once they were in the kitchen, and Harry had raced upstairs, he added over his shoulder, "Could you unpack that stuff for me?" before busying himself replying to a text on his phone.

Which made Lainey feel a bit like Cinderella, although that was unfair, since it was her job to organize their lives and do as she was told.

He'd been to an upmarket deli by the look of things. As she began to empty the bag, Lainey said, "Ooh, champagne truffles," because they were her favorite treat at Christmas. "And cheese straws — God, I love cheese straws." Next came a box containing a spherical bottle of Chambord, the blackberry liqueur she'd only discovered last year, and with it the growing suspicion that Seth must be about to get together with Dawn, because these were the kind of luxury items you took over to your glamorous girlfriend's house . . .

Unless it had already happened, and Dawn had spent the last few days with him at his flat in Clifton, having stupendous, glamorous sex and enjoying every moment of their romantic reunion.

Aware of Seth glancing at her across the room and terrified of giving herself away, Lainey pulled out a packet of smoked almonds and said overly brightly, "Oh, aren't these amazing? I can't believe you've bought them! And maraschino cherries — when I was at school, I once spent a whole week's pocket money on a jar of cherries because I couldn't believe how amazing they were — *Oh.*" And this time she stopped dead, clutching a packet of salted caramel shortbread and frowning in disbelief, because these were all items of food that anyone in their right mind would love to eat, but the last remaining item in the bottom of the bag was a jar of pickled walnuts.

She'd never in her life met another human being who liked pickled walnuts. "The penny," said Seth. "It drops at last."

Lainey looked at him, saw that he was shaking his head and trying not to laugh. "These are my all-time favorite things."

"I know. I was expecting you to have figured that out a little more quickly than you did."

"I thought you'd bought them for Dawn. I just kept thinking what an incredible co-incidence it was that she loves all the same stuff as me."

Seth said, "I broke up with Dawn, remember?"

He broke up with her and they aren't back together, la-la-la-la-laaaaa.

Before she could start beaming like an idiot, Lainey said, "But how did you know they were my favorites?"

Which was another pretty daft question, as confirmed by Seth's raised eyebrow. "I gave Kit a call and asked him to email me a list."

Lainey gave in with good grace. "Of course you did." And Kit had risen majestically to the occasion. They might only have known each other for eighteen months, but he was one of those people who paid attention to what you said and had the knack for remembering tiny details you might have mentioned in passing.

"He did a great job," Seth continued, "and I can understand most of it. But *these* . . ." He reached across the table for the jar of pickled walnuts and pulled a face. "They look like little brains in gone-off embalming fluid."

"You'll hurt their feelings. Have you ever had them before?"

"I think I can safely say no."

"Well, don't knock a pickled walnut until you've tried it," said Lainey. "Go on, now's your chance."

Seth unscrewed the lid, speared one of the walnuts with a fork, and put it in his mouth.

"And?" Lainey prompted, because his face remained expressionless.

Once he'd chewed and swallowed, he said, "They taste like little brains in gone-off embalming fluid."

"I love them."

"Clearly you do. The question is how? They're bitter." He grimaced. "And sharp."

"It's an acquired taste," Lainey admitted. "My grandparents had a huge walnut tree in their back garden. My grandad used to bottle them in the kitchen, but no one else would ever eat them. I felt sorry for him because doing all the walnut preparation took hours, so I forced myself to get used to the taste, and it just made him so happy to know that someone else liked them . . . which in turn made *me* happy, because I loved him so much." She shrugged. "And somewhere along the way, I eventually got to like them because they reminded me of him."

"Well, now you've made me feel bad. But I'm sorry, I still think they taste disgusting."

"You're allowed to think that. My Granny Ivy used to feel the same way about them. Well, most people did." Lainey took the cellophane off the Hotel Chocolat champagne truffles and held the box out to him. "Here, have one of these to take the taste away. Honestly, this is so kind — I can't believe they got you to go out and buy all these things. You'll have to give me the Gardners' phone number so I can send them a text."

After a pause, Seth said, "Why?"

"To say thank you and let them know how lovely they are!" She looked at him, confused. "Didn't they do it to thank me for getting their passports down to Southampton?"

He shook his head. "Sorry, no. It was me thanking you for doing it."

"Oh. Wow. Well, thank *you,* then."

Straight-faced, Seth said, "You can tell me how lovely I am if you want to."

Lainey croaked, "Goes without saying," then made a production of taking the box back and helping herself to one of the truffles so she couldn't blurt out anything like: *I know you are! I can't stop thinking about how lovely you are! I've been thinking it for weeks!*

Because that would be *so* undignified, and if she did ever accidentally say it, she would have to move to Australia.

She was saved by Harry bursting back in. "Violet just called me an ignoramus! What's an ignoramus? Oh cool, can I have one of those?" His eyes lit up at the sight of the chocolate truffles.

"No," said Lainey. "But if you're very good, you can have one of those little brains."

Hours later, while she was finishing loading the dishwasher after dinner, Seth came into the kitchen. "All done for the evening now?"

"Pretty much." She closed the dishwasher with a practiced swing of her hip and switched it on. "Why? Do you need me for something?"

"Only if you don't have anything else planned. And not for long."

As he said it, India's music was blaring out upstairs and they heard Violet yell, "Could you have some respect for my eardrums? Some of us are trying to do our homework here."

"God, you're such a loser," India bellowed back from her room on the other side of the landing.

CRASH went Violet's door, followed by the volume of the music in India's room being whacked up to maximum, almost but not quite drowning out the sound of Harry shouting instructions to his friends through his headset as he battled on his Xbox.

"Oh, *Glenda*," Majella wailed from the sitting room. "*Naughty* girl, look what you've done to my slipper!"

"Shall we head down to the beach?" said Seth. "It'll be quieter."

"*Aaarrrgh!*" bellowed Harry. "*You've killed me! Now I'm dead!*"

Lainey said, "Right now, New Year's Eve in Trafalgar Square would be quieter than this." She dried her hands on the sides of her skirt. "Come on, let's go."

The sand was still warm underfoot. She kicked off her yellow flip-flops and Seth removed his deck shoes so they could walk along the shoreline. The last few vacationers were packing up and leaving the beach now, and over to the west, the sun was sinking lower, spreading a tangerine glow across the duck-egg-blue sky. In unison, they swerved to avoid a small boy who was determinedly scooping handfuls of wet sand out of the shallow trench he'd dug to block the progress of the sea.

Lainey tilted her head back, loving the sensation of warmth on her face, the tang of salt in the air, and the simple fact that they were here together. Was anyone looking at them now, watching them as they walked along the sand side by side? Did they assume they were a couple? Were they wondering why they weren't holding hands?

She could almost imagine it, a ghost sensation of his fingers clasping hers, intertwining in such a way that —

"So what I want to know is why you didn't take India along with you to the Gardners' house."

The pleasurable romantic fantasy popped like a bubble.

"Sorry?" Lainey stepped sideways to veer past a clump of dried seaweed. "Oh, I think she was busy with something else."

"No. You didn't want to take her," said Seth. "When I suggested it on the phone, it wasn't even an option." He looked sideways at her. "Why?"

It was the kind of all-seeing look that made you realize it was a good job you weren't a secret agent, with your life depending on your ability to tell a flawless lie.

Lainey gave up trying. "OK, I might be completely wrong, but a few weeks ago, I saw India in the pharmacy on the esplanade.

And I think she stole a bottle of nail polish."

Seth's eyebrows rose. "You think? Did you see her do it?"

"No, but I saw her looking at it. Then she left the shop and the bottle was gone. And the next night she was wearing that exact color. She told me she bought it ages ago."

"But you didn't believe her."

Lainey shook her head. "Sorry. I haven't told anyone else because I don't have proof. I don't want to worry Majella in case I made a mistake. But there was no way I could take India with me to Bude and leave her alone in the Gardners' house. Imagine if they came home from their cruise and noticed something missing."

"Of course you couldn't. And thanks for telling me." Seth raked his hand through his hair. "Shit, though. Why would she do that?"

"No idea. Hopefully it's just a silly phase. Or a dare or something. I did try to gently warn her about consequences, but . . . well, you know what girls are like. She wasn't interested."

"Should I have a word with her, d'you think?"

"If you do, she'll know I told you. Leave it for now," said Lainey. "I'm keeping an eye on her as best I can."

"OK." He stopped walking, turned to face her. A light breeze ruffled his dark hair and the angle of the sun on his face accentuated his cheekbones. "I hope you know how much we appreciate you. And Kit too, of course."

Lainey's tongue glued itself to the roof of her mouth. She nodded like an idiot and made a high-pitched bat squeak before the saliva kicked back in. "We like it here."

"And we like having you here. Both of you." Seth hesitated, his gaze intent. "But especially you."

Lainey trembled as an avalanche of adrenaline swooshed its way through her veins. This was electrifying, even more so than when she'd woken up next to him on the sofa in Bristol. Now they really did look like a couple about to experience a deeply romantic moment on the beach. Here they were, facing each other, gazing into each other's eyes, and it felt as if they were having an entire conversation without uttering so much as a single word:

Lainey, I probably shouldn't be saying this.

No, you probably shouldn't.

But I want to kiss you.

I want to kiss you too.

Have you ever imagined how it would feel?

Honestly? Many, many times.

Me too. And I suppose there's only one way to find out if we imagined it right.

Oh my God, is this really about to happen?

I really think it is.

Well, OK then! Let's do it!

"Ach," said Seth.

Lainey's eyes had begun to close in anticipation. As he took a sudden step back, they snapped open again. Following the direction of his gaze, she glimpsed a slender dark-haired figure wearing a long white dress, her pink-and-orange scarf fluttering in the sea breeze as the waves lapped at her bare feet.

Had she chosen the scarf specially to coordinate with the sunset behind her?

If she had, it was a stroke of genius.

"It's Dawn," Seth murmured.

"Yes." Of course it was. And she'd been watching them. Crashing back into the real world, Lainey moved awkwardly to the left and pointed like a child in a school play at a small crab scurrying across the sand. "Look, a crab!"

A rueful, can-you-believe-it smile lit up Seth's face. "Well, isn't that just incredible? A crab on a beach. Whatever next?"

It was one of those situations you really wished weren't happening. Lainey made a big show of checking her watch. "I should get back. I think you're the reason she's here." Because Dawn's cottage was closer to Beachcomber Bay, which meant coming this far across town must have been deliberate.

"I'm not seeing her anymore."

"I know, but still." The moment had passed, the mood was broken. "You can't ignore her. And Kit's expecting me back; he'll be wondering where I've gotten to." Not strictly true, but it would do.

"OK." Seth exhaled slowly, then nodded. "Fine. I'll see you tomorrow."

She nodded and gave Dawn a little wave of acknowledgment before turning and heading back up the beach in the direction of Menhenick House.

It had so nearly happened. Nearly, but not quite. Oh well, maybe tomorrow . . .

CHAPTER 33

On Tuesday morning, leaving the car in the hotel parking lot until he was able to drive again, Wyatt and Penny caught the train that would get him back to London. Penny gave him a huge hug before getting off at Bristol. "Good luck. Let me know how it goes."

His parents, Betsy and Charles, had moved over from New York five years ago in order for his father to overhaul the London branch of the family investment bank. Now that Charles had finally taken retirement at his wife's insistence, they split their time between Holland Park and the dazzling twelfth-floor duplex apartment overlooking Central Park. Every time Wyatt arrived at either building, he found that Betsy, whose passion was interior design, had meticulously planned and overseen the redecoration of yet another room.

By the time he reached the house, the butterflies were really beginning to kick in. But there couldn't be any backing out; it had to be done — face-to-face and before they had a chance to hear the news by any other means.

He hauled himself awkwardly out of the taxi and made his way up the white stone steps to the glossy black front door.

"Oh, honey, whatever's happened to you? What have you done this time?"

More than you think, thought Wyatt as he kissed his mother on the cheek. "It's nothing, just a little break, same part of the ankle as before. I slipped on a path leading down to the beach." As he said it, he remembered being helped up by Kit, to whom he owed so much. It was thanks to Kit that he'd said those all-important words for the first time, and now all he had to do was keep on saying them until everyone knew.

In the vast ivory-and-silver kitchen with its marble central island as large as a billiards table, his father was filling in the *Telegraph* crossword while watching rolling CNN news on one iPad and an international golf tournament on another. "Does this mean you're off work for a bit?" He raised an eyebrow at the surgical boot.

"It's fine, Dad. I'll be back in the office tomorrow."

His mother poured him a coffee. "So how

was the wedding? And how did you and Penny get on?"

"The wedding was great. We had the best time."

"That sounds promising! Do you think there's a chance of you getting back together?"

He saw the hope in her eyes. "There's no chance of that, none at all. We're —"

"Oh, but, honey, you don't know that for sure! Give her a bit more time and she might change her mind."

"She isn't going to. And neither am I." Here we go. "Mom, Dad, the reason I've come to see you today is because there's something I need to tell you."

His mother laughed. "Oh, how funny. That's what Charlene's son Ricky said when he came home from Bali and told her he was gay!"

Wyatt's father muted CNN. For a couple of seconds, absolute silence reigned in the kitchen, until the British commentator on the second iPad exclaimed, "Oh, I say, whoops-a-daisy, straight into the bunker on the seventeenth hole! That's not ideal, is it?"

Wyatt took a breath. "Well, there's a coincidence . . ."

"Yes, but Ricky said it because he was

gay." Baffled, his mother shook her head. "You aren't gay!"

"Actually —"

"You asked Penny to *marry* you. It's not your fault she said no."

"Mom, the thing is —"

"It's such a shame. That beautiful chateau would have been the perfect setting for the wedding . . ." Her voice trailed away and she gazed at him, searching his face for clues, just as she always had when he'd gotten his exam results from school. In a quieter voice, she said hesitantly, "*Are* you gay? Is that what you're here to tell us?" Another thought belatedly struck her. "Or are you ill?"

Wyatt said, "Which would you prefer?"

His mother closed her eyes, then opened them again. "I'd rather you were gay."

"Well, that's good to know." He managed a half smile. "Your wish has been granted."

A stunned silence was eventually broken by Betsy's strangled sob, a sound that wrenched at Wyatt's heart. Her face was pale, the flats of her hands pressed to her sternum. "I'm sorry, just give me a minute . . ." she said jerkily before turning and exiting the kitchen in a rush.

They heard her feet hurrying up the stairs, and Wyatt felt sick. After a couple more seconds, his father murmured, "I'd better go and check on her," and disappeared too.

"Oh dear," chuckled the golf commentator, "and now he's landed in the water. That didn't go according to plan!"

They were gone for ten minutes, and it felt more like ten hours. Wyatt already knew from scouring the internet that you could never predict how parents would react to the news. He had to be prepared for them to cast him out of their lives, to refuse to see or speak to him again. Anxiety was rising up inside him. He'd never had a panic attack, but this could be the beginning of one. He filled a glass with ice water from the fridge, then nearly dropped it on the marble-tiled floor as the kitchen door opened once more.

"Oh, honey, I'm so sorry," his mother blurted out, her eyes red-rimmed and her arms outstretched. "It's fine, it's fine. I just knew I was going to cry and didn't want you to get the wrong idea. You're my baby boy and I love you so much . . . We both do, don't we, Charles? So long as you're happy, that's all that matters." She was hugging him now, fiercely. "I'm worried that life isn't always going to be easy for you.

But we can deal with that, one day at a time."

There were more tears after that, on both sides, an outpouring of confusion and acceptance, and love and relief. Even Wyatt's father, who categorically *wasn't* the crying kind, wiped his eyes at one point and embraced his son and tried to pretend he wasn't still half listening to the progress of the golf tournament.

"It wasn't a shock, honey," his mother said for the sixth time. "It was just a surprise, that's all."

"Mom, it's OK," he reassured her yet again. "You're allowed to be surprised. It's a pretty big thing to get used to."

"All we want is for you to be happy. Don't we, Charles?"

His father nodded and said gruffly, "Of course we do. The boy knows that."

As he was leaving, Wyatt's mother stroked his face. "Take care now, baby. We love you so much. Are you going to be all right?"

Who knew what the future held? But wasn't that the case for everyone, regardless of whether they were gay, straight, or anything else at all? Wyatt felt as if his heart might burst with love for his parents, who only wanted the best for him.

"Yes, Mom. You don't have to worry. I'll be fine."

CHAPTER 34

Majella had left work early on Tuesday afternoon to get her hair done, which meant Seth was alone in the office on the top floor of Menhenick House when the landline began to ring. As he reached along the desk to answer it, he glanced out of the window at Lainey, down in the garden, chasing after Ernie with a hose. Which meant Ernie had been rolling in fox poo again but was also thoroughly enjoying this game of making it as difficult as possible for Lainey to wash it off.

"Hello, Faulkner Travel."

"Seth? Is that you?"

"It is." He didn't immediately recognize the voice.

"Hi, darling, it's Shelley, your mum's friend. How are you, all good? Now listen, what's Christina done with her phone? I've been calling her all morning, but I can't get through."

"Who knows?" said Seth. "It's either run out of battery, or she forgot she was holding it when she jumped into a swimming pool." His mother treated phones like disposable razors and went through them at a rate of knots. "Probably easier to send her a text or an email."

"Oh, darling, my new nails are too long. I can't be bothered with all that malarkey. Anyway, I'm having my neck done this afternoon — I just wanted to update Christina with a bit of news before I forget. Could you be an angel and pass on the message?"

Wrinkle-free necks, nails too long to text . . . what a life some people led. Outside the window, Lainey let out a shriek of laughter as Ernie doubled back and cannoned into her legs, resulting in her losing her grip on the hose and showering herself with cold water. Seth picked up a pen. "Of course. Fire away."

"OK, well, it's about Matteo. He's someone we knew years ago. I already told Christina he was pretty ill . . ."

Matteo. The pen remained in midair above the notepad. "She mentioned him to me."

"That's it, Matteo with the hair, went around dressed like a rock star. Anyway, I spoke to his sister this morning and she told me why he'd become so reclusive. Poor thing, it's so sad. I'd assumed he was dying of a brain tumor or some such, but it's actually a dreadful disease, one of those ones that destroys your brain, slowly eats it away . . . Digestive? No, that's not the word . . . Oh, what is it?"

"Degenerative," said Seth.

"That's the one! And he's been in a terrible state for years, getting worse and worse, which is why he never married or had children, because it's one of those diseases that can be hereditary and his father died of the same thing. Isn't that just awful? Horrendous! And now he's so ill he's looked after by a team of nurses and can't do anything for himself, not even say his own name, so do warn Christina not to try to call him for a catch-up. God, though, isn't it just *tragic*? All these years he's been disintegrating and we never knew . . . Ooh, they're telling me the anesthetist's on his way. Let's hope he's got loads of lovely drugs to give me. Gotta love a sedative! Now, tell Christina that she won't be able to call me for the next ten days, because I'm going to be recuperating on Jerry's yacht and he's refusing to let me take my phone because apparently I spend all my time on it, like I'm an *addict* or something!"

"OK," said Seth when she stopped prattling on.

"Oh bugger, and now one of my extensions has just fallen out. How *bloody* infuriating. I only had them redone last night!"

"Did his sister mention the name of the disease Matteo has?" Seth didn't want to ask, but he needed to know before Shelley hung up.

"She did," said Shelley. "Oh, hello, Doctor. Could you be an angel and pick that extension up for me? No, not the extension plug. That strip of hair on the floor . . ."

The call had ended several minutes ago, but Seth still hadn't moved. Shelley had told him the name of the disease, and in that split second, the world had tilted on its axis. It felt as if the sun had gone in, except it hadn't. Down in the garden, both dogs were now darting back and forth, gleefully running rings around Lainey.

He exhaled, mouth dry. Lainey, the girl who'd inveigled her way into his heart, who he'd finally decided was the one for him, the girl he'd realized last night he could no longer resist.

And now this had happened, something potentially so life-altering that his brain was still struggling to take it in. Of course, Shelley had no idea of the significance of what she'd told him; to her, it was irrelevant, no more than a mildly interesting snippet of information about someone she'd known for a short period of time over three decades ago.

Seth turned away from the window, aware of the growing sense of fear in his chest. It was all very well having zero interest in ever meeting the man who could be his biological father, but this was an altogether different situation. He might share this man's — this stranger's — genetic mutation. This was the kind of dilemma no one wanted to find themselves in. He wished he didn't know, but it was too late. And there was no way of unknowing.

Right now, he was aware of being in a state of shock. He also felt as if he was never going to be able to think about anything else again. He felt sick. He felt numb and cold and alone. Above all, he wished he didn't know, in agonizing detail, just what this illness did to those in its grasp.

But he did, because he'd seen it for himself, growing up in Chelsea. He and Christina had lived at 32 Billingham Road, and next door to them at number 34 had been Mr. Kay and his wife. Mrs. Kay had asked Seth to call them Auntie Helen and Uncle Rob, though it had always been an effort to do so. She was thin and sad and anxious, understandably so, and her husband was a wheelchair-bound shell of a man in the final stages of a neurodegenerative disease, frail and unpredictable.

A nurse lived with them, helping to take care of Mr. Kay, and Mrs. Kay was always inviting the neighbors over for tea. When this happened, Christina invariably said, "Oh, I'm so sorry. I can't make it, but Seth would love to come over!" And then, when he did, poor Mrs. Kay — Auntie Helen — would get out the photo albums and show him endless photos of Uncle Rob before the illness had taken its toll . . . surfing in Portugal, climbing in the Alps, playing tennis and visibly enjoying every moment of his life. Unlike the current Uncle Rob, whose speech was unintelligible and who no longer appeared to recognize his own wife.

"I can't go over there," Christina had explained to Seth. "It's just too awful. That poor woman, I don't know how she can bear it."

Then Uncle Rob had died and his mother had said, "I'm amazed Helen's so upset. You'd think she'd be relieved it was all over."

In many ways, Seth had always been aware that his mother's thoughts and actions were self-serving and questionable. But the fact remained that he was her son and she loved him, and the news that he could be at risk of ending up like Uncle Rob would be devastating for her to hear. Being able to confide in her wouldn't be a comfort; it would just make an unbearable situation worse.

Gathering himself, he picked up his phone and called Shelley back, briefly explaining the Uncle Rob situation and concluding, "You know what Mum's like; it would really upset her to hear that Matteo has the same illness our neighbor had. So it'd be kinder not to mention it, is that OK? There's no reason for her to know."

"Of course, darling. Yes, you're quite right. I love Christina to bits but she's definitely a drama queen, isn't she? Let's not upset her. I won't breathe a word."

"Thanks."

"Ooh, the porter's just arrived to take me down to the operating room! Hello, you're a handsome lad, aren't you? Seth, you should see him. He looks like a young George Clooney!"

"Off you go," said Seth.

"Time to go and get myself a new neck! Bye, darling," Shelley trilled. "Wish me luck!"

CHAPTER 35

The day had finally arrived. It was Thursday lunchtime and Richard had been counting down the hours. He'd offered to meet Nerys off the train, but she'd turned him down flat.

"Oh, no, not in public." The idea was clearly horrifying. "People might see us."

As if the prospect of being spotted in his company was too embarrassing for words.

So instead he'd suggested the back room of the least popular café on the outskirts of St. Carys, because on a sunny summer's day, it would definitely be empty, on account of its grumpy owner, stale cakes, and lurid wallpaper covered in giant purple poppies.

"You don't know for sure it'll be empty." Nerys was clearly still concerned.

"Bring a notebook and pen," Richard told her. "You can pretend to be a journalist interviewing me."

He'd been half joking, but Nerys had exclaimed with relief, "Good plan."

And now here she was, coming through the café to meet him for the first time, checking the back room from the doorway before allowing a shy smile to light up her face as she moved toward him. Her cheeks were pink, her eyes bright, and she was indeed carrying a notebook in one hand and a black Sharpie in the other. She was wearing a pale-gray cardigan over a gray-and-cream polka-dot cotton dress.

"Oh, I can't believe this is happening," she said in her soft Welsh accent. She hesitated a few feet away. "I don't quite know what to do . . . It's a bit strange, what with you being so famous. Shall we shake hands?" She was already transferring the Sharpie from her right hand to her left.

"No." Richard shook his head and held out his arms. "No we will not. Come here."

The hug lasted a long time, and it was just as well the back room of the café was otherwise empty.

Finally, he let her go. "That perfume you're wearing." It had knocked him sideways.

"Shalimar."

"That's it, by Guerlain. I bought it for Sandy . . . she used to wear it all the time."

Nerys's smile widened. "She did? I didn't know that. She bought me a bottle for my twenty-first birthday and I fell in love with it. I've worn it ever since. Well, not every day, obviously." Because perfume was expensive. "But, you know, on special occasions."

Richard gazed down at his daughter, who so strongly resembled Sandy. "Does that mean this is a special occasion?"

"I think it probably counts as one." Nerys hastily wiped her eyes and shook her head apologetically. "I still can't believe it. If only Mum could have been here to see this."

Two hours later, there were three plates of curling sandwiches and six untouched cups of tea in front of them, and the owner of the least popular café in St. Carys was waiting to close up.

"You haven't eaten a thing." She glowered at them.

"Sorry, I was busy interviewing Sir Richard," said Nerys.

"Hmph. Well, you don't seem to have written much down."

Nerys tapped her temple. "Don't worry. It's all up here in my head."

She even tried to pay the bill when it arrived. Richard pushed her purse aside. "Will you *stop* that? Put your money away."

As they were leaving, Nerys said, "This has been amazing. Thank you so much. I'm never going to forget this day."

"Why do you keep looking at your watch?"

"I can catch the next train if I hurry. It leaves at five thirty."

"Don't go," said Richard. "Stay. I want you to meet the rest of the family."

Nerys looked alarmed. "You said they didn't know about me."

"They don't." He'd needed to meet her first, just in case it all went horribly wrong. Now, placing his arm around her shoulders, he said with pride, "But they're about to find out."

The worst café in St. Carys was a kilometer from Menhenick House. As they neared home, still talking nonstop, and paused to cross the road, they realized they were being watched.

"Oh *no.*" Nerys froze in dismay. Because there on the other side of the road, staring at them as if they were a couple of ghosts, was Pauline.

"Oh God," muttered Richard. But it was more a nuisance than a disaster. "Sorry, I completely forgot about her. Never mind, it's fine. We've nothing to hide, have we?"

Pauline's mouth was agape as she looked from Richard to Nerys, then back again. Finally finding her voice, she said, "Nerys? What's going on?"

Next to Richard, Nerys murmured, "Whatever you do, don't tell her."

"I don't understand," continued Pauline. "What are you doing in St. Carys?" She shook her head in bewilderment. "And how are you here with Sir Richard?"

"He . . . replied to my l-letter," Nerys stammered. "The one in the turquoise envelope."

"He never replies to letters."

"I did, though." Richard nodded. "I'm turning over a new leaf after what you said at the hotel last week."

"And you invited Nerys down to *see* you?"

Nerys pulled the notebook out of her bag and waved it. "I asked if I could come and interview him for our parish magazine, and he said yes."

Pauline was now gazing at him askance, as if he'd grown three heads.

Richard shrugged. "It's all thanks to you. You were the one who told me to look out for the turquoise envelope."

"Yes." Nerys nodded eagerly at Pauline. "Thanks for doing that!"

Bewildered, Pauline said, "But you didn't even tell me this was happening. All those times I've invited you down here to come and stay with me in my trailer."

"Oh, I know, but this was the only day Sir Richard could see me, and you'd already said on the group page that you were going to visit your aunt in Dorset."

"Auntie wasn't feeling well, so the trip was canceled."

"Oh, your poor aunt, I'm so sorry to hear that," Richard interjected smoothly, because he was a better liar than Nerys.

"Thank you, Sir Richard." Pauline returned her attention to Nerys. "Well, you're still very welcome to stay with me tonight if you want to."

"That's so kind of you," said Nerys, "but I have to catch the train back this evening."

Once they'd said their goodbyes to Pauline and moved on down the road, Nerys whispered, "I'm going to have to write about you for our parish magazine now."

"No you don't. And listen, you don't need to get the train home this evening either. We've got a beautiful spare room you can stay in." With a jolt, Richard realized he didn't want her to leave.

"I have to get back, though," said Nerys. "I need to be at work first thing tomorrow."

Menhenick House came into view ahead of them. He said, "I wouldn't mind you telling Pauline, you know. Once the family have gotten used to the idea, of course."

"Are you serious? Her big hobby is finding out as much as she can about you and sharing everything she knows with your other fans. She wouldn't be able to keep that kind of secret to herself for one minute."

"But it's OK." Richard frowned. "You're my daughter and I'm your father. I'm not embarrassed by that. I'm proud! It doesn't have to be a secret," he assured her, still scarcely able to believe he was saying and meaning it. "I want to tell the whole world!"

"Oh, but I don't want you to." Nerys touched his arm, clearly concerned. "Please let's not do that."

"Why not?"

"Because you're . . . *you.*" She gestured helplessly. "You're famous, and that's great for you, because you were always happy to be famous. But I'm more like Mum; I'm not one for attention. The thought of people with phones taking my photo and posting stuff about me online . . . it's just not the kind of thing I'd want to have to go through. Sorry, is that rude? I don't want to offend you. I'm so thrilled this has happened and

I'd love us to stay in touch, but the idea of being splashed across the papers is just unbearable. People would think I was looking for attention, and I couldn't bear that."

In the heat of the afternoon, her fair hair had lost its blow-dried bounce, and now Richard was able to see the point at her hairline, just above her left eyebrow, where a whorl of blond hair grew out at an angle. He'd had exactly the same whorl in that precise spot until twenty-odd years ago, when his hairline had receded like the tide.

"What are you looking at?" said Nerys. "Why are you smiling?"

"You have my cowlick." He tapped his own forehead.

She relaxed. "I know. Thanks for passing that on to me; it's been the bane of my life. At least yours has vanished now."

"And at least you don't have to worry about your hairline receding." He offered her his arm. "Let's get inside, shall we? Time to introduce you to the rest of the family. They're about to get a surprise."

When he'd gathered them outside on the terrace, it was with great pride that he was able to relay the full story to them of his relationship with Sandy.

"I had no idea, none at all," he concluded

with a lump in his throat. "But all this time I had a daughter waiting to meet me. And now it's happened, and it's just the best feeling in the world."

"Oh, Richard, what a miracle. This is just the loveliest news." Tears were shining in Majella's eyes as she jumped up and hugged him, then threw her arms around Nerys. "I'm so glad you found each other at last. Welcome, darling! Welcome to the family."

CHAPTER 36

Lainey had stayed in the kitchen while Richard, having first armed himself with a large gin and Fever-Tree tonic, asked the family to join him out in the garden. She kept busy and barely glanced out of the window at whatever might be going on out there.

At least that was the official line, if anyone were to ask. In reality, because she was only human, she glanced out at them roughly every thirty seconds, and by the time Richard returned to the kitchen, she had worked it out for herself.

Wow.

"Come on, come out and join us." Richard was beaming as he beckoned to her. "It's all thanks to you that this has happened." Once they'd reached the others, he announced proudly, "Remember the turquoise envelope? This is Nerys Davies, Sandy's daughter. And you're not going to believe this . . . she's my daughter too!"

Lainey did an excellent job of looking astonished and delighted as she greeted Nerys with a hug and listened to Richard retell the story for her benefit. But what was even more fascinating was the reaction of the rest of the family — minus Harry, whom Kit was collecting from a school friend's house in Port Isaac. Majella, busy topping up drinks and cutting more slices of orange drizzle cake, was her usual cheerful, hospitable self and clearly delighted by the news. Violet seemed happy too. But India was casting troubled glances in Nerys's direction and fidgeting with the phone in her lap, clearly not at all overjoyed by the situation. Her body was tensed up, her shoulders hunched, and she was studying the new arrival intently from behind her magenta fringe. Her hands were stained blue, Lainey noticed; if she wasn't careful, at this rate her over-dyed hair was going to start falling out in clumps.

It was Seth, though, whose reaction was the most puzzling and unexpected of all. Or rather, his lack of reaction. Because the thing about Seth was that he was never distracted, always on the ball, never failing to give anything or anyone his undivided attention. Yet here, sitting next to India while he *appeared* to be listening to Richard,

Lainey instinctively sensed that he was miles away, barely present at all, his mind otherwise occupied by something that was taking up all his attention. Or someone.

And not in a good way either. The habitual half smile and humorous glint in his eye were missing. Was this connected with Nerys's arrival? Or with something else entirely? The business, maybe. Or Dawn. It was impossible to tell.

She kept looking over at him, but he didn't meet her eye, not even once. And to think she'd thought something incredible had been about to happen between them the other night. Being so close to him had felt electrifying, alive with possibilities.

And now he wasn't so much as glancing in her direction.

It wasn't the next stage she'd been hoping for, and as a chill of disappointment slid down her spine, it dawned on her that there was a good chance the cause of Seth's altered mood was embarrassment. Worse still, that the cause of the embarrassment was because he'd changed his mind about *her*.

After Nerys explained that she really did need to catch the train back to Cardiff this evening, Majella offered to drive her to the station, and Richard went with them.

"Well, let's hope we never have to see her again," India said darkly once they'd gone.

"Why are you being so mean?" Violet frowned. "I think she's nice."

"We're fine as we are. We've already got all the family we need."

"Oh, come on. She's Dad's half sister. She's our half aunt! And look how happy Grandad is to have found her."

"She doesn't even look like him!"

"I think she does. I can see a resemblance. Anyway, you're my twin and I don't look anything like you."

"Thank God," said India. "And just you wait. I don't believe all that let's-keep-it-private stuff for one minute. Give her a few weeks and she'll be flogging her story all over the shop. Every tacky magazine she can get to listen to her, she'll be onto them. It'll be like Meghan Markle's half sister all over again."

Violet rolled her eyes. "Has anyone ever told you you're a horrible person? Oh yes, me. About a million times."

"At least I'm not gullible. They haven't even done a DNA test yet."

At this, Lainey glanced across once more at Seth, but he didn't even appear to have heard.

"I wouldn't mind getting one of those

done," said Violet. "Maybe someone took the wrong baby home from the hospital and my real twin's out there somewhere, all alone and missing me like crazy."

"If she's missing you, she really must be crazy. Anyway, shut up." India tossed back her hair. "Go and do some extra homework or something."

"And what are you going to do? Sit in front of a camera and update your vlog, then chat to a bunch of strangers about your new eye shadow, because that's *so* much more worthwhile."

"You're such a nerd."

"And you're such a loser."

The four of them headed back to the house. Reaching the kitchen, Violet helped herself to a packet of chicken slices from the fridge, then gathered up the math textbooks she'd left on the window seat and disappeared upstairs. Having grabbed a family-sized bag of chips, India announced, "She's pathetic. Am I right or am I right?" and turned to Seth for confirmation.

He shook his head. "Sorry, what?"

"Never mind. I'm right. Are *you* OK?"

He nodded. "I'm fine."

"Good." India reached up and gave him a fierce hug. "I might have a ridiculous sister and a really annoying little brother, but at least I've got you."

"You have." Seth patted her on the back. "And I'm not going anywhere."

"Who d'you love more, me or Violet?"

For the first time today, Lainey glimpsed a ghost of a smile on his face; it was evidently a question the twins had been asking him their entire lives.

Seth said solemnly, "You know the answer. I love you both exactly the same."

"But secretly I'm your favorite."

"Secretly," he gave her shoulder an affectionate squeeze, "you both are."

Lainey waited until India had gone up to her room, then took a breath and said, "You're not fine, though. Are you?"

For a fraction of a second Seth met her gaze, then he looked away again, but not before she'd caught a lightning-fast mix of emotions — surprise, pain, temptation, and denial.

Not *that* sort of temptation, the lustful kind; this was more of a wavering hesitation, swiftly followed by the decision to absolutely deny that there was any kind of problem at all.

"It's nothing. Just pressure of work."

"Is it to do with Christina?"

A shake of his head. "No."

"Dawn?"

"No."

"Anyone else?"

His jaw tensed. "I told you. Everything's OK."

Is it me? Lainey couldn't bring herself to ask the question aloud, but she was running out of options. He was tired of the interrogation and had closed himself off. On Monday evening on the beach, she'd felt so close to him, had experienced a connection between them so strong it had seemed inevitable something magical was about to happen . . .

Until Dawn had turned up at exactly the wrong moment. And yes, Seth had maintained it was all over between the two of them now, but he'd also said he'd see Lainey the next day, and that hadn't happened. She'd waited with bated breath, but he hadn't appeared. And what was she meant to do about that? What did it mean?

Looking at the way he was behaving today, something pretty major clearly *had* happened.

Lainey's palms were damp. Unless she'd got it all horribly wrong again, fantasizing that her feelings for Seth were reciprocated. How unbearable would it be if the silent conversation on the beach had in fact only taken place inside her own head?

Oh, but it had felt so *real*. Had she been so carried away thinking tumultuous thoughts that she hadn't even realized Seth's mind was occupied with such prosaic matters as what was happening at work, whether or not to download that new film everyone was talking about, and when he should book his car in for its next service?

From upstairs came the sound of loud pounding music and barking. Soon Majella and Richard would be back from dropping Nerys at the station. Once again, Menhenick House wasn't the ideal place to have a private conversation. But the beach was there, two minutes away and always perfect for the job.

"Look, I don't know what's going on, but something's wrong." Lainey looked directly at Seth. "And it's probably none of my business, so I'm not going to ask any more questions. If you don't want to talk about whatever it is, that's fine." She paused, silently willing him to react. "But if you do want to talk, about anything at all . . . well, I'm here. And you can trust me, you know you can."

Silence in the kitchen. Above them, India's music continued to blare out *thud-thud-thud*. From the corner of her eye, Lainey saw

Seth's knuckles gleam white through tanned skin as his hand gripped the back of one of the kitchen chairs, then glimpsed the faint shake of his head as if he'd been on the brink of saying something before deciding not to.

"OK." She gave it one last try. "I'm going to go down to the beach. Have a walk, get some fresh air. If you want to join me, that'd be great." In the past, while either sitting side by side on the sand or making their way along the shoreline, conversation between them had flowed naturally; maybe the beach was their happy place and this was what they needed. To spur him into action, she crossed to the kitchen door, opened it, and turned to glance over her shoulder. "It's still sunny, may as well make the most of it. Fancy coming along?"

In her head, she added: *Remember what so nearly happened on Monday evening? Remember how you nearly kissed me? Because I know I didn't imagine that.*

"Thanks," said Seth, and for a dizzy moment she thought she'd won . . . before he shook his head. "But I'll give it a miss. Got some work to do upstairs. You go ahead," he added shortly. "Enjoy your walk."

CHAPTER 37

"Aaarrrgh!" Harry let out a bloodcurdling howl. "I've been jellyfished!"

It was a drizzly Sunday afternoon, and Lainey, busy throwing a Frisbee for Ernie and Glenda, hadn't planned on going in for a swim. But Harry was panicking, windmilling his arms and shrieking in his panic to get away from the attacking creature. She tore off her sneakers and launched herself into the sea in her sweatshirt and jeans, heading toward where he was splashing his way over to the rocks at the end of the beach and hoping she wouldn't end up getting stung herself.

"Ow," wailed Harry, having reached the rocks and slipping as he attempted to haul himself up out of the water.

"It's OK, don't panic, just hang on . . ." It wasn't easy to shout words of reassurance when you were doing a fast front crawl and waves kept splashing into your mouth.

Lainey put her head down and concentrated on reaching him. When she was only a few meters away, she saw him scramble out of the water, stumble and fall back a second time.

"Right, I've got you. Lean on me and climb out slowly." She braced herself against the barnacle-encrusted rocks and allowed Harry to use her as a climbing frame, wincing at the swirling cloud of blood he was leaving behind in the water.

At last he was safe and she was able to haul herself up too. He winced as she swiftly checked him over. There was a nasty gash on his knee, presumably barnacle related, a second smaller one on the sole of his left foot, and a long graze down his skinny right arm.

"You'll live." She ruffled his wet hair. "I can't see any signs of jellyfish stings."

"I felt its tentacles against my leg."

Lainey pointed to a tattered remnant of supermarket bag floating in the water.

Plastic, the scourge of the sea. "Might have been that." The trouble with hearing a mention on the radio that jellyfish had been spotted locally was that everything that brushed against you instantly felt like tentacles.

"Oh, maybe. Look how much I'm bleeding." Fascinated, Harry gazed at the mixture of blood and seawater seeping down his shin. "Good job there weren't any killer sharks around!"

Eleven-year-olds and their ghoulish imaginations. Lainey laughed. "Let's get you home. I'm going to carry you over the rocks and down onto the beach, OK?"

"OK." Harry nodded as she readied herself to lift him into her arms. "But mind you don't drop me."

Seth was in his bedroom, throwing clothes into an open suitcase before heading up to Bristol for a few days, when he glanced out of the window at the beach. Thanks to the rain, it was largely deserted, but over at the far end two figures were making their way slowly across the rocks, and the bright-orange board shorts of the smaller figure, being carried by the taller one, were instantly recognizable.

What had happened? What was going on? Snatching up the binoculars on the window ledge, he peered through the curtain of gray drizzle and saw that the taller figure was Lainey, fully clothed and dripping wet. He focused in on Harry and spotted the injuries to his arm and leg. And there were the dogs, barking like crazy from the shoreline as if intent on guiding the two of them home.

His heart had already given a jolt at the unexpected sight of Lainey. Now, as he watched, she briefly lost her footing and stumbled, and his heart crashed against his rib cage again. The plan to avoid her entirely for the next few days clearly wasn't going to work. He needed to get down there and help.

By the time he reached them, the drizzle had turned to hard driving rain.

Lainey's sodden jeans were liberally stained with the blood that was dripping down Harry's skinny leg.

"Is he OK? Did he hit his head?"

"I didn't hit my head," said Harry. "But soon I might not have much blood left." He peered avidly at his injuries. "I reckon I've lost quite a few liters by now."

Lainey said, "He's fine. It looks worse than it is." She eased her way carefully down the sloping rocks and onto the beach.

"Don't put me down on the sand! I don't want sand in my bad foot!"

"You're heavy," Lainey protested. "My arms are dropping off."

Seth said, "Here, give him to me."

"I'll get blood on you," Harry warned.

"I'll survive." As Seth reached out to take him and Lainey began to pass him over, inevitably they made contact and he had to angle his face away in case she saw the effect on him. "Now let's get you home and cleaned up." He glanced at Lainey, her lashes made spiky by the rain, and felt the coldness of her hands against his forearms. "Right, I've got him. Good job. Ernie, get *down.*"

"Waaah," cried Harry as both dogs leaped up, tails wagging madly. "They're licking the blood off my feet and it *tickles . . .*"

When they arrived back at the house, Seth said to Lainey, "You're shivering. Why don't you towel the dogs down, then go and have a shower? I'll get Harry cleaned up, see if he needs stitches."

Whereupon Harry, who was renowned for his many sporting injuries and intensely proud of his own bravery, retorted, "Of course I'll need stitches. I always do."

Fifteen minutes later, showered and changed into dry clothes, Lainey returned to the house and came upstairs to the main bathroom.

"He definitely needs it seen to," said Seth. "Looks like he's sliced his foot open on a mussel shell." He'd wrapped a clean tea towel around the worst injury and stuck Harry's foot in a shopping bag for good measure.

"Do you want to take him to the emergency room, or shall I?" Lainey looked at him, and he felt his resolve weaken.

Harry said, "You could both take me if you want."

"Lainey can take you. I need to get up to Bristol." This was an outright lie; it wasn't a matter of needing to be there — he was just desperate to get away from Lainey. Seth gave Harry a fist bump. "You be brave, OK?"

Harry did a disbelieving eye roll. "I'm the bravest person in this house."

Seth exhaled; just now, he could well be right.

Lainey helped Harry downstairs and into the car. Once he'd heard them drive off up the road, Seth turned his attention back to the bathroom, which looked like a crime scene.

It occurred to him that his mother's idea during her last visit to St. Carys might not have been such a bad one after all. At the time, he'd had no interest in finding out the identity of his biological father. But now the situation was different and infinitely more serious. Under these new circumstances, maybe he did need to know.

He selected the most heavily bloodstained

of the two hand towels he'd used to stem Harry's bleeding. Feeling somewhat repulsed as he did so, he rolled it up, took it into his own room and placed it in a bag at the back of the wardrobe. It might not be the aboveboard way to go about it, but what other choice did he have? They were either half brothers or unrelated; it wouldn't be hard to find out which.

Oh God, though, the creeping fear that hadn't left him since he'd taken the devastating phone call from Shelley was once more pressing down on his chest, constricting his lungs. The last thing he wanted to know was whose son he was, but could he bear to live without knowing the truth?

CHAPTER 38

So here she was then, a living, breathing triumph of hope over experience, yet again giving someone else the opportunity to change her life.

Maybe this one wouldn't be as completely disastrous as the others. On the bright side, he surely couldn't be worse.

For what felt like the hundredth time, Majella checked her watch. She hadn't even had time to mentally prepare herself for this one; downloading the dating app last night had been Violet's bright idea because — in her daughter's blithe words — it'd be a laugh, was worth a shot, and what did she have to lose? Then Lainey had gotten involved, and an hour later, after a couple of bucket-sized glasses of wine and much swiping and laughter, she'd somehow found herself agreeing to meet Niall, a forty-six-year-old former financial adviser from London who now lived in Padstow and painted full-time, because the world was a beautiful place and life was too short not to make the most of every single day and every opportunity that came along.

Well, it was a sentiment she agreed with, in theory at least. And where was the harm in giving it a whirl? She knew she couldn't spend the rest of her life regretting the fact that she'd let a man in a kitten T-shirt slip through her fingers; Dan might have been the perfect one for her, but he'd gone back to wherever it was he lived, and she hadn't even managed to get his surname. Which just went to show what a complete amateur she was, and also meant Dan was a ship that had well and truly sailed off and disappeared over the horizon.

Anyway, being positive, who was to say that Niall wouldn't be better? Maybe this evening would be the start of something magical and miraculous and amazing.

They could gaze into each other's eyes and both experience a *coup de foudre,* that thunderclap of mutual attraction, and every single thing about him might be perfect . . .

Oh God, and here he was now, heading down the hill toward her. Awash with nerves, Majella straightened her spine and prepared to meet her date. One good thing: at least he looked like his photograph.

Although, hang on, was that a guitar on his back?

"Hey! Wow, you're gorgeous, how nice to meet you! What can I get you to drink? Sorry, how rude of me, I'm Niall. And let me tell you, this dating app business is off to a flying start. This is my first go and I'm well impressed!"

Twenty minutes later, Majella found herself starting to relax. Niall was chatty and easygoing, with a wide smile and well-shaped hands. The reason he'd brought his guitar along with him was because he'd been giving a friend's son a lesson earlier and hadn't wanted to leave it in the car in case it got stolen. Playing the guitar was another of his life-enhancing hobbies, he explained, along with songwriting. Did she have any idea how incredible her cheek-bones were? And the curves of her mouth?

Had she ever had her portrait painted? Because she really should; it was a special experience.

"Seriously, I'd love to paint you." He eyed her with the speculative air of an expert. "Your eyes are hypnotic. Oh God, listen to me getting carried away. My sister's been warning me to stay cool, calm, and in control. Ignore me, forget I said that about your eyes. It's just I'm a heart-on-my-sleeve kind of guy." He shook his head by way of apology. "This might sound stupid, but it didn't even occur to me that I'd meet someone I really like."

"It's fine." Majella smiled, slightly embarrassed but at the same time charmed by his honesty. "All that game playing. It's so complicated, isn't it?"

Niall's blue eyes crinkled at the corners. "I'd rather just come out with it and say what's on my mind. And this is turning into the kind of evening I'm not going to forget in a hurry." He reached for his guitar, resting on the chair next to him, and slung the strap over his shoulder. Within seconds, he was strumming chords and gazing directly at her.

Oh no, please no, don't say he was about to start *singing.* Majella's skin prickled in alarm, and she shrank back like a slug being showered with salt.

"Your eyes, your beautiful eyes," he crooned, rocking gently from side to side and smiling dreamily. "And your mouth, such a wonderful mouth . . ."

Aaarrrgh, people at nearby tables were turning to see what was going on.

"But it's your soul, Maj-ellaaa, that's won my heart . . ."

Nooo, make it *stop.*

"You and me together now, never apaaaart . . ."

Majella's toes weren't just curling; they were turning themselves into spirals of mortification, and now Niall was launching into the second verse with increased vigor, as if she'd passed some kind of test and deserved an extra-special treat. Was she meant to be looking at him or not? Smiling as if enraptured, or deadly serious and brimming with emotion? Could the people behind her see the expanding damp patch on the back of her blue silk shirt where perspiration was trickling down her shoulders and spine?

Finally, after what felt like fourteen hours of mental torture, the song came to an end. An awkward smattering of applause broke out around them, and Niall thanked his audience with a raised hand and a modest smile of acknowledgment.

"That was . . . wow." Majella swallowed. "Did you write it yourself?"

"I did. I've been waiting for someone to sing it to." His eyes sparkled. "This evening finally felt like the right time."

"Well, it's . . . great." If they carried on seeing each other, she'd just have to break it to him gently that being sung to in public wasn't her thing and basically she'd rather dive into an alligator swamp.

It was OK, though; the experience might have been excruciating, but it didn't need to be a deal breaker. Much like her very first date with Tony twenty years ago, when he'd turned up wearing a truly terrible Kermit-green corduroy jacket. A couple of months later, she'd surreptitiously donated it to a charity shop and had steered Tony in the right direction when they'd gone shopping together to buy a replacement.

Compromise, that was what a truly happy relationship was all about.

"Are you hungry?" said Niall. "Or do you want to stay here for another drink?"

He hadn't put the guitar down; it was still there, its strings mere centimeters from his playing hand, as if at any moment he might launch into another song. To be on the safe side, Majella said, "Actually, I am quite hungry. Shall we find somewhere to eat? I mean, they do food here if you want . . ."

"I noticed." Niall indicated the plates that had been brought out to a neighboring table, then leaned forward and said discreetly, "But this is a special occasion, isn't it? I think we can do a bit better than burgers and fries."

They arrived at Montgomery's ten minutes later. Majella couldn't help feeling flattered and impressed; the new restaurant overlooking Beachcomber Bay had rapidly become known as one of the best in Cornwall, a bit of a foodie's paradise. The chef was by all accounts wildly talented. She'd not eaten here herself since its doors had opened in December but had heard great things about the place. And the decor, in shades of bronze, dove gray, and mulberry, was luxurious.

Best of all, though, was knowing that if Niall was so keen to bring her here, it must mean he liked her too. It was such a relief to know she didn't have to spend the rest of the evening hoping he did. He'd already told her he would be happy to pay for dinner and she'd explained that she would be more comfortable splitting the bill, but wasn't it lovely of him to have made the gesture? Plus, he'd asked the maître d' to store his guitar in a safe place, so she no longer had to worry that he might be about to whip it out and serenade her again in the middle of the restaurant.

A pretty young waitress handed them their menus and Majella boggled a bit at the prices.

"Cheers!" When their wine had been poured, Niall clinked his glass against hers. "This feels like the start of something special, doesn't it? Here's to you and me."

Despite her rosy glow, Majella couldn't help noticing that the pretty waitress seemed to be keeping a close eye on her. Every time she glanced up, the girl was still watching, like an out-in-the-open secret agent. Maybe being superattentive was all part of the service here. She returned her attention to the menu, debating whether to go for lobster and pomegranate salad or the scallops with prosciutto to start, then looked up again because the waitress was now hovering behind Niall, discreetly pointing in the direction of the back of the restaurant and mouthing the word *bathroom.*

Majella blinked, puzzled.

"Problem?" Niall looked concerned.

The waitress turned away, then looked back at her and nodded urgently before heading over to clear one of the other tables.

"No problem! It all looks so lovely, I just can't decide." She pushed back her chair. "Sorry, just going to nip to the bathroom. Back in a minute."

Still mystified, she waited in the cool marble bathroom. A minute later, the door swung open and the waitress joined her.

"Hi, sorry, this might be none of my business." The girl kept her voice low. "But is this the first time you've met that guy you're with?"

Majella nodded. "Well . . . yes."

"Did he find you on a dating app?"

"Yes."

"OK, can I just warn you, he's been here twice before and both times he asks for the bill at the end of the meal, then suddenly discovers he's forgotten to bring his wallet with him."

What?

"Oh no." Majella's hand flew to her mouth as the realization sank in.

"I mean, maybe he's remembered to bring it with him this time. But like my mum says, once a scam artist, always a scam artist. I didn't know whether to tell you." The girl wrinkled her nose. "But it's not nice, is it? Ordering dinner and a couple of bottles of, like, really expensive wine, then making you pay for the whole lot."

Appalled, Majella said, "*Making* me pay?"

"I don't mean, like, at gunpoint. But he's being all charming and keen, isn't he? That's how he was with the other women he brought here. Then he made out he was mortified when he realized he'd left his wallet at home, and they felt so sorry for him they insisted on getting their credit cards out. We couldn't believe he had the nerve to do it twice," she went on. "Two weeks running. But *three* times, that's just taking the . . . well, you know what I mean. Some men reckon they're God's gift, don't they, and just take it for granted that single women are so desperate they'll fall for any old —"

"Bastard." Majella belatedly realized from the widening of the girl's eyes that she hadn't just thought it inside her own head. "Sorry, I can't believe this is happening to me. I feel like such an idiot. I'm just trying to work out what to do."

"Well, you could disappear." The girl indicated the small window at the other end of the bathroom. "That'd be good. Could you manage to wriggle through that, d'you think?"

Majella's mind instantly went back to the house in Bude, when Lainey had climbed in through the bathroom window and then they'd met Dan, whom she now thought of as the one who got away.

But that was life for you; it was never straightforward, was it? Also, this bathroom window was smaller than the one at the Gardners' house, and there was no way she could squeeze through a gap that size.

As she shook her head, the waitress continued brightly, "Or you could confront him in the restaurant and pour a jug of water over his head."

"It's a nice idea." Majella looked rueful. "But a messy one."

"I wouldn't mind clearing it up."

She didn't want to create a scene, though. They left the bathroom and the waitress slipped back into the kitchen. Majella returned to the table and sat back down.

"There you are." Niall flashed his winning smile. "I was beginning to think you'd run away. Shall we order now?"

There was no time to waste. She couldn't let the restaurant start preparing their food. Mentally bracing herself, she said, "Sorry if this is a weird question, but we did agree we'd be splitting the bill, didn't we?"

Niall looked startled. "Yes. I mean, if you've changed your mind, that's absolutely fine. I'm more than happy to pay for you too."

He sounded so believable. What if he was telling the truth? She might be about to ruin a potentially perfect relationship.

"Well, that's really lovely." She swallowed. "And of course I'm happy to go Dutch. But can I . . . could I just ask you to show me your wallet?"

The quizzical smile abruptly vanished from Niall's handsome face and his eyes darted in the direction of the maître d'.

"What a strange thing to say. My wallet's in my pocket."

Her stomach lurched. "Can I see it?"

"Why would you want to?"

Majella kept her voice low. "Because I want to make sure you haven't accidentally forgotten to bring it with you." Pause. "Again."

"I haven't forgotten. But thanks for showing me the kind of person you really are. You've made me realize I don't want to have dinner with you after all." Rising to his feet, Niall said evenly, "No wonder you're single."

"At least I'm not a liar and a con artist," said Majella.

He knocked back the rest of his wine, eyed her coldly, and put the empty glass down on the table. "You can pay for the drinks. Bye."

Once he'd retrieved his guitar and stalked out of the restaurant, the young waitress came over. "I still think you should've chucked water all over him."

"He might have thrown something back." Or worse, sung another song at her. "Can I just have the bill for the wine, please?"

It wasn't until the girl glanced at the name on her credit card that recognition dawned.

"I knew I knew you from somewhere — you're India and Violet's mum! I go to school with them!"

"Oh, right." Majella winced; did this mean tonight's disastrous date was about to be spread throughout the school? She'd be a laughingstock.

"I'm Rochelle Harris." The girl beamed, delighted to have placed her. "You tried to chat up my mum's boyfriend a while back, in the supermarket. You asked him out on a date and he was so embarrassed because he didn't know how to say no!"

Gerry. Oh no, this was going from bad to worse.

"I'm so sorry," said Majella. "I had no idea he was seeing someone. I would never have done it if I'd known."

"No worries. Mum thought it was hilarious. She went out with a few iffy men before meeting Gerry."

"Not as iffy as the ones I've managed to meet." Majella vowed to knock the dating scene on the head; she'd tried and failed, and it clearly wasn't for her.

"You'll get there in the end." Having run the card through the machine, Rochelle handed it back along with the receipt. "Hey, is India OK?"

"I think so. Isn't she?"

The girl shrugged. "Sorry, just thought I'd ask in case there was anything we should know. She's been a bit quiet lately, not as cheerful as usual. I didn't know if maybe something was up."

"I don't think so." Majella frowned.

"I did ask Violet, but she said it's India's fault if she hasn't studied for her exams. Anyway, I'm sure everything's fine. Sometimes I get carried away, thinking there are problems when there aren't any. Forget I said it . . . Yes, of course." Rochelle nodded efficiently as a diner at another table asked to see the dessert menu. "I'll get it for you now."

She went off to deal with the request, and Majella left her a big tip. *Was* something troubling India? Her more extrovert daughter had never been the type to worry about anything, but she'd been spending more time at home shut away in her room recently and had lost a bit of weight. Maybe she should have a chat with her, see if anything was bothering her.

Ding went her phone as she left the restaurant and began the walk home along the seafront. Taking it out of her bag, she saw it was a notification from the dating app, letting her know that a fifty-year-old science teacher from Plymouth was interested in meeting her. His name was Dylan, he was very fond of golf, bell-ringing, and exotic reptiles, and was looking for a lady with a sense of humor and —

No, she couldn't do it. Life was complicated enough without having to meet men who would only turn out to be disappointing. Stopping dead in her tracks, she shielded her eyes from the evening sunshine and deleted first the message, then the app.

There, gone.

She'd rather be single for the rest of her life than endure another date like tonight's.

CHAPTER 39

The sky was velvet black and studded with stars. The graceful curves of the suspension bridge were still lit up as Seth made his way toward it. At this time of night, only a few cars were visible below, snaking their way along the Portway running adjacent to the light-reflecting river.

He'd barely been able to sleep for the last ten days. This evening, his exhausted brain was still refusing to switch off, intent instead on going over and over the life that could lie ahead of him. The eternal presence of the internet wasn't helping either, but like an addict, he found himself unable to stay away from the endless pages of information about people's experience of the disease for which there was no cure. It was one of the cruelest in existence. And until a week and a half ago, he'd had no idea that this could be his fate. All his life he'd striven to achieve, had worked hard and enjoyed turning his fledgling business into a success. He was accustomed, too, to attracting admiring glances and attention from beautiful women.

And now, for the first time, he'd found someone who made him feel increasingly certain that she was the one he wanted to love and spend the rest of his life with . . . More than that, in fact: the one with whom he couldn't imagine *not* sharing the rest of his life.

Except that was when the rest of his life had been something to look forward to, the kind you'd *want* to share.

But how could he even contemplate starting a relationship with Lainey when all he could offer her was —

The lights on the suspension bridge switched off, letting him know it was midnight. He carried on walking until he reached the center of the bridge, exactly where he and Lainey had stood holding hands alongside Grace and the boys. Even now, as he gazed across at the twinkling lights of Clifton village on the left-hand side of the Avon Gorge, he could remember every detail of that sunny afternoon with absolute clarity. Closing his eyes, he relived the moment Lainey had slipped her hand into his. Not because she'd wanted to, but because Ned had ordered her to do it. Seth had nevertheless felt the electrifying sensation at that moment of contact and had wondered if Lainey was experiencing it too. At the time it had seemed almost impossible that she hadn't. And as for the other evening, down on the beach . . . well, who knows what might have happened if Dawn hadn't chosen that precise moment to come along?

Maybe, though, knowing what he knew now, it was a good job she had. "Hello." The gentle voice came from a few meters away, startling him. "Are you OK?"

Seth's eyes snapped open. A woman was approaching with care, moving slowly forward with one arm half outstretched.

"I'm fine."

"Look, all the lights have gone off. It's late. Shall we head back now?"

Head back? The woman was wearing jeans and a thin cotton hoodie. Why was she treating him like a dog who might be about to bolt?

"Please, come with me. We can have a chat if you like. Or just walk, if you'd prefer. Sometimes it's easier to talk to someone you don't know . . ."

Belatedly Seth realized that she thought he'd come to the suspension bridge at midnight in order to throw himself off it. As he opened his mouth to explain, he recalled the statistic he'd read on the internet, that 26 percent of patients who'd developed the illness made serious efforts to commit suicide. At that moment, a lone car came toward them across the bridge, its headlights illuminating the face of his would-be rescuer and the genuine concern in her eyes.

"It's OK, I'm fine." He shook his head and forced a smile to allay her fears. "Really. I just came up to admire the view."

"Are you sure?" The middle-aged woman looked relieved.

"Absolutely." This time Seth nodded. Ending his own life might be something he chose to do at some stage in the future, but not now. Not yet. "I'm going home now. Thanks, though," he added, turning in the direction of his flat and giving her one last nod of gratitude over his shoulder. "It was good of you to check."

The time had come to move on. By a stroke of luck, moving on was what Dawn was good at. Emotionally, rather than physically, although she could do either at a push. But St. Carys had captured her heart and she was keen to stay here, working for Berry and Dexter and hopefully advancing her career, because Malcolm Berry had already dropped several heavy hints about his retirement next year.

There was no future for her with Seth; she knew that now. It had been obvious from the moment she'd spoken to him last week on the beach. She'd asked him about whether he was already sleeping with Lainey and he'd said no, he wasn't, nothing like that had happened between them. And she'd believed him, because when she'd gone on to ask if he *wanted* to sleep with Lainey, he hadn't replied but had given her the kind of look that unequivocally said yes.

"Well, good luck," she'd told him, because it was always better to be magnanimous than resentful and a sore loser.

"Thanks." He'd nodded, then added, "You'll find someone amazing."

Dawn smiled at the memory, proud of the way she'd been able to reply cheerfully and with dignity, "Oh, I know I will."

And it was true, because once she made up her mind to do something, she made sure it happened. Plus, last week's Face-Time conversation with Aunt Yvonne now meant she had to get a move on.

Yvonne had moved to New Zealand a decade ago, but they still maintained contact, exchanging emails and speaking to each other several times a year. Calling to wish her aunt a happy seventieth birthday, Dawn had ended up telling her about the end of her oh-so-promising relationship with Seth.

"Oh, angel, that's a shame. But listen, I thought you were a diehard career girl like me. I had no idea you were keen on the idea of popping out babies."

Yvonne was a high-flying accountant who'd never married or entertained the possibility of children.

"I am a career girl." Dawn looked down at her flat stomach. "And I never did want kids. But now I've realized I do. And it's no big deal. I can have both."

"Oh boy! Well, I'm glad that ticking clock thing never reared its ugly head with me. I mean, good luck to you, my angel, but you're going to have to get a move on. How old are you now? Thirty-six?"

For a high-flying accountant, her aunt had a terrible memory for figures. "Thirty-seven," said Dawn. *Nearly thirty-eight.*

"Then you need to get an extra-speedy wiggle on. Your mum went crashing into the menopause at thirty-six and was all done and dusted by thirty-eight. Are you still having periods, angel?"

"Yes!"

"Well, maybe you should get yourself checked out, because who knows how many eggs you have left? Get them frozen or something. Or better still, find someone who's already got kids of their own, then you won't have to go through any of that nasty messy business. I mean, have you *seen* those TV shows about giving birth? Jeez, I'm telling you, it's like *The Texas Chainsaw Massacre*!"

Dawn loved her aunt dearly, but empathy and understanding weren't her forte.

She hadn't known about the early menopause either; her mum had died suddenly fifteen years ago of a heart attack, and discussions about fertility had never arisen.

Now, though, the issue clearly did need to be addressed, so Dawn had done what she always did when important decisions had to be made and had written a list of pros and cons.

She'd suggested it to Seth out of sheer desperation but really didn't want to freeze her eggs, and she didn't want to marry someone with kids either. Nor, ideally, would she choose to outsource the task to a surrogate.

She wanted her own baby, she wanted to carry it herself, and she needed it as soon as possible.

The one thing she didn't need was a long-term partner; a sperm donor would do just fine. But not an anonymous one off the internet; she knew it would have to be someone she'd at least met in person, seen with her own eyes, and had a conversation with.

In fact, a bit more than a conversation.

This was the decision she'd made a week ago, and tonight's unwitting applicant for the position was due any minute now. The last three hadn't made the grade; Dawn reminded herself she wasn't so desperate she didn't still have standards.

Waiting at a table outside the wine bar where they'd arranged to meet up, she redid her lipstick. If number four didn't fit the bill, she still had a few more lined up before the meeting with the fertility expert at the private clinic in Exeter. Oh yes, every base was covered.

"Hi, Dawn? Wow, my evening's looking up. You're beautiful!"

Turning to assess him, she took in the blond hair, thickly lashed blue eyes, ready smile, and excellent teeth. Tick, tick, tick.

"Niall. Good to meet you." He had a guitar with him for some reason. But musicality was a definite plus, and she already knew he was artistic too. So far, so very good.

"If this is what happens when you download a dating app, I'm all for it. My first match and I think I've just hit the jackpot." He gestured at her in admiration before greeting her properly with a brief kiss on each cheek. "I should have done this years ago, except then I wouldn't have been matched up with you!"

It was a corny line, but somehow she didn't mind. He was forty-six years old and had a nice voice, neat ears, and beautifully shaped hands. When they'd spoken on the phone to arrange this evening's meet up, she'd suggested he come to St. Carys so they could have dinner at Montgomery's, but Niall had said he'd had a disappointing meal there and wasn't keen on going back, so why didn't they try this new place he'd heard great things about in Padstow instead?

Which meant he had a discerning palate too. Another big tick.

"I can't get over how amazing you look," he told her once they'd ordered their drinks. "Sorry, I don't usually do this, but . . ."

He was picking up his guitar, looking as if he were about to play it. Alarmed, Dawn blurted out, "What are you *doing*?"

"You're so beautiful, you make me want

to sing you a little something I wrote."

"Oh, please don't. I can't stand it when people sing at me. If you start playing that thing, I'm out of here." Dawn shook her head. "I mean it."

Niall stopped and looked at her as if he couldn't believe what she was saying. Shit, was he mortally offended? Had she just blown her chances with him? Physically, he was miles better than the last three.

Then he broke into a huge smile and put the guitar down. "I like a woman who knows her own mind."

Giant tick. "I definitely know my own mind."

"There's a lot to be said for honesty." His eyes were sparkling. "Can I be honest too? Until you said that, you were a nine out of ten for me. But now you've gone up to a nine point five."

Phew.

"I'd put you at an eight," said Dawn, "but that allows room for improvement and it's a higher mark than I usually give."

He laughed. "You're fantastic."

"I know. Aren't you lucky?"

And when it was time for them to leave the wine bar to head over to the restaurant, it seemed completely natural for him to hold her hand in his. It felt right.

"One thing I have to get out of the way," Dawn told him. "I looked at the website for this restaurant, and it's a pretty fancy place."

"Only the best for you." His hip bumped gently against hers as they crossed the road that curved round the harbor. "I already know you're worth it."

"I am." She nodded. "But I'm not comfortable letting you foot the bill. I want to be the one who pays for this meal. Can you understand why I need to do that?"

Niall paused. "You mean you don't want to feel beholden, as if you owe me something? Is that it?"

"Exactly." She nodded, grateful that he seemed surprised rather than offended.

"Well, this is a first." There was that beautiful tender smile again. "I can't pretend it won't feel a bit weird." He studied her face, then touched her cheek, and she quivered at the sensation of his warm breath against her mouth. "But I suppose if I want to keep you happy, I'm just going to have to give in and go along with it."

Good manners, honesty, charm, looks . . . who could ask for more? Well, hopefully he'd be good in bed too. With a surge of triumph, Dawn returned his smile. "I insist."

If she was going to get what she wanted

from him, it would be worth every penny.
Oh yes.

CHAPTER 40

"Sorry, love, I didn't know whether to mention this to you, but I think I should."

"What is it?" Majella couldn't imagine what Arthur from the newsagent's might be doing on her doorstep looking so serious; he was normally a cheerful soul. "Oh no, did I forget to pay last month's paper bill?"

"No, love, nothing to do with you. It's your girl, India. I caught her taking a packet of chewing gum from the shop, and it wasn't an accident. I saw her put it in her pocket."

"What?"

"I know. I made her put it back, and of course I'm not going to do anything about it, but I thought you ought to know. Sometimes this kind of thing needs to be nipped in the bud, d'you know what I mean? Before it gets out of hand."

"Arthur, I'm so sorry." Majella's heart was thudding. "When did this happen?"

"Just ten minutes ago. Don't get upset. It's not your fault." Arthur was a kind man.

"Thanks for telling me," said Majella. She wasn't upset; she was furious.

Having hurriedly left the house, she spotted her daughter twenty minutes later, dawdling along the esplanade. Each time India paused to browse in a shop window, Majella's breath caught in her throat. If she entered the shop, should she race in after her to ensure no pilfering occurred? But she couldn't handcuff herself to her daughter 24/7. Why was India doing it, though? It made no sense at all.

After discreetly following her for a few minutes more, still wondering what on earth could be going on, Majella saw her turn away from the shops and head for the steps that led down to the beach. She watched from a distance, taking in the droop of her daughter's shoulders and her air of . . . what? Defeat? Unhappiness? More to the point, was it unhappiness at having been caught and told off by Arthur, or as a result of something else?

On the dry, silvery sand, India sat down and pulled a plastic bottle of Coke from her bag. She took a couple of big swigs, then gazed out to sea. From the top of the steps, it occurred to Majella that her daughter would normally take out her phone within seconds and be glued to it, but this didn't happen. She was thinking too hard about something to want the distraction of a phone.

It also occurred to her to wonder if there was rum in that bottle of Coke.

As she approached, India turned. "You'd make a terrible secret agent. I saw you ages ago, lurking outside the flower shop."

"What's going on, India?"

"Nothing."

"Arthur came to see me."

"Of course he did. I didn't mean to do it. It was an accident. I just wasn't thinking."

"Arthur's run that shop for the last thirty years. He's had enough practice to be able to tell the difference."

"Better call the police, then. Chuck me in a cell and throw away the key. After all, it was an entire packet of chewing gum costing sixty-five whole pence."

Majella's fury had abated; the tone might be defiant, but there was genuine pain in her daughter's eyes and she was trembling. "Oh, sweetheart, what's wrong?"

"Nothing." India hugged her knees, shaking her head and continuing to gaze out to sea.

"You've known Arthur your whole life.

How could you steal from him? He's the loveliest man."

Tears brimmed in India's eyes.

"I'm thirsty." Majella nudged the plastic bottle of Coke. "Can I have a swig?" She unscrewed the lid and sniffed the contents.

"I'm not a secret drinker, if that's what you're thinking."

Majella took a swallow anyway. It was just Coke. "Whatever the problem is, you can tell me. We can sort it out."

Another shake of the head. "Are you on drugs?"

"No."

"Pregnant?"

"No."

"Boyfriend trouble? Problems at school? You haven't been yourself lately. Is it the exams you're worried about?" Majella was running out of options. "Are you being bullied?"

"None of those. It's nothing." A tear overflowed and ran down India's cheek as she said it. "I'm fine."

Majella felt her own throat tighten with emotion. "Does Violet know what's going on?"

India briefly closed her eyes and shook her head.

"Well, if you won't tell me, will you at least

talk to her about it?"

Another shake. "No. Mum, please, don't ask me again. I'll be OK."

A text pinged up on Seth's phone on Thursday afternoon as he was heading back to Bristol following a long meeting in Bath. Pulling over, he saw that it was from Majella: Just took a call from someone in the office — says she's a friend of your mum's and needs to speak to you. I said you'd call her back. Her name's Shelley and here's her number . . .

He braced himself and rang the number Majella had sent him.

"Seth? Darling, I swear to God your mother's driving me to distraction. I've been calling and leaving messages since yesterday, and *again* I'm just not getting any reply. Does she just hate me, is that it?"

"She's gone to a spa retreat," Seth explained. "Some detox place in the Cotswolds where they confiscate your phone on arrival. She's booked herself in for the next ten days, if there isn't a mass breakout before then. It's all yoga and meditation and drinking liquidized grass, apparently, so that could happen."

"She's mad!" Shelley gave a shriek of laughter. "Why would anyone want to do that to themselves? Anyway, so what d'you think I should do, because I wanted to tell her that Matteo died and if she felt like sending flowers to the funeral I've got the address? His sister messaged me yesterday morning to let me know, but it's not going to be a big flashy ceremony, so Christina wouldn't want to fly over for it anyway. Family only, his sister said."

Seth digested the news, so casually imparted, in silence. So that was it, then. The man who was probably his father was now dead. Because in all honesty, with his dark hair and dark eyes, the odds were that he was indeed Matteo's son.

"Hello? Hello? Are you still there, darling?"

"Yes, still here." He took a deep breath. "Thanks for telling me. Look, if you text me the details, I'll get in touch with the spa and find a way to let Mum know."

Lainey was busy washing the cars on the driveway when she became aware that she was being watched. Across the road, a thin woman of maybe forty was hovering, peering in through the gates.

Seeing that she'd been noticed, the woman made her approach. "Hello, I'm looking for someone and I think this could be where they live . . ."

"He's asleep at the moment," said Lainey, because Richard had been out for a long lunch with an old director friend and was now snoring gently on his favorite chaise longue in the back garden with his hat tilted over his face.

"It's not a he," said the woman. "I'm looking for someone called Majella."

"Oh, sorry!" Not another member of the fan club, then. "Yes, this is the right house, but I'm afraid she's out with a client at the moment. You can leave a message with me if you like, and I'll make sure she gets it."

The woman said, "Actually, you might be able to help. Do you work for Majella?"

"Yes." Lainey was trying to guess what this could be about. She hoped it wasn't something to do with India, about whom Majella was increasingly concerned. *Please don't let it be more shoplifting.*

"Did you break into a house in Bude the other week?"

"Well, yes." Wrong-footed, Lainey added, "But not in a burglar-y way."

"You were looking for some lost passports," said the woman, "and my ex-husband found them lying in the road."

"Yes! You mean Dan's your ex-husband? He was a star!" Lainey exclaimed. "Completely saved the day. I got the passports down to Southampton with minutes to spare. Is he here with you?"

"No, I came down on my own — Oh, good grief." Staring over Lainey's shoulder, the woman did a double take. "Is that . . . ?"

"Lainey?" Richard called from the side of the house. "Got a bit of a headache, can't think why. Could you be an angel and bring me out a couple of aspirin with a cup of tea?"

"Of course. Give me two minutes."

"Who's that?" He pointed at the stranger. "Not another long-lost daughter, I hope."

"Blimey," said Dan's ex-wife when Richard had returned to the back garden. "Dan did mention there was an old chap here who looked a bit like Richard Myles. He didn't realize it *was* him."

Lainey dropped the car-cleaning sponge into the bucket of soapy water. "Come on inside. He'll be grumpy if I don't make him his cup of tea. We'll have one too."

Once Richard's tray had been delivered to him, they sat down together at the kitchen table. "So why are you here?" Lainey asked.

Dan's wife, whom she now knew was called Sara, said, "Well, I hope this doesn't sound a bit weird, but when Dan dropped Majella back here, she was all excited about meeting some amazing new guy her friend had matched her up with." She hesitated, looked embarrassed. "And I . . . well, I kind of wondered how it went."

"Total disaster. He was awful," Lainey said promptly. "Awful *and* a drug dealer."

"Oh no, that's terrible! Well," Sara amended, "terrible for her at the time, but probably good in the long run." She paused again to stir her tea, then said in a rush, "The thing is, I think Dan really likes Majella."

Wow. Was this a *Fatal Attraction* scenario? Proceeding with caution, Lainey said, "And . . . is that a problem?"

"God no! Not at all! I want him to be happy. That's why I'm here. Every time he mentions her, I see his face change. It kind of lights up. So I told him he should come over here and ask her out, but he won't do it in case he's gotten it all wrong and she's not interested. But honestly, he's a lovely man . . . If you could just persuade her to give him a chance, I promise she wouldn't regret it."

"Shall I tell you something?" Lainey broke into the broad smile she'd been working so hard to suppress. "Ever since that day, Majella's been kicking herself for not getting Dan's number. She didn't have any way of tracking him down; all she knew was that he lived in Exeter. Hearing you saying this is just . . . brilliant."

And now they were both grinning at each other like idiots, unable to control themselves.

"If we tell them we've fixed them up, they might refuse to go along with it. I know what Majella's like. She'll be too scared in case it all goes wrong."

"Same with Dan. The more something matters to him, the more terrified he gets."

"We need to come up with a plan," said Lainey.

"We're like a pair of fairy godmothers," said Sara, "and we're going to do this." Triumphantly, she took a cookie out of the tin and waved it like a wand. "Honestly, I thought I might be a bit mad coming here today. But now I'm so glad I did."

CHAPTER 41

"Oh no, please no." Majella knew she had to be firm, stand her ground. "Don't try to make me change my mind, because it's not going to happen. I said no more blind dates and I meant it." Honestly, why wouldn't people believe her?

"But this one isn't from a dating app." Lainey had her wide-eyed, earnestly persuasive face on. "And it isn't really blind, because I've seen him and you know you can trust me."

"I thought I could trust my friend Judi, and look how well that turned out." With a shudder, Majella said, "She thought I'd get on like a house on fire with her cokehead cousin. I mean, what was she even *thinking*?"

"Well, I'm way better at matching people up than Judi. And I promise you'll like this one. As soon as we got chatting, I knew he'd be perfect for you. Honestly, it was like love at first sight by proxy — when you meet him, you'll be so glad I did this."

Majella shook her head. "I'm not going to meet him and I can't believe you thought this was a good idea. How could you set me up without even asking me first? It's just *wrong.*"

"It's called being spontaneous," Lainey exclaimed. "It's called seizing the moment, rather than doing nothing and letting a brilliant opportunity slip by. Didn't I tell you I'd sort you out and find you a man?" Her eyebrows disappeared up beneath her bangs, and Majella's spirits sank at the realization that she had clearly set her heart on this hideous meeting going ahead.

"And where *did* you find him?"

"On Mariscombe Beach! I was throwing the Frisbee for Ernie and Glenda, and I accidentally clonked him on the back of the head, but he was really nice about it, and we got talking about mad accidents and dogs, and he thought Ernie and Glenda were brilliant — and they loved him too, by the way — and then we chatted about St. Carys, how I'd happened to find my way here and how much I loved working for you . . . I mean, we ended up talking for ages," Lainey rattled on, "and the whole time I just kept thinking how perfect you two would be for each other. And then remember when you met Dan and you couldn't ask him for his number because you were too shy and it would've been too embarrassing if he'd said no?"

There it was, the awful recurring pang of disappointment and regret. Dan, whom she hadn't been able to stop thinking about and who, she was now certain, had been her perfect man. Majella nodded sadly. "Yes."

"Well, it's a lot easier to ask someone out on a date with somebody else. So I told him all about you and said would he like to meet you, and he was completely up for it!"

"And I still don't want to go."

"Look, I can't force you. But if you don't meet him, I really think you'll be missing out. He'll be waiting for you outside Paddy's Café at midday tomorrow. All you have to do is have a quick cup of coffee with him. Ten minutes, tops. Then if you want to leave, you can, and I hereby promise never to set you up on a date again." Lainey shrugged. "So how about that for an offer you can't refuse?"

This was her special skill, persuading people to do things they didn't want to do.

Feeling resentful and hopelessly outmaneuvered, Majella said, "I don't even know what he looks like."

"He looks . . . friendly and kind and *nice.*"

"I meant, how would I recognize him?"

"No worries." Lainey was triumphant. "I'll walk down with you."

That had been yesterday. Now it was today. As she and Lainey made their way along the curving esplanade, the jitters rose like a cloud of locusts inside Majella's rib cage and she wished more than ever that she had stood her ground.

The church bells began to chime; it was twelve o'clock exactly. Feeling like Cinderella in reverse, Majella muttered, "If I don't like the look of him, I'm not even going to sit down. I'll be turning around and going straight back home."

"Fine," said Lainey. "But I think you'll like the look of him."

"I feel sick."

"No you don't. Just relax. It'll be fun."

"One cup of coffee, that's all. And no spying on us from a distance. It's going to be bad enough as it is without worrying about you sneaking around corners, watching us like monkeys in a zoo."

"No spying, I promise."

They rounded the curve and there was Paddy's Café. Scanning the tables outside, Majella saw only one man on his own, but he was ancient. Which meant her date was either late, or sitting inside, or not coming. Torn between relief and outrage, she said, "If he's stood me up . . ."

Then the words died in her throat and her ears began to buzz, because there, seated at a table for four along with a laughing brunette woman and two young girls, was Dan.

Dan.

Oh goodness, it really was him, here with his family, his wife and daughters, and it was so wonderful to see him again, but also completely awful.

"What's wrong?" said Lainey, because Majella had stopped dead in her tracks.

She unstuck her tongue from the roof of her mouth. "It's . . . him."

"Who?"

"Look. With the woman and the girls. *Dan.*"

"Wow, so it is. Fantastic!"

At that moment, a tall man emerged from inside the café, carrying a coffee and heading for an empty table. Majella said fearfully, "Is that him? Is that the one I'm supposed to be meeting? Oh God, I can't do it now, how can I sit there and talk to a stranger in front of Dan, there's no way I could —"

"He's seen us! Come on!" Clutching Majella's arm, Lainey called out, "Hellooo!" and dragged her along the pavement. Majella was simultaneously mortified by the awfulness of the situation and awash with adrenaline because Dan was now less than twenty meters away. Although he and his supposedly ex-wife were looking so relaxed in each other's company that she was probably about to find out that he was still happily married to her after all.

"You'll have to tell the other one I can't do it." She was doing her best to dig her heels in. The man was now looking over at them, and at closer quarters, he bore a startling resemblance to a horse.

"Hey, remember what I told you? Relax," said Lainey. "I wouldn't choose someone you didn't like."

Except she'd evidently chosen someone with a *really* long face and enormous yellow teeth. Perspiration prickled at the back of Majella's neck as she pretended not to have noticed Dan and his family. But to her surprise, Lainey steered her right past the horse-faced man and said cheerfully, "Well, it took a bit of persuading, but I got her here in the end! Now, shall we leave them to it?"

And within a minute, she found herself

seated opposite Dan at an otherwise unoc-cupied table littered with half-finished soft drinks. Lainey, Dan's ex-wife, and the two girls had disappeared together in the direc-tion of the beach.

"Well," Dan said at last. "Looks like we've been set up."

"I'm confused." Majella's hands were trembling. "I don't know how this has hap-pened."

He paused, meeting her gaze. "When your friend said it took a bit of persuading to get you here, was that because you knew you were going to see me?"

"What? No! I didn't want to come here because Lainey told me she'd fixed me up with a stranger! I thought it was *him.*" Furtively Majella indicated the man on his own, reading a paper, over to their left.

"He looks like a donkey," Dan murmured.

"I *know.*" So many questions were bub-bling up. "Are you really divorced?"

"Sure am. How did it go with the guy at your friend's party?"

"He offered me half-price cocaine. And no, that isn't a good thing." Majella gri-maced. "He was repulsive."

"Well, *that's* a good thing." Dan smiled for the first time.

"I'm sorry, I'm still trying to work this

out. Did you know I was going to be here?"

He shook his head. "I may have casually mentioned you once or twice to Sara. Or maybe three or four times," he amended, his tone rueful. "Yesterday she said why didn't we come down to Cornwall and have a day out in St. Carys, because we hadn't been here for years, and I was happy to do that. Secretly I was hoping we might bump into you, because . . . well, I suppose because I wanted to see you again."

"So your wife . . . ex-wife, she arranged this? With Lainey?" Majella was still trying to make sense of the situation.

"When I dropped you off last time, I spotted the name of the house. I must have mentioned it to Sara. Might even have pointed it out to her on Google Earth. You know, just in a casual way."

If he could be honest, so could she. Majella heard herself say, "I was planning to go to Bude next June, to see if I could accidentally bump into you again."

"Really?"

She blushed; now she sounded like a complete stalker. "This way's much better, though."

"I agree. Quicker too. You're looking great, by the way." Dan indicated her turquoise sundress, her hair and face. "A bit different from last time. Not that you didn't look great then . . . eurgh, sorry, I didn't mean it like that."

"I'm wearing makeup and clean clothes." Majella grinned. "And I don't have a giant spider in my hair. I hope."

"Your eyebrows are different too. Symmetrical."

"I just thought I'd try them that way for a change." She nodded at his bottle-green polo shirt. "No kittens."

His eyes danced. "It's a miracle we even recognized each other."

Paddy came over to see what Majella wanted to drink, and they ordered more coffee. As Dan carried on figuring out how the two of them had been set up, she found herself beginning to relax at last. A warm glow of happiness was spreading through her body. Against the odds, they'd found each other again, and it felt every bit as natural and thrilling and perfect as she'd hoped it would during her daydreams about something like this happening. It just seemed so right.

"You knew where I lived, so you could have driven down here to see me at any time," said Majella, once Dan had worked out that Sara had come down to St. Carys and met Lainey.

"But I wouldn't have been brave enough to do that; it would've felt too presumptuous. I didn't know if you were with that other guy or if you'd even be interested in me. You might have laughed in my face. If that had happened, I'd never have had the nerve to look at another woman again, let alone ask her out."

A flicker of a smile lifted the corners of his mouth, and Majella had to force herself not to say, *Maybe you won't need to. You've got me now.*

Because it might be what she was thinking and hoping, but it wouldn't do to scare him off completely. Instead she said, "I wouldn't have laughed."

"Well, that's reassuring. But I was too scared to take the risk."

He had a beautiful upper lip. Majella stirred her coffee, then rested her right hand palm down on the table. She watched as Dan did the same with his left hand, his fingertips a couple of centimeters from hers. Crazy though it was, her stomach flipped with anticipation, because other than lifting the spider from her hair, there had been zero physical contact between the two of them.

No contact whatsoever.

Sometimes you had to force yourself,

didn't you, to take the risk.

Majella gave her fingers a tiny experimental wiggle and moved them a couple of millimeters closer to Dan's.

He watched them, then looked up at her and edged his own fingers fractionally toward hers.

Now they were both smiling. Thanks to Sara having made the first move, they could relax and enjoy what was happening. Together they slid their hands forward until their fingertips touched.

And *zinggg,* there it was, and just like that, all the bad dates of the past few weeks were canceled out. This moment, this perfect moment, was all that mattered — Majella jumped out of her skin as her phone burst into life, playing Sir Mix-a-Lot's "I Like Big Butts" song at maximum volume. Just what you needed at a moment like this. Scrabbling in her bag to make it stop, she said, "Sorry, my eleven-year-old changed my ringtone. It's his favorite song . . . Oh, it's a text from Lainey." She shielded the screen from the overhead sun and read aloud, " 'This is your emergency get-out option. If you're hating every minute, text me and I'll come and rescue you. If you're happy, give us a wave — we're down on Mariscombe Beach.' "

Dan, opposite her, slanted his eyebrows. "Which is it going to be? The suspense is killing me."

Together they rose to their feet and made their way across to the left-hand section of the terrace, from where they could gaze over the beach. And there they were, Lainey and Sara with the two girls, all waving madly up at them.

As Majella and Dan waved back, Dan slid his free arm around her waist and Majella felt her heart swell with joy, because it felt even more wonderful than just touching fingertips.

He said, "Sara's going to be so smug about this," as his daughters jumped up and down on the sand.

"So's Lainey."

And just at that moment, another text arrived: What did I tell you? Sorry, couldn't resist!

CHAPTER 42

The atmosphere at Menhenick House was mixed, to say the least. Lainey was thrilled for Majella; since meeting Dan on Saturday, she'd been fizzing with happiness. But as counterbalance there was Seth, back from Bristol and acting as if everything were fine, although clearly everything *wasn't*. Furthermore, the connection between Seth and herself had been abruptly turned off like a switch in a fuse box.

Which was why, at breakfast on Tuesday morning, she really wished Kit weren't trying so hard to be helpful.

"I'm fine," she insisted. It was her day off, and she was heading up to the Cotswolds to visit her grandmother. "Honestly, I don't mind catching the train."

"Trainzzz, plural," Kit emphasized. "It's going to take how many hours to get there?" He had to have one of the cars for the school runs, and Majella needed the other for work. Having heard that Seth would be driving up past Cirencester to visit his mother at her spa, Kit said, "But Lainey's gran isn't far from there. You could drop her on the way and pick her up afterward. Doesn't that make more sense?"

And once he'd appealed to Seth, who was practically forced to agree to take her, Lainey found herself, in turn, forced to accept. Even though it was painfully obvious that this was the last thing either of them wanted to happen.

The journey from Cornwall to Cirencester was blissfully free of traffic holdups but still awkward. His manner distant, Seth explained briefly that Matteo had died in Italy and he needed to tell his mother in person, hence today's trip. He then inquired politely about Lainey's Granny Ivy and, equally politely, Lainey explained that she liked to go and visit her at least a couple of times a year.

For the rest of the trip she plugged in earbuds, closed her eyes, and pretended to be asleep. Which wasn't easy when you were sitting next to someone whose physical presence made you quiver, for whom you'd had such high hopes and who had decided for whatever reason that he was no longer remotely interested in you.

"Anywhere here's fine," she said when they reached Market Place, in the center of Cirencester.

"Are you sure?" Seth pulled over to drop her off. "Right, it's one o'clock. I'll be back at four thirty if that's OK with you. Any problems, give me a call."

It was as if he could hardly bear to look at her. Lainey unfastened her seat belt. "That's fine. I'll wait for you here. Thanks for the lift."

Seth nodded, knuckles gleaming white as he gripped the steering wheel. "No worries. Have a good time."

"You too. Sorry." She winced, because he was on his way to give his mother tragic news and a good time was highly unlikely for either of them. "I hope it isn't too difficult."

Another brusque nod; he was gazing directly ahead, not so much as glancing in her direction. "Thanks. See you later."

As soon as he'd driven off up the road and disappeared from view, Lainey hitched the strap of her bag over her shoulder and made her way across to the taxi office on the other side of the road.

As Seth drove away from Cirencester, the sudden absence of Lainey in the car hit him like a physical force every bit as intense as the agony he'd endured traveling up here from St. Carys with her at his side.

Carrying on a cheerful, easy conversation with her as if nothing had changed in his life simply hadn't been possible. He was exhausted, sleep-deprived, and filled with a sensation of perpetual dread as to what the future might hold. His feelings toward her hadn't changed, but he could no longer allow himself to act upon them. If you loved someone, how could you risk causing them years, decades even, of untold pain and anguish?

And not just Lainey either. There was also the rest of the family to consider.

They would be devastated too.

As he continued to drive along on autopilot, he ran through the options available to him for what felt like the millionth time. First, undergo the DNA test that would confirm to him that he was Matteo's son. Next, make an appointment with a geneticist and begin the long, arduous process of getting tested to see if he would develop the disease — and there was a fifty-fifty chance that he would. Nor was it a simple, straightforward process; the rules stated that many months of careful professional counseling were required before the testing could even be carried out.

Which meant the impermeable block of ice currently lodged in his chest was going to remain there for a good few months yet. And after that? Well, either all would be well and life could return to normal . . .

Or not.

He took a deep breath and buzzed down his window, because the faint scent of Lainey's perfume still lingered in the car, bringing back memories of being with her on the beach, deliberately delaying the moment when he would make that first move from which there could be no going back.

So much for the best-laid plans and thinking that the future couldn't be more perfect . . .

The spa retreat was situated in the depths of the countryside between Lechlade and Fairford. He'd looked it up online last night, and it had sounded exactly as expected: an idyllic getaway from the pressures of the outside world, enabling you to relax, expand your awareness, find your center, and nurture your soul.

Claptrap, basically, and staggeringly expensive claptrap at that, but the kind his mother was keen on. After months of drinking, partying, and jet-setting around the holiday hot spots of the world, she liked to atone by devoting herself to a restorative fortnight of lettuce, mineral wraps, yoga, meditation, aura cleansing, and an awful lot of obnoxiously green smoothies.

Apparently it did wonders for one's spiritual well-being. Seth, who would rather swallow razor blades, was pretty sure it wouldn't do it for him.

Pausing at the imposing stone-pillared entrance to the luxury retreat, he took a phone out of the glove compartment and slid it into his shirt pocket, out of sight beneath his jacket.

"Darling, what a lovely surprise!" Christina greeted him at the entrance to her huge, high-ceilinged suite on the third floor. In keeping with her surroundings, she was wearing layers of ivory linen, soft and floaty. Her blond hair was slicked back from her face, which was unmade-up and glowing with health. "Mind my skin. I've just had an oil treatment and it has flecks of gold leaf in it. What are you doing here?"

"I was in the area." Seth landed a tentative kiss on one shimmering cheekbone. "Thought I'd call in and see how you're getting on."

"Well, it's completely ghastly, of course, no alcohol and nothing anyone in their right mind would ever choose to eat, but that's the whole point. The place is stunning, though. Some of the people are a bit dreary, going on and on about the wonders of spirulina like they've got shares in the stuff . . . oh, but there's a gorgeous chap I've got my eye on. So that helps!"

There was always some new gorgeous chap or other in Christina's life. Seth indicated the table and chairs next to the open sash window. "Shall we sit down?"

"Of course! I can't offer you anything exciting to drink, but we've got plenty of this stuff." She opened the mini fridge and held up a jug of what looked like pureed Savoy cabbage. "It has twenty-seven different vitamins in it!"

"No thanks." He briefly debated telling her there *weren't* twenty-seven different vitamins.

"And eighty-three enzymes and micronutrients, apparently. We had an hour-long lecture about it." She nodded vigorously and grabbed two clean glasses. "Try some. You might be surprised. It gives you a whole-body boost!"

Once they were sitting down with the untouched smoothies in front of them, Seth said, "Mum, Shelley was wondering where you were. She was trying to get in touch."

"Well, that's not my fault. I told you," said Christina, "they don't let us have our phones in here. Did you know, every time you go on social media, your brain is bombarded with literally trillions of negative electrical thingummies? I had no idea."

"I don't think that's quite right." Seth shook his head.

"It is, though! This psychotherapist guy called Zebedee gave us a talk about it yesterday. He knows everything there is to know about negative electricity."

"Mum, Shelley couldn't get hold of you, so she called me."

"Oh for heaven's sake, is this about the liposuction? She wants me to go along with her so we can have our legs done at the same time, but the thing is, I don't *need* lipo on my legs."

"It isn't about that." Seth waited until he had his mother's attention. "It's Matteo. Shelley had another text from his sister. I'm sorry," he said gently. "Matteo died."

"Oh." Christina sat back, silver bangles clinking as her hand fluttered to her mouth. "Oh, right. Well, that's sad. Poor Matteo."

"Yes." Seth exhaled.

"How about you? Are you . . . OK?"

He nodded. "I'm OK."

A tear trickled down her tanned, shimmering cheek, and she wiped it away with the back of her hand. "We knew it was going to happen. I can't believe I'm this upset. But he was a lovely boy. Always fun to be with. And such beautiful eyes." She raised her gaze, and Seth knew she was comparing his eyes with Matteo's.

"It's a private funeral," he explained. "Family only. But if you want, you can send flowers. I mean, I could send them on your behalf."

"Yes, darling, that's a nice idea. I'd definitely like to do that. Where's the funeral being held?"

"Santa Maria Rezzonico." Seth reached into his jacket pocket and took out his mobile.

Christina's eyes widened. "Oh my God! How did they not take that off you?"

"They asked me to hand my phone over at reception, so I gave them my old one." He switched on the phone and found what he was looking for. "Here you go. Shelley forwarded the email from Matteo's sister so we'd have all the details."

He passed his mother the phone, displaying the photo of the death notice in an Italian newspaper, and gazed out of the window at the tranquil rose garden below while she read it. Beyond the rose garden, in a far corner of the grounds, a tai chi class was in progress. Over to the right, people were sitting cross-legged in a circle, presumably meditating. In the distance, a tiny plume of gray-blue smoke drifted up from a clump of bushes, indicating that some desperate soul was hiding behind them having a forbidden cigarette.

Glancing back at his mother, Seth saw that she was bent over the phone, texting at lightning speed. "Mum, what are you *doing*?" He whisked it from her grasp in case she was messaging something hideously inappropriate to Matteo's sister, then checked the screen and shook his head in despair. "Facebook? Are you serious?"

"I'm sorry. I just couldn't help myself. It's *hard* going cold turkey. OK, fine." Christina heaved a long-suffering sigh. "You can delete it."

The message was to one of her female friends, complaining that the retreat didn't serve wine with dinner and the nearest shop was miles away, which meant she hadn't even been able to sneak out to buy chips and chocolate.

Clearly not that devastated about Matteo then.

Seth deleted what she'd typed and returned to the email from Matteo's sister.

This time he angled the screen so Christina could see it, but made sure he held on to the phone.

She leaned closer, reading for several seconds in silence. Seth waved aside a bluebottle that had just flown in through the open sash window and landed on the table. The fly darted around ninja style before alighting on the rim of his smoothie glass, which gave him an even better excuse not to try it.

"This says Matteo Romano." His mother looked up at him, puzzled. "Who's that?"

"It's him," said Seth.

Christina's hoop earrings jangled. "Well, that's not right. My Matteo was Matteo Mancini."

Seth blinked. "What? But Shelley said it was him. Matteo with the hair."

"Yes, he had hair! Long hair, loads of it, like a rock star!"

Inside his chest, Seth's heart rate began to speed up, because this wasn't making any sense. "But his sister sent the email. She knows who her own brother is."

"Well, this is just weird. It's definitely not his surname." Christina pointed at the death notice on the screen. "And that isn't his date of birth either."

"Are you *sure*?" Remembering birth dates

had never been her forte.

She looked outraged that he could doubt her. "Of course I'm sure. Matteo's birthday was New Year's Eve, that's why I wouldn't forget it."

CHAPTER 43

Seth's heart was by now thudding like the blades of a helicopter preparing for takeoff. Grabbing the phone back, he scrolled down to the photograph that had been attached to the bottom of the email. With an unsteady hand, he held it up in front of Christina, who peered intently at the screen then let out a yelp of recognition.

"Oh my God, this is so wild," she exclaimed. "That's not him. That's the other Matteo!"

The other Matteo . . .

"I remember him," she went on triumphantly. "I don't think I ever even heard his surname, but he used to go to all the same clubs as us, so we knew him to chat to. He was one of the Carnaby Street punks, darling, bright-blue hair in a foot-high Mohawk. I mean, he was a lovely boy but I never slept with him." She wrinkled her nose. "Bit too skinny for me. Poor Mattie, though. It's sad that he's died. We'll still send some flowers, shall we, even though it's the wrong one?"

Seth couldn't trust himself to fully comprehend what he was hearing. He'd almost forgotten to breathe. When people discovered that the numbers on their lottery tickets matched the winning ones, how many times did they feel the need to double-check and check again before finally believing they'd won?

Christina was tapping his arm. "Seth? Will you call a florist and organize it? Something big and flashy, lots of red and blue?"

He nodded, looking again at the photograph of Matteo-who-wasn't-his-biological-father, who had never slept with his mother and therefore whose genes he categorically didn't share. The photo had been taken decades ago, presumably before the illness had taken hold. He had prominent cheekbones, short dark hair, and a large aquiline nose, but it was those dark eyes that had convinced Seth of the resemblance when Shelley had forwarded the email to him the other day.

Without thinking, he reached for the glass on the table and almost took a gulp of putrid-looking green smoothie before spotting the upturned fly on the foamy surface.

Stone dead, which didn't bode well for any resident tempted to drink the stuff.

"Ha, how funny!" Christina was now chuckling to herself. "Imagine if I'd traveled all that way and turned up at a funeral for the wrong Matteo!"

One last check. It had to be done. Seth said, "So the other one's surname is Mancini."

"*My* Matteo, yes." She nodded and waved her arms extravagantly around her head. "Long dark hair like a lion. And a beautiful chest." Reminiscing fondly, she added, "He used to wear black leather trousers too."

Seth keyed the name into Google and came up with several options so went to Images instead and showed his mother the page of photographs.

"I did have a go at looking him up a few years ago but couldn't find him . . . Ooh, now *he's* rather gorgeous!" She pointed to a Californian orthopedic surgeon. "But it's not him, worse luck. Hmm, not him, nor him . . . eurgh, *definitely* not that one. Oh . . ."

"What?" said Seth, because she'd suddenly gone quiet.

"Found him."

"Really?"

His mother nodded. "Oh yes, this is him. Wow."

Seth sat back; from this angle, he couldn't see the screen. "What does *wow* mean?"

"He has a restaurant in Naples. And a big family. He looks . . . older." She sounded put out. Sometimes she still had the ability to astound him.

Having never been remotely interested in learning any details about the man who could well be his biological father, Seth now reached across and angled the phone so they could both see the photo. The family were posing in front of their restaurant, arms around each other's shoulders as they beamed for the photographer. Two strapping sons, three striking daughters, a curvaceous, dark-haired wife . . . and Matteo Mancini, the proud father, with thick graying hair swept back from his face and a broad smile that felt instantly, subliminally familiar.

"He's gone gray *and* put on a few pounds." Christina's lip curled.

Seth clicked on the link beneath the photo, which took him to a website. This in turn led them to a gallery containing more photographs of staff and diners at the cheerfully decorated restaurant. He scrolled through the photos, stopping at an extra-celebratory one featuring a banner with *FE-LICE ANNO NUEVO!* written across it and Matteo taking center stage beneath balloons bearing the words *BUON COMPLEANNO!*

Happy New Year and Happy Birthday. Which was pretty much case closed.

"I mean, I suppose he's still good-looking," said Christina, "but he was even better when he had all that wild hair."

There was a knock at the door and she called out, "Come in," before belatedly realizing Seth still had the phone in his hand. He dropped it into his jacket pocket and they both turned as the door opened.

"Sorry to disturb you, but I've brought tomorrow's menu choices." A smilingly serene woman approached them with a sheet of paper. "I can *thoroughly* recommend the tofu and dandelion stir-fry with wheatgrass and —"

Seth's phone began to ring and the woman's smile promptly vanished. "Sorry," said Seth, not sorry at all.

"We don't allow phones at this retreat, sir. I think you already know that."

"I didn't realize I had it on me."

"If you hand it to me for safe keeping, you may continue with your visit and collect it from reception when you leave."

Seth pushed back his chair and rose to his

feet. "Thanks, but there's no need. I'm leaving now anyway."

Once out of the grounds of the retreat, he drove for a few miles before pulling over at the side of the road and switching off the ignition.

His head was buzzing with adrenaline, relief, the realization that he'd been given back his life. He felt free and overwhelmingly grateful. The horror and the agony had been lifted, leaving him filled with joy and new appreciation for . . . well, just about everything.

But especially his family.

And even more especially Lainey.

Oh God, though, how indescribably lucky he was. Now he found himself considering all those less fortunate than himself, who didn't get the kind of get-out-of-jail-free card he'd just been handed. A great wave of sympathy swept through him; for every two people who underwent the genetic testing, one would receive the news they and their families feared most of all.

Life was cruel, life was unfair — sometimes almost unbearably so. But he knew he'd never forget how he'd felt for the past three weeks. Nor would he ever stop thinking about those affected by such a devastating diagnosis.

He gazed through the windshield at the waving field of corn spread out ahead of him, at the birds flying high in a turquoise sky, and felt his throat begin to tighten. He hadn't shed so much as a tear for years, not since Tony — his *real* father — had died, but it could be about to happen now. The overwhelming relief was breaking him. His own life wasn't in pieces after all.

Shedding a few tears, it turned out, was cathartic. Who knew? Once the pent-up grief was out of his system, he wiped his eyes and checked his watch. Much as he wanted to call Lainey and tell her he needed to see her now, the reason for her coming up here with him was because she was paying a visit to her grandmother.

The thought of calling her — which he mustn't do, not yet — belatedly reminded him of the phone call that had got him kicked out of the retreat.

Or enabled him to escape.

It had been from Grace, mother of Ned, Stevie, and Bay, and he knew why she'd wanted to speak to him — today was Ned's eleventh birthday and he'd sent him a box of *Star Wars* LEGOs.

Time to call her back.

Once the effusive thanks were over, Grace

said cheerily, "And are you still up there in the Cotswolds, or are you on your way home now?"

Seth was amused. "And how do you know where I am today? Or has Ned fitted a tracker to my car?"

"You aren't the only one who sent him a present, you know. Lainey had a T-shirt specially made, with Ned's face in among a load of *Star Wars* characters on the front, and I don't think he's ever going to take it off. I called to thank her and asked if she'd like to come over for tea, to see the boys. That's when she told me you'd given her a lift up there so she could visit her Granny Ivy."

"Ah, right. Yes, I did. It wasn't out of my way."

"Don't you just love the sound of that place, Goosebrook? Oops, don't do that, Stevie! I'd better go," said Grace over the sound of clattering furniture. "Tell Lainey to be careful and not go falling out of any trees! And thanks again for Ned's LEGOs."

The call had ended, but Seth was still staring at the phone in his hand. Finally, he looked at Google Maps and saw that while the journey from Cirencester to the spa retreat was more or less a straight line,

Goosebrook was several miles over to the left.

Goosebrook. Surely not . . .

He drove into the village forty minutes later, remembering random familiar details as he spotted them: the pub sign swinging in the light breeze outside the Black Swan . . . the cobalt-blue paint on the propped-open door of the village shop . . . the huge domed chestnut trees casting pools of shadow across the grass as they stood sentinel on either side of the whitewashed village hall.

How long was it since he'd last been here? His mother and her boyfriend at the time had rented a holiday cottage bordering the village green, and he'd been forced to spend a weekend with them. It must have been twenty years ago, he worked out. He'd been twelve.

Now, he parked at the roadside and climbed out of the car, taking a more detailed look at the buildings lining the main street. The Old Schoolhouse, Bay Cottage, the B and B with a trellis of white roses around the door. Over there on the other side of the green were the grand Cotswold-stone pillars flanking the entrance to Fox Court, and to the right of them stood the church, with its tree-shaded higgledy-piggledy graveyard.

A tall woman in her sixties, with a black cat walking at her heels, was heading along the pavement toward him. Her eyes narrowing at the sight of a stranger, she regarded him with suspicion. "Are you looking for someone?" Clearly checking in case he was a burglar intent on breaking into one of the houses in the vicinity.

Actually, why stop at one? May as well go through the whole lot, see what he could get.

But nothing now could spoil his mood. "I'm fine, thanks," he said good-naturedly. "Going to have some lunch in the pub. Beautiful cat."

The woman's sharp features softened in an instant. "Thank you." She made her way past him with the cat swishing its tail alongside her, then stopped and turned. "By the way, they do a good chicken pie."

From her manner, it sounded as if she wasn't quite used to being friendly but was doing her best.

"Thanks," said Seth.

The woman hadn't been wrong: the homemade chicken pie was excellent. By the time he left the Black Swan, it was half past three. Setting out on foot, he explored the rest of the village, recalling more details of his previous visit along the way. Reaching the outskirts, after crossing the brook and following a narrow path, he came to a field with sheep in it. And yes, there behind a high dry-stone wall at the other end of the field was the cottage he remembered so well.

He could still be wrong, of course, but somehow he sensed he wasn't. Taking out his phone, he rang Lainey's number.

"Yes?" She sounded cautious.

"Grace called me. She said your Granny Ivy lives in Goosebrook. Where are you now?"

Silence. Then, "Goosebrook."

"Why did you let me drop you in Cirencester?"

"I didn't want to take you out of your way."

"Idiot." He smiled into his phone. "Look, I'll see you there at four thirty. I'll be waiting on the bench outside the village hall, OK?"

Still cautious, Lainey said, "OK. You sound . . . different."

"Do I?"

"Hang on, how do you know there's a bench outside the village hall?"

"Google Maps. See you there," said Seth. "Don't be late." And he ended the call.

CHAPTER 44

She was early. It was still only 4:15 when he saw her making her way down the street before crossing the village green and heading toward him. It felt like a good sign.

Reaching the bench, she said, "You were already here when you called me, weren't you?"

Seth nodded and indicated that she should sit down next to him. "I was."

"Is your mum OK?"

"She's fine. Very . . . detoxed. And how's Granny Ivy?"

"Brilliant. Ninety years old and probably going to live until she's two hundred." Lainey was watching him intently. "You still sound different. And you look different too. Something's happened. What's going on?"

Oh, nothing much. Just got my life back, that's all. He took a deep breath. "It's about Matteo."

When he'd finished relaying the whole

story, Lainey raked her fingers through her hair, pushing it back from her forehead. "My God, I can't believe it. Two Matteos. So for the last three weeks you've been going through hell. I can't imagine what that must have felt like. And now . . ." Her voice trailed away as she searched his face.

"I feel like the luckiest person in the world. I don't have to worry about it anymore." And as he held her gaze, Lainey's eyes filled with tears.

"Sorry," she said, "but I really need to hug you."

"Not nearly as much as I want you to hug me."

He wondered if it would feel awkward, but it didn't; it was the opposite of awkward. The sensation was intoxicating, everything he could have wished for. He could feel Lainey trembling as she wrapped her arms around him. Inhaling the scent of her skin, her hair, he closed his eyes and held her tight, committing every tiny detail to memory. The urge to find her mouth with his own was intense, almost overwhelming, but he mustn't do it, not yet, not quite yet. There were small children racing around the village green and a group of teenagers stretched out on the grass, chatting and listening to music. The first time had to be perfect, and whistles and catcalls from easily amused teenagers wouldn't help.

He drew back finally, sensing that Lainey was as reluctant as he was to let go. Which was good.

She was still trembling too.

"When did you find out about the disease?" There was a catch in her voice. "I mean, when exactly?"

"The day after Dawn saw us on the beach." He knew she was putting two and two together. Just when the next stage of their relationship had seemed inevitable, his world had come crashing down and for both their sakes he'd had to step away.

"Right." She nodded slowly. "I thought it was me, getting it wrong. Or I thought I'd *done* something wrong."

There was no point in pretending otherwise; they both knew what had been on the verge of happening between them.

"Neither of those," said Seth.

"I'm glad to hear it." She smiled and ran an index finger lightly over the back of his hand.

"There is one thing, though. Something I do need to ask you."

"Go on."

"When you were six or seven, did you have one of those toys where you pull a cord and the fairy flies up into the air?"

Confused, Lainey said, "I did, but . . . that's not the kind of question I thought you were going to ask."

"This fairy of yours. Was it green and pink?"

"Yes . . ." She hesitated, and her eyes slowly widened in disbelief. "Oh no, you can't be . . . *no* . . ."

"You'd flown the fairy out of your bedroom window, and it got caught in the branches of the tree," Seth reminded her.

"But . . . but it *can't* have been you!"

"And you were so desperate to get it back, you climbed out of the window into the tree. Then found out you were stuck and couldn't get down or back inside."

Her eyes were like saucers now. "There was a boy in the field behind the house, and he jumped over the wall . . ."

"Good-looking boy, age twelve," Seth prompted. "And it was a pretty high drystone wall."

"He rescued me," whispered Lainey. "He climbed the tree, helped me down . . ."

"And he rescued the flying fairy, don't forget that. Total hero."

"Then he called me an idiot."

Seth raised an eyebrow. "Maybe he was right. If he hadn't spotted you, you could have broken your neck."

"Was it really you?"

"As soon as Grace mentioned Goose-brook, I remembered the name of the place. I came here with Mum and one of her boyfriends for a weekend getaway. Then Grace said on the phone to tell you not to go falling out of any trees . . . and that was it. I knew."

"I always remembered you," Lainey said, marveling. "It was like my brain took a picture of your face. I can see you now, helping me down the tree, with the sun behind you, shining through the branches . . . and your eyes . . . and the way you looked at me when you called me an idiot. Then you gave me back my fairy, climbed over the wall at the end of the garden, and disappeared."

Seth nodded. "We left the next day, went back to London."

"I was terrified you might turn up again and tell Granny Ivy what I'd done. She still doesn't know to this day."

"Promise me you'll never climb out of a bedroom window again."

"I won't." Playfully she added, "Not unless you're there to catch me."

"Try not to do it anyway."

"I've just remembered — the first day we

511

met you at Menhenick House, I felt as if I knew you from somewhere." Lainey shook her head. "And I did. It was here. It was you all along. *Wow.*"

Seth took her hand, interlinking his fingers with hers, reveling in the sensation and recalling the last time it had happened. "This thing. You and me. Just so you know, I wouldn't be doing this if I didn't think it was going to last."

"And if it all goes horribly wrong, you'll sack me." Lainey's mouth twitched. "So I'm kind of hoping it works out too."

They made their way back to the car. Once inside, Seth drew her toward him and kissed her for the first time. It was everything he could have hoped for and definitely worth the wait.

He had a feeling this was going to work out.

Eventually they heard a bark and broke apart. Observing them from a few meters away was a man of roughly his own age, with dark hair and electric-blue eyes, walking an ancient, whiskery dog on a lead. Breaking into a dazzling grin, the man winked at Lainey before continuing on down the main street.

Cheeky sod.

Over on the village green, Seth discovered,

they were also now being watched with interest by the group of teenagers. He said drily, "I feel like a tourist attraction. Time to go."

Her eyes sparkling, Lainey gave his arm a squeeze. "How weird is it that a few months ago I'd never even heard of St. Carys? And now all I want to do is go back there with you."

CHAPTER 45

A fortnight later, the stage was set to celebrate Richard's eightieth birthday. Always up for a party, he'd invited over two hundred people to Menhenick House.

Thankfully, after three cloudy, drizzly days in a row, the skies had cleared, the sun was now blazing down, and the garden, thanks to Kit's loving attention over the course of the summer, had never looked better.

The guest list comprised an eclectic assortment of family, fellow actors and arty types, and friends acquired over the decades, ranging from long ago to those made more recently during his time here in St. Carys. Even a couple of ex-wives — the calmer ones who could be trusted not to make a scene — had been invited along to join in with the celebrations.

"You've done wonders. Everything's perfect," said Majella as they surveyed the scene. Lainey had strung colored bunting around the yard, along with garlands of fairy lights to come on later when it grew dark.

"Seth helped me. I couldn't have done it without him." Just saying his name still gave Lainey a warm glow, not to mention the thought of that magical first weekend they'd spent together at his flat in Bristol. The last fortnight had been the happiest of her life.

"And we couldn't do anything without you." Majella squeezed her arm and whispered, "How's it going? All OK?"

Lainey smiled, because although Majella had tried her best to be pleased for her and Seth, at the same time, she had been worried that if the relationship didn't work out, it would make life at Menhenick House difficult for all concerned. She'd explained apologetically that she couldn't bear the thought that if it went wrong, Lainey might up sticks and leave.

"So far, so good. In fact, better than OK."

"Well make sure you keep it that way, please." Majella gave her arm another squeeze. "And I am starting to relax, just so you know. I've never seen Seth so happy. I mean, when he was with Dawn they seemed to get on well, but he was still . . . himself, you know? This time it's different. He can't stop looking at you and his eyes light up in a way I've never seen before. It's like you truly *belong* together."

"I hope so." Secretly, Lainey felt it too.

"*Ooh,* I haven't had a chance to tell you." Majella brightened. "Guess who I saw when I popped into the post office at lunchtime?"

"Hugh Jackman?" Well, you never knew; maybe Richard had given his good friend Hugh a call, casually made a last-minute addition to the guest list.

"Dawn! Sitting outside Paddy's Café! And you'll never guess who she was with."

"Umm . . . Kate Winslet?"

"No! *Niall.*" Majella pulled an *eek!* face and strummed an imaginary guitar. "I couldn't believe it! And it didn't look like a first-date scenario either . . . she was draped all over him, as if they knew each other *really* well."

Lainey boggled. "Wow, we'd heard she'd started seeing someone." Which had been good news as far as she and Seth were concerned. "But we didn't know who it was."

"Let's just hope he's nicer to her than he was to me. Anyway, Dan's going to be here soon." Majella beamed and patted her heart. "I still can't believe it's happened. Honestly, he makes me feel like a teenager again."

"Things are looking up around here," said Lainey.

"For us. But not for India." The smile faded from Majella's face, because India continued to worry them and was flatly refusing to confide in anyone about whatever it was that was clearly still troubling her. She was quiet and withdrawn, not her usual exuberant self at all, and over the last few days had become noticeably more on edge whenever anyone had mentioned today's party. Which, to be fair, had happened a lot.

"We're keeping an eye on her," Lainey's tone was reassuring. "It's all we can do. Whatever it is, we'll get her through it."

Although quite how, when they were so in the dark about the problem and India flatly refused to talk to anyone or consider any kind of professional help, she wasn't entirely sure.

People started arriving at six, and by seven the garden was filling up nicely. Lainey carried out plates of hors d'oeuvres and began offering them to the guests, helped by Nerys, who was still adamant she didn't want to be introduced to anyone as Richard's daughter. "Oh no, really, I couldn't be doing with the attention." She winced at the hideous prospect. "All those people giving me the once-over and coming out with ridiculous questions . . . it's not my cup of tea at all. If anyone asks, just say I'm a friend of the family, that Mum and Sir Richard worked together years ago."

Which just went to show, Lainey realized, that some secrets were better coming out while others were far happier staying hidden.

Oh, but she still wished she knew what was troubling India.

A cry of "Wyatt!" went up behind her, and Lainey turned to see Majella and Richard greeting the latest arrival. When Kit had mentioned that Wyatt was coming down to Cornwall this weekend, they'd insisted he be invited along to the party. And being Wyatt and partial to an over-the-top gesture, he was carrying a dramatic arrangement of tropical flowers.

Kit embraced him as Lainey made her way over to them. Richard, rakish in a cobalt-blue linen suit worn over a bright-pink shirt and with a pink rose in his buttonhole, said, "Flowers for me, young man? Most kind, but I'd have preferred something I could drink."

"Which is why these are for Majella." Wyatt presented them to her with a gentlemanly flourish, then turned back to Richard. "I couldn't manage to carry yours out here because it's a crate of Perrier-Jouët. It's sitting in the kitchen."

Richard landed a smacking kiss on each of Wyatt's cheeks and declared expansively, "Did I ever tell you you're my favorite American?"

Wyatt's cheeks glowed as he turned to include Lainey and Kit in the conversation. "Actually, I've got a piece of news for you two. Think you're going to like it."

Lainey clutched his arm with delight. "You've got yourself a boyfriend? Yay, that's brilliant! Isn't it brilliant?" She beamed at Kit, but Wyatt was already shaking his head, looking pleased with himself.

"No, not that. I won't say it's better than that, but it's still good." He paused, then said, "Mom and Dad have just bought the Chateau de Rafale."

"Oh my God! Are you *serious*?" Lainey's mouth fell open. "That's amazing . . . Biddy and Bill will be *so* relieved."

"They are. And they're going to be staying on to run it as a business."

"Wow . . ."

"Pop needs a project to keep him occupied. He put in the research, and it's a sound financial investment. Biddy and Bill love the place, so why would they need to leave? It works out well for everyone, and they're planning to turn it into a really high-end destination. I didn't tell you before, in case the deal fell through, but they completed the sale yesterday. It's a done deal and everyone's delighted."

"This is the best news." Lainey threw her arms around Wyatt and wondered what it must be like to belong to a family capable of just buying a French chateau outright because retirement was a bit boring and you fancied opening a hotel. Imagine if she'd been a completely different kind of person, the ruthlessly gold-digging kind who couldn't be bothered to save up their own money in order to start up a business; never mind that he was gay, she could have married Wyatt Hilstanton herself.

"And of course we'll be doing weddings there," Wyatt whispered into her ear as Seth made his way across the lawn toward them. "So if things carry on going as well as Kit tells me they're going . . . you know where to find us."

Lainey said, "Very funny." It was far too soon, of course, but deep down, the thought that it could conceivably happen one day made her heart flutter.

An hour later, they heard the roar of a

powerful sports car pulling up outside, and Christina made her late but show-stopping entrance in a full-length, slinky white dress and more silver necklaces than Harrods. Spyros, the Lamborghini-owning boyfriend, was dressed all in black and kept casting covert glances in the direction of the other attractive female guests, which didn't bode well.

Once Christina had finished greeting Richard, his ex-wives, and several of his more famous actor friends, she collected a fresh glass of champagne and sauntered across the lawn to join Seth and Lainey.

"Here we go," Seth murmured as she approached. "Mum, hi, you're looking great."

"I should hope so, darling, after all those weeks of detox in a no-fun retreat! Still, no pain no gain, and at least my liver's had a rest. Now it's as good as new and ready to rock and roll again. Cheers!" She clinked her glass against both theirs, then turned to Lainey. "And this is a turnup for the books, isn't it? Seth tells me you two are a couple now! Which is wonderful, obviously, but you'll have to keep an eye on him — my son's almost as bad as I am when it comes to settling down."

"Actually, I'm not," said Seth.

"Only joking, my darling. And this one's

lovely, so I definitely approve. So tell me how it happened, how you two got together." Christina fixed her heavily mascaraed gaze on Lainey, bright with expectation. "I want to hear everything, *all* the details!"

Since there was no way *that* was going to happen, Lainey said lightly, "Well, I was visiting my Granny Ivy in the Cotswolds and Seth gave me a lift up there, then at the end of the day he came to pick me up from Goosebrook, and that was when we discovered —"

"Goosebrook? That name rings a distant bell. Now why does it sound familiar?"

"Yes, it was the most brilliant coincidence, because that was when we realized it was —"

"Oh, was this the day you came up to the retreat to tell me about Matteo?" Christina turned to Seth and clapped her hands in delight. "So really it's all thanks to me!"

It was the suddenness of the movement that caught Lainey's eye. India, sitting alone on a bench beneath a pergola overhung with honeysuckle, had dropped her phone on the grass and her head had jerked up. Now she was staring at Christina like a mongoose hypnotized by a snake.

"Yes, it was that day." As if sensing that

522

Lainey was distracted, Seth took over the story about their first meeting, twenty years earlier, up a tree in a back garden in Goosebrook.

"Well, isn't that just wonderful?" Christina's many bangles jangled as she clapped her hands. "Bravo! And I'm going to take *all* the credit!"

"I did tell you about it at the time," Seth reminded her.

"Did you, darling? I don't remember. Oh, now look at that. Empty." She regarded her glass with dismay. "I'd better go and find Spyros and pick up a refill."

The moment she'd tottered off, India was on her feet.

"What was Christina talking about just then?" She was looking at Seth, her jaw visibly tense.

He laughed. "When Lainey got stuck in the tree, you mean?"

"Not that. When she said you went to see her to tell her about Matteo." India's rib cage was rising and falling as if she'd run a marathon. "Who's Matteo?"

Seth hesitated. "He was a friend of hers from years ago. Why?"

"But who *was* he? Did you know him too? Have you . . . met him?"

Lainey checked to make sure no one else

was within earshot. No, all clear.

What was going on here? The color had drained from India's face and she was practically hyperventilating with the need to know about Matteo.

Seth clearly understood that something significant was happening too. Taking care not to say the wrong thing, he shook his head. "I . . . didn't meet Matteo, no."

They were staring at each other now. As far as the two of them were concerned, the party no longer existed.

"Why are you asking?" Seth went on. "What does the name mean to you?"

India's gaze slid to Lainey, then back again. In an unsteady voice she said, "Seth, tell me who Matteo is. If you know more than you're saying . . . please just say it. I need to know."

"First," Seth replied slowly, "you have to tell me where you heard his name."

CHAPTER 46

Lainey held her breath; it was like those cycling races in a velodrome where neither rider wants to make the first move.

At last India said, "I saw a message on Facebook."

"From?"

"Your mum."

He closed his eyes briefly. "Of course."

"Don't get her back over here. It was an accident." India shook her head. "I was never meant to see it. She was replying to something from one of her old girlfriends and typed it into my inbox by mistake. Then ten seconds later, it vanished. She'd deleted it." India tilted her head back, her eyes swimming with tears. "If I hadn't been on my account at that moment I'd never have seen it, never known what it said." She swallowed with difficulty. "But I *was* on there, so I did."

"It's OK," said Seth. "I know what it was."

He also knew that this was unconnected with the medical diagnosis; it only concerned the other Matteo.

"I want you to already know, more than anything. But what if you only think you do?"

"Fine, I'll say it. My mother slept with some guy called Matteo, and he might be my biological father. But it doesn't matter one bit." Seth's voice was low and reassuring. "And it doesn't change *anything,* because my dad was your dad and you and Violet are my sisters and . . . Oh don't cry, please don't, you mustn't. *I love you . . .*"

"I can't believe it. I can't believe you already knew." India fell into his arms, sobbing in earnest now with relief. "When did you find out?"

"When I was about your age."

"What?" She did a horrified double take. "Oh God, how awful for you."

"Not awful at all." Seth rocked her like a baby as she continued to drip tears and mascara down the front of his white shirt. "Like I said, it makes no difference. Thanks." He took the tissues Lainey passed him and began mopping at India's cheeks. "When did you see the Facebook message?"

"F-five weeks ago. It was so awful, because I thought you didn't know, so there was no one I could tell, and I was just bottling it all up inside me and wishing I'd never seen it, and then I couldn't stop worrying and panicking because we all know what Christina's like, and if she could let it slip once, sooner or later it was bound to happen again, only the next time you'd be the one who found out . . ."

Beyond them, the party was in full swing, carrying on without them. "Everything just seemed to be happening at once," India went on, her voice cracking. "And then Nerys turned up, which just made it a hundred times worse, because if Grandad found out you weren't related to him, would he even bother with you anymore now he'd gotten a new daughter instead?"

Lainey's heart went out to her. India had been conjuring up worst-case scenarios for weeks, spiraling into panic and despair. And now Violet was on her way over, clearly having spotted that something was going on. She took one look at her sister's wet, makeup-streaked face, and said, "Oh God, what's happened? Tell me."

India looked at Seth, who nodded. So between much sniffing and eye wiping, India did.

By the time she'd finished, Violet was in tears too. She hugged her twin fiercely. "I can't believe you kept it to yourself. You didn't even tell *me.*"

Lainey passed over a second handful of tissues.

"You were the last person I'd tell. I wanted to so much, but then you'd have been as miserable as me, and I couldn't bear to do that to you."

Taking the long way around, the four of them slipped back to the house so Seth could change his mascara-stained shirt and the girls could repair their makeup.

On the landing, India turned suddenly to Lainey. "I'm so sorry about the nail polish and the chewing gum. And there was a fridge magnet too, but it only cost a pound. I'm going to go back to all the shops and apologize and pay them back. I just felt so helpless, not knowing what to do about the Matteo thing, but I can stop worrying now. And I feel so much better already." She heaved a happy sigh. "I promise I'm never ever going to do it again."

"I know you won't." Lainey smiled as she found herself wrapped in her first ever embrace from India.

"Thanks. I'm glad you're here and I'm glad you and Seth are together. Promise me you'll never break up."

Seth appeared at the top of the stairs. He raised his dark brows a fraction and waited.

"We'll do our best," said Lainey.

As the sun sank lower in the sky, flooding the horizon with shades of gold, the music was turned down, and Richard tapped a fork against the side of his glass to gain everyone's attention.

"Right, so if you lot thought you were going to get away without having to listen to a speech, I'm afraid you're sadly mistaken."

Cries of mock horror went up, and he continued, "Luckily for you, this isn't the Oscars, and I'll be brief."

Lainey, standing beside Seth, caught her breath as she felt their fingers slotting together as if they were a perfect fit. Would this simple gesture always have such an effect on her? Oh, she hoped so.

"So, thank you all for coming. After a lifetime of debauchery, it's a miracle I'm still here, but there you go. I'm eighty today, and the Grim Reaper hasn't caught up with me yet." Richard chuckled and paused in an actorly way. "Life's had its ups and downs, but overall I've been a lucky bugger. I have the most wonderful family anyone could wish for, and I love every last one of them." His gaze swept around the lawn, encompassing each member in turn, and Lainey's heart gave a squeeze of affection as she saw him include Nerys with a discreet nod and a wink. "I've also had more than my fair share of friends —"

"And wives," called out the husband of an elegant actress called Evelyn who'd been briefly married to Richard in the 1980s.

"Some of them were even my own," Richard riposted, provoking more laughter. "And I could still add to the total. So, Evelyn, if you ever get tired of him, you know where I am."

"Eurgh," India whispered in Lainey's left ear. "He'd better not be talking about sex. That's gross."

Serious now, Richard continued. "The greatest sadness in my life, of course, was losing Tony, and when that happened, I wondered how on earth we'd all get through it. But somehow we did, and I'm lucky enough to have the best daughter-in-law in the world, as well as four wonderful grandchildren." He paused to blow them a kiss. "I love you all, and I'm so very glad to still be here, sharing my life with you. So here's to family." He raised his glass, and everyone followed suit. "And here's to all of us, and the absolute miracle of me reaching eighty."

■ ■ ■ ■

Seth had discussed it with the girls, and they'd decided between them that the time for keeping secrets was over. Well, maybe not every secret, but as many as possible.

Once the party had wound down and Harry had gone up to bed, he gathered the family for a nightcap in the living room. It was unfair to expect India and Violet to keep what they'd learned to themselves, which meant Majella needed to hear the story too; it was the only way.

The clock struck eleven out in the hall, and from the kitchen came the distant clink and clatter of Lainey and Kit washing glasses, loading the dishwasher, and generally cleaning up. The cats were curled up on the rug in front of the purple sofa, while Ernie lay stretched out on his side over by the window, paws scrabbling furiously as he chased imaginary seagulls along the beach. Glenda was ensconced like a small queen on India's lap, and Richard was pouring himself another cognac, because his capacity for one last drink was limitless.

Holding Majella's hand in his as she sat beside him on the sofa, Seth relayed the story of the secret Christina had let slip about his possible parentage.

"That mother of yours," said Richard. "Sorry to say this, but she's been a liability since day one." He stopped, frowned a bit. "Actually, I'm not sorry to say it at all. She just *is.*"

"Grandad," Violet chided, fair-minded to the last. "Pot, kettle."

Seth shook his head. "She might never win Mother of the Year, but it doesn't matter." He turned to Majella. "It never did matter, because I had you. Dad was brilliant, and you were the best stepmum in the world. Always."

"Oh, darling, I tried my best." Majella's eyes swam. "I loved you from the first time I met you."

"I knew that, and I knew you weren't just putting it on either." Seth's arm was around her shoulders now. "It meant everything to me. You're my family, and that's never going to change." He nodded at Violet, who reached behind her for a tattered gray shoebox and passed it over to him.

"Oh God, what's this? I'm not sure I can cope with any more surprises." Majella blew her nose and looked worried.

Seth smiled down at her. "It isn't a surprise. You're the one who wrote them."

She lifted the lid of the shoebox, saw the

piles of envelopes bearing old stamps and familiar handwriting. "My goodness, these are the letters I sent you when you were at school. I had no idea you'd even kept them. I can't believe there are so *many* . . ."

"Christina sent me a letter once. Well, it was a postcard." Seth no longer had it, but he could still remember every hastily scrawled word. "It said: 'Sorry, baby, won't be able to see you this summer, off to Bali! Exciting!' " He paused, then took out a handful of the letters carefully addressed to him at the boarding school in Kent that Christina had insisted he attend. "But you wrote to me twice a week, every week. And they were the *best* letters . . ." For a moment his throat tightened with emotion, because no one who hadn't been in his position could ever really understand how much they'd meant to him. They had been long, chatty letters interspersed with jokes and funny little drawings, brimming with love and updates about everything that had been going on in the family's lives.

They shared them out now, reading snippets aloud and remembering stories from the past. Then India asked if she could look at the photo on Seth's phone again, and he passed it to her so she could study the Mancini family. There was no need to exclaim over the similarity of their features; it was there for all to see. "Do you really not want to meet them?" Violet was curious.

He shook his head. "You're my family. I don't need another one."

"Not even if they're nicer than us?" India grinned, resting her head on Majella's shoulder, and Seth's spirits lifted still further because he could see that the old, sparky, mischief-making India was well and truly back.

He knew that maybe one day he might change his mind. At some stage in the future, ten or twenty years from now, his interest could be piqued and the temptation might be there to learn more about the Mancinis, but for now, he felt no inclination to do so. He looked from his sisters to Majella. "I'll stick with what I know."

From his position by the mantelpiece, Richard caught his eye, raised his glass and mouthed, *Love you.*

And at his side, with the shoebox still resting on her lap, Majella reached for his hand and held it in hers.

CHAPTER 47

The people on the ground were looking up, having evidently heard the helicopter's approach before it came into view over the tops of the trees. The powerful juddering *thud thud thud* of the rotor blades was even more thrilling from up here as they hovered above the Chateau de Rafale, surrounded by acres of manicured grounds in the depths of the French countryside.

Beside herself with excitement, Lainey shielded her eyes from the bright sun and exclaimed, "There they are. I can see Biddy and Bill on the steps! Can you believe how beautiful it all looks? And there's Wyatt . . . Oh, this is just out of this world. I never dreamed I'd get the chance to ride in one of these things, and now it's happening!" She strained forward against the seat belt, waving madly with both hands at Wyatt.

"Don't lean. You'll tip us off balance."

From the seat behind her, Seth pulled her back.

Lainey let out a yelp of alarm. "Oh my God, I'm so sorry!"

To her right, the pilot said with a grin, "He's having you on."

Of course he was. Half turning, Lainey's gaze met Seth's and she experienced the jolt of love that had shown no sign of abating so far. "Can you believe it's a year since Kit and I left this place? A ten-hour bus trip all the way from Paris to London. And now this." She gestured expansively. "Here I am in an actual helicopter, about to land in front of the chateau. It's just crazy that so much has happened since then."

"You got yourself a boyfriend," Seth reminded her.

"I did, that's true."

"What's he like?"

Lainey paused. "Thinks he's funnier than he is. But he's OK, I suppose. How about your girlfriend?"

"You can tell her anything and she'll believe it," said Seth. "Totally gullible."

Everyone on the ground was watching them now, as the pilot brought the silver-and-blue helicopter down, settling it skillfully in the very center of the landing pad.

When the blades had slowed to a halt, they

jumped out and joined the party assembled on the steps of the chateau.

"Thank you." Lainey embraced Wyatt, whose idea it had been to arrange the helicopter trip from Charles de Gaulle airport. "That was amazing."

"My pleasure." His eyes crinkled. "None of this would have happened if it wasn't for you."

And in a weird, fateful, convoluted way, Lainey realized, this was true.

Because if she hadn't inadvertently brought that oversized diamond ring back to the UK with her, Wyatt would never have traveled down to St. Carys and ended up breaking his ankle . . .

Would never have got talking to Kit at the wedding reception and plucked up the courage to come out . . .

Would never have discovered that this place was on the market.

It just went to show how one seemingly tiny action could set off a domino chain of consequences.

The change in Wyatt himself was heartwarming too. He radiated happiness.

Lainey said, "Is Penny here yet?"

"She is." He turned and pointed. "Over there with the new boyfriend, talking to Mom."

"Ooh, what's he like?"

"Name's Tim, lives in Kidderminster, and he's a geography teacher. Luckily, he doesn't look like one." Wyatt nodded genially. "Couldn't have chosen a better guy myself. I approve."

Later, Bill and Biddy took Seth and Lainey on a tour of the chateau. In its previous incarnation, shabby chic had been the order of the day, but the absolute fortune plowed into it by the Hilstantons had brought the place up to five-star standard. Each room was gleaming, spotless, and perfect. Sumptuous furnishings and painstakingly restored architectural details dazzled the eye at every turn. There were flower arrangements the size of trees.

"You have to see the brochures." The couple were like proud parents. "So *glossy*. And you won't believe the inquiries we've been getting. Elton John's already booked the place for a week in September. Oh, and you can't imagine how blissful it is when anything expensive goes wrong. All we have to do is find the best local tradesmen and let Mr. Hilstanton know, and he pays them to fix it!"

Tonight a lavish party was being thrown to celebrate the reopening of the chateau.

Guests were arriving from all over. The Hilstantons had invited Lainey and Seth, Majella and Dan, and Penny and her geography teacher to join them for the event. India and Violet were back in St. Carys, studying for their imminent exams and looking after Harry and the animals. Richard had been invited too, but was over in LA, filming a cameo appearance in an upcoming big-budget superhero movie and had taken Nerys along with him as his PA in order to show her the city where he'd met her mother.

Upstairs in their suite on the third floor, Lainey boggled at the phone in her hand. "We never had superfast Wi-Fi in our day. This is fantastic. I'm going to send the girls that video of us in the helicopter — Oh!" Her phone went *ting* as a text arrived.

"Who's that? Not work, I hope," said Seth.

Work was something else that had changed over the course of the last six months. Lainey had begun helping Seth with Faulkner Travel, while Majella scaled back in order to spend more time with Dan. Lainey was the one who'd come up with the idea of expanding into activity holidays for single-parent families, and bookings had taken off like a rocket.

But no, she saw the name on the screen

and breathed a sigh of relief. "It's Dawn. Crikey, she says the contractions have started, her water has just broken, and she's on her way to the hospital, all systems go."

She swiftly texted back: Wow, good luck! And then smiled, because the friendship that had developed between Dawn and herself had been as nice as it was unexpected. Dawn's whirlwind romance with Niall might only have lasted a few weeks before he'd revealed his true colors, but it had nevertheless had the desired result. A week after discovering his devious skinflint ways and giving him the boot, she'd discovered she was pregnant. With no regrets whatsoever, she had begun to prepare with characteristic efficiency for single parenthood. As she'd explained to Lainey when they'd run into each other on the beach shortly after Niall's departure, men were fickle creatures who could come and go, but a baby was for life. She had let Niall know the state of play; he couldn't have been less interested, and that was absolutely fine by her. From now on, becoming a mother was all that mattered.

Lainey had found herself admiring her honesty and can-do attitude.

"Come and look at this." Seth beckoned her over to join him at the window.

"Dawn's about to have the baby."

"So I gathered. I'm sure she'll be brilliant at it." Seth was less interested in hearing the details of Dawn's labor than Lainey was. He slid his arm around her waist and pointed out of the window at the group of three people below. "Isn't this great? Something else that's changed in the last year."

Lainey leaned against him and smiled. "Just so you know, I'm planning on taking all the credit for that happy ending too."

On the freshly mown lawn below, Wyatt's mother was proving unstoppable, shouting orders like a sergeant major, taking endless photos, and showing no signs of stopping anytime soon.

"Now turn your head a little to the left, honey, that's right . . . Rest your right hand on the back of the chair and smile . . . No, not that much!"

Wyatt was doing his best to obey orders, but really, how could he not smile that much when he was bursting with happiness? After so many years of trying to please his parents and get on with living a life that didn't come naturally, what a relief it had been to discover how blissfully easy it was to be his true self. It was as if the pieces of an impossible-to-complete jigsaw had morphed into new shapes, leaving everything fitting and feeling right at last.

He said, "Mom, have you taken enough now?" Because she was still darting around like a studio photographer. "You've got plenty."

"Just a few more, honey. Now turn to face each other and look into each other's eyes. I need you both in profile."

This was no hardship. Wyatt turned and did as he was told.

"Don't worry. It'll be over soon," Kit murmured, struggling to keep a straight face.

"C'mon, you two. Stop talking. I want a really great one to go on Instagram."

Amused, Wyatt said, "Don't tell me, Charlene had one of Ricky and his boyfriend on hers and you want yours to be better."

"And why not? You and Kit *are* better! Now just let me do this . . . Place your left hand on Kit's hip . . . Oh yes, that's it, that's *perfect.*"

Who could have imagined that his mother would have become his greatest cheerleader? Against all expectations, and probably at least in part because of the long-standing rivalry between herself and Charlene, she had embraced his sexuality with enthusiasm. His brothers had teased him, of course, because they were his brothers and that was what they'd always done, but there had been acceptance too. And when, over Christmas, his friendship with Kit had grown and eventually blossomed into a relationship, it had felt like a miracle to both of them, a dream come true. Kit had worried at first that being so newly gay, Wyatt should really be getting out and about, widening his social circle and gaining experience. But Wyatt wasn't like that, had never been that kind of operator. A relationship with someone he cared for was what he craved, far and away above casual dates and meaningless sex.

Which was nice, because that was how Kit felt too.

Even better, upon meeting Kit's mother early in the new year, they'd gotten on wonderfully well together, and then his own mom had pretty much fallen in love with Kit from the word go.

"These are great." Finished at last, she scrolled through the dozens of photos, then, eyes shining, darted between the two of them and cried, "Now a selfie of the three of us! Oh my beautiful boys, aren't we having the best time? This is one of the happiest days of my life!"

CHAPTER 48

It was midnight and the party had ended, following a firework display that had lit up the sky with dazzling chrysanthemum bursts of color choreographed to accompany Stravinsky's *Firebird.*

It had been truly spectacular; even the local dignitaries had been impressed. Seth listened to the murmur of voices in the distance as doors closed, limousines departed, and those guests staying overnight made their way upstairs to their bedrooms. Now it was just the two of them left outside, gazing up at the star-studded sky and listening to the sound of crickets chirruping in the grass nearby.

Lainey, lying next to him on one of the garden sofas with her head resting on his chest, said, "I could stay out here forever."

He stroked her hair. "We don't have to go in."

"But I want to go in." Sitting up, she

rolled over and rose to her feet.

"What are you doing?" As he asked the question, she was already lifting her strappy oyster silk dress over her head in one smooth movement.

"I want to go *in* the pool." Standing there in her pale-pink bra and panties, she wiggled her bare toes and dropped the dress to the ground.

"You're mad. That water's cold." Wyatt's parents had made the decision not to heat it just yet, in order to dissuade partygoers from jumping in.

Lainey's eyes sparkled. "So maybe you should come in and warm me up."

Seth watched as she made her way over to the pool, glowing iridescent turquoise thanks to the underwater lighting, and dived in. She swam a full length underwater like a mermaid, before coming up for air at the far end, slicking back her hair and bursting out laughing at the look on his face.

"Is it *very* cold?"

"Nooo!"

He bent over at the side of the pool, testing the temperature. "I think you're lying to me."

"I would never do that."

"You'll be even colder when you get out."

"Hey, you two!" In the upper reaches of

the chateau, a window had been flung open and Majella's head popped out. "You're completely mad."

"*She's* mad." Seth shook his head, pointing to Lainey. "I'm the sensible one."

"Here, have these." There was movement behind the window, then two white terry cloth robes came tumbling down like dancing ghosts. "Enabler," said Seth.

Majella gave him a cheery wave. "Night!"

He collected the robes, then returned to the side of the pool.

"Help, help," whispered Lainey, beckoning. "I'm drowning. You need to rescue me."

Seth gazed down at this woman whom he loved beyond measure, more than he'd ever imagined possible. Over the last year, those feelings had only deepened; when he wasn't with her, his mind was able to conjure up a mosaic of images that never failed to fill his heart . . .

Lainey dancing in and out of the surf with the dogs along Menhenick Beach, doubling up with laughter in the kitchen at one of Richard's outrageous comments, putting on an impromptu puppet show with a crab and a king prawn to entertain Grace's boys, taking part in a piggyback race along the sand with Harry bouncing along like a jockey on her back . . .

Oh, there were so many unforgettable snapshot moments. And hopefully a million more to come.

He stripped off and dived in. Fuck, it was freezing.

When he reached Lainey, her teeth were chattering. She wrapped her icy arms around his neck and murmured, "My hero, you came to rescue me."

But in reality, she was the one who'd rescued him, and he knew how lucky he was. In *every* way. He kissed her on the mouth, which was cold on the outside but warm on the inside. Her body was pressed against his and her hair was fanned out around her in the illuminated water. Anyone looking out of the window would have a clear view of them.

"Come on, we need to warm up." He disentangled himself. "Let's swim."

And for the next ten minutes, they did, chasing each other up and down the pool, splashing, twisting, turning, and raising their body temperatures by a much-needed couple of degrees before climbing out of the water and wrapping themselves in the thick robes.

Lainey was squeezing water from her hair, her teeth still chattering like castanets. "See?" She grinned at him. "Wasn't that fun? Don't you just feel more alive?"

Her sparkling eyes, those wet lashes clumped together, that incorrigible joie de vivre . . .

"Are you going to marry me?" said Seth.

She had been laughing and shivering; now she abruptly stopped. "I don't know. Are you going to ask me?"

"Well, you're the only woman I'm going to love for the rest of my life. You've ruined me for anyone else. And you make me a better person. So yes." He clasped her icy hands in his and drew her against him. "I am asking and really hoping you're planning on saying yes."

Lainey gazed up at him, eyes wide.

After several seconds, Seth cleared his throat. "I can't help noticing you haven't said anything yet."

"Shh." A flicker of a smile. "I'm fixing this moment in my mind so I never forget it."

The crickets were still chirping around the pool. Overhead, the stars continued to shine.

"It's actually been quite a few moments now."

"Has it?" The smile spread across Lainey's face. "In that case, I'd better say yes before you change your mind."

"Good choice. Now come here." He kissed

her again, aware of the pulse beating at the base of her throat, matching the beat of his own heart. "I love you."

"I love you too."

"Love you more." He paused. "I haven't bought you a ring."

"You absolute cheapskate."

"I was going to buy one and wrap it up in a hankie, then slip it into your pocket, but . . ."

"I know. I might have thrown it away, never to be seen again."

"And I thought we should choose one together. So you end up with one you'll be happy to wear."

"That's a better idea."

"Majella thought of it."

"I love your family," said Lainey.

"They're going to be your family too before long. You're still shivering," said Seth.

"Still waiting for you to warm me up."

He took her hand. "I think it's time we went inside."

"What are we going to do when we get inside?" Lainey slid her arm around his waist and leaned against him.

"Celebrate," said Seth.

ABOUT THE AUTHOR

With over eleven million copies sold, *New York Times* and *USA Today* bestselling author **Jill Mansell** writes irresistible, funny, poignant, and romantic tales for women in the tradition of Marian Keyes, Sophie Kinsella, and Jojo Moyes. She lives with her partner and their children in Bristol, England.